ANDRE R. FRATTINO

JESSE LEE

WITHDRAWN

IN MEMORY OF MY BUBBIE, LILLIAN KUCHINSKI, WHO SHARED
AND NURTURED MY JEWISH CULTURE AND HERITAGE.
— ANDRE

FOR MY WIFE, WHO GRANTS ME STRENGTH EVERY DAY.
— JESSE

AND TO THE OVER 17 MILLION PEOPLE PERSECUTED AND MURDERED DURING
THE HOLOCAUST. JEWS, INTELLECTUALS, ROMANI, HOMOSEXUALS AND
ALL THE OTHERS WHO WERE CONSIDERED "UNDESIRABLES"...

WE WILL NEVER FORGET.

IMAGE COMICS, INC. • Robert Kirkman: Chief Operating Officer • Erik Larsen: Chief Financial Officer • Todd McFarlane: President • Marc Silvestri: Chief Executive Officer • Jim Valentino: Vice President • Eric Stephenson: Publisher / Chief Creative Officer • Jeff Boison: Director of Publishing Planning & Book Trade Sales • Chris Ross: Director of Digital Sales • Jeff Stang: Director of Direct Market Sales • Kat Salazar: Director of PR & Marketing • Drew Gill: Art Director • Heather Doornink: Production Director • Nicole Lapalme: Controller • IMAGECOMICS.COM
• Deanna Phelps: Production Artist for SIMON SAYS • Melissa Gifford: Content Manager for SIMON SAYS •

SIMON SAYS, VOL. 1. First printing. September 2019. Published by Image Comics, Inc. Office of publication: 2701 NW Vaughn St., Suite 780, Portland, OR 97210. Copyright © 2019 Andre Frattino & Jesse Lee. All rights reserved. "Simon Says," its logos, and the likenesses of all characters herein are trademarks of Andre Frattino & Jesse Lee, unless otherwise noted. "Image" and the Image Comics logos are registered trademarks of Image Comics, Inc. No part of this publication may be reproduced or transmitted, in any form or by any means (except for short excerpts for journalistic or review purposes), without the express written permission of Andre Frattino & Jesse Lee, or Image Comics, Inc. All names, characters, events, and locales in this publication are entirely fictional. Any resemblance to actual persons (living or dead), events, or places, without satirical intent, is coincidental. Printed in the USA. For information regarding the CPSIA on this printed material call: 203-595-3636. For international rights, contact: foreignlicensing@imagecomics.com. ISBN: 978-1-5343-1319-4.

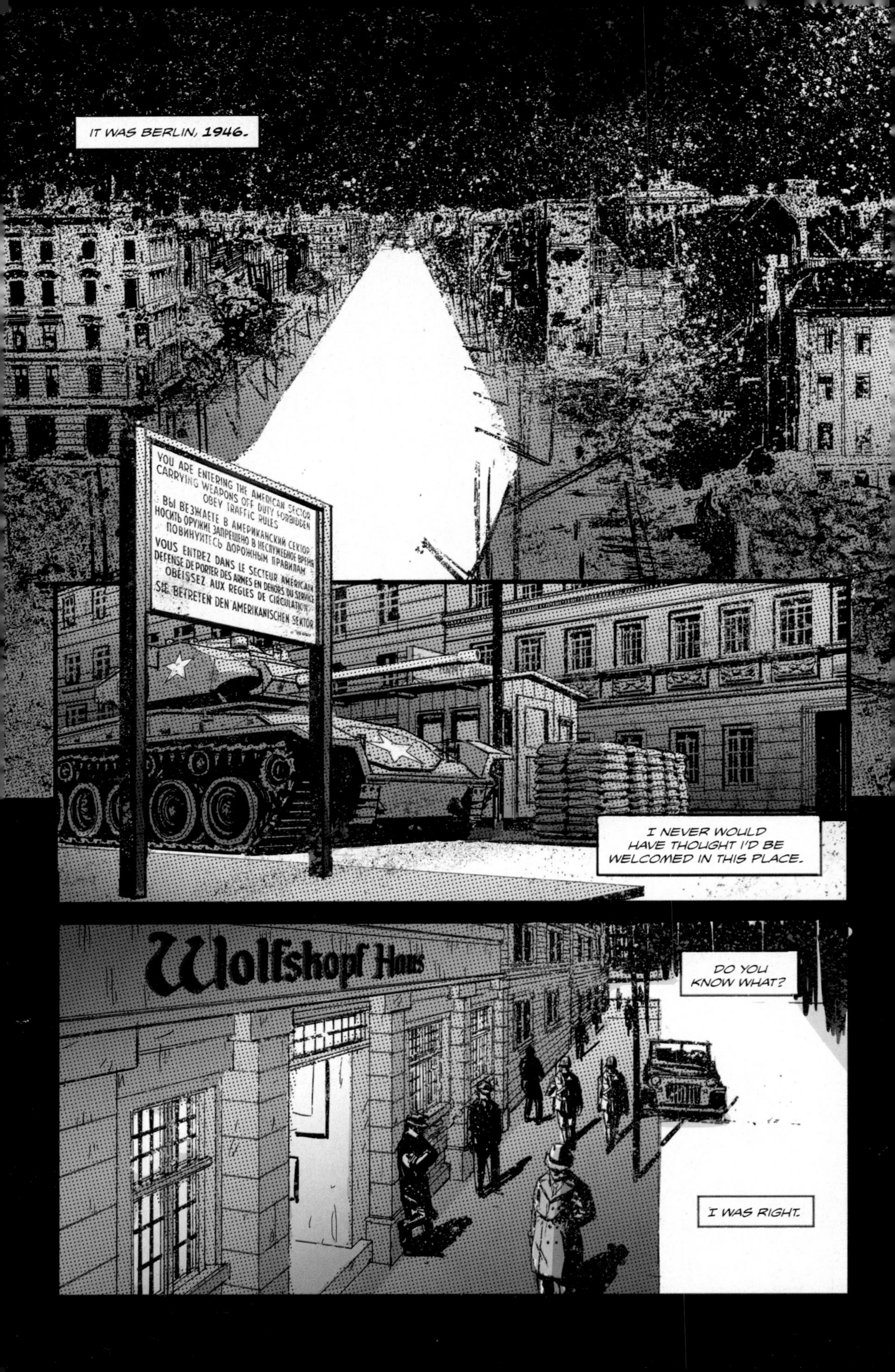
IT WAS BERLIN, 1946.
YOU ARE ENTERING THE AMERICAN SECTOR
CARRYING WEAPONS OFF DUTY FORBIDDEN
OBEY TRAFFIC RULES
ВЫ ВЕЗЖАЕТЕ В АМЕРИКАНСКИЙ СЕКТОР
НОСИТЬ ОРУЖИЕ ЗАПРЕЩЕНО В НЕСЛУЖЕБНОЕ ВРЕМЯ
ПОВИНУИТЕСЬ ДОРОЖНЫМ ПРАВИЛАМ
VOUS ENTREZ DANS LE SECTEUR AMERICAIN
DEFENSE DE PORTER DES ARMES EN DEHORS DU SERVICE
OBEISSEZ AUX REGLES DE CIRCULATION
SIE BETRETEN DEN AMERIKANISCHEN SEKTOR
I NEVER WOULD HAVE THOUGHT I'D BE WELCOMED IN THIS PLACE.
Wolfshopf Haus
DO YOU KNOW WHAT?
I WAS RIGHT.

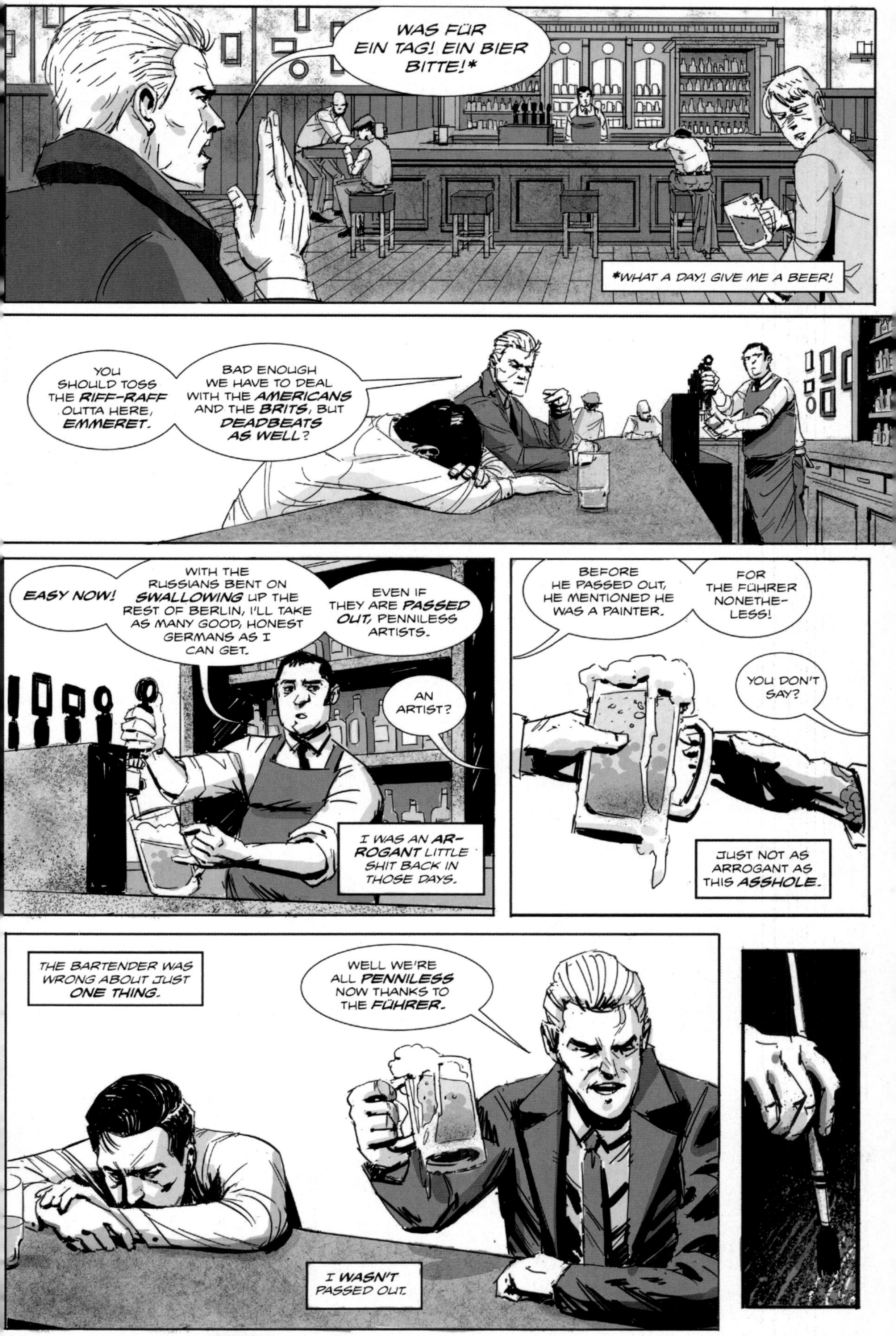
WAS FÜR EIN TAG! EIN BIER BITTE!*
*WHAT A DAY! GIVE ME A BEER!
YOU SHOULD TOSS THE RIFF-RAFF OUTTA HERE, EMMERET.
BAD ENOUGH WE HAVE TO DEAL WITH THE AMERICANS AND THE BRITS, BUT DEADBEATS AS WELL?
EASY NOW!
WITH THE RUSSIANS BENT ON SWALLOWING UP THE REST OF BERLIN, I'LL TAKE AS MANY GOOD, HONEST GERMANS AS I CAN GET.
EVEN IF THEY ARE PASSED OUT, PENNILESS ARTISTS.
AN ARTIST?
I WAS AN ARROGANT LITTLE SHIT BACK IN THOSE DAYS.
BEFORE HE PASSED OUT, HE MENTIONED HE WAS A PAINTER.
FOR THE FÜHRER NONETHELESS!
YOU DON'T SAY?
JUST NOT AS ARROGANT AS THIS ASSHOLE.
THE BARTENDER WAS WRONG ABOUT JUST ONE THING.
WELL WE'RE ALL PENNILESS NOW THANKS TO THE FÜHRER.
I WASN'T PASSED OUT.

I WAS AN ARTIST. *AM* AN ARTIST.

WENT TO UNIVERSITY FOR IT AND EVERYTHING.

MY FAVORITE CLASS WAS *ART HISTORY*.

LOVE THE STORIES BEHIND THE PAINT.

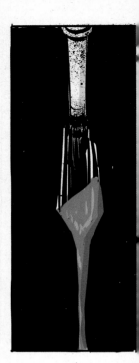

FOR INSTANCE, THAT BEAUTY THERE TELLS ME HE'S PART OF THE *U.S. NAVY.* SUBMARINE DIVISION.

LIKELY COMES FROM A FARM OUT IN AMERICA, NEVER EVEN SAW THE OCEAN BEFORE THE WAR.

HE'LL WEAR IT *PROUDLY.* TELL HIS GRANDCHILDREN ALL ABOUT HIS ADVENTURES WHEN HE'S OLD AND GRAY.

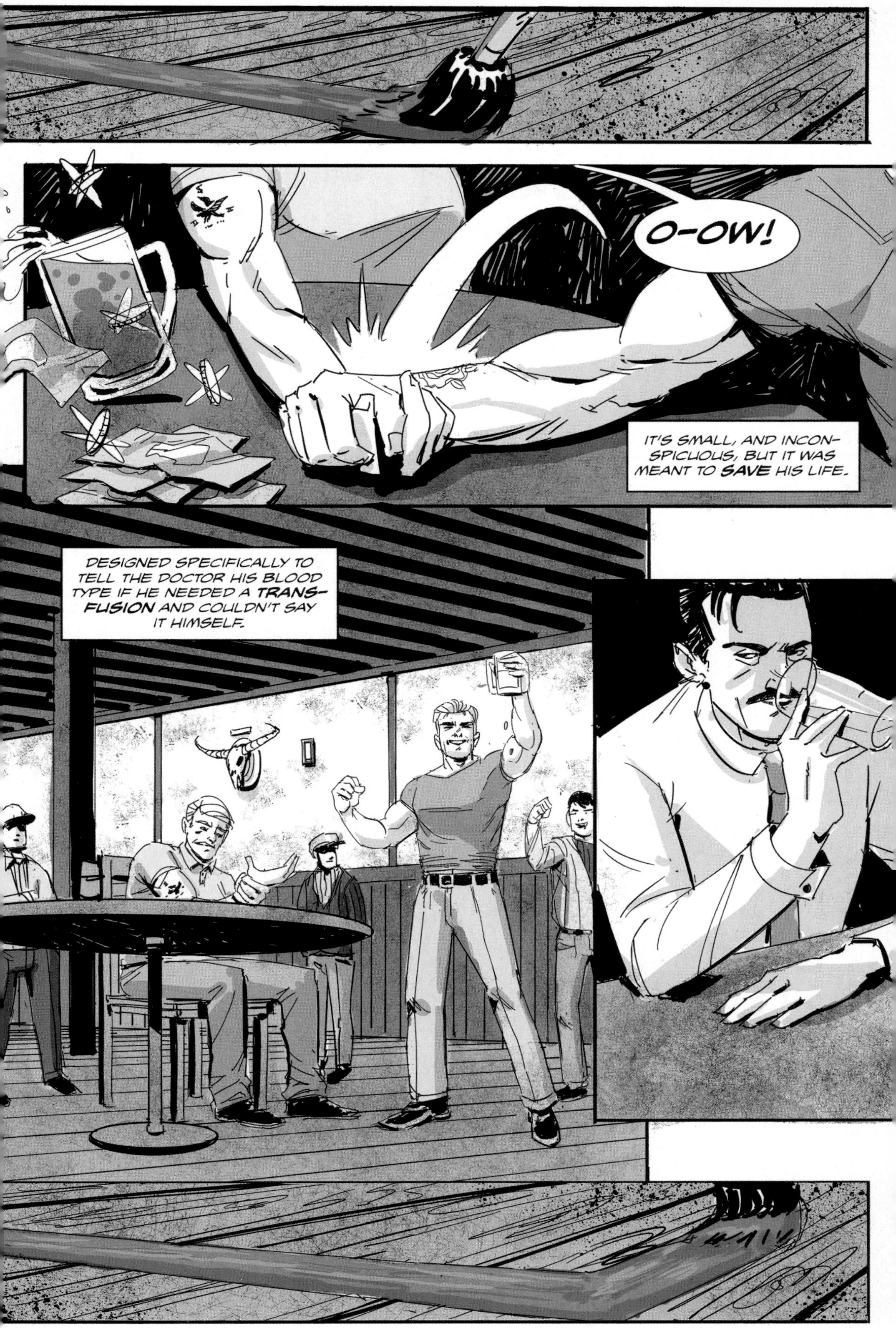
O-OW!
IT'S SMALL, AND INCON-SPICUOUS, BUT IT WAS MEANT TO **SAVE** HIS LIFE.
DESIGNED SPECIFICALLY TO TELL THE DOCTOR HIS BLOOD TYPE IF HE NEEDED A **TRANS-FUSION** AND COULDN'T SAY IT HIMSELF.

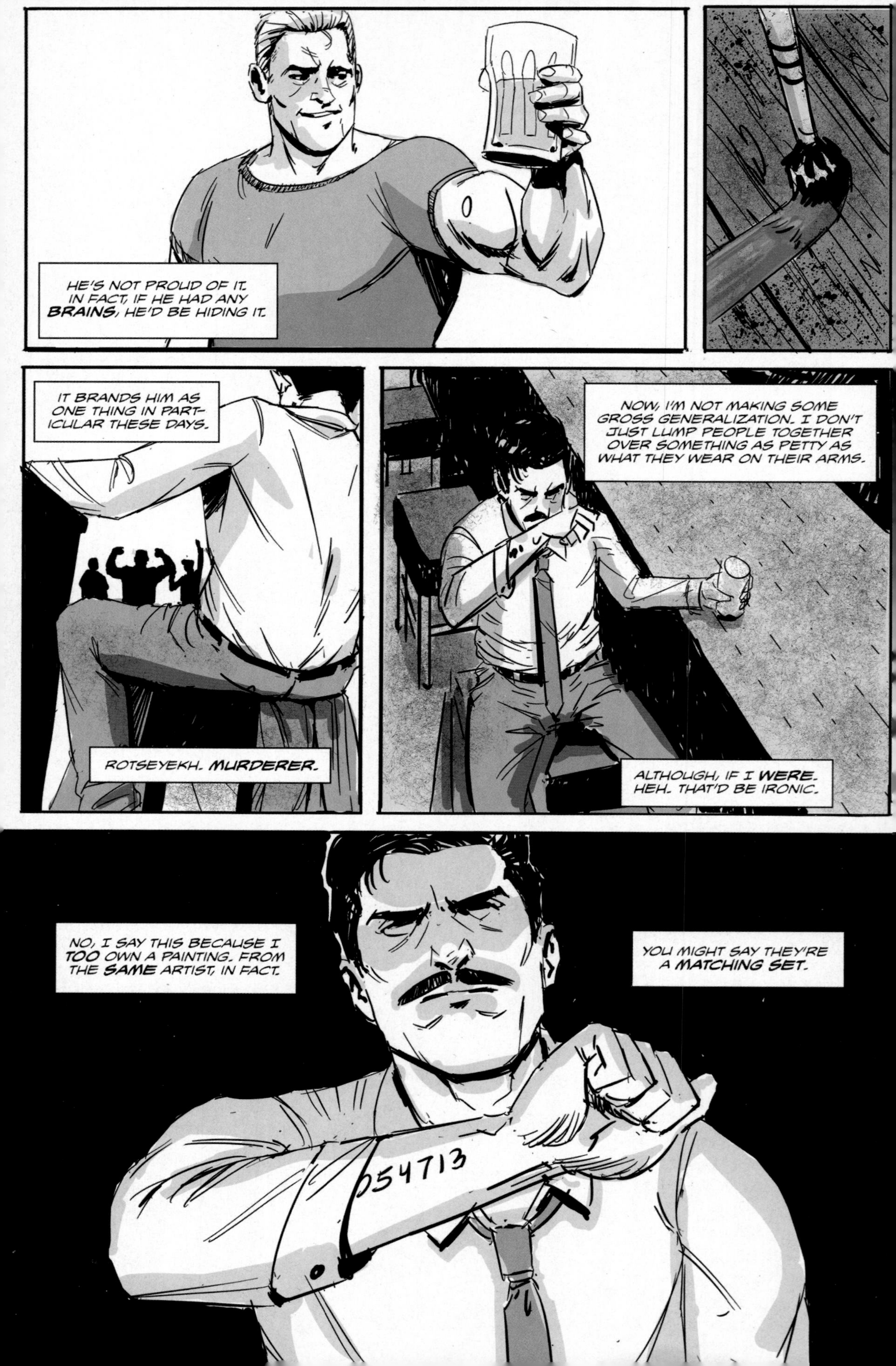
HE'S NOT PROUD OF IT. IN FACT, IF HE HAD ANY **BRAINS**, HE'D BE HIDING IT.
IT BRANDS HIM AS ONE THING IN PART-ICULAR THESE DAYS.
ROTSEYEKH. **MURDERER.**
NOW, I'M NOT MAKING SOME GROSS GENERALIZATION. I DON'T JUST LUMP PEOPLE TOGETHER OVER SOMETHING AS PETTY AS WHAT THEY WEAR ON THEIR ARMS.
ALTHOUGH, IF I **WERE**. HEH. THAT'D BE IRONIC.
NO, I SAY THIS BECAUSE I **TOO** OWN A PAINTING. FROM THE **SAME** ARTIST, IN FACT.
YOU MIGHT SAY THEY'RE A **MATCHING SET**.
054713

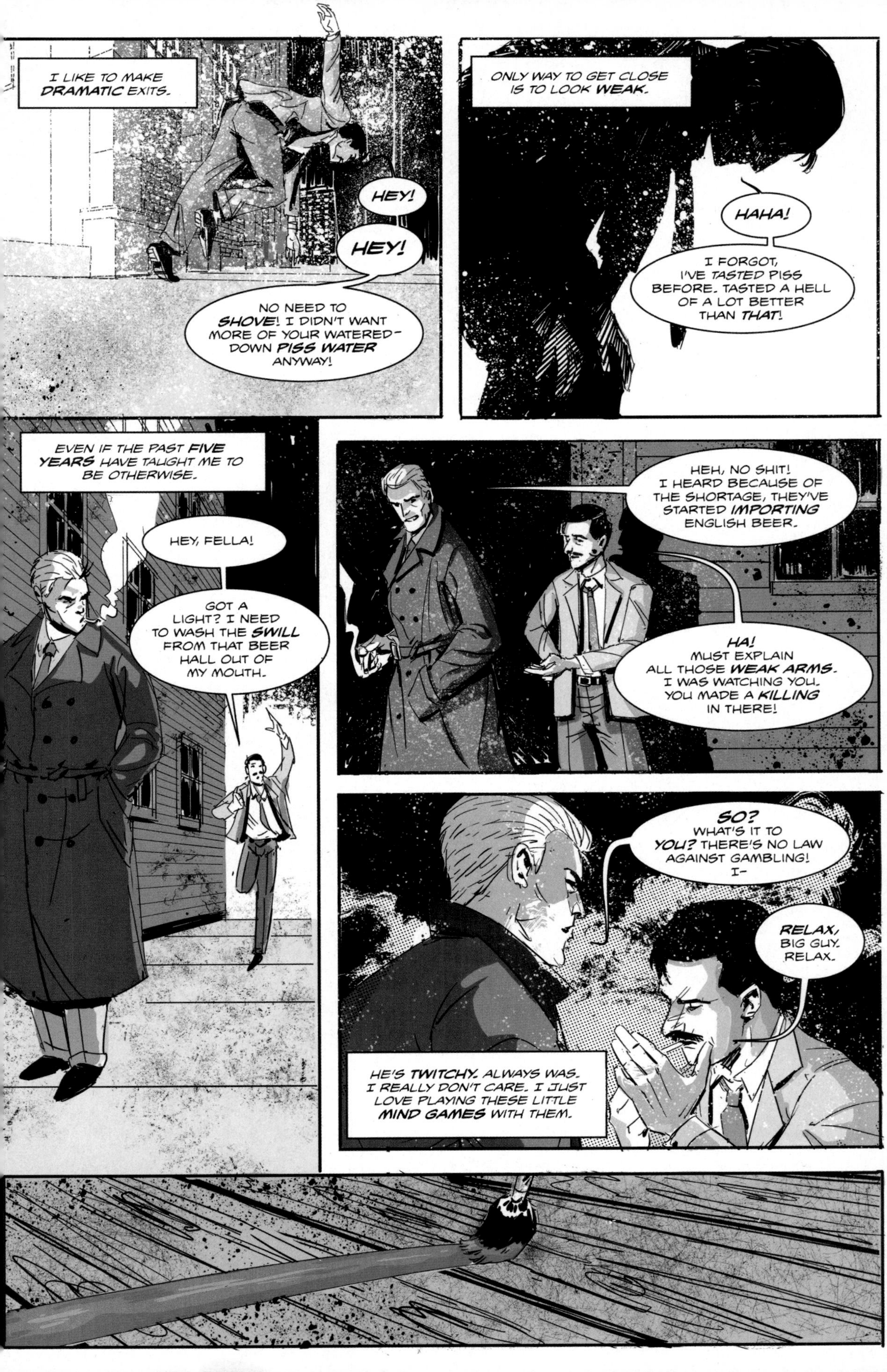
I LIKE TO MAKE DRAMATIC EXITS.
HEY!
HEY!
NO NEED TO SHOVE! I DIDN'T WANT MORE OF YOUR WATERED-DOWN PISS WATER ANYWAY!
ONLY WAY TO GET CLOSE IS TO LOOK WEAK.
HAHA!
I FORGOT, I'VE TASTED PISS BEFORE. TASTED A HELL OF A LOT BETTER THAN THAT!
EVEN IF THE PAST FIVE YEARS HAVE TAUGHT ME TO BE OTHERWISE.
HEY, FELLA!
GOT A LIGHT? I NEED TO WASH THE SWILL FROM THAT BEER HALL OUT OF MY MOUTH.
HEH, NO SHIT! I HEARD BECAUSE OF THE SHORTAGE, THEY'VE STARTED IMPORTING ENGLISH BEER.
HA! MUST EXPLAIN ALL THOSE WEAK ARMS. I WAS WATCHING YOU. YOU MADE A KILLING IN THERE!
SO? WHAT'S IT TO YOU? THERE'S NO LAW AGAINST GAMBLING! I-
RELAX, BIG GUY. RELAX.
HE'S TWITCHY. ALWAYS WAS. I REALLY DON'T CARE. I JUST LOVE PLAYING THESE LITTLE MIND GAMES WITH THEM.

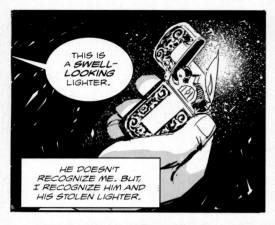

THIS IS A *SWELL-LOOKING* LIGHTER.

HE DOESN'T *RECOGNIZE* ME. BUT, I *RECOGNIZE* HIM AND HIS *STOLEN* LIGHTER.

REMINDS ME OF A FRIEND OF MINE'S, *LUCA.*

HE *LOVED* THAT DAMN THING. GREAT GUY! SMOKED LIKE A *CHIMNEY* THOUGH!

IT WAS HIS ONLY VICE. SMOKING. HE WAS ACTUALLY VERY RELIGIOUS. THE LIGHTER HAD GENESIS 3:1-3 ENGRAVED IN HEBREW ON THE BACK.

HEY, *JUST* LIKE THIS ONE, LOOK AT THAT!

YOU KNOW GENESIS, *RIGHT?* FROM THE BOOK OF CREATION? YOU KNOW WHAT THIS SAYS IN HEBREW?

OF COURSE HE DOESN'T. TALL, BLOND ARYAN LIKE *HIM?* PROBABLY NEVER EVEN HEARD OF A BOOK! TOO BUSY *BURNING* THEM ALL.

LUCA COULD HAVE TOLD YOU.

BEFORE YOU *PLUCKED* IT FROM HIS DEAD BODY. RIGHT *TONY?*

I DON'T HAVE TO LOOK UP TO SEE THAT I'M *SEC-ONDS* AWAY FROM *DEATH.*

WHO THE *FUCK* ARE YOU? HOW DO YOU KNOW MY *NAME?*

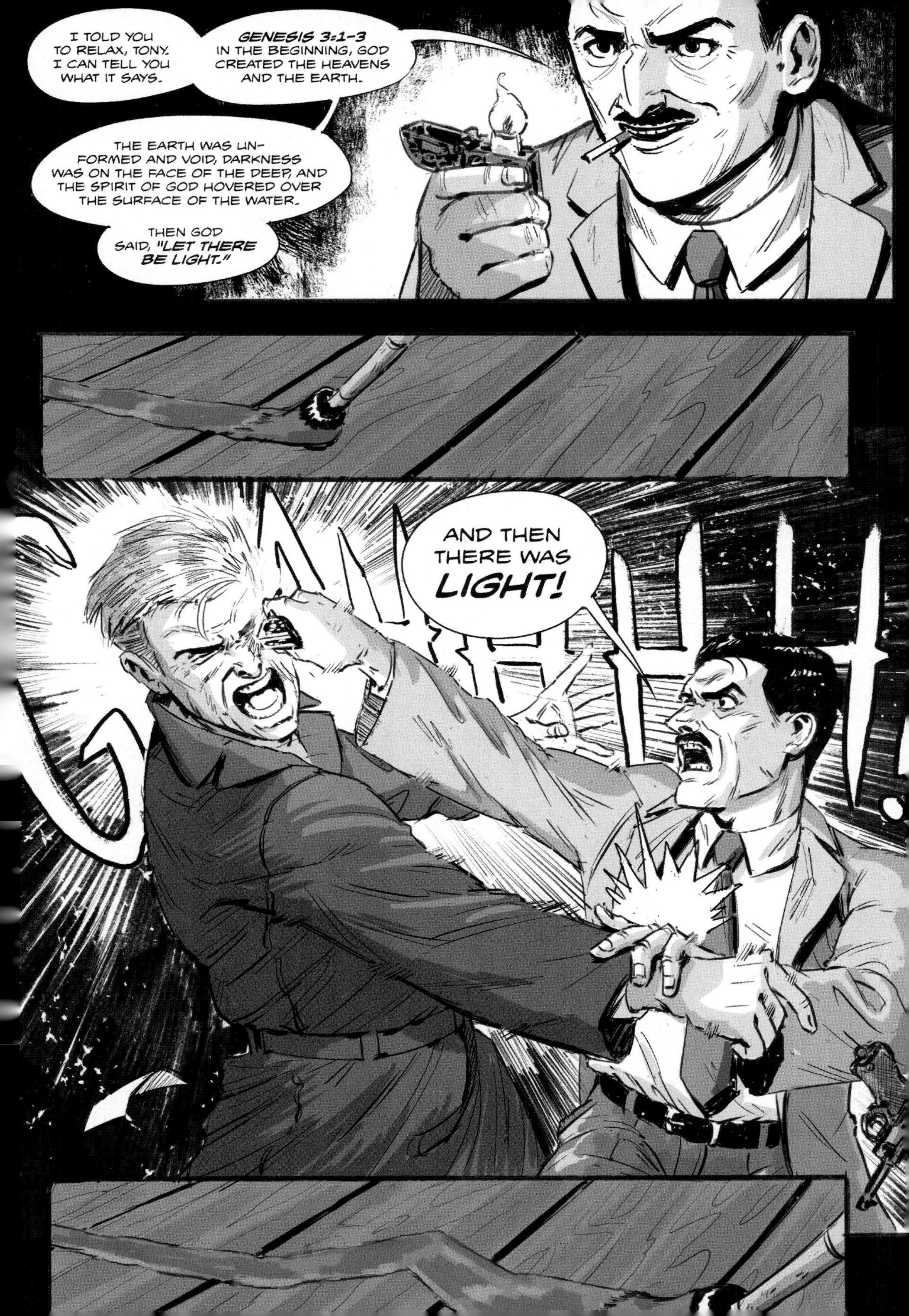
I TOLD YOU TO RELAX, TONY. I CAN TELL YOU WHAT IT SAYS.
GENESIS 3:1-3 IN THE BEGINNING, GOD CREATED THE HEAVENS AND THE EARTH.
THE EARTH WAS UN-FORMED AND VOID, DARKNESS WAS ON THE FACE OF THE DEEP, AND THE SPIRIT OF GOD HOVERED OVER THE SURFACE OF THE WATER.
THEN GOD SAID, "LET THERE BE LIGHT."
AND THEN THERE WAS LIGHT!

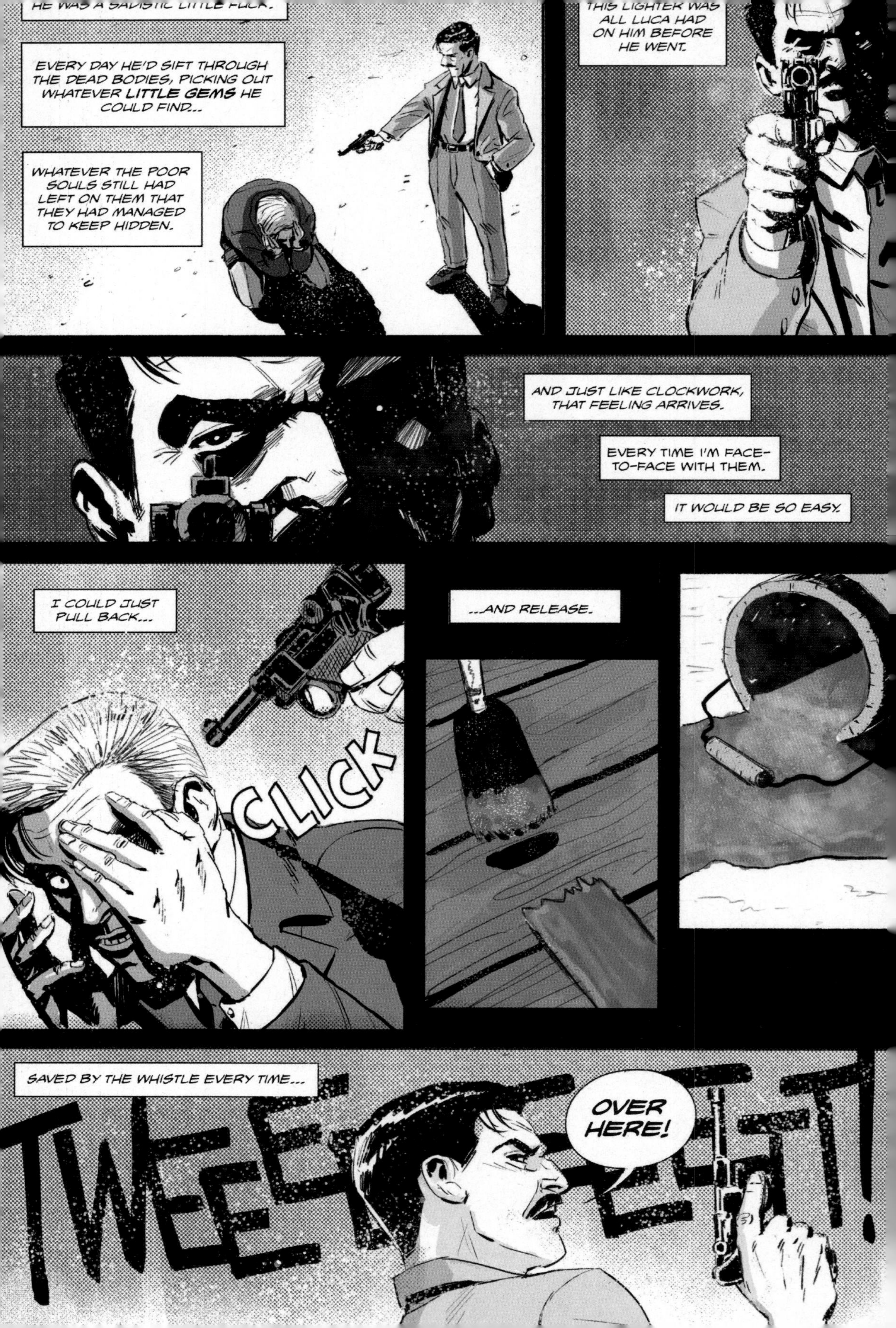
HE WAS A SADISTIC LITTLE FUCK.
EVERY DAY HE'D SIFT THROUGH THE DEAD BODIES, PICKING OUT WHATEVER LITTLE GEMS HE COULD FIND...
WHATEVER THE POOR SOULS STILL HAD LEFT ON THEM THAT THEY HAD MANAGED TO KEEP HIDDEN.
THIS LIGHTER WAS ALL LUCA HAD ON HIM BEFORE HE WENT.
AND JUST LIKE CLOCKWORK, THAT FEELING ARRIVES.
EVERY TIME I'M FACE-TO-FACE WITH THEM.
IT WOULD BE SO EASY.
I COULD JUST PULL BACK...
CLICK
...AND RELEASE.
SAVED BY THE WHISTLE EVERY TIME...
OVER HERE!

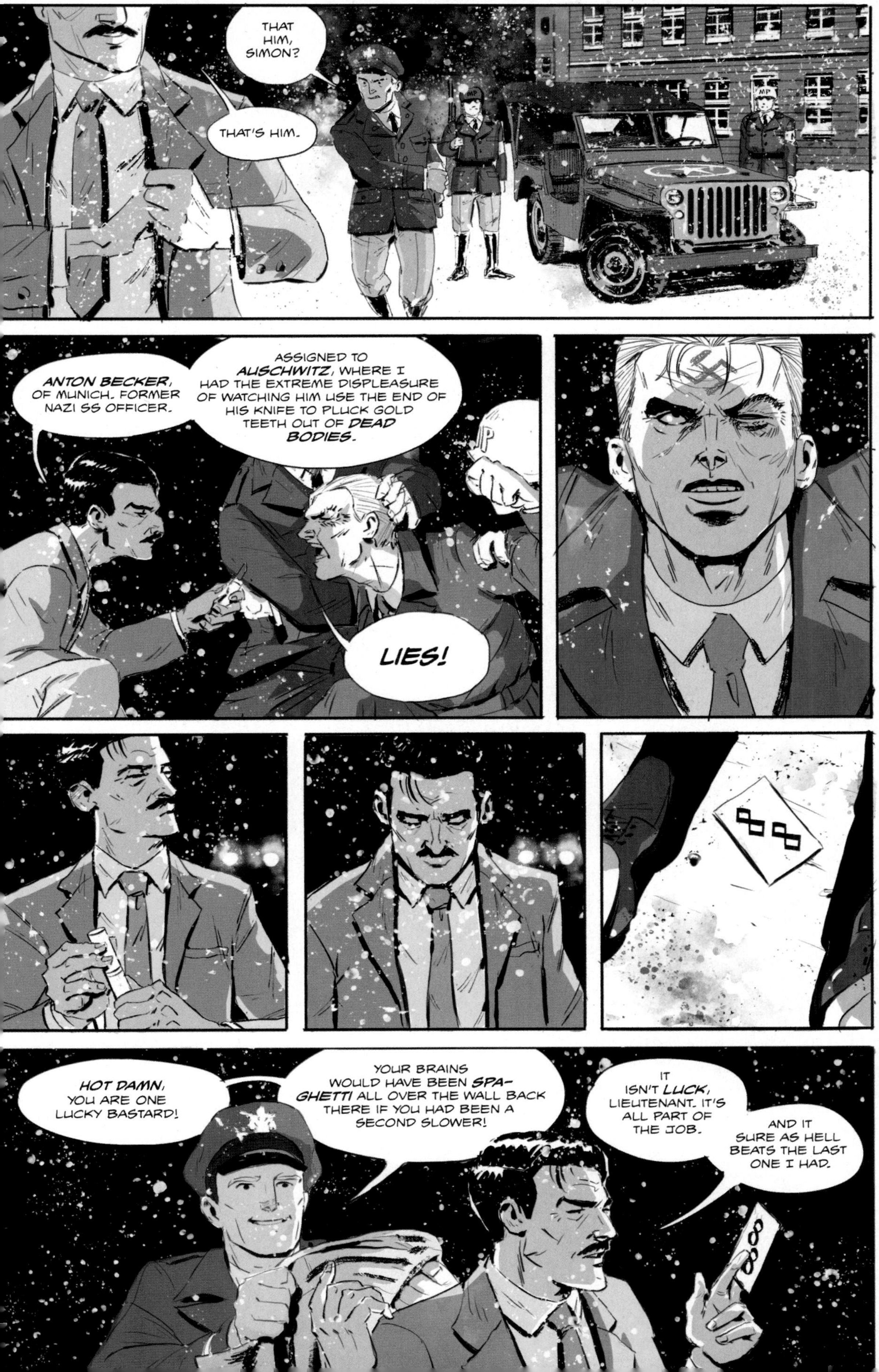
THAT HIM, SIMON?
THAT'S HIM.
ANTON BECKER, OF MUNICH. FORMER NAZI SS OFFICER.
ASSIGNED TO AUSCHWITZ, WHERE I HAD THE EXTREME DISPLEASURE OF WATCHING HIM USE THE END OF HIS KNIFE TO PLUCK GOLD TEETH OUT OF DEAD BODIES.
LIES!
HOT DAMN, YOU ARE ONE LUCKY BASTARD!
YOUR BRAINS WOULD HAVE BEEN SPA-GHETTI ALL OVER THE WALL BACK THERE IF YOU HAD BEEN A SECOND SLOWER!
IT ISN'T LUCK, LIEUTENANT. IT'S ALL PART OF THE JOB.
AND IT SURE AS HELL BEATS THE LAST ONE I HAD.

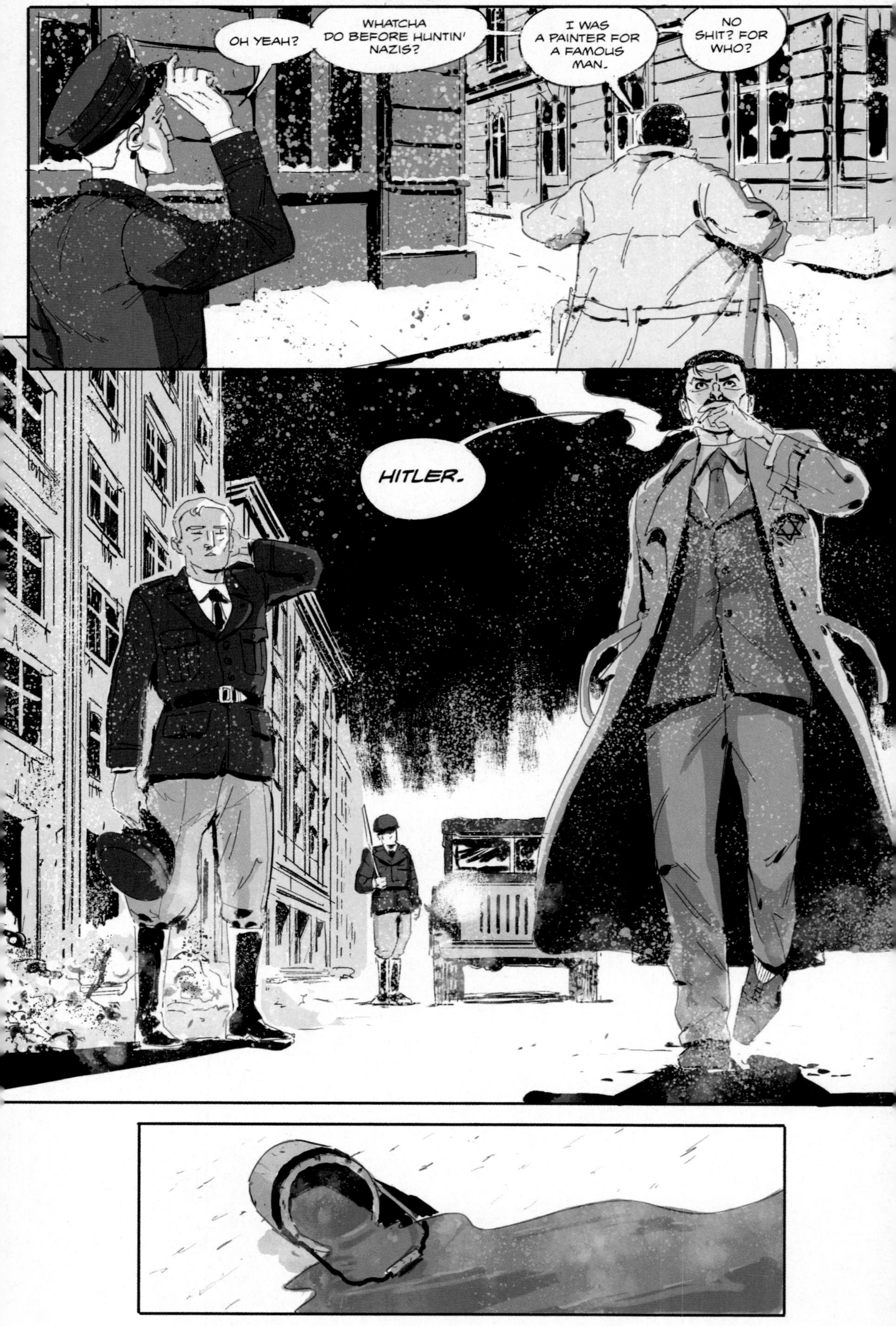
OH YEAH?
WHATCHA DO BEFORE HUNTIN' NAZIS?
I WAS A PAINTER FOR A FAMOUS MAN.
NO SHIT? FOR WHO?
HITLER.

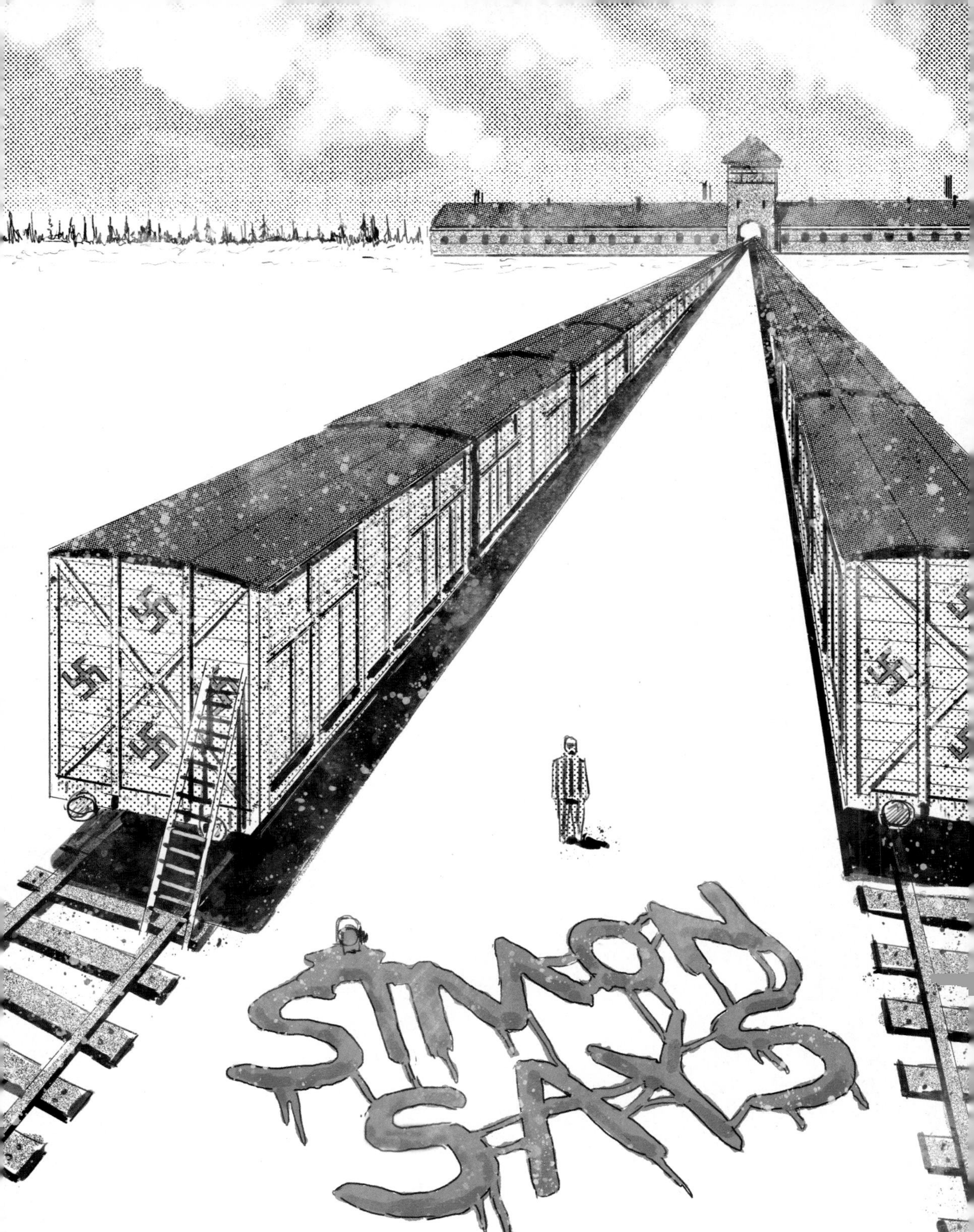
SIMON SAYS

ANDRE R. FRATTINO WRITER
JESSE LEE ARTIST/LETTERING

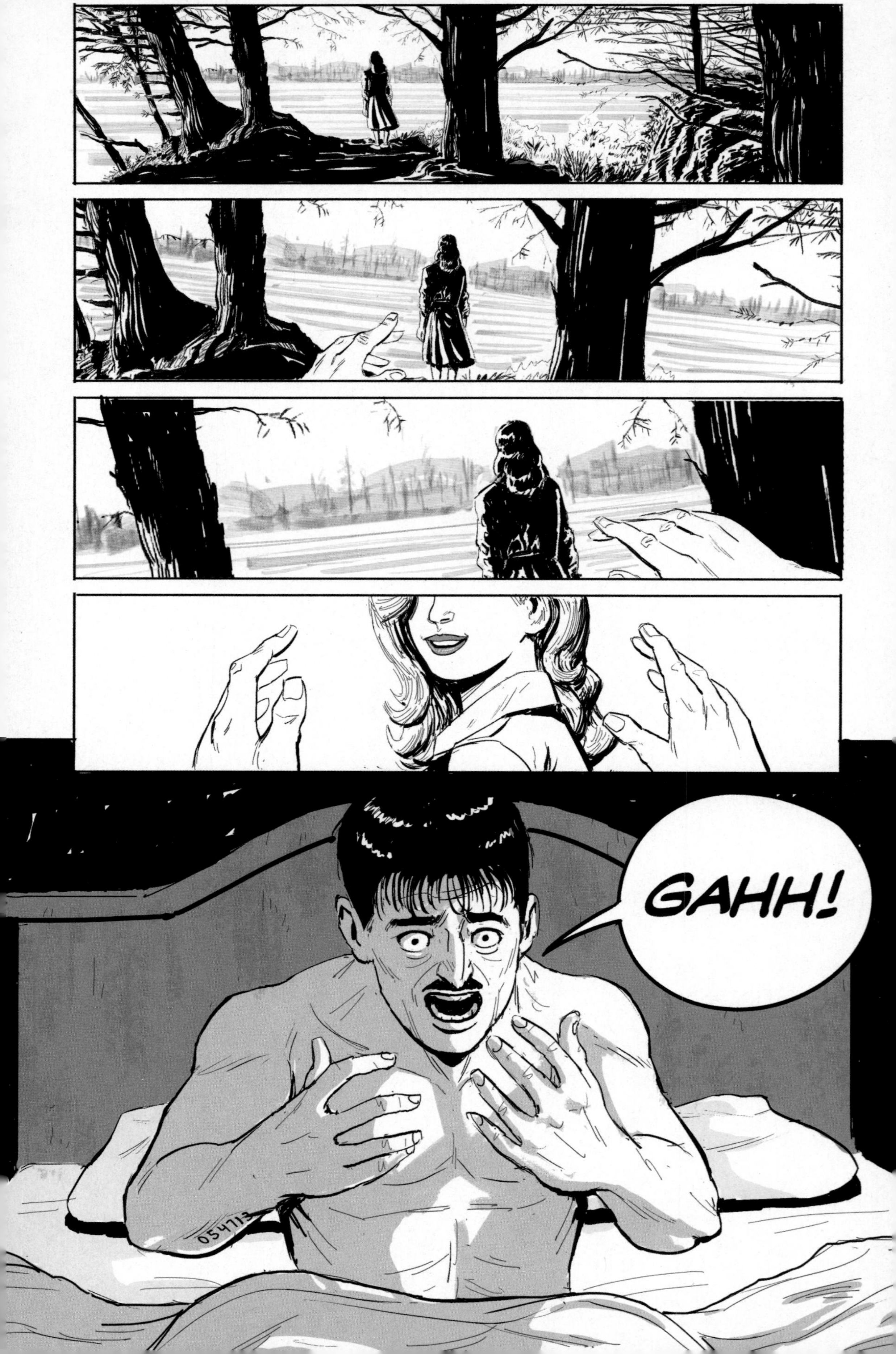
GAHH!

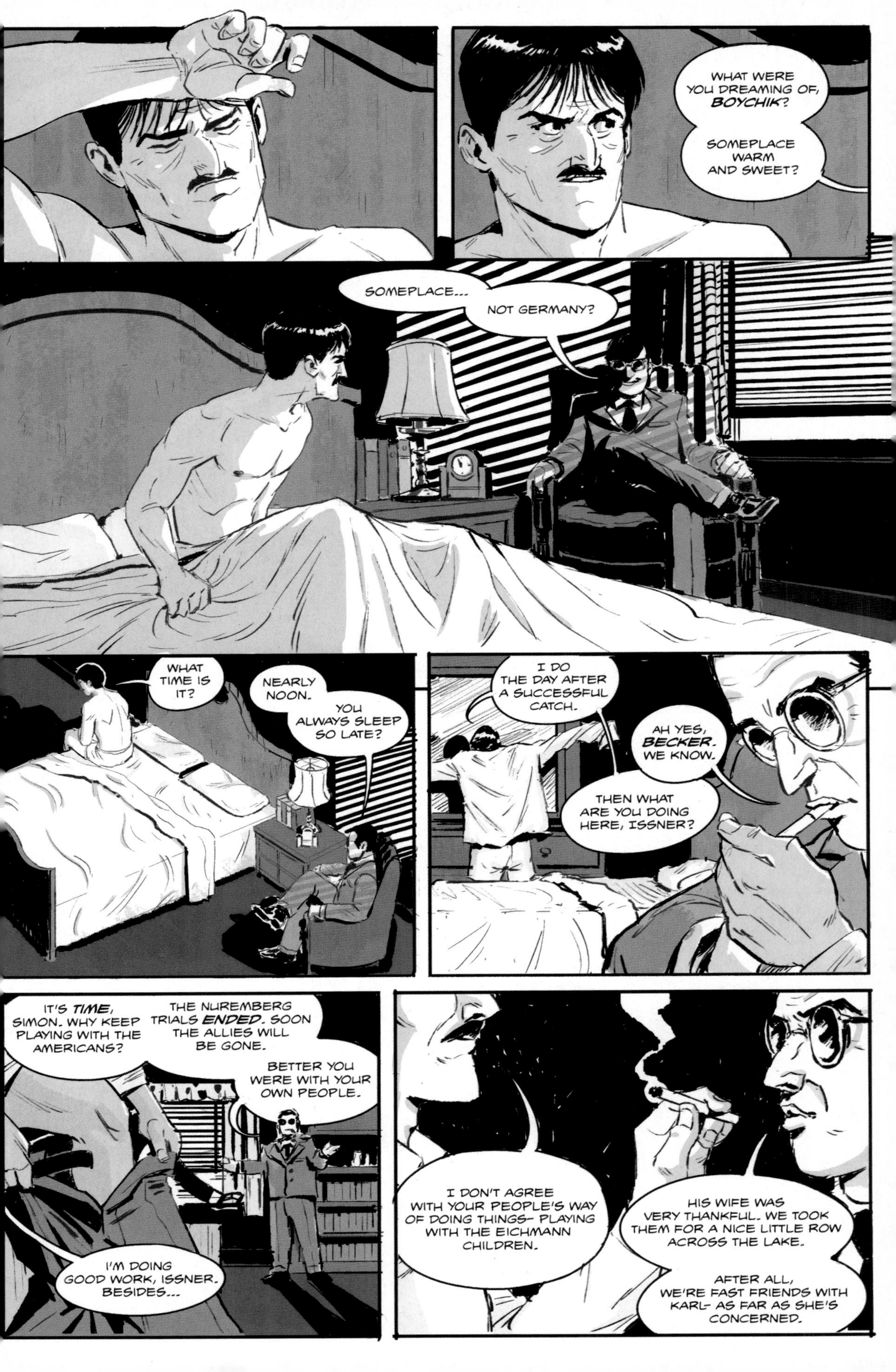
WHAT WERE YOU DREAMING OF, ***BOYCHIK***?
SOMEPLACE WARM AND SWEET?
SOMEPLACE...
NOT GERMANY?
WHAT TIME IS IT?
NEARLY NOON.
YOU ALWAYS SLEEP SO LATE?
I DO THE DAY AFTER A SUCCESSFUL CATCH.
AH YES, ***BECKER***. WE KNOW.
THEN WHAT ARE YOU DOING HERE, ISSNER?
IT'S ***TIME***, SIMON. WHY KEEP PLAYING WITH THE AMERICANS?
THE NUREMBERG TRIALS ***ENDED***. SOON THE ALLIES WILL BE GONE.
BETTER YOU WERE WITH YOUR OWN PEOPLE.
I'M DOING GOOD WORK, ISSNER. BESIDES...
I DON'T AGREE WITH YOUR PEOPLE'S WAY OF DOING THINGS-- PLAYING WITH THE EICHMANN CHILDREN.
HIS WIFE WAS VERY THANKFUL. WE TOOK THEM FOR A NICE LITTLE ROW ACROSS THE LAKE.
AFTER ALL, WE'RE FAST FRIENDS WITH KARL-- AS FAR AS SHE'S CONCERNED.

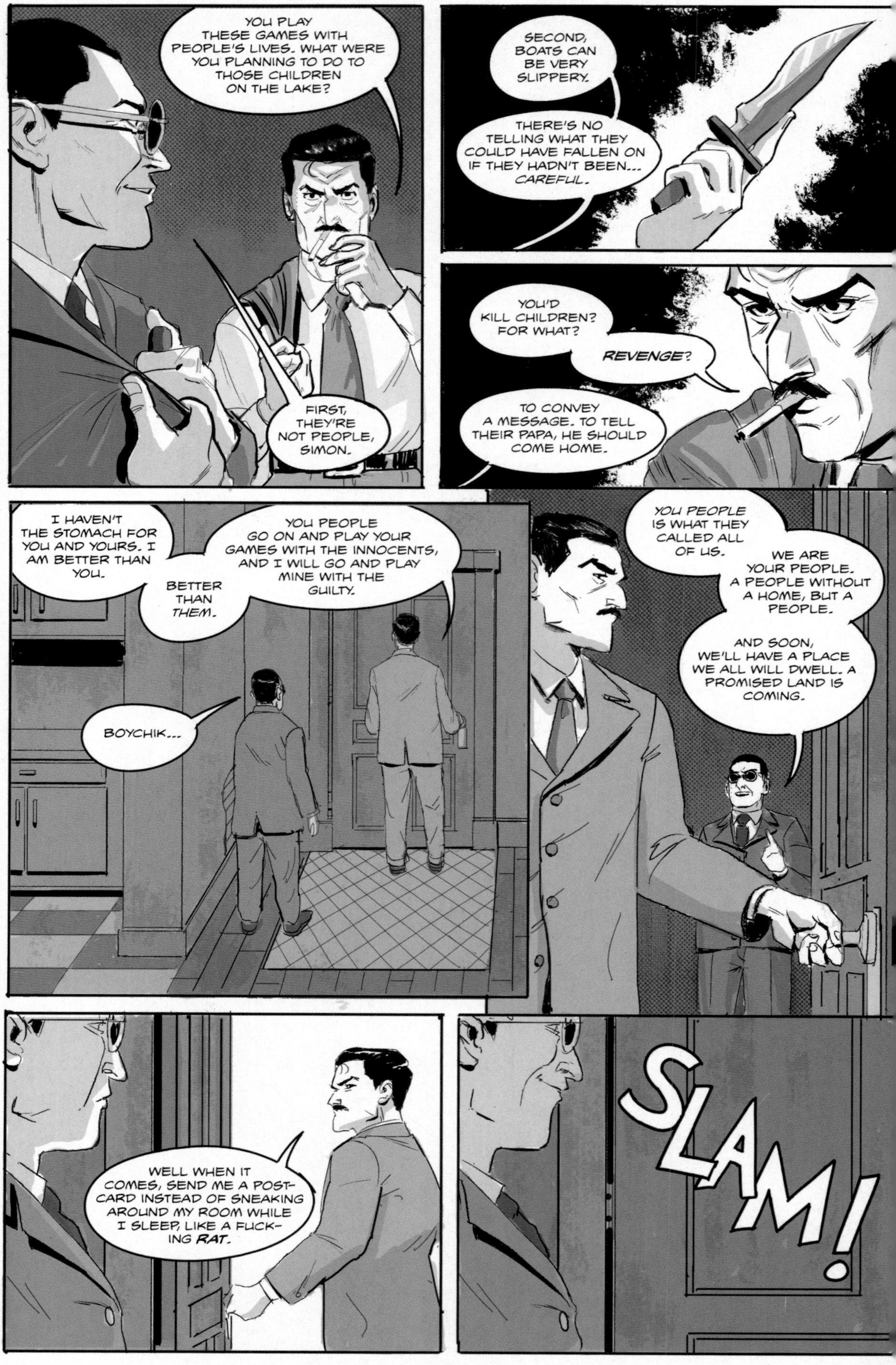
YOU PLAY THESE GAMES WITH PEOPLE'S LIVES. WHAT WERE YOU PLANNING TO DO TO THOSE CHILDREN ON THE LAKE?
FIRST, THEY'RE NOT PEOPLE, SIMON.
SECOND, BOATS CAN BE VERY SLIPPERY.
THERE'S NO TELLING WHAT THEY COULD HAVE FALLEN ON IF THEY HADN'T BEEN... *CAREFUL*.
YOU'D KILL CHILDREN? FOR WHAT?
REVENGE?
TO CONVEY A MESSAGE. TO TELL THEIR PAPA, HE SHOULD COME HOME.
I HAVEN'T THE STOMACH FOR YOU AND YOURS. I AM BETTER THAN YOU.
BETTER THAN *THEM*.
YOU PEOPLE GO ON AND PLAY YOUR GAMES WITH THE INNOCENTS, AND I WILL GO AND PLAY MINE WITH THE GUILTY.
BOYCHIK...
YOU PEOPLE IS WHAT THEY CALLED ALL OF US.
WE ARE YOUR PEOPLE. A PEOPLE WITHOUT A HOME, BUT A PEOPLE.
AND SOON, WE'LL HAVE A PLACE WE ALL WILL DWELL. A PROMISED LAND IS COMING.
WELL WHEN IT COMES, SEND ME A POST-CARD INSTEAD OF SNEAKING AROUND MY ROOM WHILE I SLEEP, LIKE A FUCKING *RAT*.
SLAM!

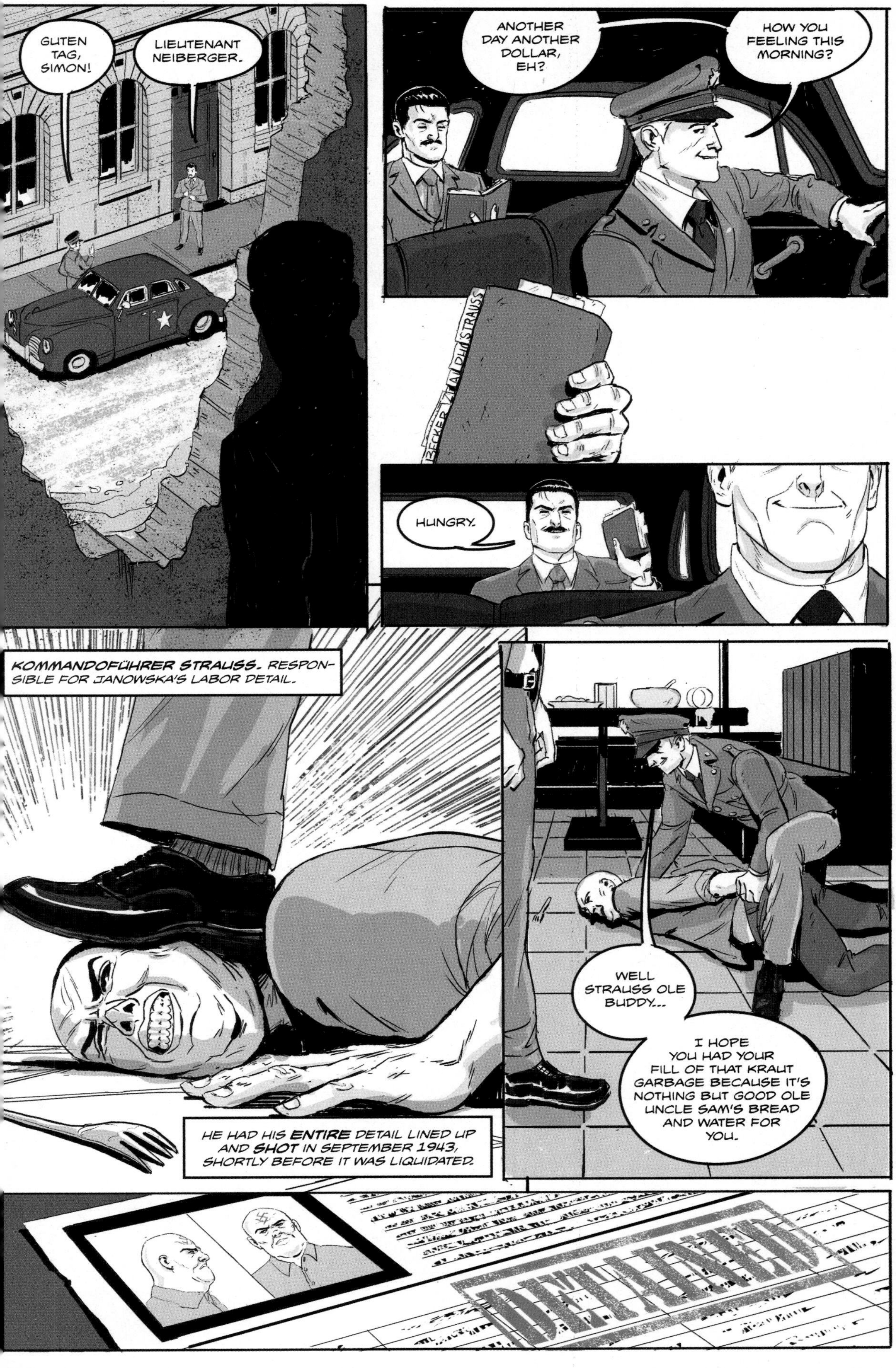
GUTEN TAG, SIMON!
LIEUTENANT NEIBERGER.
ANOTHER DAY ANOTHER DOLLAR, EH?
HOW YOU FEELING THIS MORNING?
BECKER
STRAUSS
HUNGRY.
KOMMANDOFÜHRER STRAUSS. RESPONSIBLE FOR JANOWSKA'S LABOR DETAIL.
HE HAD HIS ENTIRE DETAIL LINED UP AND SHOT IN SEPTEMBER 1943, SHORTLY BEFORE IT WAS LIQUIDATED.
WELL STRAUSS OLE BUDDY...
I HOPE YOU HAD YOUR FILL OF THAT KRAUT GARBAGE BECAUSE IT'S NOTHING BUT GOOD OLE UNCLE SAM'S BREAD AND WATER FOR YOU.
DETAINED

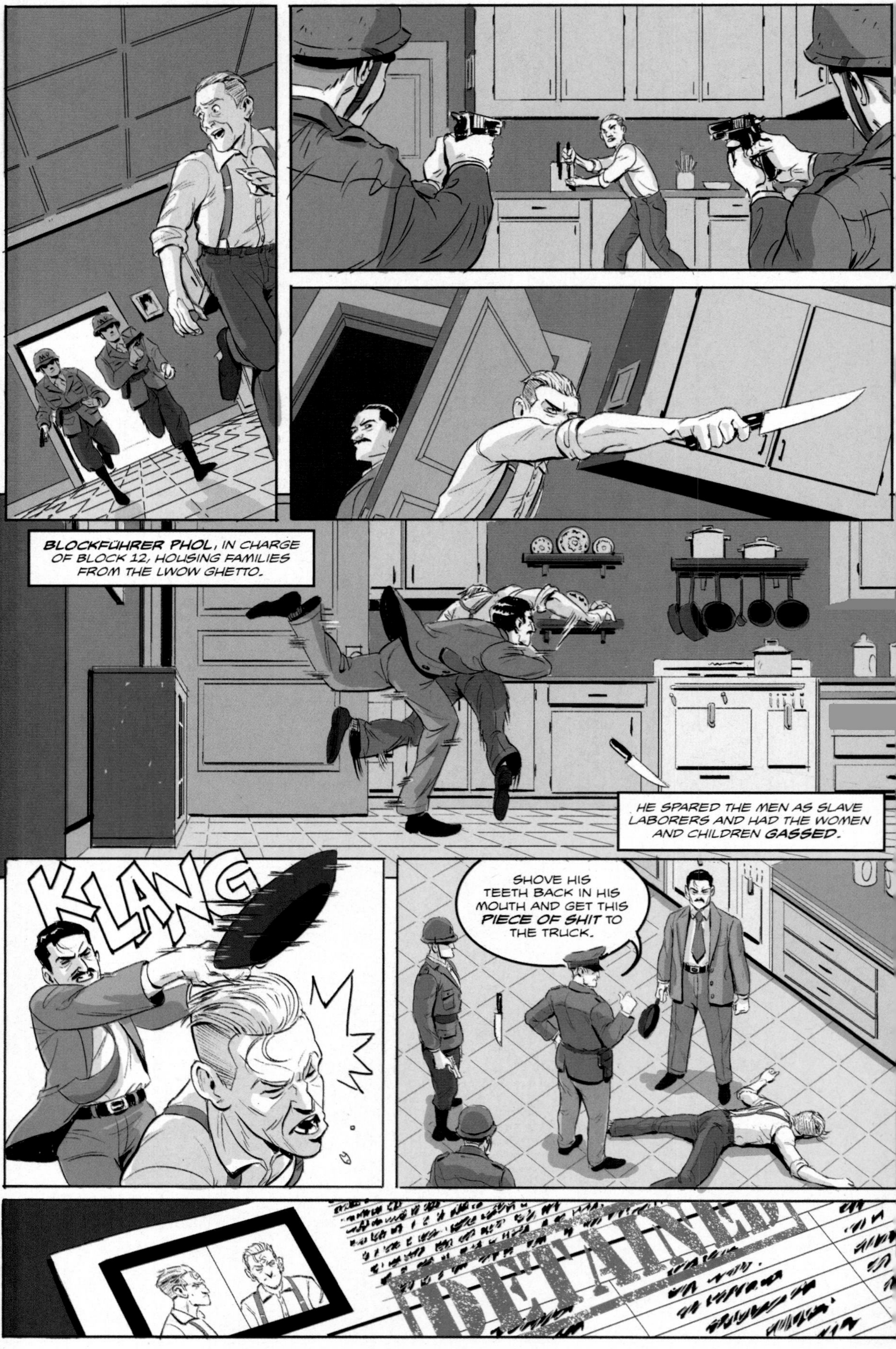
BLOCKFÜHRER PHOL, IN CHARGE OF BLOCK 12, HOUSING FAMILIES FROM THE LWOW GHETTO.
HE SPARED THE MEN AS SLAVE LABORERS AND HAD THE WOMEN AND CHILDREN GASSED.
KLANG
SHOVE HIS TEETH BACK IN HIS MOUTH AND GET THIS PIECE OF SHIT TO THE TRUCK.
DETAINED

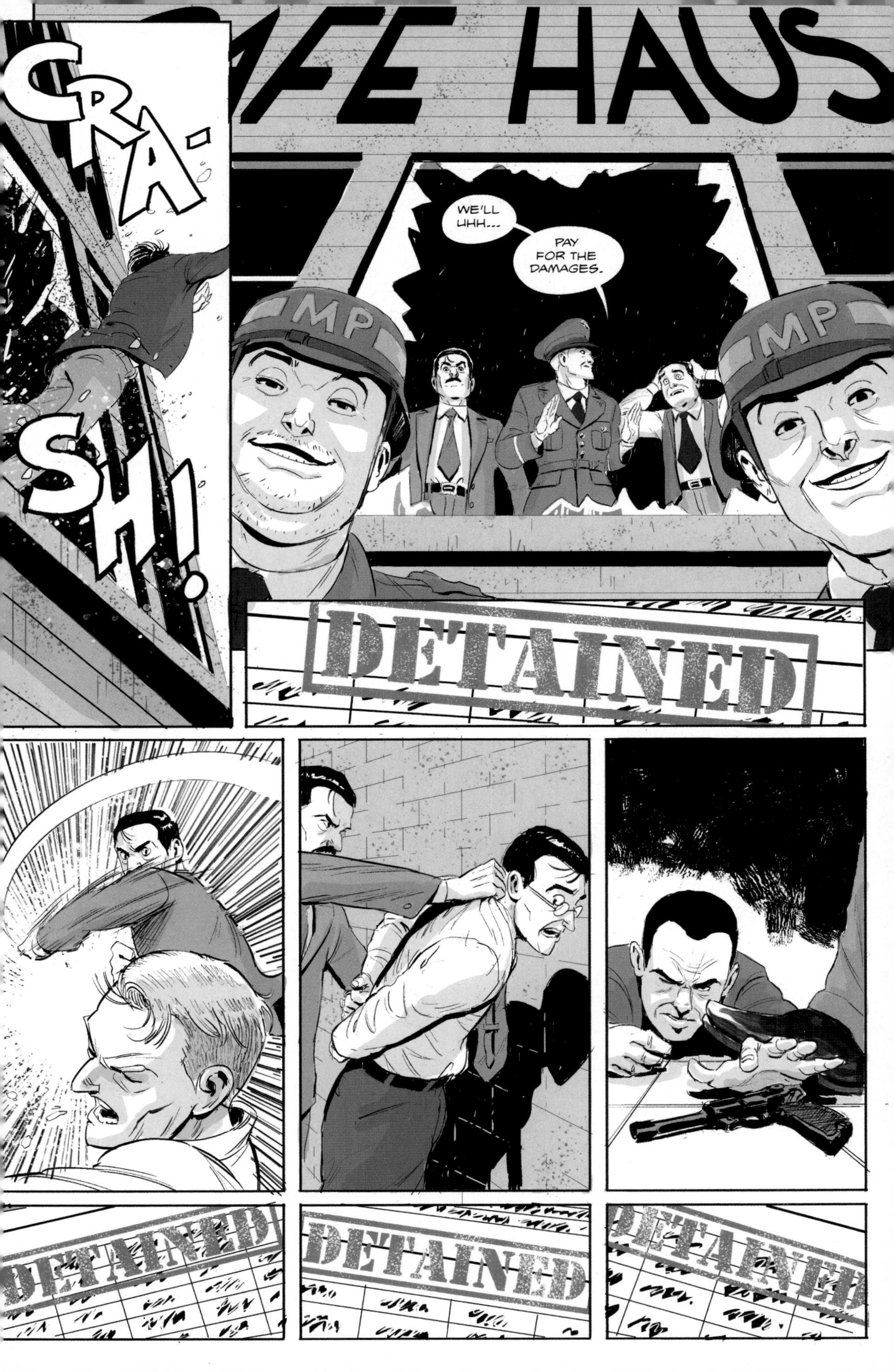
CAFE HAUS
CRA-
SH!
WE'LL UHH...
PAY FOR THE DAMAGES.
MP
MP
DETAINED
DETAINED
DETAINED
DETAINED

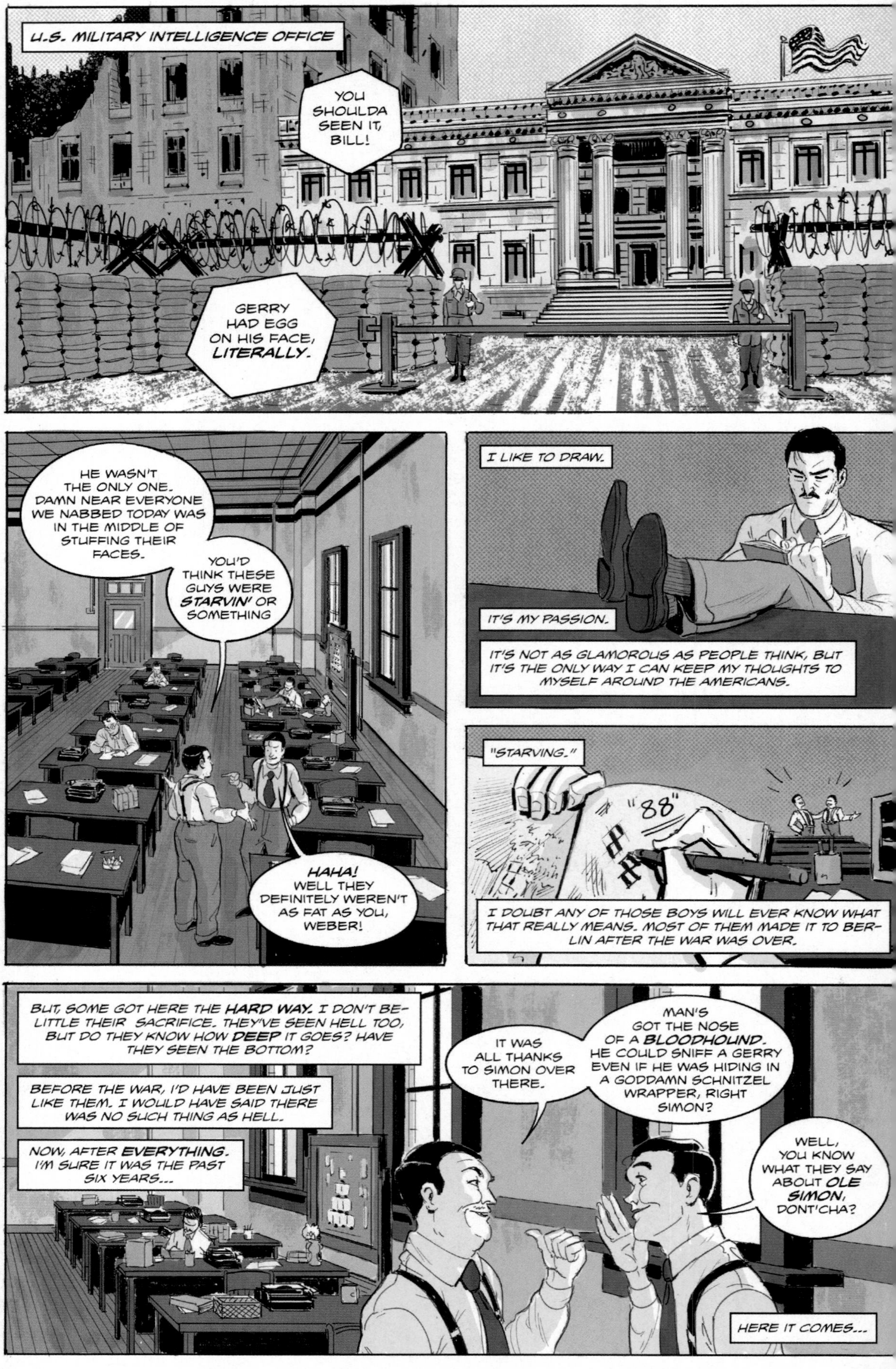
U.S. MILITARY INTELLIGENCE OFFICE
YOU SHOULDA SEEN IT, BILL!
GERRY HAD EGG ON HIS FACE, LITERALLY.
HE WASN'T THE ONLY ONE. DAMN NEAR EVERYONE WE NABBED TODAY WAS IN THE MIDDLE OF STUFFING THEIR FACES.
YOU'D THINK THESE GUYS WERE STARVIN' OR SOMETHING
HAHA! WELL THEY DEFINITELY WEREN'T AS FAT AS YOU, WEBER!
I LIKE TO DRAW.
IT'S MY PASSION.
IT'S NOT AS GLAMOROUS AS PEOPLE THINK, BUT IT'S THE ONLY WAY I CAN KEEP MY THOUGHTS TO MYSELF AROUND THE AMERICANS.
"STARVING."
"88"
I DOUBT ANY OF THOSE BOYS WILL EVER KNOW WHAT THAT REALLY MEANS. MOST OF THEM MADE IT TO BER-LIN AFTER THE WAR WAS OVER.
BUT, SOME GOT HERE THE HARD WAY. I DON'T BE-LITTLE THEIR SACRIFICE. THEY'VE SEEN HELL TOO, BUT DO THEY KNOW HOW DEEP IT GOES? HAVE THEY SEEN THE BOTTOM?
BEFORE THE WAR, I'D HAVE BEEN JUST LIKE THEM. I WOULD HAVE SAID THERE WAS NO SUCH THING AS HELL.
NOW, AFTER EVERYTHING. I'M SURE IT WAS THE PAST SIX YEARS...
IT WAS ALL THANKS TO SIMON OVER THERE.
MAN'S GOT THE NOSE OF A BLOODHOUND. HE COULD SNIFF A GERRY EVEN IF HE WAS HIDING IN A GODDAMN SCHNITZEL WRAPPER, RIGHT SIMON?
WELL, YOU KNOW WHAT THEY SAY ABOUT OLE SIMON, DONT'CHA?
HERE IT COMES...

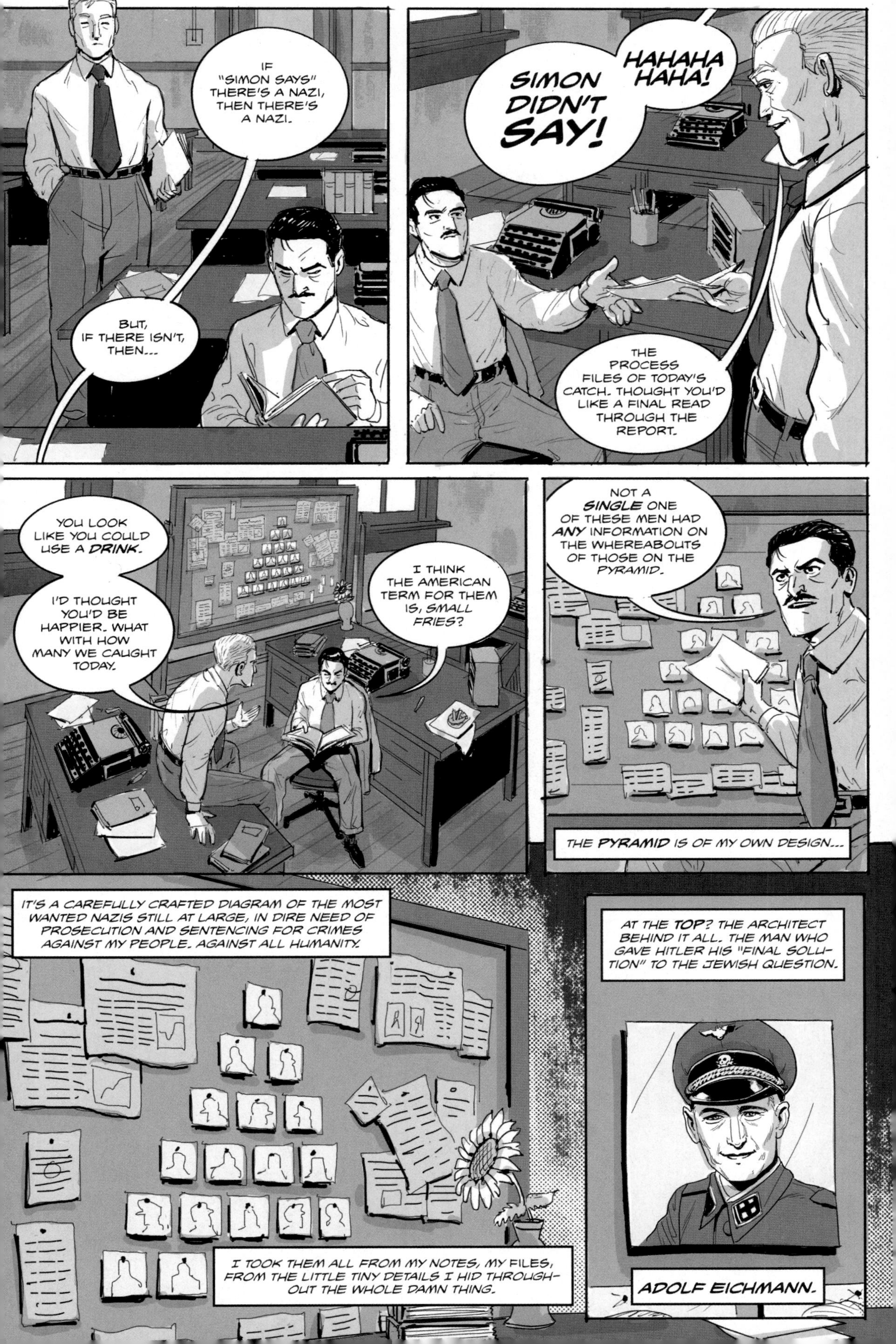
IF "SIMON SAYS" THERE'S A NAZI, THEN THERE'S A NAZI.
BUT, IF THERE ISN'T, THEN...
SIMON DIDN'T SAY!
HAHAHA HAHA!
THE PROCESS FILES OF TODAY'S CATCH. THOUGHT YOU'D LIKE A FINAL READ THROUGH THE REPORT.
YOU LOOK LIKE YOU COULD USE A DRINK.
I'D THOUGHT YOU'D BE HAPPIER. WHAT WITH HOW MANY WE CAUGHT TODAY.
I THINK THE AMERICAN TERM FOR THEM IS, SMALL FRIES?
NOT A SINGLE ONE OF THESE MEN HAD ANY INFORMATION ON THE WHEREABOUTS OF THOSE ON THE PYRAMID.
THE PYRAMID IS OF MY OWN DESIGN...
IT'S A CAREFULLY CRAFTED DIAGRAM OF THE MOST WANTED NAZIS STILL AT LARGE, IN DIRE NEED OF PROSECUTION AND SENTENCING FOR CRIMES AGAINST MY PEOPLE. AGAINST ALL HUMANITY.
I TOOK THEM ALL FROM MY NOTES, MY FILES, FROM THE LITTLE TINY DETAILS I HID THROUGH-OUT THE WHOLE DAMN THING.
AT THE TOP? THE ARCHITECT BEHIND IT ALL. THE MAN WHO GAVE HITLER HIS "FINAL SOLU-TION" TO THE JEWISH QUESTION.
ADOLF EICHMANN.

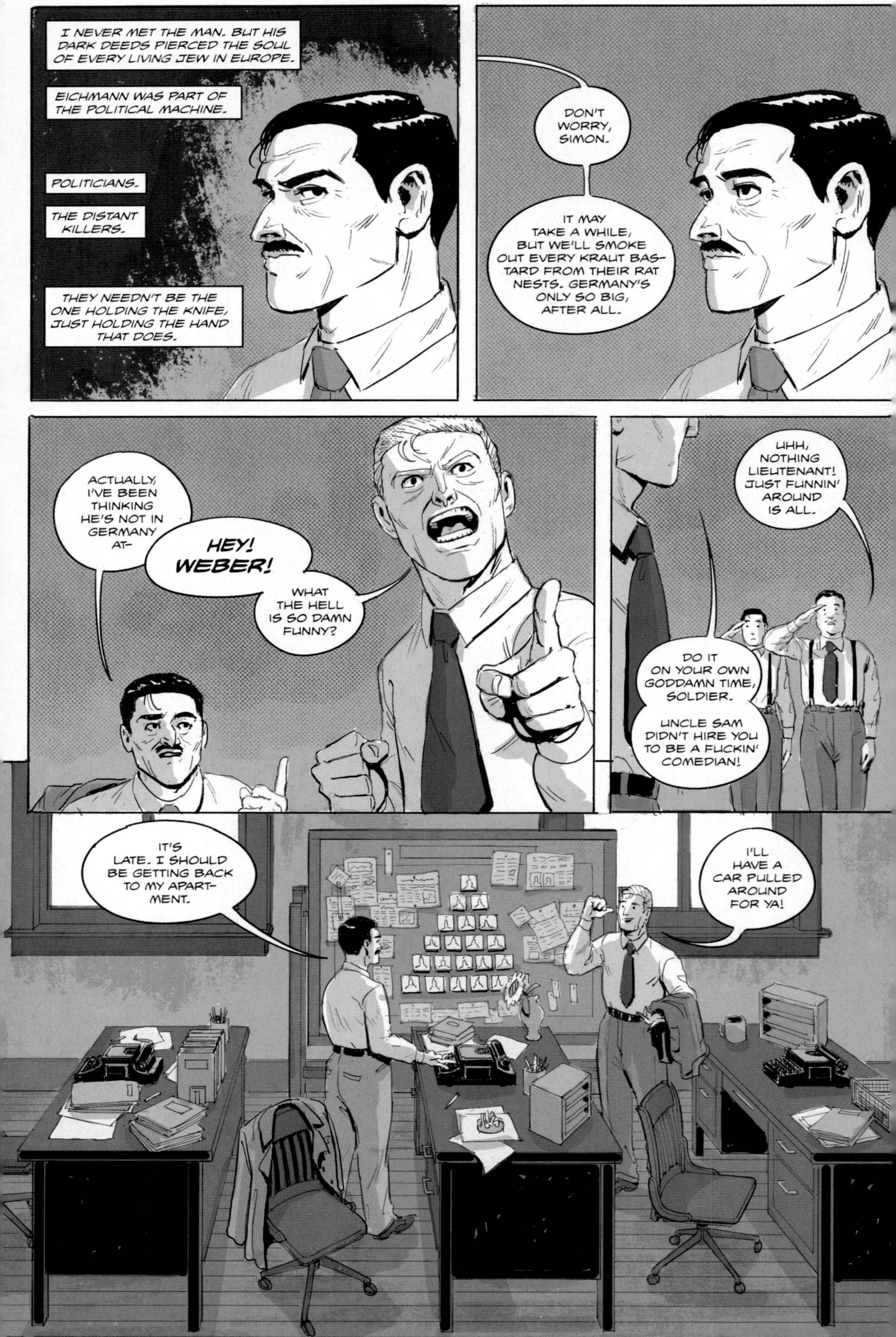
I NEVER MET THE MAN. BUT HIS DARK DEEDS PIERCED THE SOUL OF EVERY LIVING JEW IN EUROPE.
EICHMANN WAS PART OF THE POLITICAL MACHINE.
POLITICIANS.
THE DISTANT KILLERS.
THEY NEEDN'T BE THE ONE HOLDING THE KNIFE, JUST HOLDING THE HAND THAT DOES.
DON'T WORRY, SIMON.
IT MAY TAKE A WHILE, BUT WE'LL SMOKE OUT EVERY KRAUT BAS-TARD FROM THEIR RAT NESTS. GERMANY'S ONLY SO BIG, AFTER ALL.
ACTUALLY, I'VE BEEN THINKING HE'S NOT IN GERMANY AT-
HEY! WEBER!
WHAT THE HELL IS SO DAMN FUNNY?
UHH, NOTHING LIEUTENANT! JUST FUNNIN' AROUND IS ALL.
DO IT ON YOUR OWN GODDAMN TIME, SOLDIER.
UNCLE SAM DIDN'T HIRE YOU TO BE A FUCKIN' COMEDIAN!
IT'S LATE. I SHOULD BE GETTING BACK TO MY APART-MENT.
I'LL HAVE A CAR PULLED AROUND FOR YA!

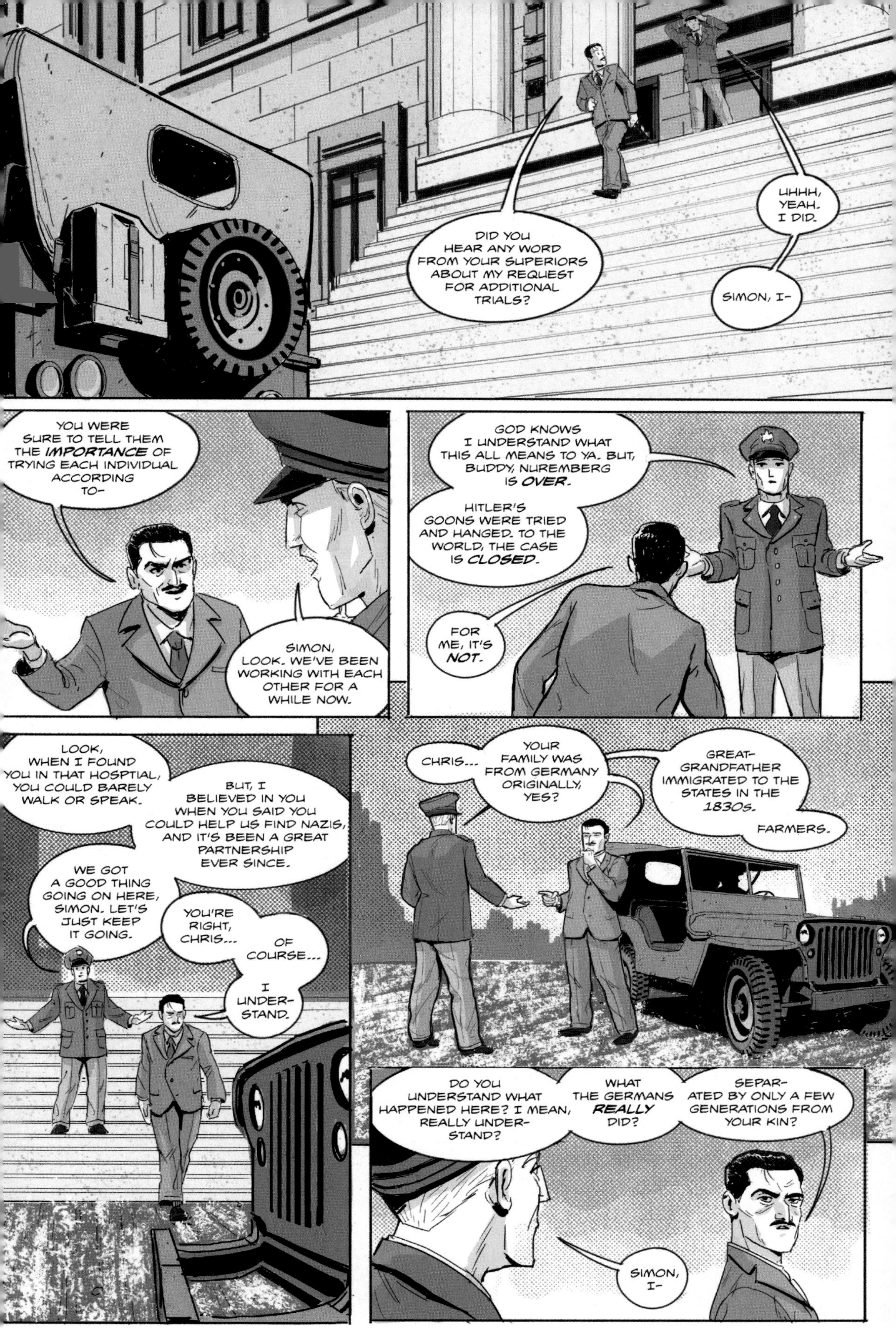
DID YOU HEAR ANY WORD FROM YOUR SUPERIORS ABOUT MY REQUEST FOR ADDITIONAL TRIALS?
UHHH, YEAH. I DID.
SIMON, I-
YOU WERE SURE TO TELL THEM THE *IMPORTANCE* OF TRYING EACH INDIVIDUAL ACCORDING TO-
SIMON, LOOK. WE'VE BEEN WORKING WITH EACH OTHER FOR A WHILE NOW.
GOD KNOWS I UNDERSTAND WHAT THIS ALL MEANS TO YA. BUT, BUDDY, NUREMBERG IS *OVER*.
HITLER'S GOONS WERE TRIED AND HANGED. TO THE WORLD, THE CASE IS *CLOSED*.
FOR ME, IT'S *NOT*.
LOOK, WHEN I FOUND YOU IN THAT HOSPTIAL, YOU COULD BARELY WALK OR SPEAK.
BUT, I BELIEVED IN YOU WHEN YOU SAID YOU COULD HELP US FIND NAZIS, AND IT'S BEEN A GREAT PARTNERSHIP EVER SINCE.
WE GOT A GOOD THING GOING ON HERE, SIMON. LET'S JUST KEEP IT GOING.
YOU'RE RIGHT, CHRIS...
OF COURSE...
I UNDERSTAND.
CHRIS...
YOUR FAMILY WAS FROM GERMANY ORIGINALLY, YES?
GREAT-GRANDFATHER IMMIGRATED TO THE STATES IN THE *1830s*.
FARMERS.
DO YOU UNDERSTAND WHAT HAPPENED HERE? I MEAN, REALLY UNDERSTAND?
WHAT THE GERMANS *REALLY* DID?
SEPARATED BY ONLY A FEW GENERATIONS FROM YOUR KIN?
SIMON, I-

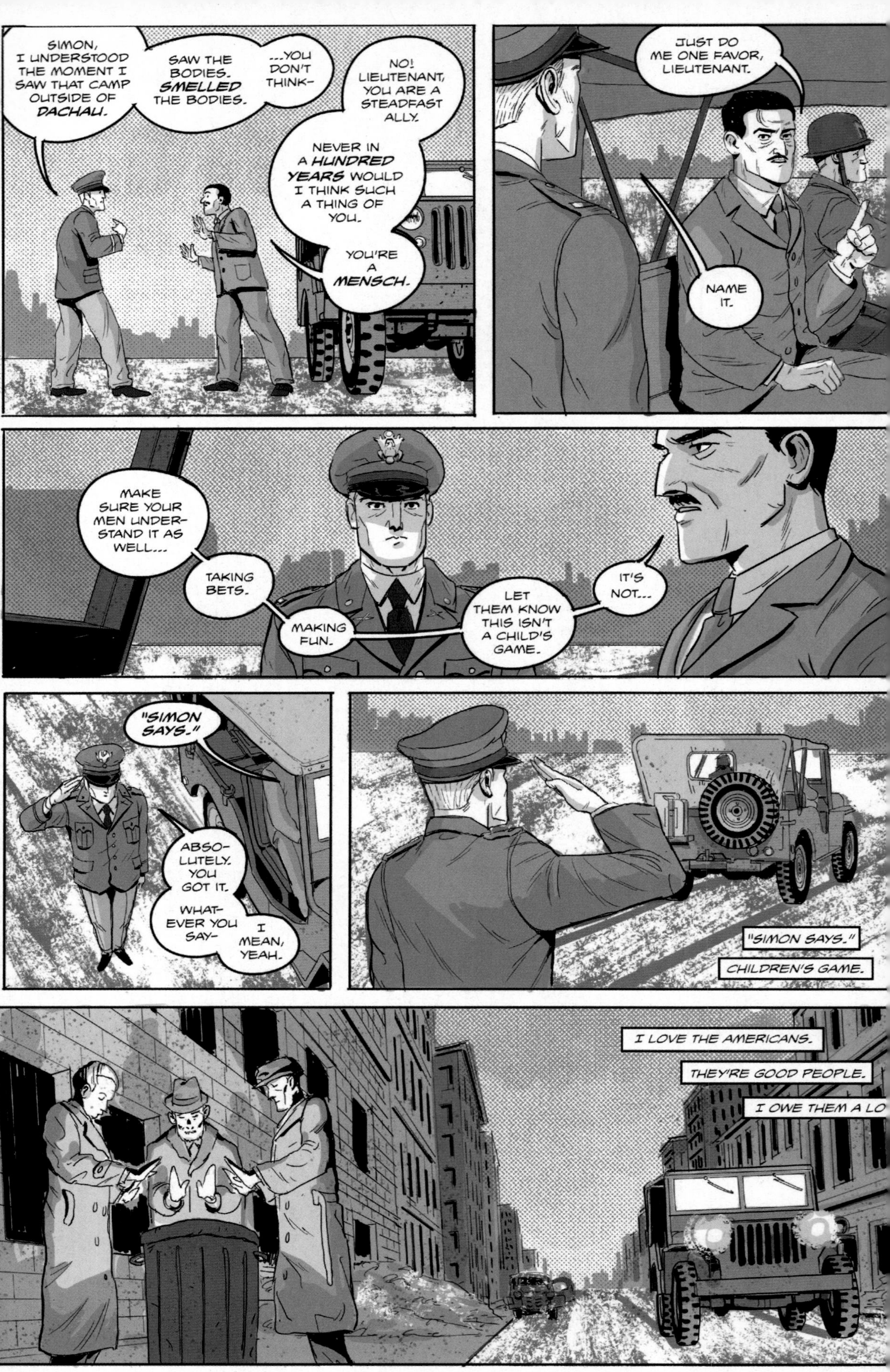
SIMON, I UNDERSTOOD THE MOMENT I SAW THAT CAMP OUTSIDE OF DACHAU.
SAW THE BODIES. SMELLED THE BODIES.
...YOU DON'T THINK-
NO! LIEUTENANT, YOU ARE A STEADFAST ALLY.
NEVER IN A HUNDRED YEARS WOULD I THINK SUCH A THING OF YOU.
YOU'RE A MENSCH.
JUST DO ME ONE FAVOR, LIEUTENANT.
NAME IT.
MAKE SURE YOUR MEN UNDER-STAND IT AS WELL...
TAKING BETS.
MAKING FUN.
LET THEM KNOW THIS ISN'T A CHILD'S GAME.
IT'S NOT...
"SIMON SAYS."
ABSO-LUTELY. YOU GOT IT.
WHAT-EVER YOU SAY-
I MEAN, YEAH.
"SIMON SAYS."
CHILDREN'S GAME.
I LOVE THE AMERICANS.
THEY'RE GOOD PEOPLE.
I OWE THEM A LO

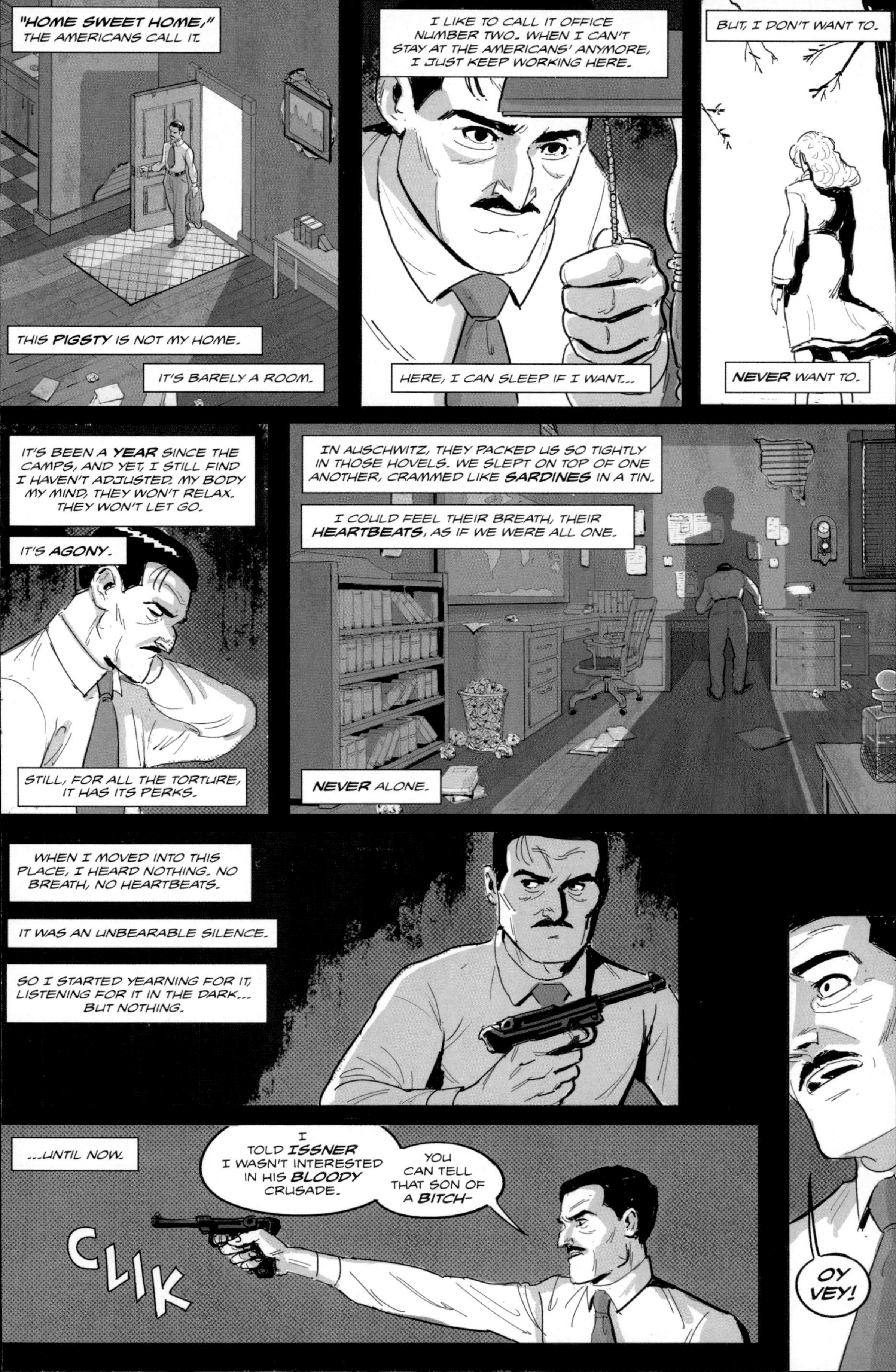
"HOME SWEET HOME," THE AMERICANS CALL IT.
THIS PIGSTY IS NOT MY HOME.
IT'S BARELY A ROOM.
I LIKE TO CALL IT OFFICE NUMBER TWO. WHEN I CAN'T STAY AT THE AMERICANS' ANYMORE, I JUST KEEP WORKING HERE.
HERE, I CAN SLEEP IF I WANT...
BUT, I DON'T WANT TO.
NEVER WANT TO.
IT'S BEEN A YEAR SINCE THE CAMPS, AND YET, I STILL FIND I HAVEN'T ADJUSTED. MY BODY MY MIND, THEY WON'T RELAX. THEY WON'T LET GO.
IT'S AGONY.
STILL, FOR ALL THE TORTURE, IT HAS ITS PERKS.
IN AUSCHWITZ, THEY PACKED US SO TIGHTLY IN THOSE HOVELS. WE SLEPT ON TOP OF ONE ANOTHER, CRAMMED LIKE SARDINES IN A TIN.
I COULD FEEL THEIR BREATH, THEIR HEARTBEATS, AS IF WE WERE ALL ONE.
NEVER ALONE.
WHEN I MOVED INTO THIS PLACE, I HEARD NOTHING. NO BREATH, NO HEARTBEATS.
IT WAS AN UNBEARABLE SILENCE.
SO I STARTED YEARNING FOR IT, LISTENING FOR IT IN THE DARK... BUT NOTHING.
...UNTIL NOW.
I TOLD ISSNER I WASN'T INTERESTED IN HIS BLOODY CRUSADE.
YOU CAN TELL THAT SON OF A BITCH-
CLIK
OY VEY!

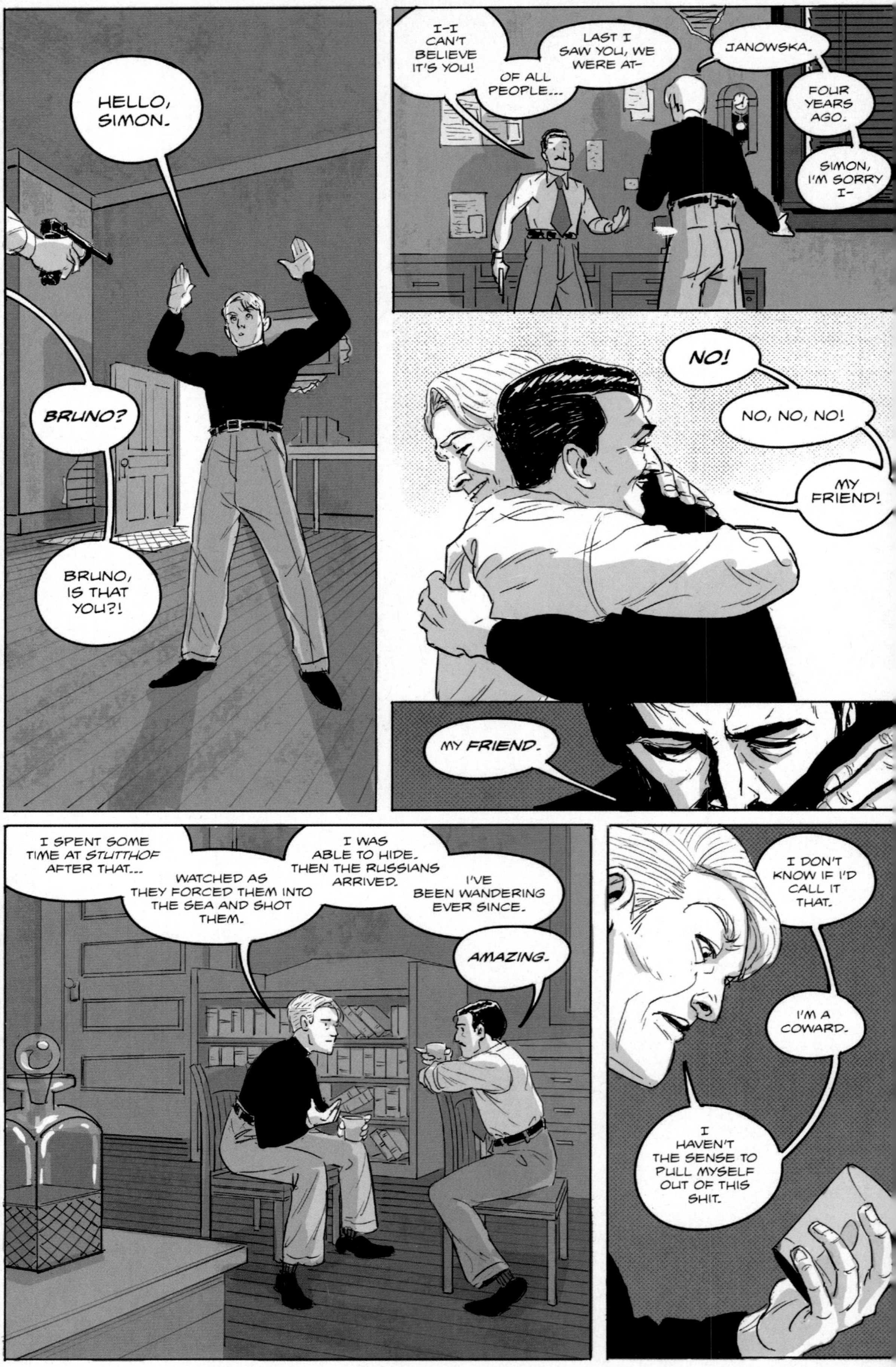
HELLO, SIMON.
BRUNO?
BRUNO, IS THAT YOU?!
I-I CAN'T BELIEVE IT'S YOU!
OF ALL PEOPLE...
LAST I SAW YOU, WE WERE AT-
JANOWSKA.
FOUR YEARS AGO.
SIMON, I'M SORRY I-
NO!
NO, NO, NO!
MY FRIEND!
MY FRIEND.
I SPENT SOME TIME AT STUTTHOF AFTER THAT...
WATCHED AS THEY FORCED THEM INTO THE SEA AND SHOT THEM.
I WAS ABLE TO HIDE. THEN THE RUSSIANS ARRIVED.
I'VE BEEN WANDERING EVER SINCE.
AMAZING.
I DON'T KNOW IF I'D CALL IT THAT.
I'M A COWARD.
I HAVEN'T THE SENSE TO PULL MYSELF OUT OF THIS SHIT.

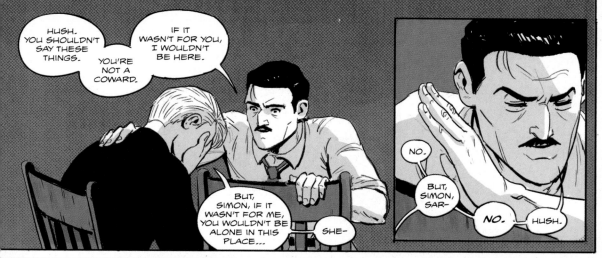

HUSH. YOU SHOULDN'T SAY THESE THINGS.

YOU'RE NOT A COWARD.

IF IT WASN'T FOR YOU, I WOULDN'T BE HERE.

BUT, SIMON, IF IT WASN'T FOR ME, YOU WOULDN'T BE ALONE IN THIS PLACE...

SHE—

NO.

BUT, SIMON, SAR—

NO.

HUSH.

WHAT NOW, BRUNO? WHERE WILL YOU GO FROM HERE?

THAT'S WHY I'M HERE. I WAS HOPING YOU COULD HELP ME.

ME? WHAT CAN I DO?

I'VE BEEN FOLLOWING YOU, YOUR EXPLOITS.

ALREADY, PEOPLE ARE TALKING.

YOU WORK WITH THE AMERICANS.

I CAN'T STAY IN BERLIN.

OR THE COUNTRY FOR THAT MATTER. IT STILL ISN'T SAFE.

IF YOU COULD MAYBE SPEAK TO YOUR CONTACTS THERE—

THERE'S NOTHING THEY CAN DO.

LET ME MAKE A CALL.

I HAVE A CONTACT IN SWITZERLAND.

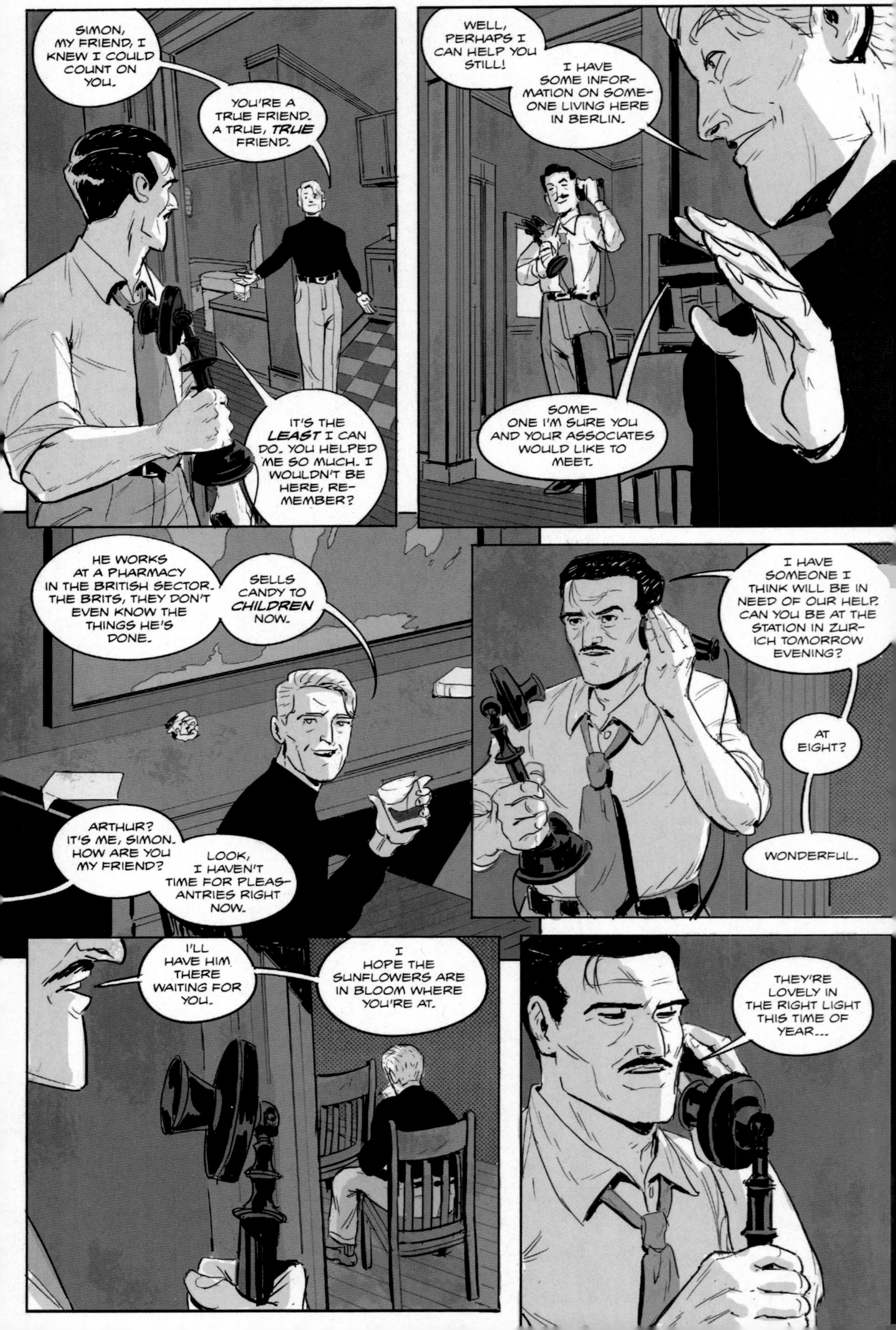
SIMON, MY FRIEND, I KNEW I COULD COUNT ON YOU.
YOU'RE A TRUE FRIEND. A TRUE, TRUE FRIEND.
IT'S THE LEAST I CAN DO. YOU HELPED ME SO MUCH. I WOULDN'T BE HERE, RE-MEMBER?
WELL, PERHAPS I CAN HELP YOU STILL!
I HAVE SOME INFOR-MATION ON SOME-ONE LIVING HERE IN BERLIN.
SOME-ONE I'M SURE YOU AND YOUR ASSOCIATES WOULD LIKE TO MEET.
HE WORKS AT A PHARMACY IN THE BRITISH SECTOR. THE BRITS, THEY DON'T EVEN KNOW THE THINGS HE'S DONE.
SELLS CANDY TO CHILDREN NOW.
ARTHUR? IT'S ME, SIMON. HOW ARE YOU MY FRIEND?
LOOK, I HAVEN'T TIME FOR PLEAS-ANTRIES RIGHT NOW.
I HAVE SOMEONE I THINK WILL BE IN NEED OF OUR HELP. CAN YOU BE AT THE STATION IN ZUR-ICH TOMORROW EVENING?
AT EIGHT?
WONDERFUL.
I'LL HAVE HIM THERE WAITING FOR YOU.
I HOPE THE SUNFLOWERS ARE IN BLOOM WHERE YOU'RE AT.
THEY'RE LOVELY IN THE RIGHT LIGHT THIS TIME OF YEAR...

BERLIN, BRITISH SECTOR

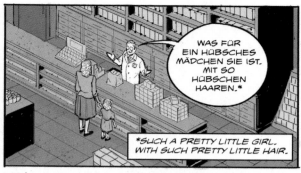

WAS FÜR EIN HÜBSCHES MÄDCHEN SIE IST. MIT SO HÜBSCHEN HAAREN.*

*SUCH A PRETTY LITTLE GIRL. WITH SUCH PRETTY LITTLE HAIR.

HIER VERDIENST DU EINE BELOHN-UNG DAFÜR SO SÜß ZU SEIN.*

*HERE, YOU DESERVE A RE-WARD FOR BEING SO SWEET.

DANKE, HERR MULLER.*

NA, NA KIND-CHEN.

ALLES GUT DER WELT GEHT. ZUCKER HEILT ALLE.**

*THANK YOU, MISTER MULLER.

**THERE NOW LITTLE ONE. ALL IS WELL IN THE WORLD. SUGAR CURES ALL.

ICH WERDE AM ANFANG DER WOCHE EINE LIE-FERUNG VON TOI-LETTENARTIKELN HABEN.

SCHÖNEN TAG!*

*I WILL HAVE A SHIPMENT OF TOILETRIES FIRST OF THE WEEK. HAVE A GOOD DAY!

YES, IT IS TRUE...

IT IS VERY TRUE...

SUGAR CURES ALL.

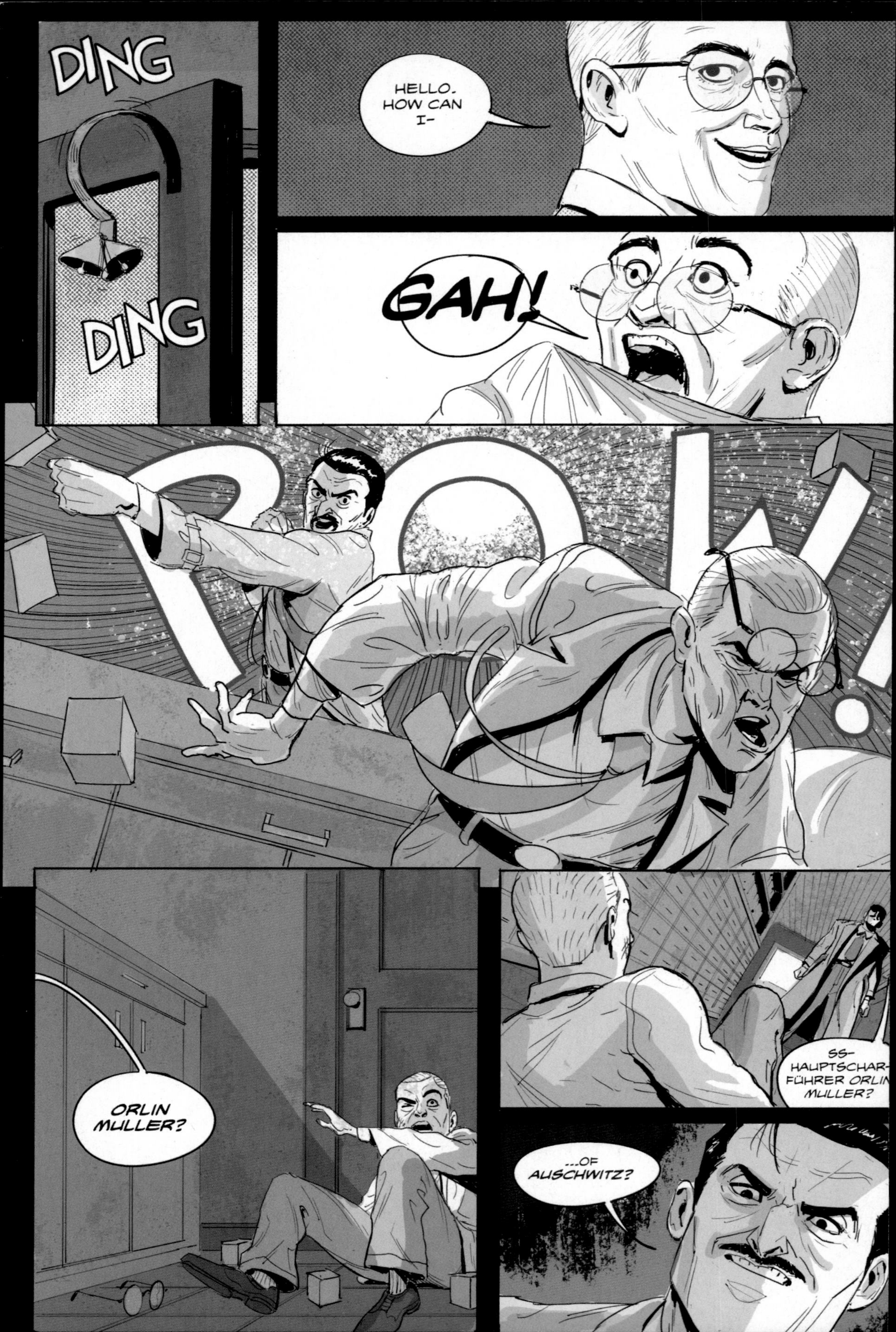
DING
DING
HELLO. HOW CAN I-
GAH!
ORLIN MULLER?
SS-HAUPTSCHAR-FÜHRER ORLIN MULLER?
...OF AUSCHWITZ?

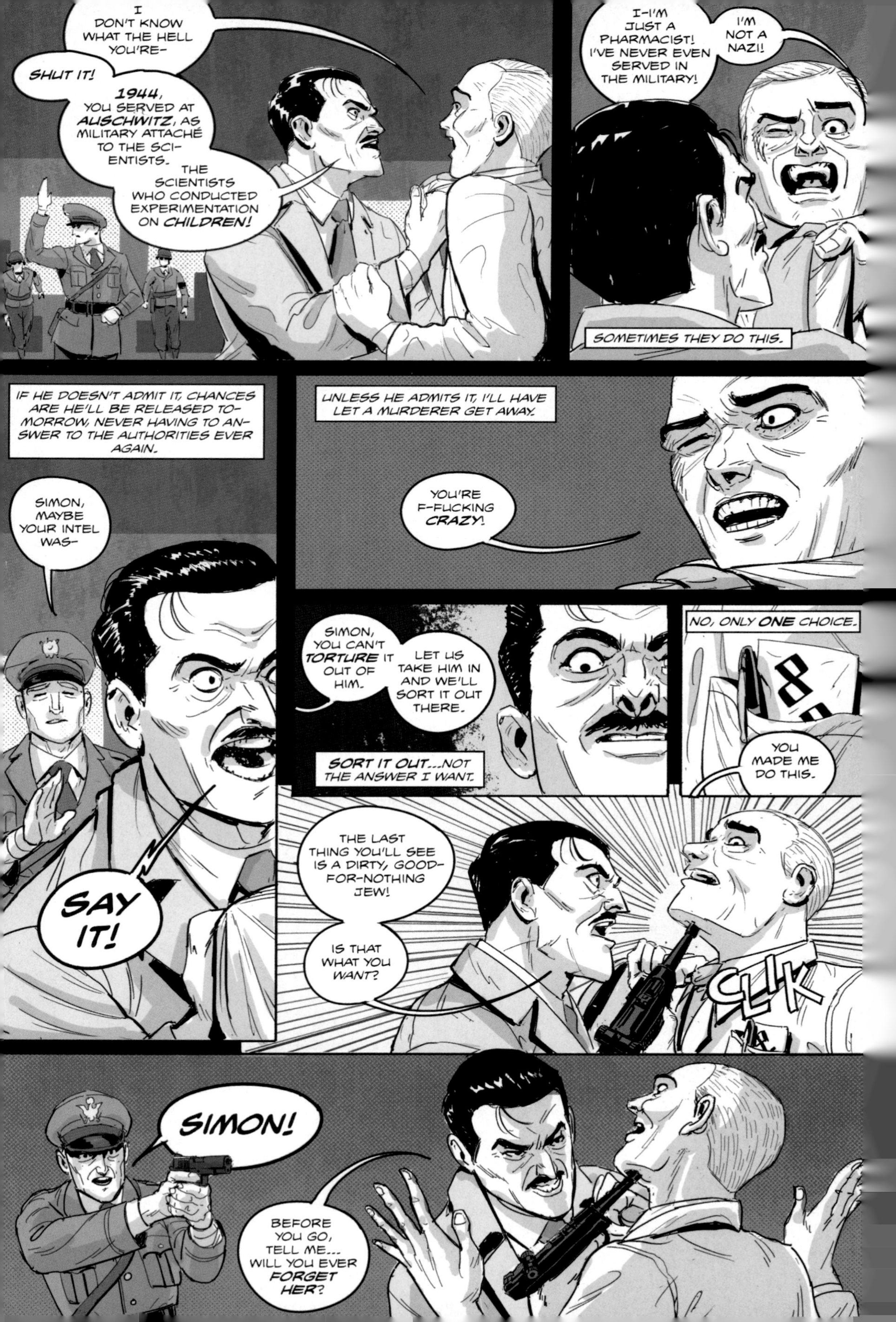
I DON'T KNOW WHAT THE HELL YOU'RE-
SHUT IT!
1944, YOU SERVED AT AUSCHWITZ, AS MILITARY ATTACHÉ TO THE SCI-ENTISTS.
THE SCIENTISTS WHO CONDUCTED EXPERIMENTATION ON CHILDREN!
I-I'M JUST A PHARMACIST! I'VE NEVER EVEN SERVED IN THE MILITARY!
I'M NOT A NAZI!
SOMETIMES THEY DO THIS.
IF HE DOESN'T ADMIT IT, CHANCES ARE HE'LL BE RELEASED TO-MORROW, NEVER HAVING TO AN-SWER TO THE AUTHORITIES EVER AGAIN.
SIMON, MAYBE YOUR INTEL WAS-
SAY IT!
UNLESS HE ADMITS IT, I'LL HAVE LET A MURDERER GET AWAY.
YOU'RE F-FUCKING CRAZY!
SIMON, YOU CAN'T TORTURE IT OUT OF HIM.
LET US TAKE HIM IN AND WE'LL SORT IT OUT THERE.
SORT IT OUT... NOT THE ANSWER I WANT.
NO, ONLY ONE CHOICE.
YOU MADE ME DO THIS.
THE LAST THING YOU'LL SEE IS A DIRTY, GOOD-FOR-NOTHING JEW!
IS THAT WHAT YOU WANT?
CLIK
SIMON!
BEFORE YOU GO, TELL ME... WILL YOU EVER FORGET HER?

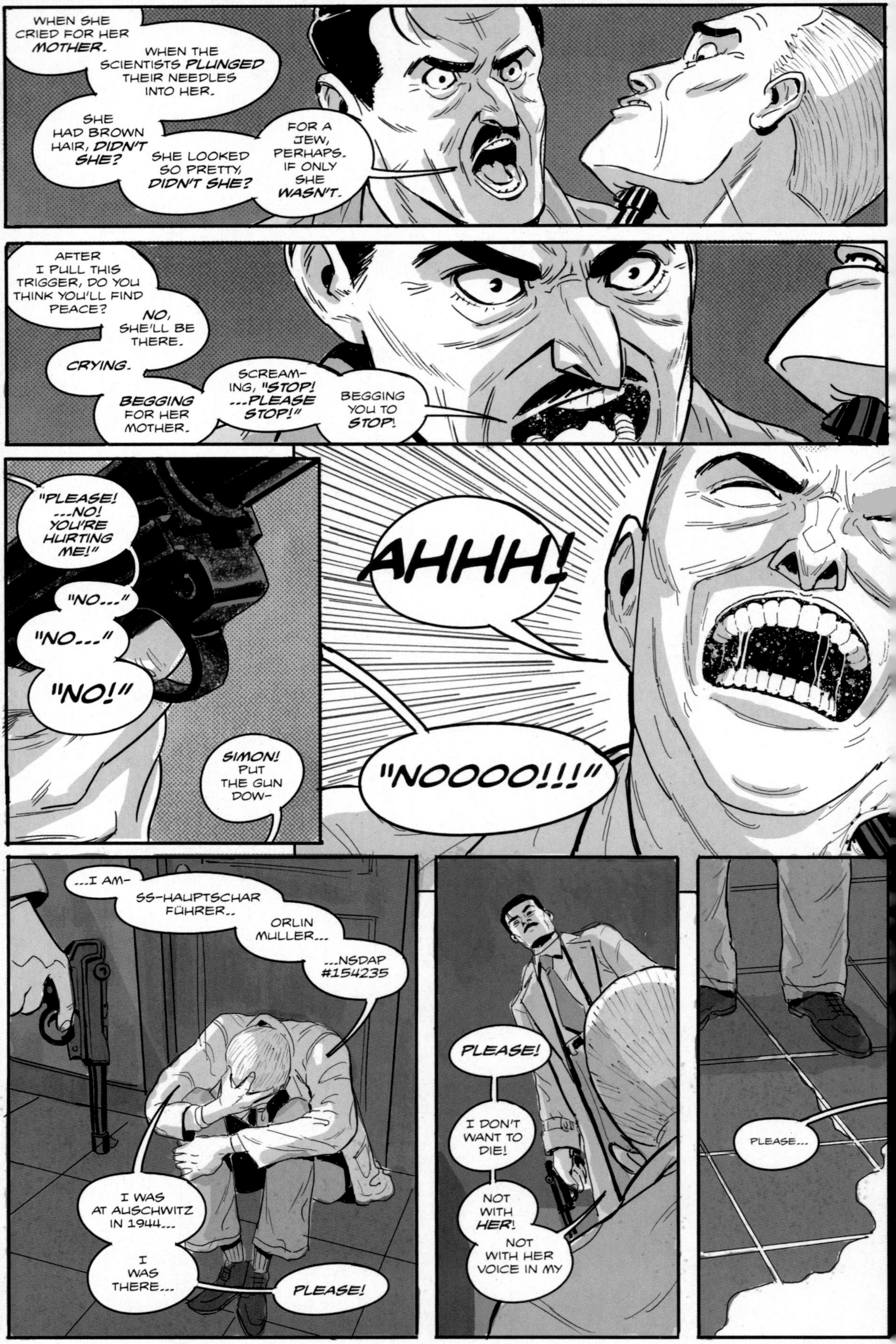

WHEN SHE CRIED FOR HER MOTHER.
WHEN THE SCIENTISTS PLUNGED THEIR NEEDLES INTO HER.
SHE HAD BROWN HAIR, DIDN'T SHE?
SHE LOOKED SO PRETTY, DIDN'T SHE?
FOR A JEW, PERHAPS. IF ONLY SHE WASN'T.
AFTER I PULL THIS TRIGGER, DO YOU THINK YOU'LL FIND PEACE?
NO, SHE'LL BE THERE.
CRYING.
BEGGING FOR HER MOTHER.
SCREAMING, "STOP! ...PLEASE STOP!"
BEGGING YOU TO STOP!
"PLEASE! ...NO! YOU'RE HURTING ME!"
"NO..."
"NO..."
"NO!"
AHHH!
"NOOOO!!!"
SIMON! PUT THE GUN DOW-
...I AM-
SS-HAUPTSCHAR FÜHRER..
ORLIN MULLER...
...NSDAP #154235
I WAS AT AUSCHWITZ IN 1944...
I WAS THERE...
PLEASE!
PLEASE!
I DON'T WANT TO DIE!
NOT WITH HER!
NOT WITH HER VOICE IN MY
PLEASE...

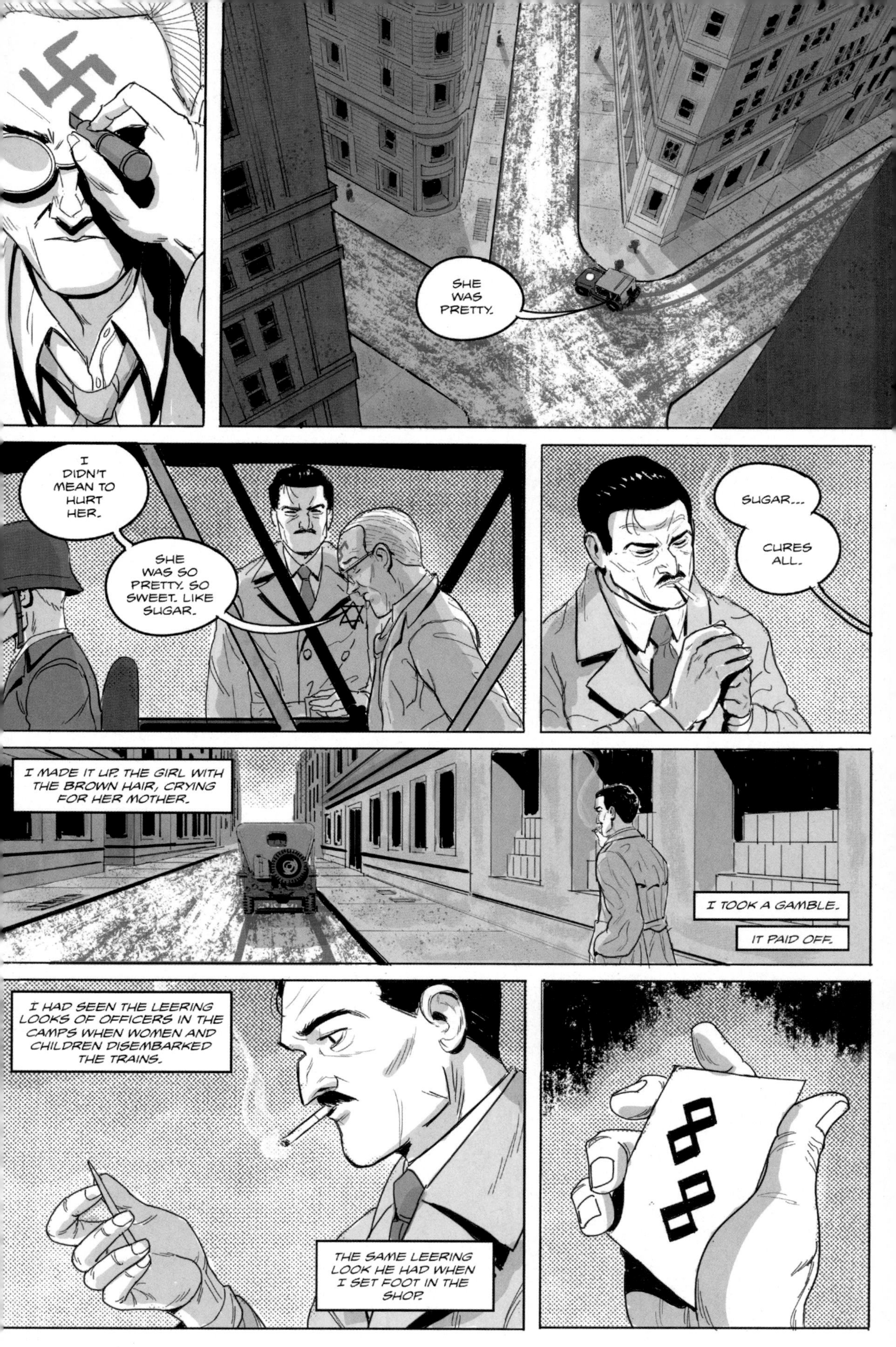
SHE WAS PRETTY.
I DIDN'T MEAN TO HURT HER.
SHE WAS SO PRETTY. SO SWEET. LIKE SUGAR.
SUGAR...
CURES ALL.
I MADE IT UP. THE GIRL WITH THE BROWN HAIR, CRYING FOR HER MOTHER.
I TOOK A GAMBLE.
IT PAID OFF.
I HAD SEEN THE LEERING LOOKS OF OFFICERS IN THE CAMPS WHEN WOMEN AND CHILDREN DISEMBARKED THE TRAINS.
THE SAME LEERING LOOK HE HAD WHEN I SET FOOT IN THE SHOP.

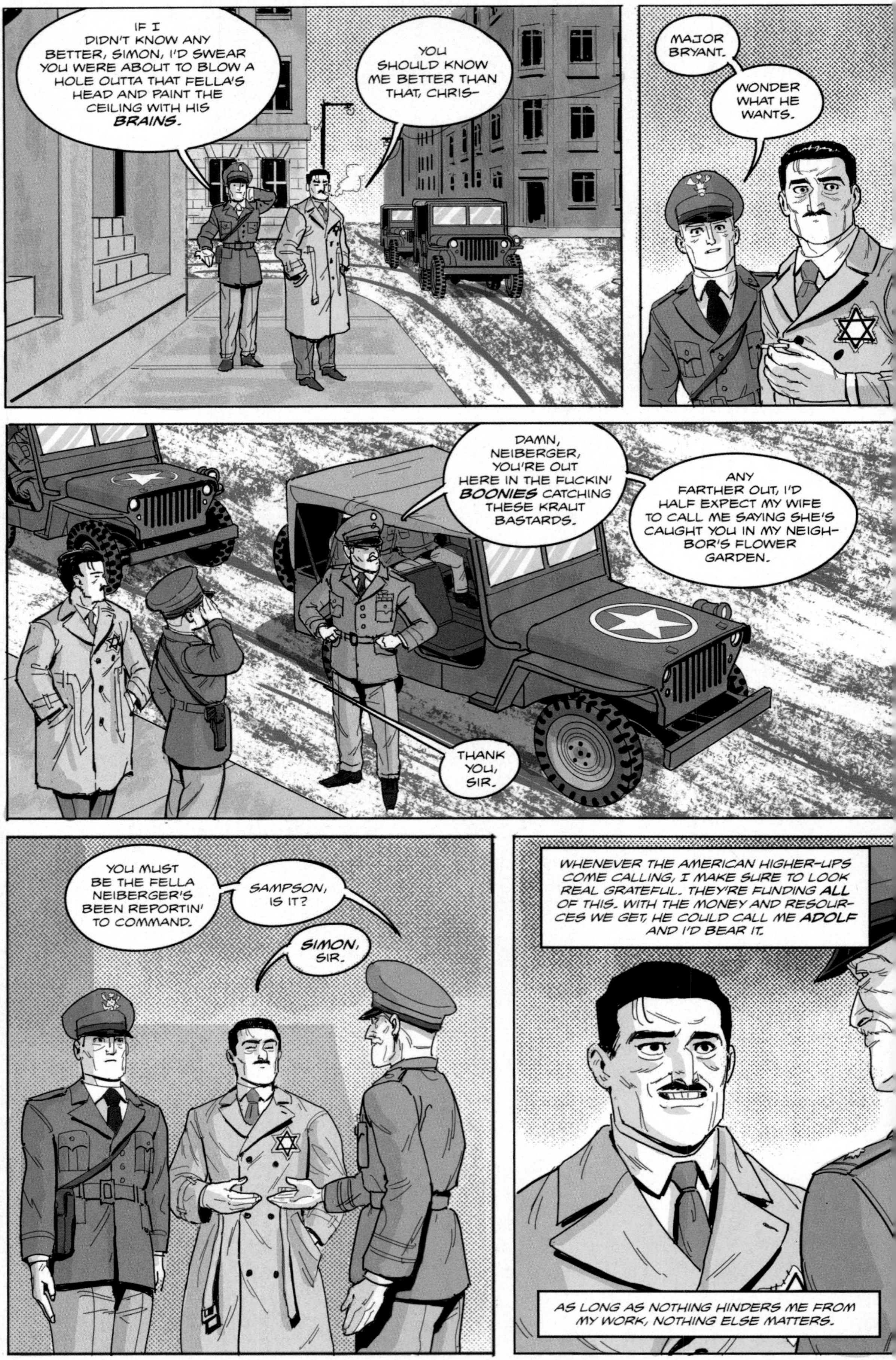
IF I DIDN'T KNOW ANY BETTER, SIMON, I'D SWEAR YOU WERE ABOUT TO BLOW A HOLE OUTTA THAT FELLA'S HEAD AND PAINT THE CEILING WITH HIS BRAINS.
YOU SHOULD KNOW ME BETTER THAN THAT, CHRIS-
MAJOR BRYANT.
WONDER WHAT HE WANTS.
DAMN, NEIBERGER, YOU'RE OUT HERE IN THE FUCKIN' BOONIES CATCHING THESE KRAUT BASTARDS.
ANY FARTHER OUT, I'D HALF EXPECT MY WIFE TO CALL ME SAYING SHE'S CAUGHT YOU IN MY NEIGHBOR'S FLOWER GARDEN.
THANK YOU, SIR.
YOU MUST BE THE FELLA NEIBERGER'S BEEN REPORTIN' TO COMMAND.
SAMPSON, IS IT?
SIMON, SIR.
WHENEVER THE AMERICAN HIGHER-UPS COME CALLING, I MAKE SURE TO LOOK REAL GRATEFUL. THEY'RE FUNDING ALL OF THIS. WITH THE MONEY AND RESOURCES WE GET, HE COULD CALL ME ADOLF AND I'D BEAR IT.
AS LONG AS NOTHING HINDERS ME FROM MY WORK, NOTHING ELSE MATTERS.

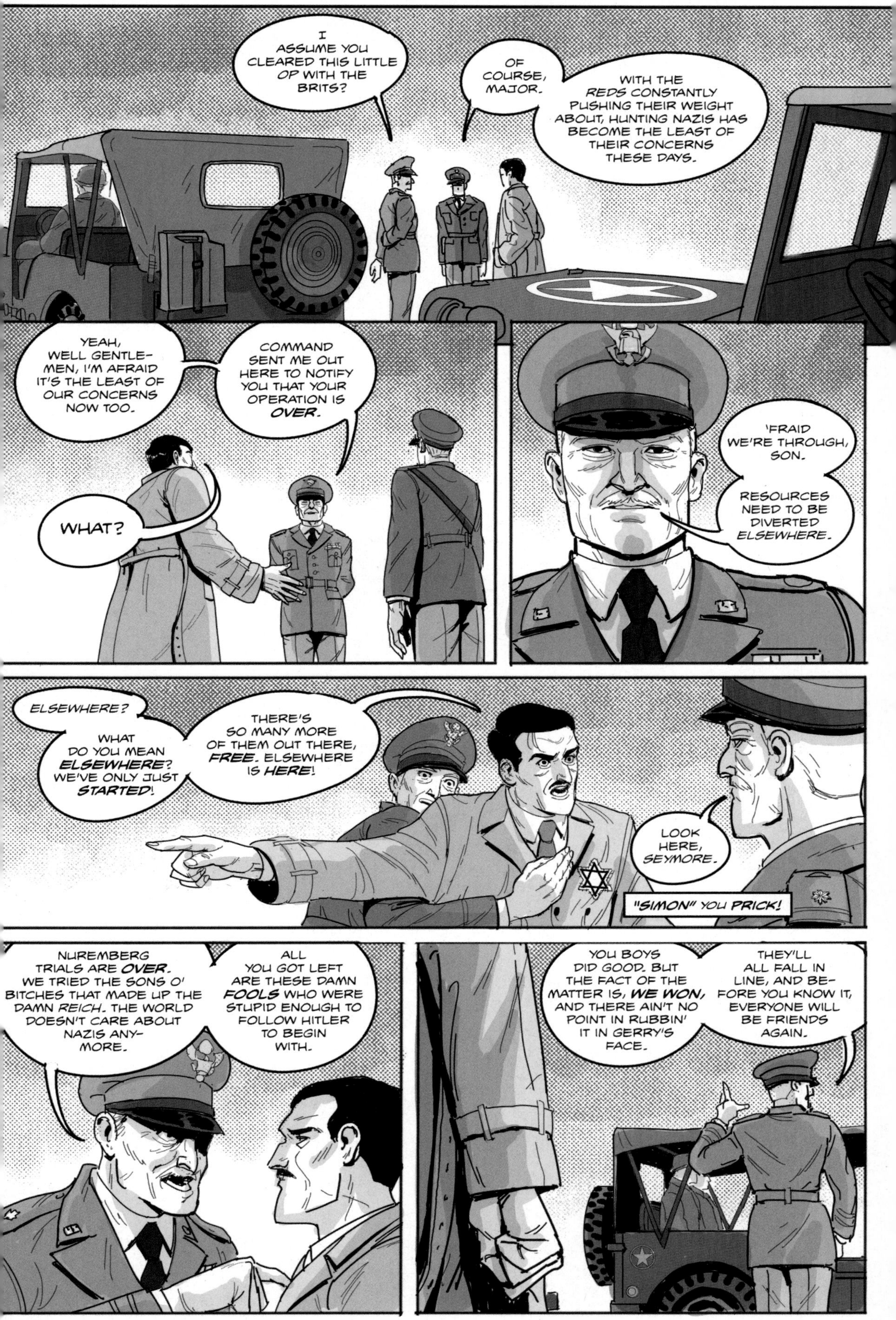
I ASSUME YOU CLEARED THIS LITTLE *OP* WITH THE BRITS?
OF COURSE, MAJOR.
WITH THE *REDS* CONSTANTLY PUSHING THEIR WEIGHT ABOUT, HUNTING NAZIS HAS BECOME THE LEAST OF THEIR CONCERNS THESE DAYS.
YEAH, WELL GENTLEMEN, I'M AFRAID IT'S THE LEAST OF OUR CONCERNS NOW TOO.
COMMAND SENT ME OUT HERE TO NOTIFY YOU THAT YOUR OPERATION IS ***OVER***.
WHAT?
'FRAID WE'RE THROUGH, SON.
RESOURCES NEED TO BE DIVERTED *ELSEWHERE*.
ELSEWHERE?
WHAT DO YOU MEAN ***ELSEWHERE***? WE'VE ONLY JUST ***STARTED***!
THERE'S SO MANY MORE OF THEM OUT THERE, ***FREE***. ELSEWHERE IS ***HERE***!
LOOK HERE, *SEYMORE*.
"SIMON" YOU **PRICK!**
NUREMBERG TRIALS ARE ***OVER***. WE TRIED THE SONS O' BITCHES THAT MADE UP THE DAMN *REICH*. THE WORLD DOESN'T CARE ABOUT NAZIS ANYMORE.
ALL YOU GOT LEFT ARE THESE DAMN ***FOOLS*** WHO WERE STUPID ENOUGH TO FOLLOW HITLER TO BEGIN WITH.
YOU BOYS DID GOOD. BUT THE FACT OF THE MATTER IS, ***WE WON***, AND THERE AIN'T NO POINT IN RUBBIN' IT IN GERRY'S FACE.
THEY'LL ALL FALL IN LINE, AND BEFORE YOU KNOW IT, EVERYONE WILL BE FRIENDS AGAIN.

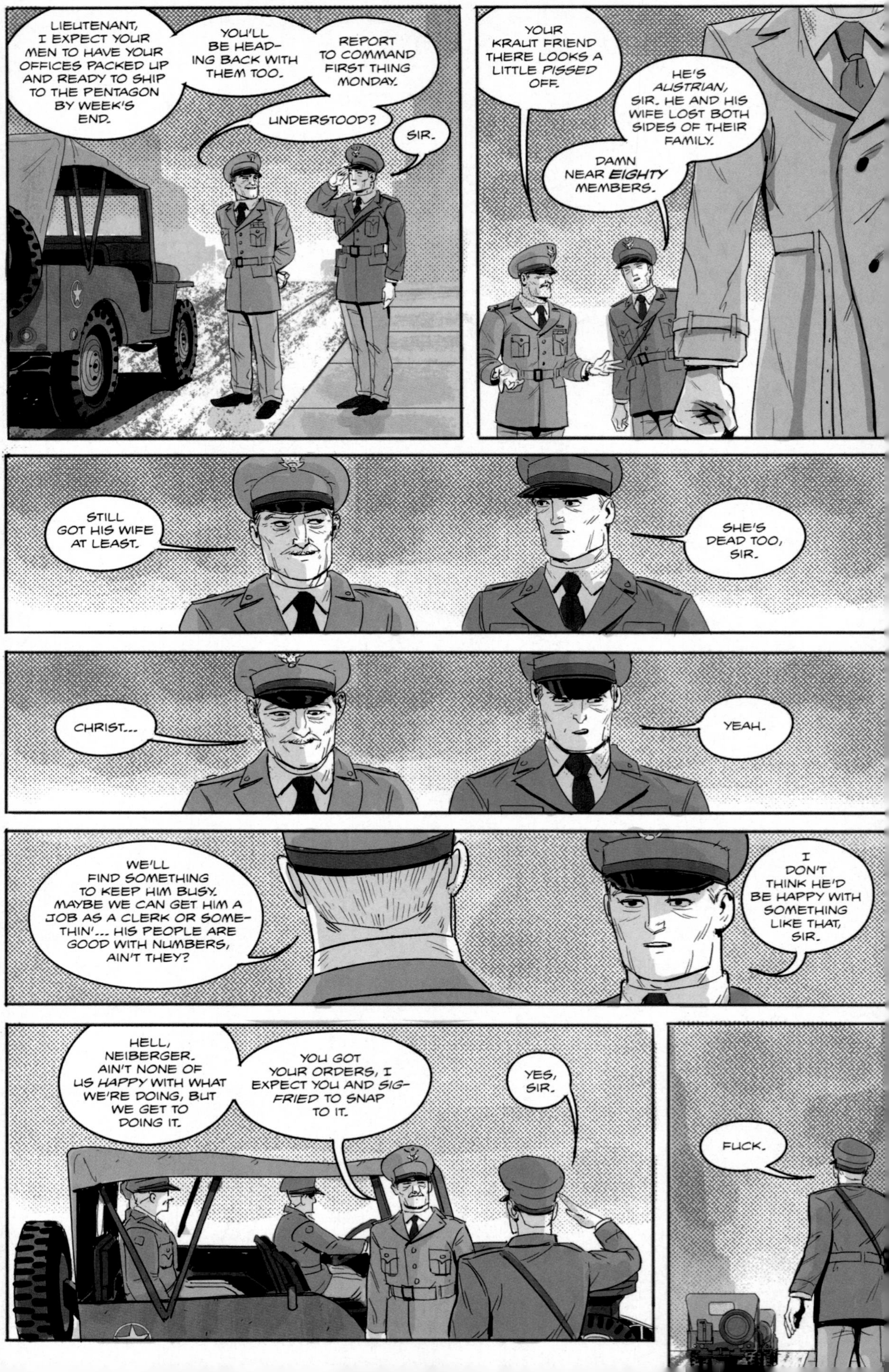

LIEUTENANT, I EXPECT YOUR MEN TO HAVE YOUR OFFICES PACKED UP AND READY TO SHIP TO THE PENTAGON BY WEEK'S END.
YOU'LL BE HEAD-ING BACK WITH THEM TOO.
REPORT TO COMMAND FIRST THING MONDAY.
UNDERSTOOD?
SIR.
YOUR KRAUT FRIEND THERE LOOKS A LITTLE *PISSED* OFF.
HE'S *AUSTRIAN,* SIR. HE AND HIS WIFE LOST BOTH SIDES OF THEIR FAMILY.
DAMN NEAR ***EIGHTY*** MEMBERS.
STILL GOT HIS WIFE AT LEAST.
SHE'S DEAD TOO, SIR.
CHRIST...
YEAH.
WE'LL FIND SOMETHING TO KEEP HIM BUSY. MAYBE WE CAN GET HIM A JOB AS A CLERK OR SOME-THIN'... HIS PEOPLE ARE GOOD WITH NUMBERS, AIN'T THEY?
I DON'T THINK HE'D BE HAPPY WITH SOMETHING LIKE THAT, SIR.
HELL, NEIBERGER. AIN'T NONE OF US *HAPPY* WITH WHAT WE'RE DOING, BUT WE GET TO DOING IT.
YOU GOT YOUR ORDERS, I EXPECT YOU AND *SIG-FRIED* TO SNAP TO IT.
YES, SIR.
FUCK.

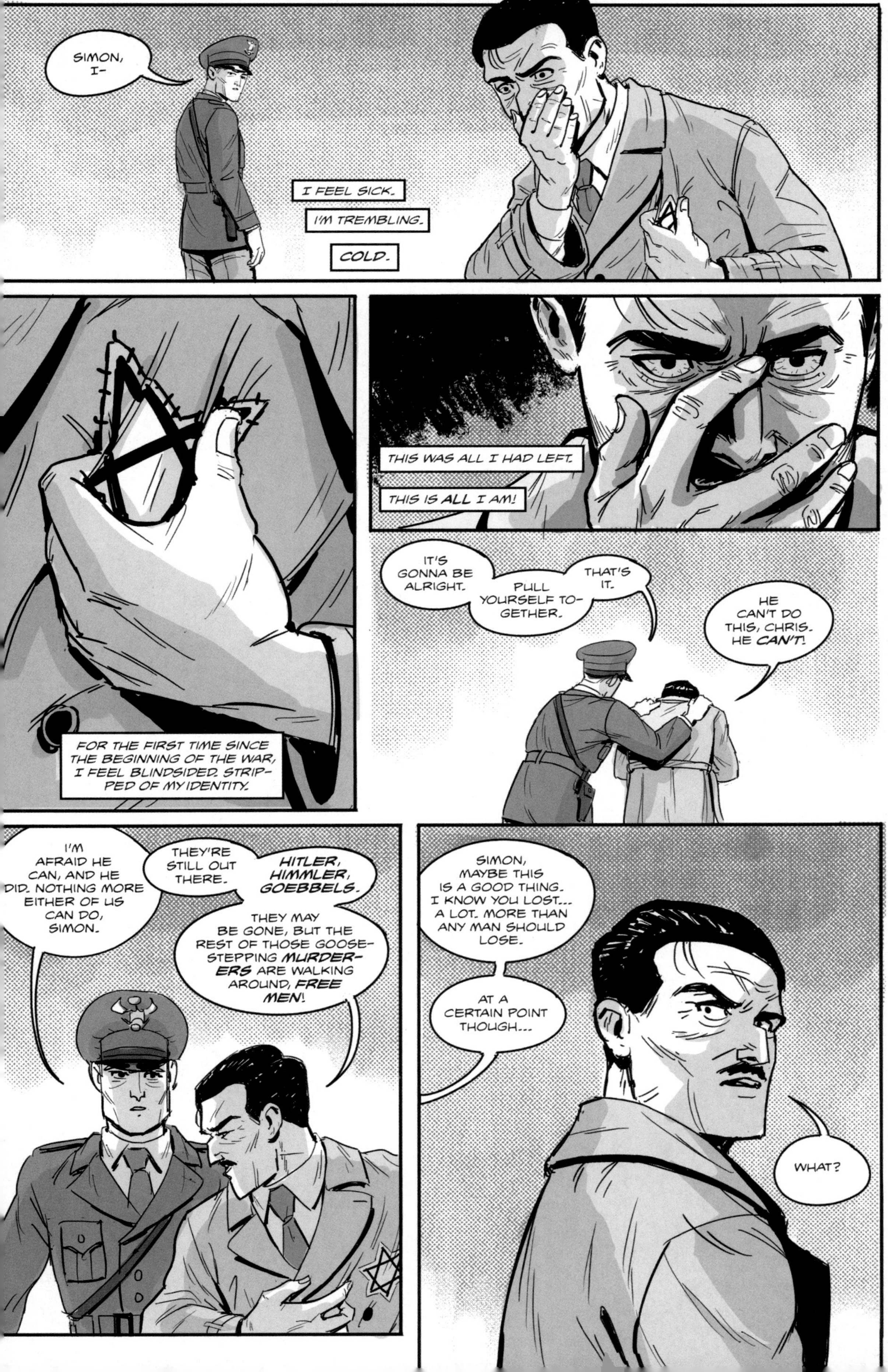
SIMON, I-
I FEEL SICK.
I'M TREMBLING.
COLD.
FOR THE FIRST TIME SINCE THE BEGINNING OF THE WAR, I FEEL BLINDSIDED. STRIPPED OF MY IDENTITY.
THIS WAS ALL I HAD LEFT.
THIS IS ALL I AM!
IT'S GONNA BE ALRIGHT.
PULL YOURSELF TOGETHER.
THAT'S IT.
HE CAN'T DO THIS, CHRIS. HE CAN'T!
I'M AFRAID HE CAN, AND HE DID. NOTHING MORE EITHER OF US CAN DO, SIMON.
THEY'RE STILL OUT THERE.
HITLER, HIMMLER, GOEBBELS.
THEY MAY BE GONE, BUT THE REST OF THOSE GOOSE-STEPPING MURDERERS ARE WALKING AROUND, FREE MEN!
SIMON, MAYBE THIS IS A GOOD THING. I KNOW YOU LOST... A LOT. MORE THAN ANY MAN SHOULD LOSE.
AT A CERTAIN POINT THOUGH...
WHAT?

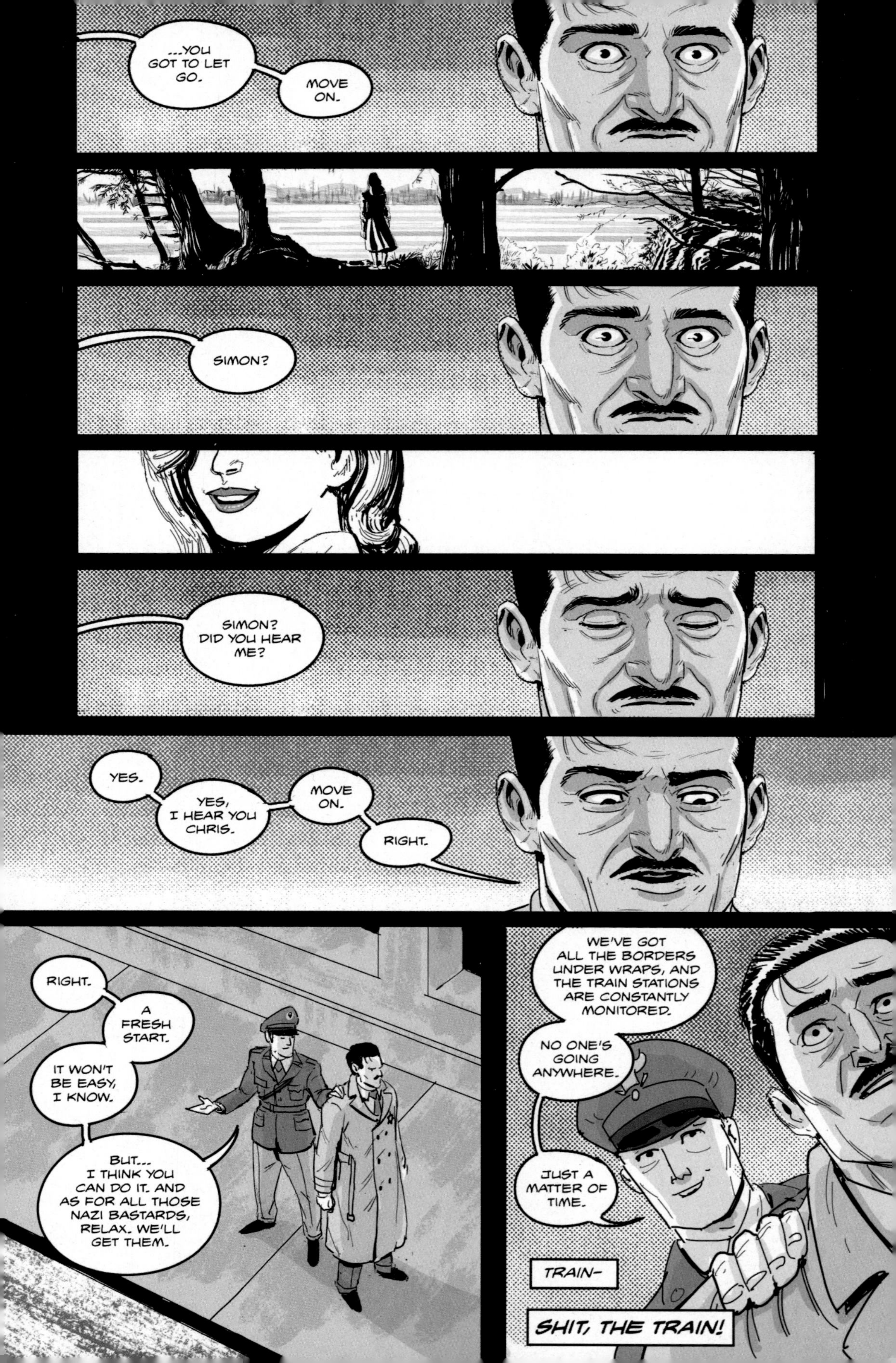
...YOU GOT TO LET GO.
MOVE ON.
SIMON?
SIMON? DID YOU HEAR ME?
YES.
YES, I HEAR YOU CHRIS.
MOVE ON.
RIGHT.
RIGHT.
A FRESH START.
IT WON'T BE EASY, I KNOW.
BUT... I THINK YOU CAN DO IT. AND AS FOR ALL THOSE NAZI BASTARDS, RELAX. WE'LL GET THEM.
WE'VE GOT ALL THE BORDERS UNDER WRAPS, AND THE TRAIN STATIONS ARE CONSTANTLY MONITORED.
NO ONE'S GOING ANYWHERE.
JUST A MATTER OF TIME.
TRAIN-
SHIT, THE TRAIN!

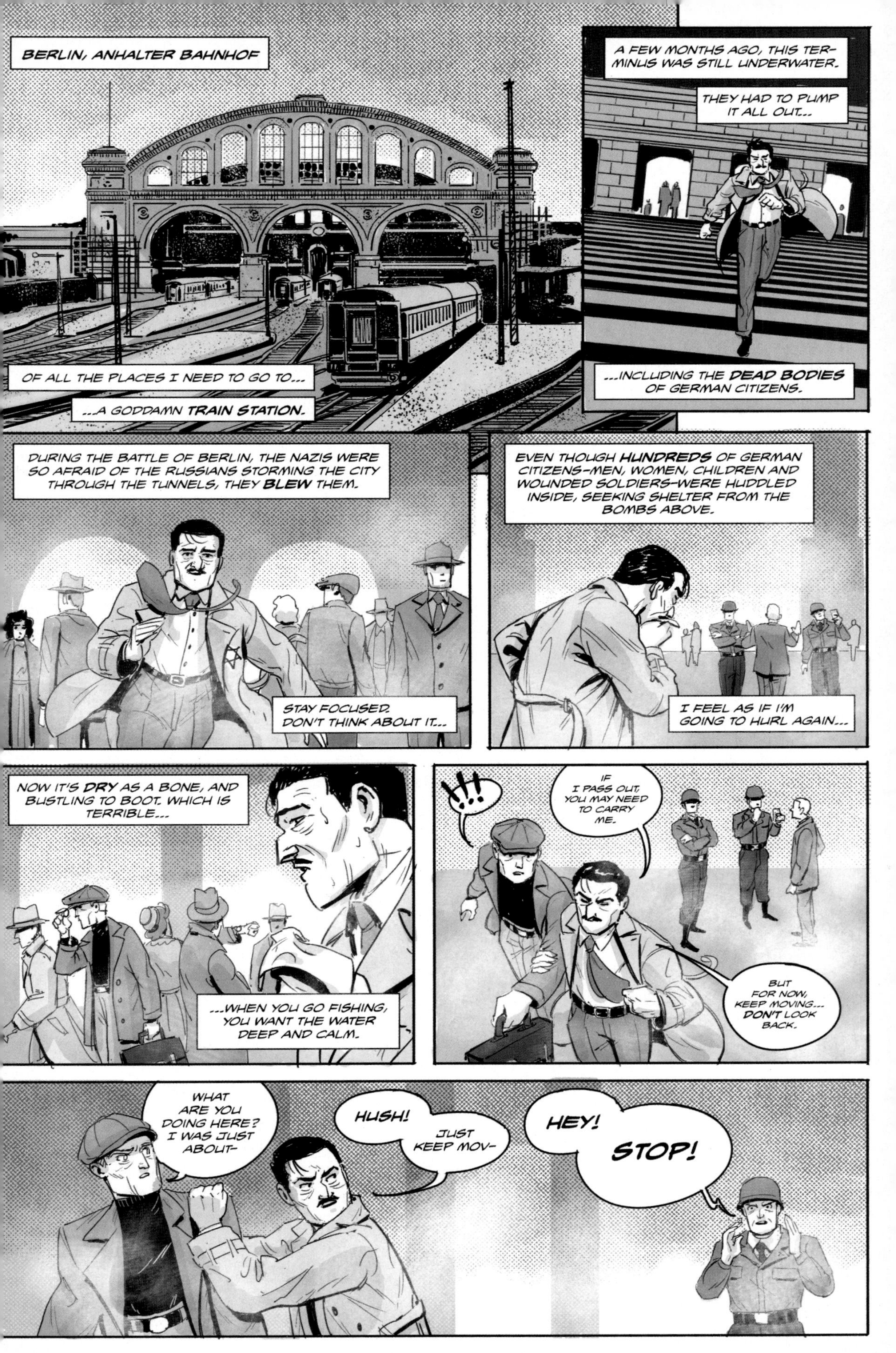
BERLIN, ANHALTER BAHNHOF
OF ALL THE PLACES I NEED TO GO TO...
...A GODDAMN TRAIN STATION.
A FEW MONTHS AGO, THIS TERMINUS WAS STILL UNDERWATER.
THEY HAD TO PUMP IT ALL OUT...
...INCLUDING THE DEAD BODIES OF GERMAN CITIZENS.
DURING THE BATTLE OF BERLIN, THE NAZIS WERE SO AFRAID OF THE RUSSIANS STORMING THE CITY THROUGH THE TUNNELS, THEY BLEW THEM.
STAY FOCUSED. DON'T THINK ABOUT IT...
EVEN THOUGH HUNDREDS OF GERMAN CITIZENS—MEN, WOMEN, CHILDREN AND WOUNDED SOLDIERS—WERE HUDDLED INSIDE, SEEKING SHELTER FROM THE BOMBS ABOVE.
I FEEL AS IF I'M GOING TO HURL AGAIN...
NOW IT'S DRY AS A BONE, AND BUSTLING TO BOOT. WHICH IS TERRIBLE...
...WHEN YOU GO FISHING, YOU WANT THE WATER DEEP AND CALM.
!!
IF I PASS OUT, YOU MAY NEED TO CARRY ME.
BUT FOR NOW, KEEP MOVING... DON'T LOOK BACK.
WHAT ARE YOU DOING HERE? I WAS JUST ABOUT—
HUSH!
JUST KEEP MOV—
HEY!
STOP!

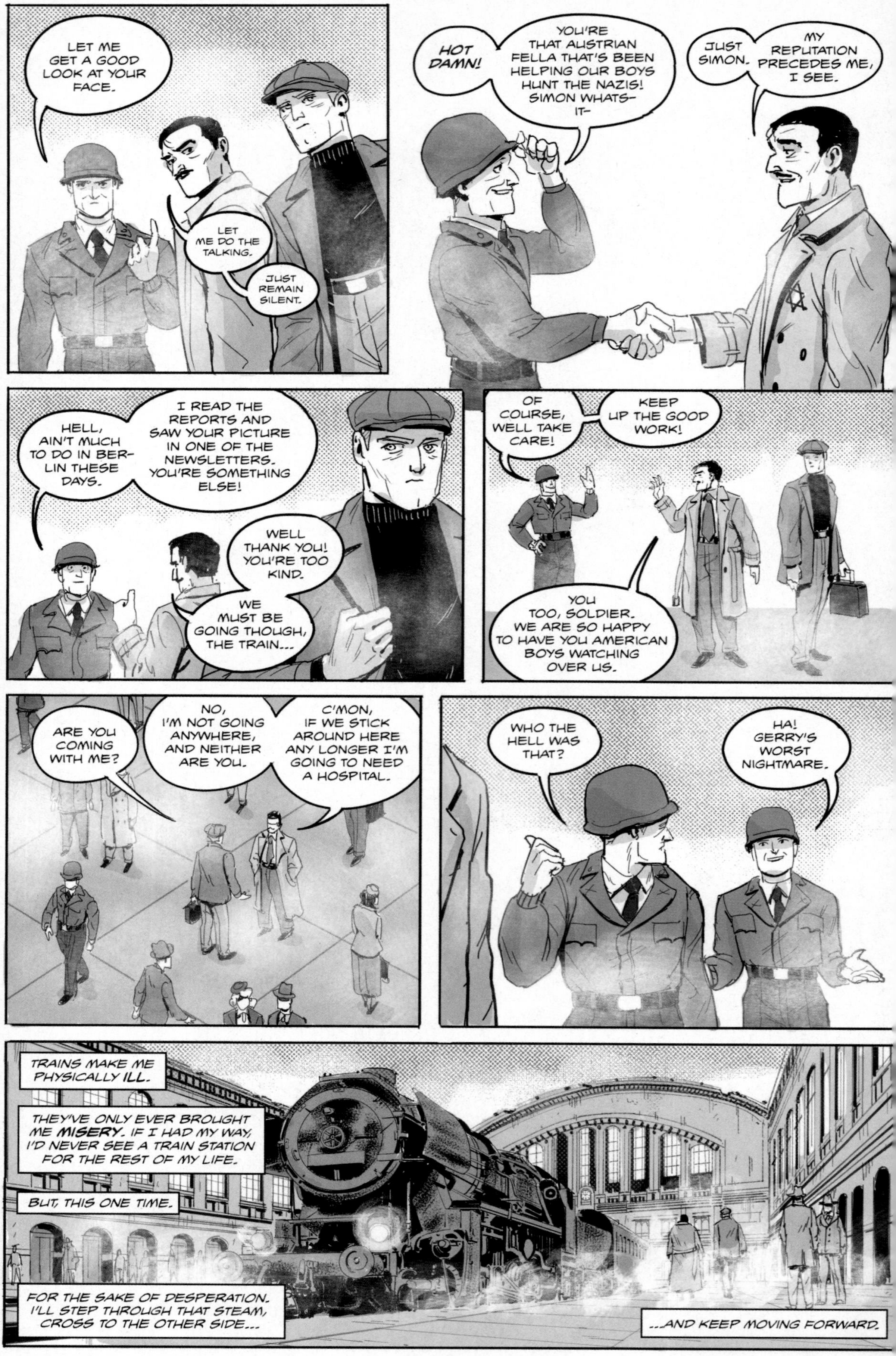
LET ME GET A GOOD LOOK AT YOUR FACE.
LET ME DO THE TALKING.
JUST REMAIN SILENT.
HOT DAMN!
YOU'RE THAT AUSTRIAN FELLA THAT'S BEEN HELPING OUR BOYS HUNT THE NAZIS! SIMON WHATS-IT-
JUST SIMON.
MY REPUTATION PRECEDES ME, I SEE.
HELL, AIN'T MUCH TO DO IN BER-LIN THESE DAYS.
I READ THE REPORTS AND SAW YOUR PICTURE IN ONE OF THE NEWSLETTERS. YOU'RE SOMETHING ELSE!
WELL THANK YOU! YOU'RE TOO KIND.
WE MUST BE GOING THOUGH, THE TRAIN...
OF COURSE, WELL TAKE CARE!
KEEP UP THE GOOD WORK!
YOU TOO, SOLDIER. WE ARE SO HAPPY TO HAVE YOU AMERICAN BOYS WATCHING OVER US.
ARE YOU COMING WITH ME?
NO, I'M NOT GOING ANYWHERE, AND NEITHER ARE YOU.
C'MON, IF WE STICK AROUND HERE ANY LONGER I'M GOING TO NEED A HOSPITAL.
WHO THE HELL WAS THAT?
HA! GERRY'S WORST NIGHTMARE.
TRAINS MAKE ME PHYSICALLY ILL.
THEY'VE ONLY EVER BROUGHT ME MISERY. IF I HAD MY WAY, I'D NEVER SEE A TRAIN STATION FOR THE REST OF MY LIFE.
BUT, THIS ONE TIME.
FOR THE SAKE OF DESPERATION. I'LL STEP THROUGH THAT STEAM, CROSS TO THE OTHER SIDE...
...AND KEEP MOVING FORWARD.

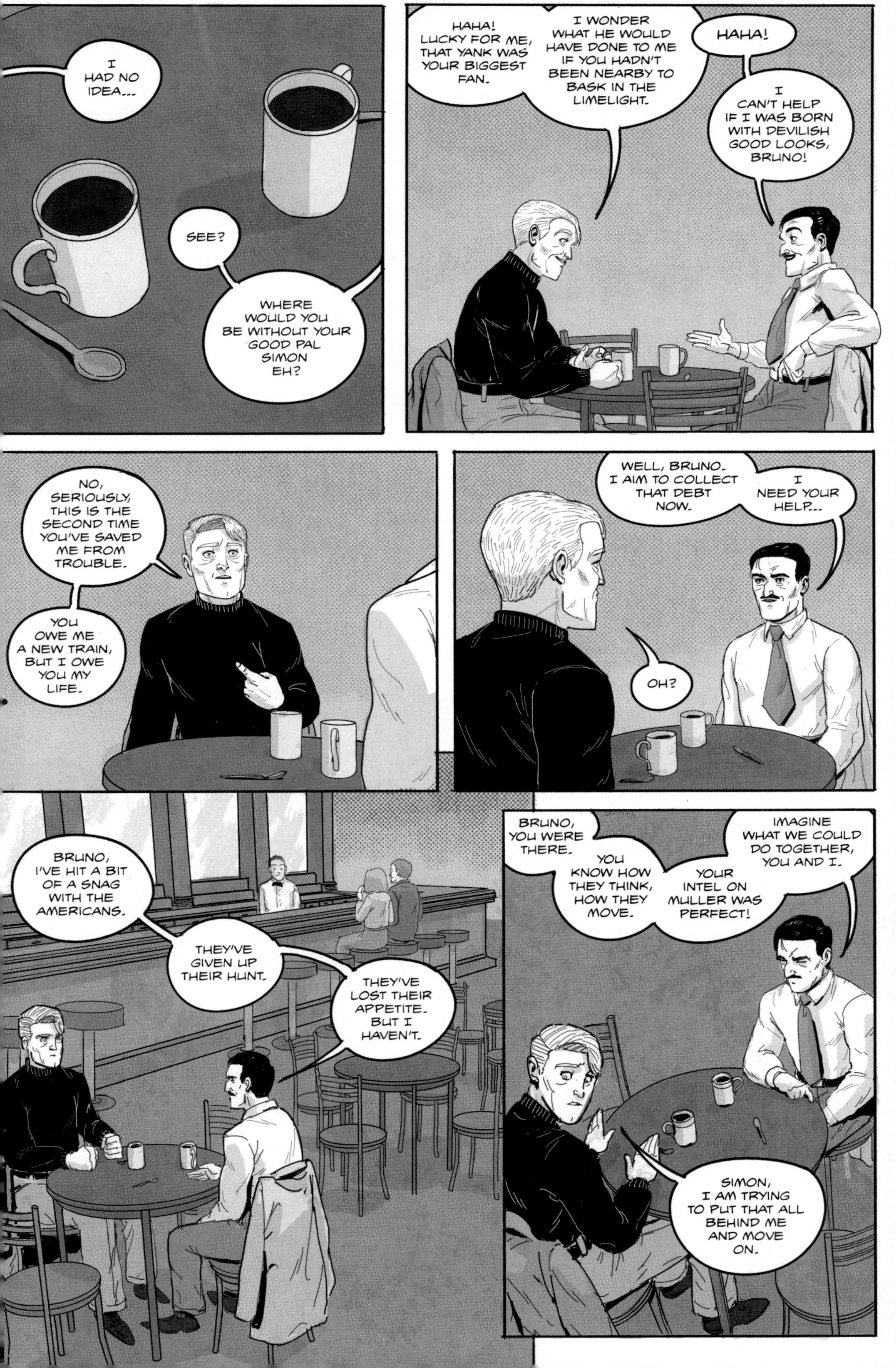

I HAD NO IDEA...
SEE?
WHERE WOULD YOU BE WITHOUT YOUR GOOD PAL SIMON EH?
HAHA! LUCKY FOR ME, THAT YANK WAS YOUR BIGGEST FAN.
I WONDER WHAT HE WOULD HAVE DONE TO ME IF YOU HADN'T BEEN NEARBY TO BASK IN THE LIMELIGHT.
HAHA!
I CAN'T HELP IF I WAS BORN WITH DEVILISH GOOD LOOKS, BRUNO!
NO, SERIOUSLY, THIS IS THE SECOND TIME YOU'VE SAVED ME FROM TROUBLE.
YOU OWE ME A NEW TRAIN, BUT I OWE YOU MY LIFE.
WELL, BRUNO. I AIM TO COLLECT THAT DEBT NOW.
I NEED YOUR HELP...
OH?
BRUNO, I'VE HIT A BIT OF A SNAG WITH THE AMERICANS.
THEY'VE GIVEN UP THEIR HUNT.
THEY'VE LOST THEIR APPETITE. BUT I HAVEN'T.
BRUNO, YOU WERE THERE.
YOU KNOW HOW THEY THINK, HOW THEY MOVE.
YOUR INTEL ON MULLER WAS PERFECT!
IMAGINE WHAT WE COULD DO TOGETHER, YOU AND I.
SIMON, I AM TRYING TO PUT THAT ALL BEHIND ME AND MOVE ON.

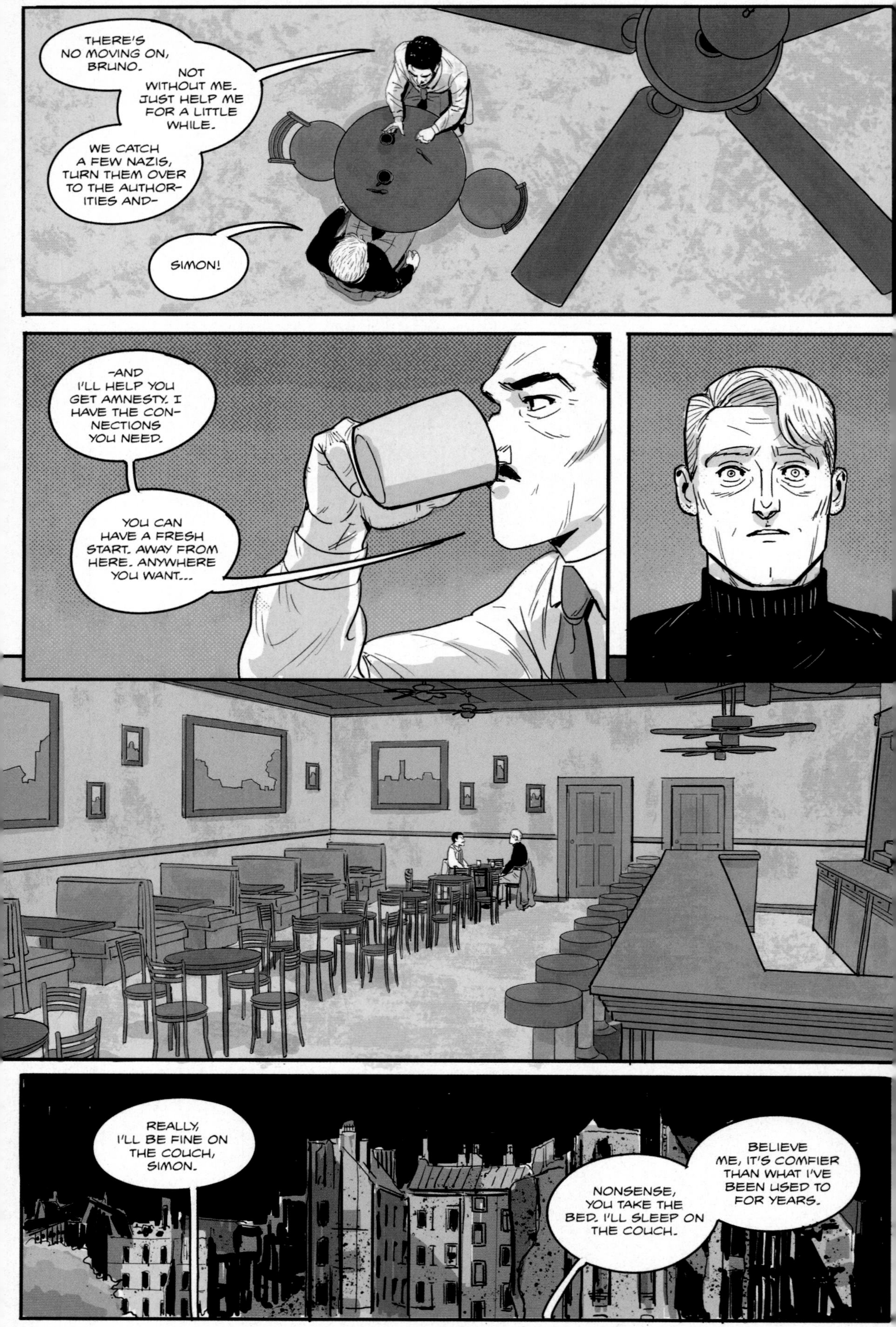
THERE'S NO MOVING ON, BRUNO.
NOT WITHOUT ME. JUST HELP ME FOR A LITTLE WHILE.
WE CATCH A FEW NAZIS, TURN THEM OVER TO THE AUTHOR-ITIES AND-
SIMON!
-AND I'LL HELP YOU GET AMNESTY. I HAVE THE CON-NECTIONS YOU NEED.
YOU CAN HAVE A FRESH START. AWAY FROM HERE. ANYWHERE YOU WANT...
REALLY, I'LL BE FINE ON THE COUCH, SIMON.
NONSENSE, YOU TAKE THE BED. I'LL SLEEP ON THE COUCH.
BELIEVE ME, IT'S COMFIER THAN WHAT I'VE BEEN USED TO FOR YEARS.

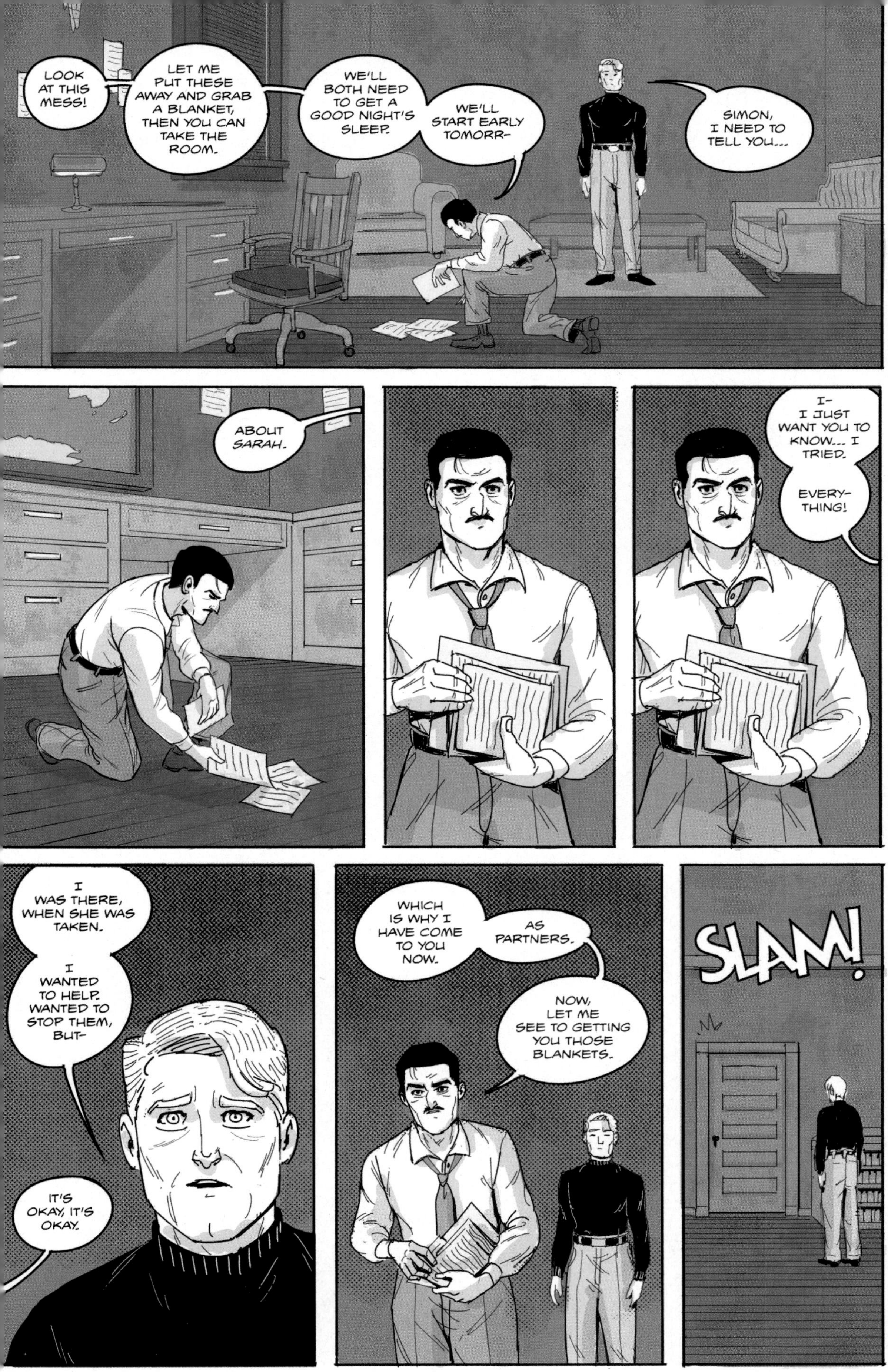
LOOK AT THIS MESS!
LET ME PUT THESE AWAY AND GRAB A BLANKET, THEN YOU CAN TAKE THE ROOM.
WE'LL BOTH NEED TO GET A GOOD NIGHT'S SLEEP.
WE'LL START EARLY TOMORR-
SIMON, I NEED TO TELL YOU...
ABOUT SARAH.
I- I JUST WANT YOU TO KNOW... I TRIED.
EVERY-THING!
I WAS THERE, WHEN SHE WAS TAKEN.
I WANTED TO HELP. WANTED TO STOP THEM, BUT-
IT'S OKAY, IT'S OKAY.
WHICH IS WHY I HAVE COME TO YOU NOW.
AS PARTNERS.
NOW, LET ME SEE TO GETTING YOU THOSE BLANKETS.
SLAM!

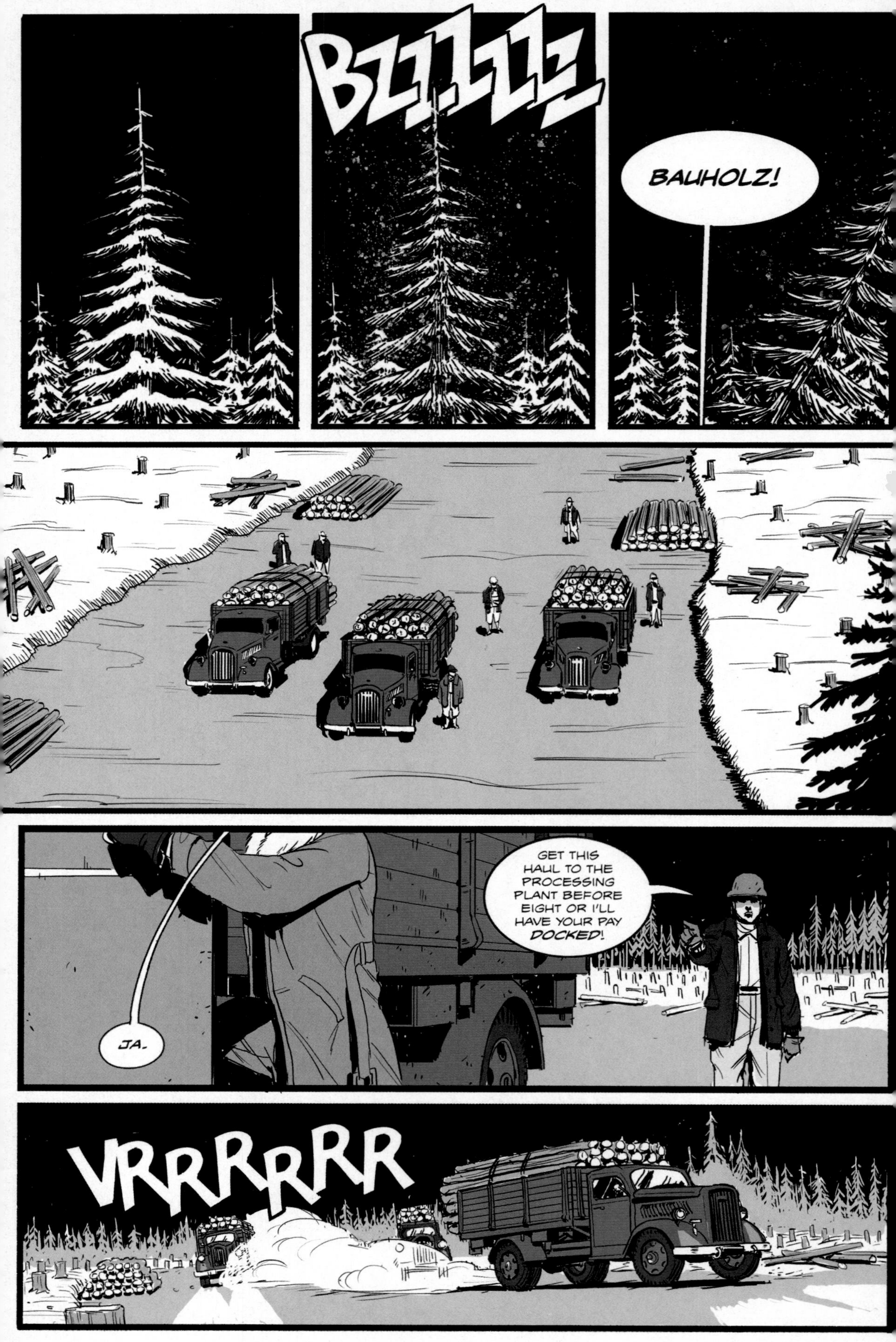
BZZZZZ
BAUHOLZ!
GET THIS HAUL TO THE PROCESSING PLANT BEFORE EIGHT OR I'LL HAVE YOUR PAY *DOCKED*!
JA.
VRRRRRR

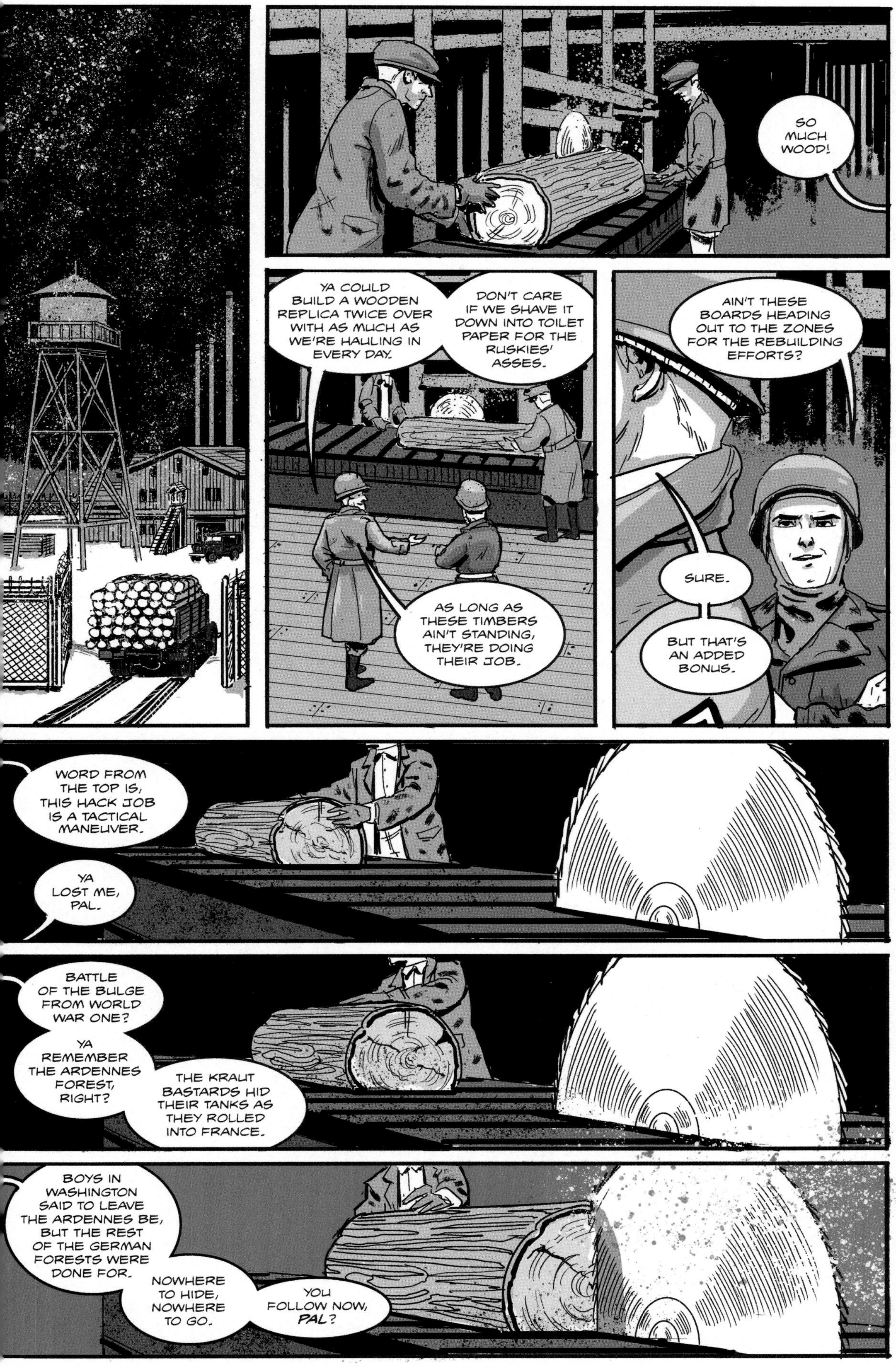
SO MUCH WOOD!
YA COULD BUILD A WOODEN REPLICA TWICE OVER WITH AS MUCH AS WE'RE HAULING IN EVERY DAY.
DON'T CARE IF WE SHAVE IT DOWN INTO TOILET PAPER FOR THE RUSKIES' ASSES.
AS LONG AS THESE TIMBERS AIN'T STANDING, THEY'RE DOING THEIR JOB.
AIN'T THESE BOARDS HEADING OUT TO THE ZONES FOR THE REBUILDING EFFORTS?
SURE.
BUT THAT'S AN ADDED BONUS.
WORD FROM THE TOP IS, THIS HACK JOB IS A TACTICAL MANEUVER.
YA LOST ME, PAL.
BATTLE OF THE BULGE FROM WORLD WAR ONE?
YA REMEMBER THE ARDENNES FOREST, RIGHT?
THE KRAUT BASTARDS HID THEIR TANKS AS THEY ROLLED INTO FRANCE.
BOYS IN WASHINGTON SAID TO LEAVE THE ARDENNES BE, BUT THE REST OF THE GERMAN FORESTS WERE DONE FOR.
NOWHERE TO HIDE, NOWHERE TO GO.
YOU FOLLOW NOW, *PAL*?

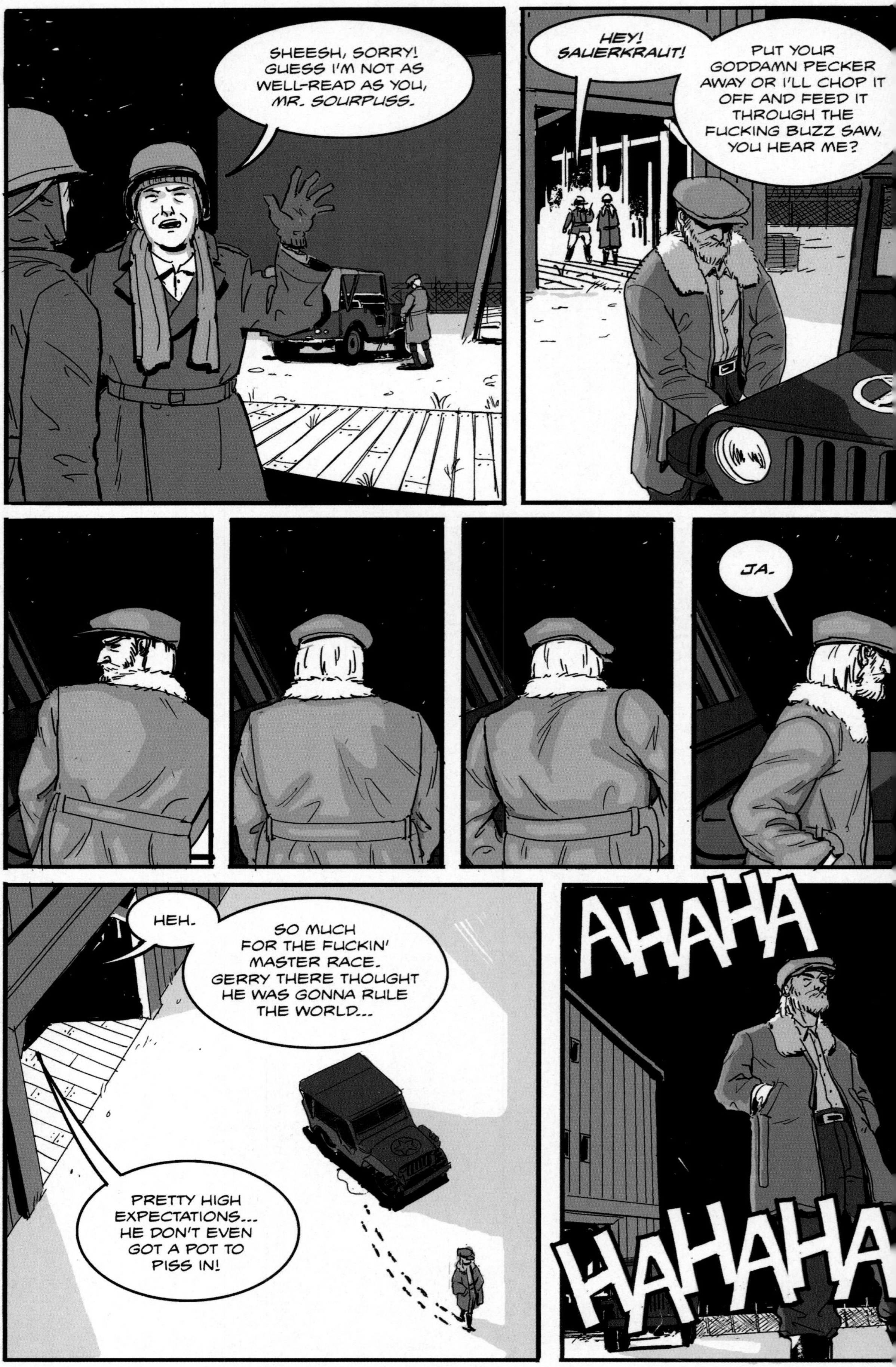
SHEESH, SORRY! GUESS I'M NOT AS WELL-READ AS YOU, MR. SOURPUSS.
HEY! SAUERKRAUT!
PUT YOUR GODDAMN PECKER AWAY OR I'LL CHOP IT OFF AND FEED IT THROUGH THE FUCKING BUZZ SAW, YOU HEAR ME?
JA.
HEH.
SO MUCH FOR THE FUCKIN' MASTER RACE. GERRY THERE THOUGHT HE WAS GONNA RULE THE WORLD...
PRETTY HIGH EXPECTATIONS... HE DON'T EVEN GOT A POT TO PISS IN!
AHAHA
HAHAHA

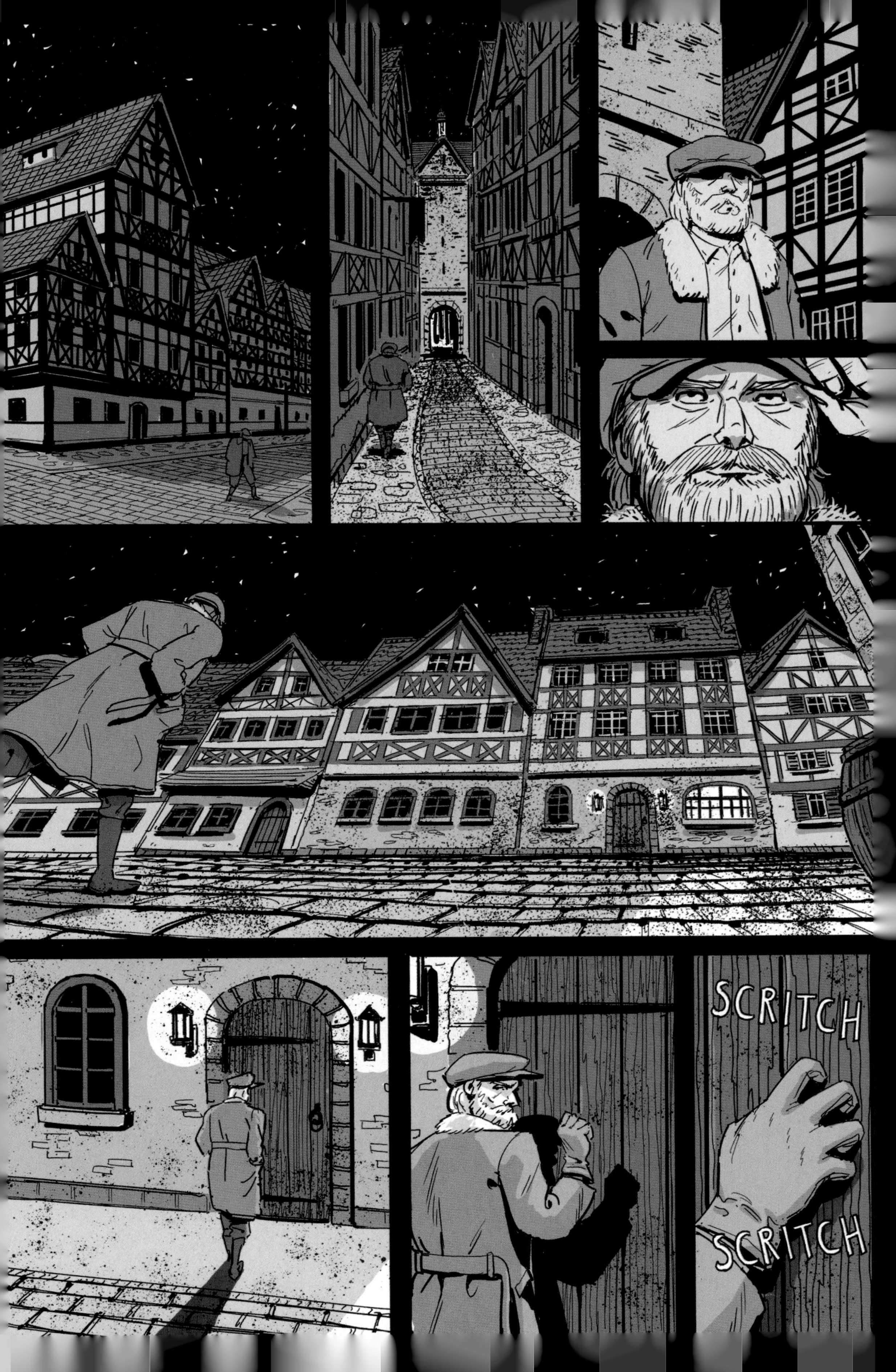
SCRITCH
SCRITCH

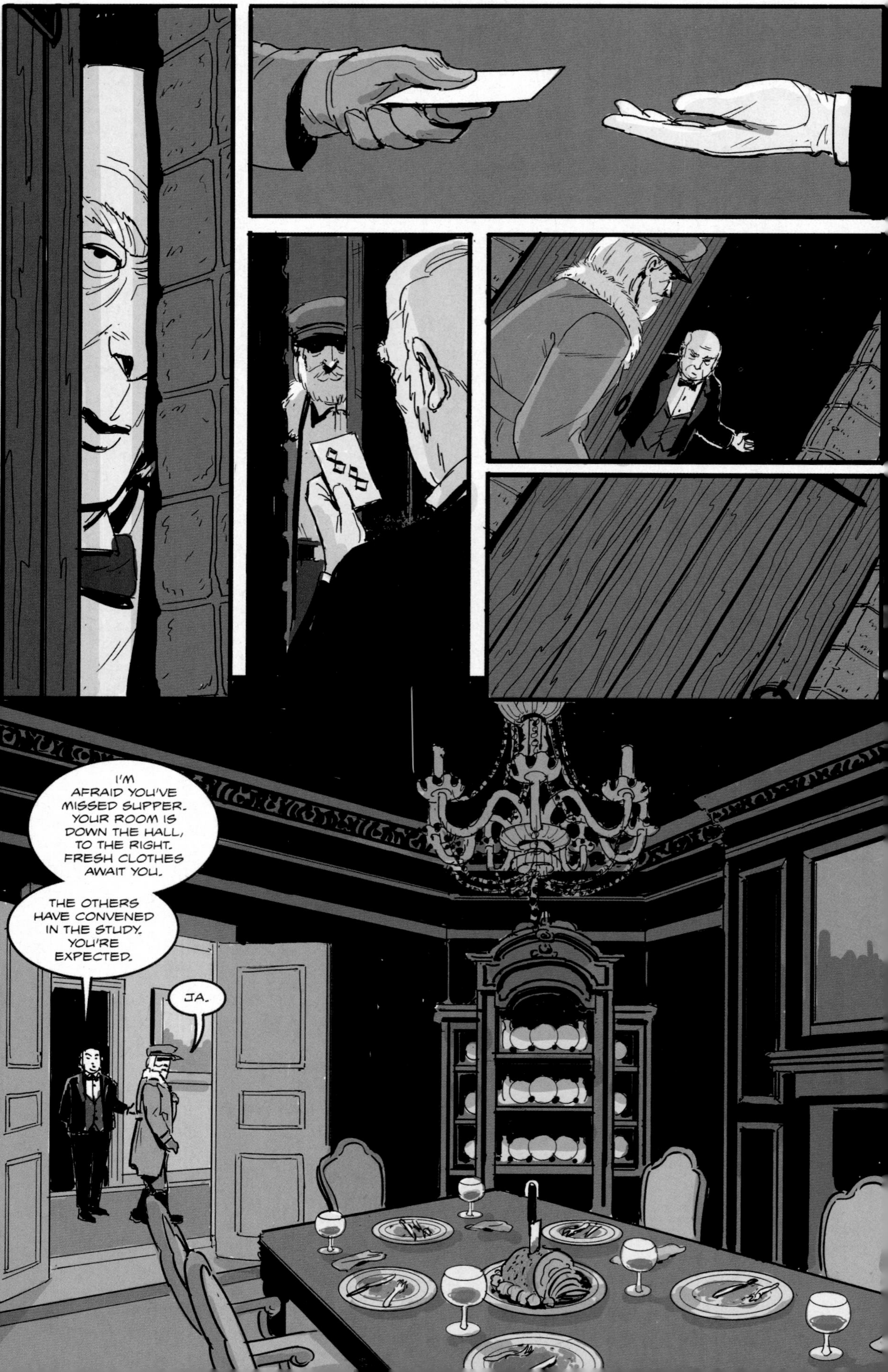
I'M AFRAID YOU'VE MISSED SUPPER. YOUR ROOM IS DOWN THE HALL, TO THE RIGHT. FRESH CLOTHES AWAIT YOU.
THE OTHERS HAVE CONVENED IN THE STUDY. YOU'RE EXPECTED.
JA.

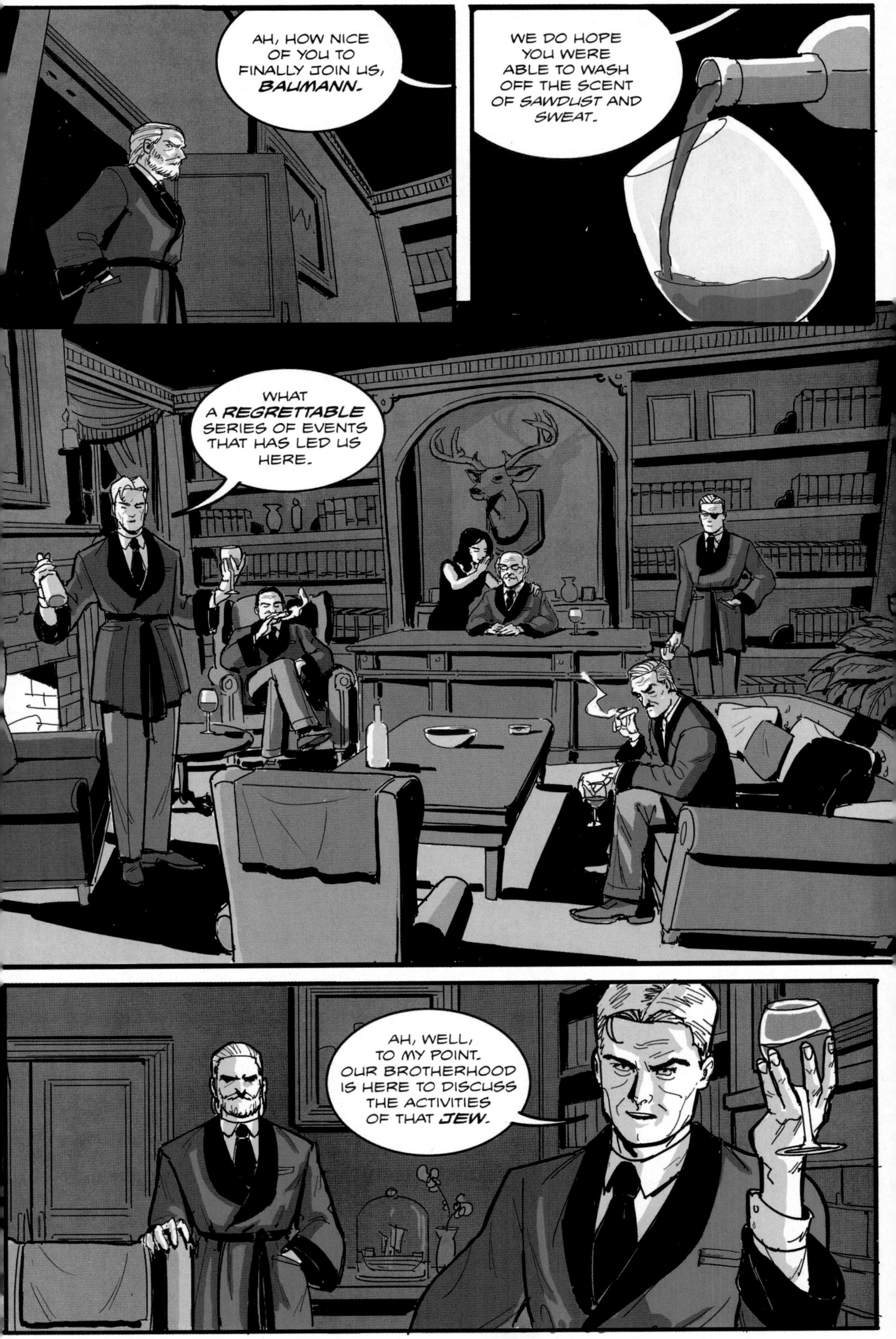
AH, HOW NICE OF YOU TO FINALLY JOIN US, BAUMANN.
WE DO HOPE YOU WERE ABLE TO WASH OFF THE SCENT OF SAWDUST AND SWEAT.
WHAT A REGRETTABLE SERIES OF EVENTS THAT HAS LED US HERE.
AH, WELL, TO MY POINT. OUR BROTHERHOOD IS HERE TO DISCUSS THE ACTIVITIES OF THAT JEW.

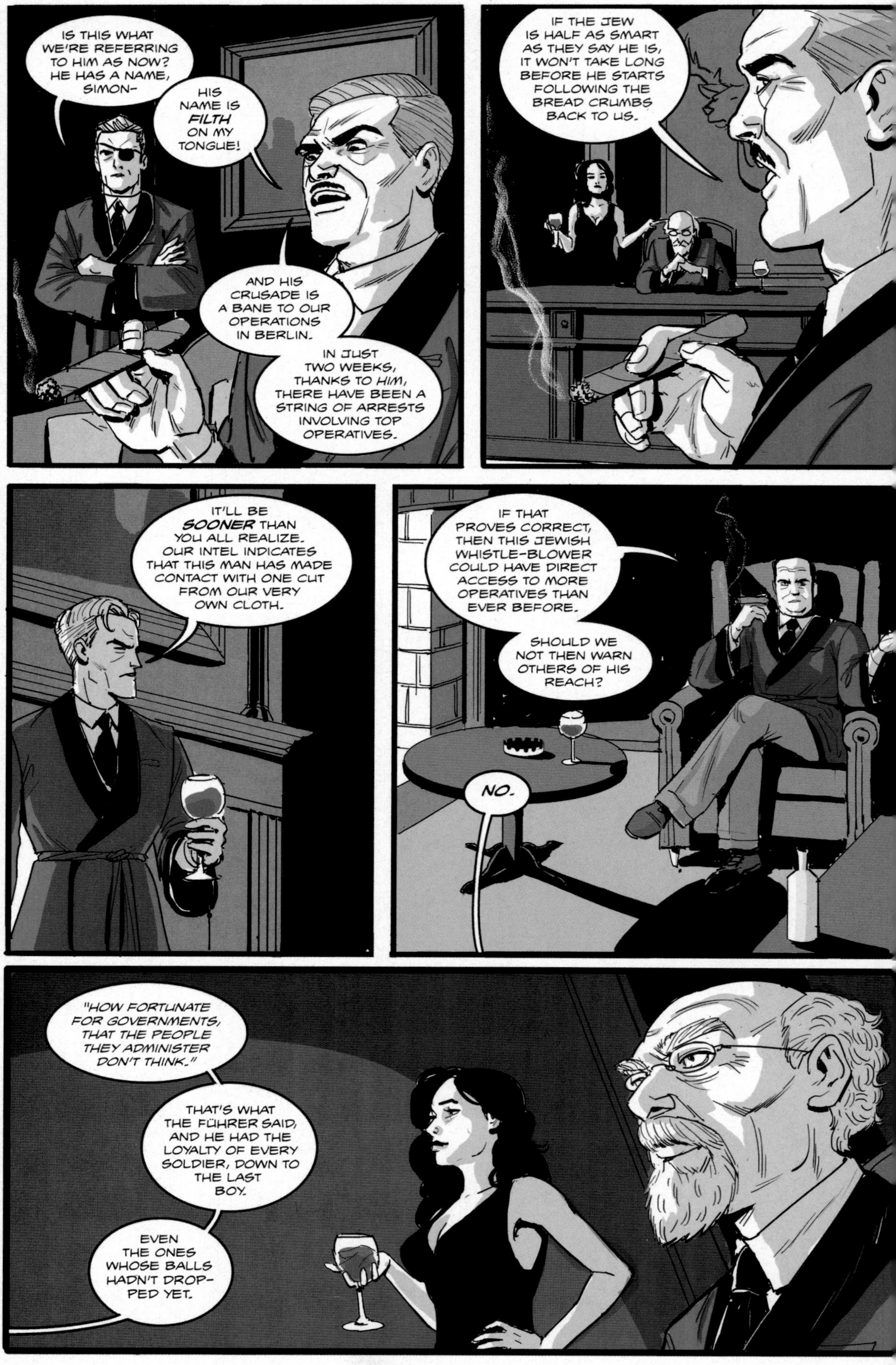
IS THIS WHAT WE'RE REFERRING TO HIM AS NOW? HE HAS A NAME, SIMON-
HIS NAME IS *FILTH* ON MY TONGUE!
AND HIS CRUSADE IS A BANE TO OUR OPERATIONS IN BERLIN.
IN JUST TWO WEEKS, THANKS TO *HIM*, THERE HAVE BEEN A STRING OF ARRESTS INVOLVING TOP OPERATIVES.
IF THE JEW IS HALF AS SMART AS THEY SAY HE IS, IT WON'T TAKE LONG BEFORE HE STARTS FOLLOWING THE BREAD CRUMBS BACK TO US.
IT'LL BE *SOONER* THAN YOU ALL REALIZE. OUR INTEL INDICATES THAT THIS MAN HAS MADE CONTACT WITH ONE CUT FROM OUR VERY OWN CLOTH.
IF THAT PROVES CORRECT, THEN THIS JEWISH WHISTLE-BLOWER COULD HAVE DIRECT ACCESS TO MORE OPERATIVES THAN EVER BEFORE.
SHOULD WE NOT THEN WARN OTHERS OF HIS REACH?
NO.
"HOW FORTUNATE FOR GOVERNMENTS, THAT THE PEOPLE THEY ADMINISTER DON'T THINK."
THAT'S WHAT THE FÜHRER SAID, AND HE HAD THE LOYALTY OF EVERY SOLDIER, DOWN TO THE LAST BOY.
EVEN THE ONES WHOSE BALLS HADN'T DROP-PED YET.

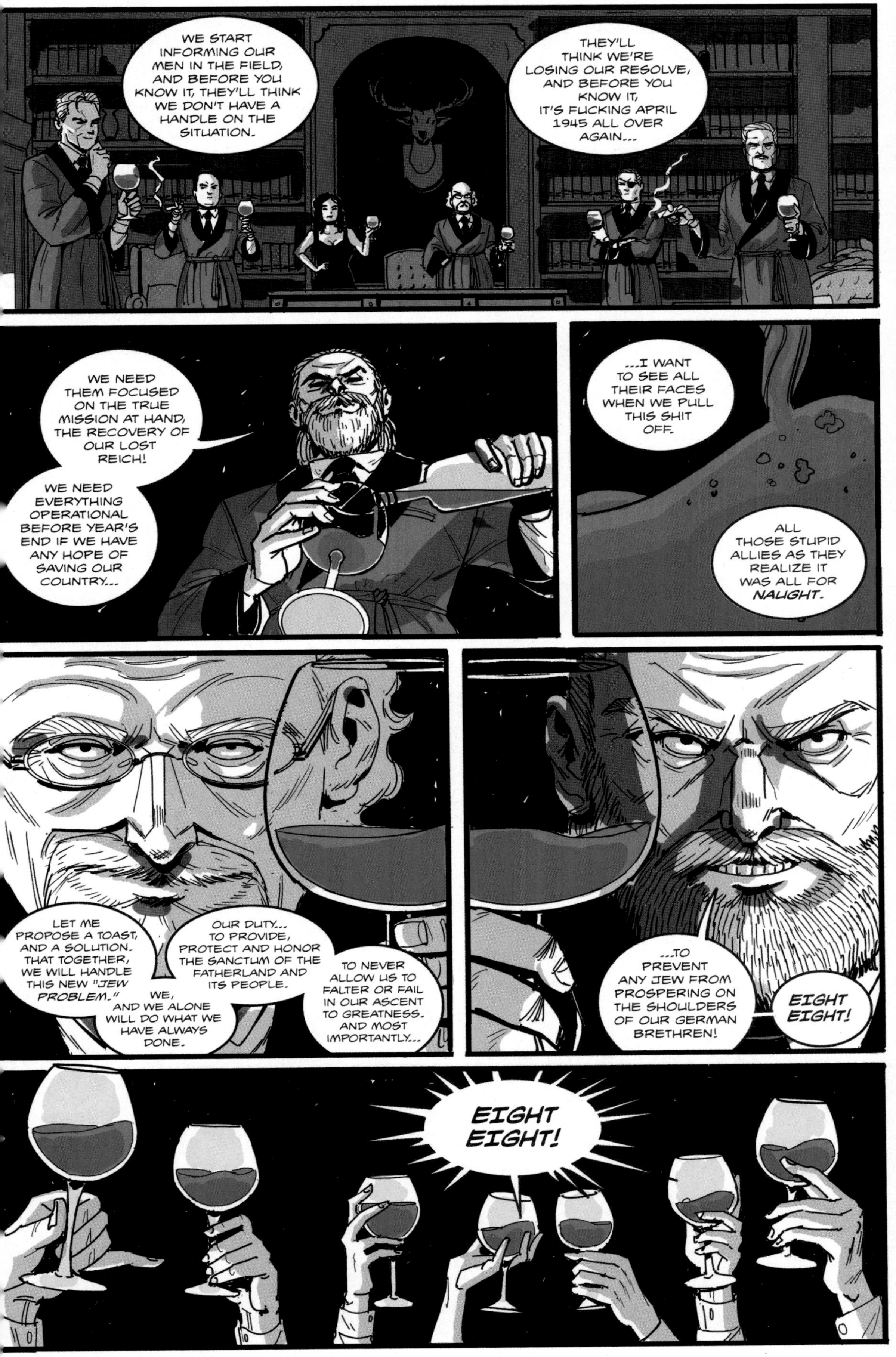
WE START INFORMING OUR MEN IN THE FIELD, AND BEFORE YOU KNOW IT, THEY'LL THINK WE DON'T HAVE A HANDLE ON THE SITUATION.
THEY'LL THINK WE'RE LOSING OUR RESOLVE, AND BEFORE YOU KNOW IT, IT'S FUCKING APRIL 1945 ALL OVER AGAIN...
WE NEED THEM FOCUSED ON THE TRUE MISSION AT HAND, THE RECOVERY OF OUR LOST REICH!
WE NEED EVERYTHING OPERATIONAL BEFORE YEAR'S END IF WE HAVE ANY HOPE OF SAVING OUR COUNTRY...
...I WANT TO SEE ALL THEIR FACES WHEN WE PULL THIS SHIT OFF.
ALL THOSE STUPID ALLIES AS THEY REALIZE IT WAS ALL FOR NAUGHT.
LET ME PROPOSE A TOAST, AND A SOLUTION. THAT TOGETHER, WE WILL HANDLE THIS NEW "JEW PROBLEM."
WE, AND WE ALONE WILL DO WHAT WE HAVE ALWAYS DONE.
OUR DUTY... TO PROVIDE, PROTECT AND HONOR THE SANCTUM OF THE FATHERLAND AND ITS PEOPLE.
TO NEVER ALLOW US TO FALTER OR FAIL IN OUR ASCENT TO GREATNESS. AND MOST IMPORTANTLY...
...TO PREVENT ANY JEW FROM PROSPERING ON THE SHOULDERS OF OUR GERMAN BRETHREN!
EIGHT EIGHT!
EIGHT EIGHT!

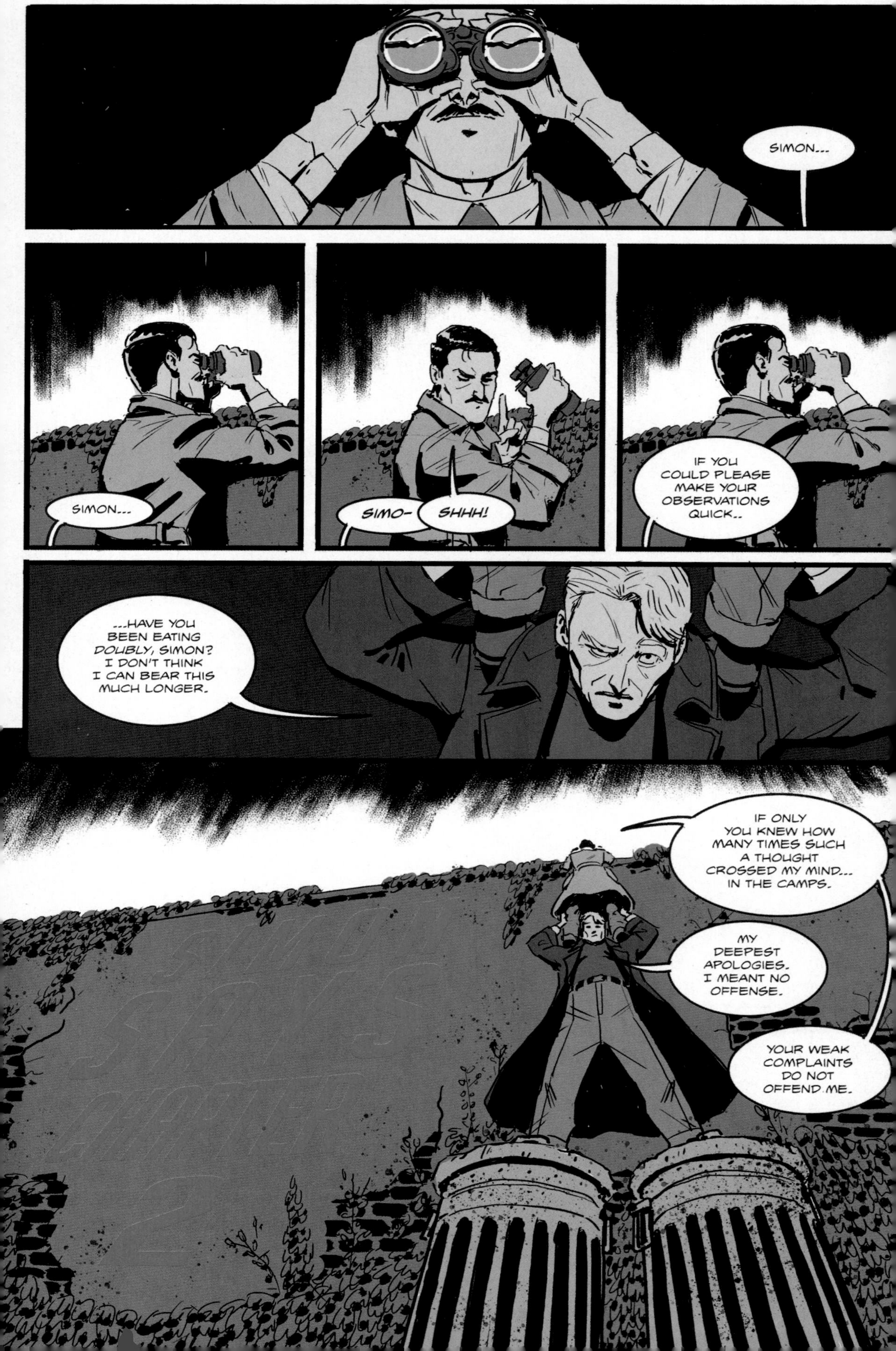
SIMON...
SIMON...
SIMO-
SHHH!
IF YOU COULD PLEASE MAKE YOUR OBSERVATIONS QUICK..
...HAVE YOU BEEN EATING DOUBLY, SIMON? I DON'T THINK I CAN BEAR THIS MUCH LONGER.
IF ONLY YOU KNEW HOW MANY TIMES SUCH A THOUGHT CROSSED MY MIND... IN THE CAMPS.
MY DEEPEST APOLOGIES. I MEANT NO OFFENSE.
YOUR WEAK COMPLAINTS DO NOT OFFEND ME.

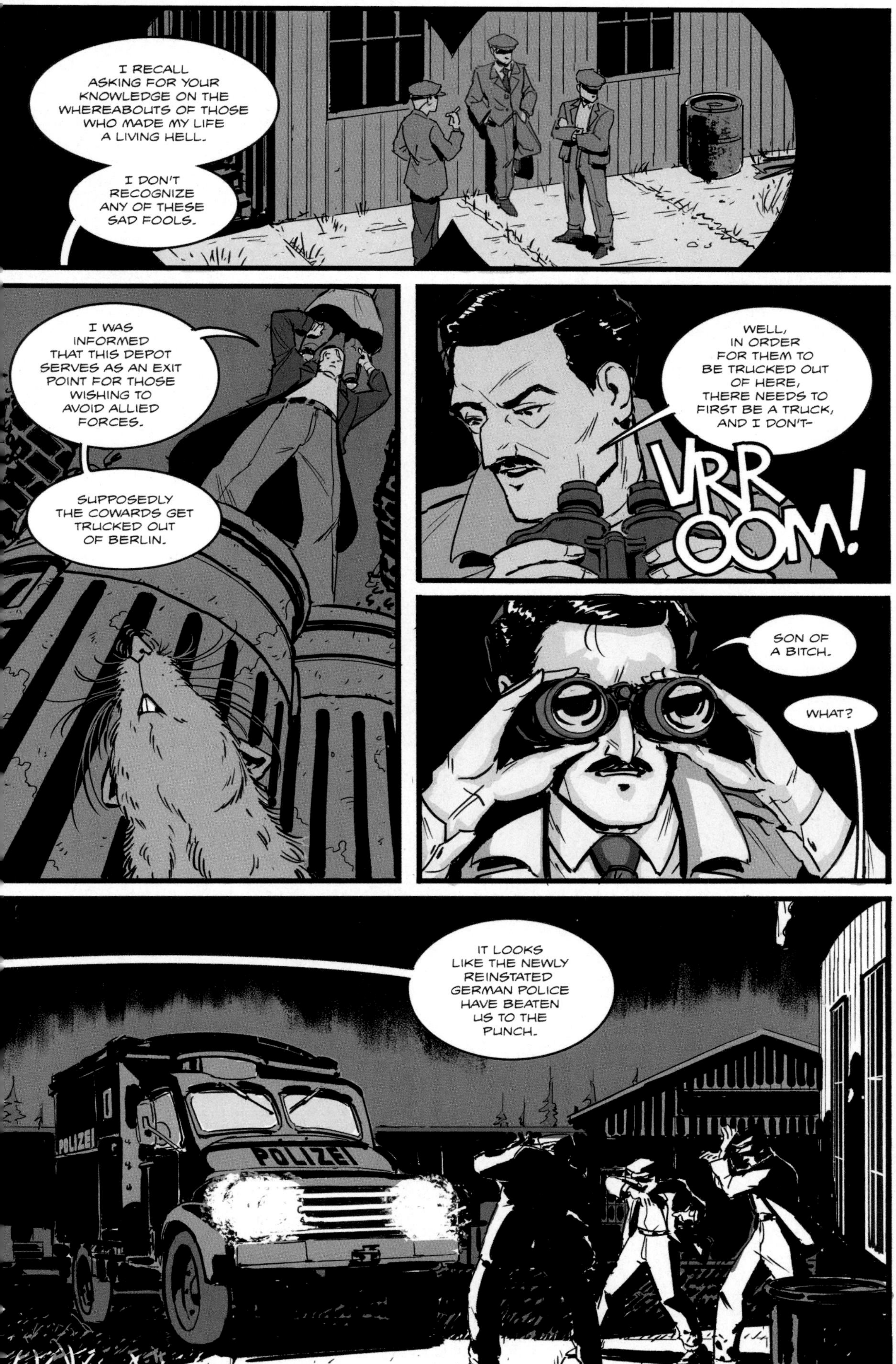
I RECALL ASKING FOR YOUR KNOWLEDGE ON THE WHEREABOUTS OF THOSE WHO MADE MY LIFE A LIVING HELL.
I DON'T RECOGNIZE ANY OF THESE SAD FOOLS.
I WAS INFORMED THAT THIS DEPOT SERVES AS AN EXIT POINT FOR THOSE WISHING TO AVOID ALLIED FORCES.
SUPPOSEDLY THE COWARDS GET TRUCKED OUT OF BERLIN.
WELL, IN ORDER FOR THEM TO BE TRUCKED OUT OF HERE, THERE NEEDS TO FIRST BE A TRUCK, AND I DON'T-
VRROOM!
SON OF A BITCH.
WHAT?
IT LOOKS LIKE THE NEWLY REINSTATED GERMAN POLICE HAVE BEATEN US TO THE PUNCH.
POLIZEI
POLIZEI

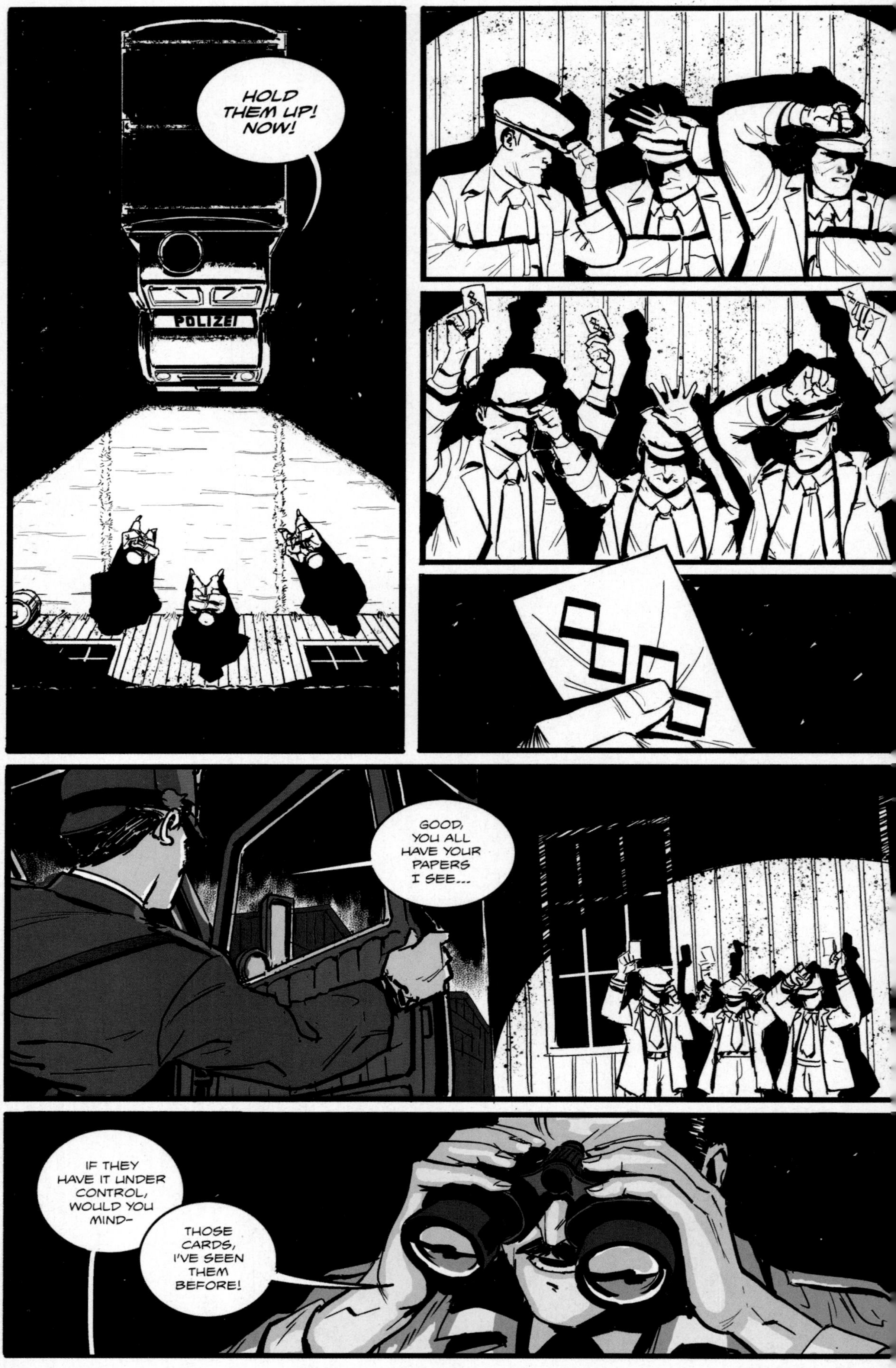
HOLD THEM UP! NOW!
POLIZEI
GOOD, YOU ALL HAVE YOUR PAPERS I SEE...
IF THEY HAVE IT UNDER CONTROL, WOULD YOU MIND-
THOSE CARDS, I'VE SEEN THEM BEFORE!

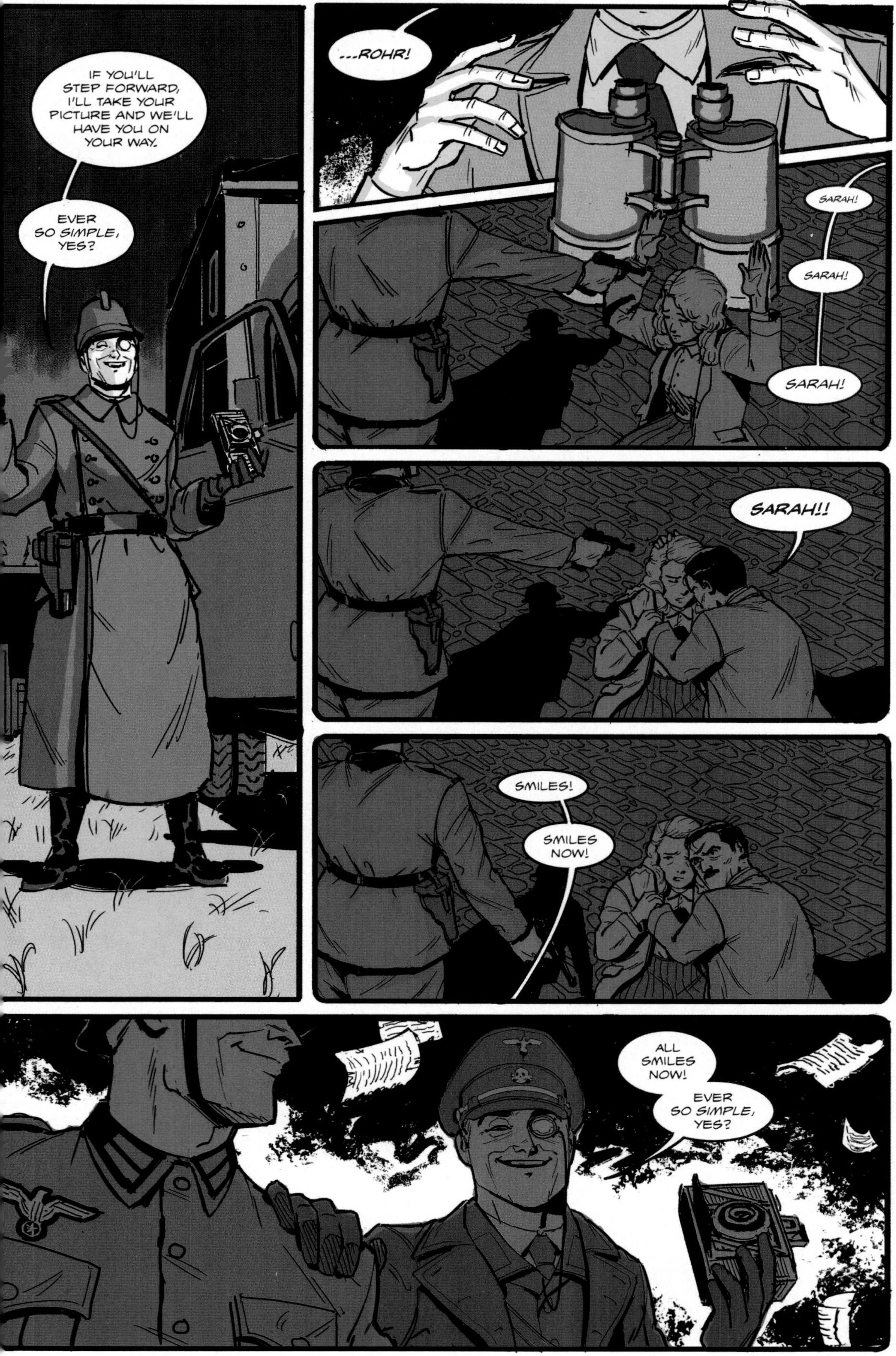
IF YOU'LL STEP FORWARD, I'LL TAKE YOUR PICTURE AND WE'LL HAVE YOU ON YOUR WAY.
EVER SO SIMPLE, YES?
...ROHR!
SARAH!
SARAH!
SARAH!
SARAH!!
SMILES!
SMILES NOW!
ALL SMILES NOW!
EVER SO SIMPLE, YES?

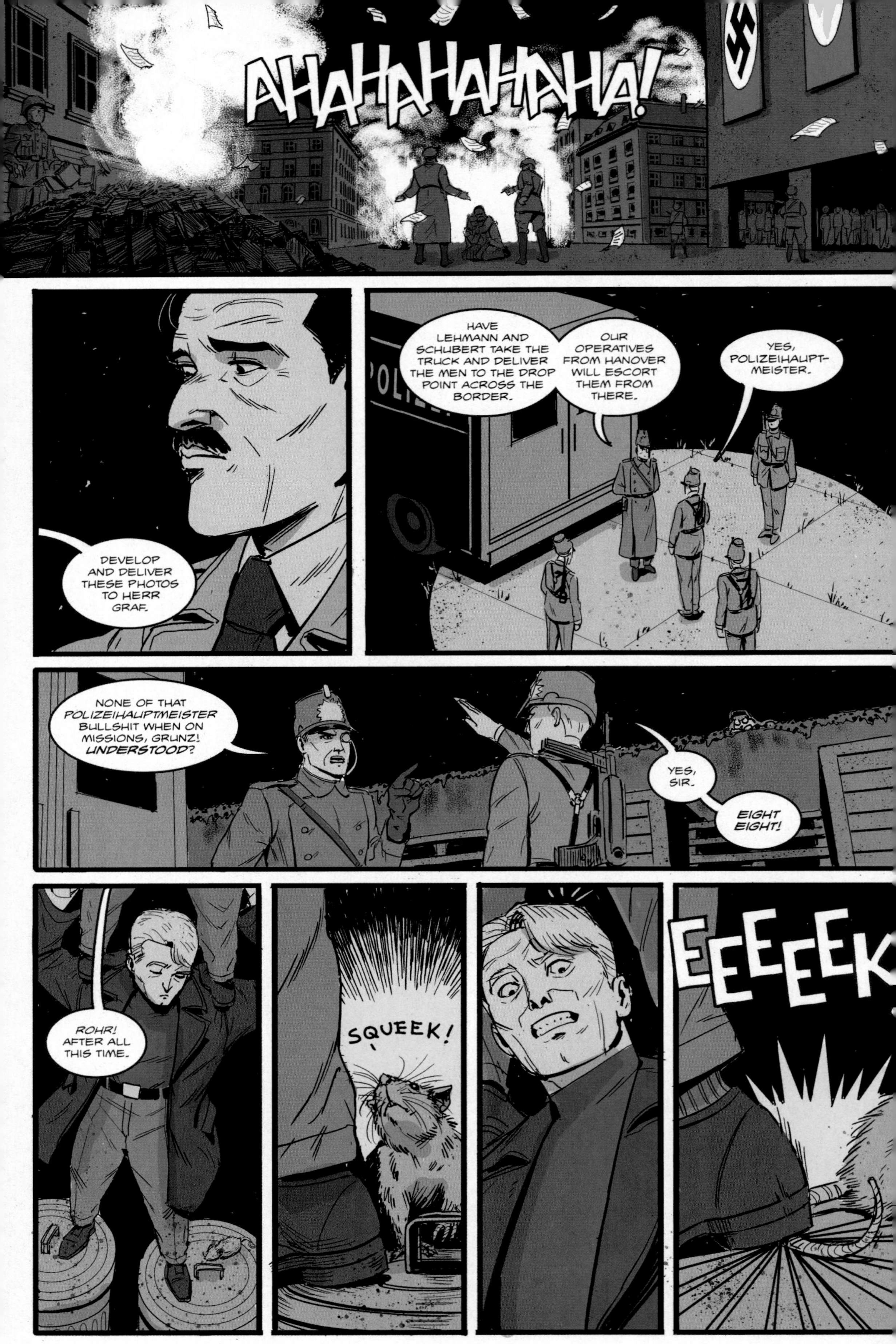
AHAHAHAHAHAHA!
DEVELOP AND DELIVER THESE PHOTOS TO HERR GRAF.
HAVE LEHMANN AND SCHUBERT TAKE THE TRUCK AND DELIVER THE MEN TO THE DROP POINT ACROSS THE BORDER.
OUR OPERATIVES FROM HANOVER WILL ESCORT THEM FROM THERE.
YES, POLIZEIHAUPT-MEISTER.
POLIZEI
NONE OF THAT *POLIZEIHAUPTMEISTER* BULLSHIT WHEN ON MISSIONS, GRUNZ! *UNDERSTOOD?*
YES, SIR.
EIGHT EIGHT!
ROHR! AFTER ALL THIS TIME.
SQUEEK!
EEEEEK

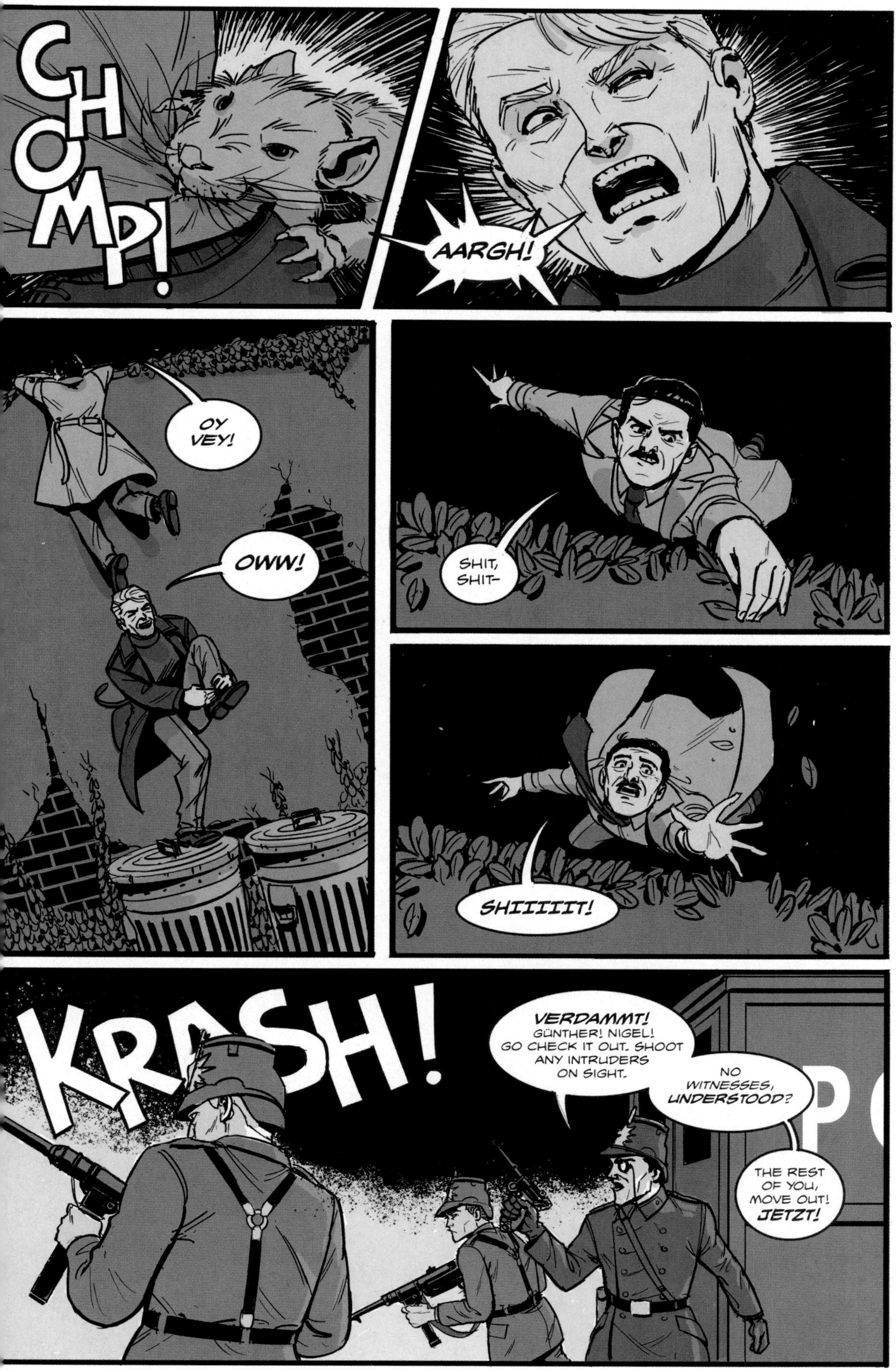
CHOMP!
AARGH!
OY VEY!
OWW!
SHIT, SHIT-
SHIIIIIT!
KRASH!
VERDAMMT! GÜNTHER! NIGEL! GO CHECK IT OUT. SHOOT ANY INTRUDERS ON SIGHT.
NO WITNESSES, UNDERSTOOD?
THE REST OF YOU, MOVE OUT! JETZT!
PO

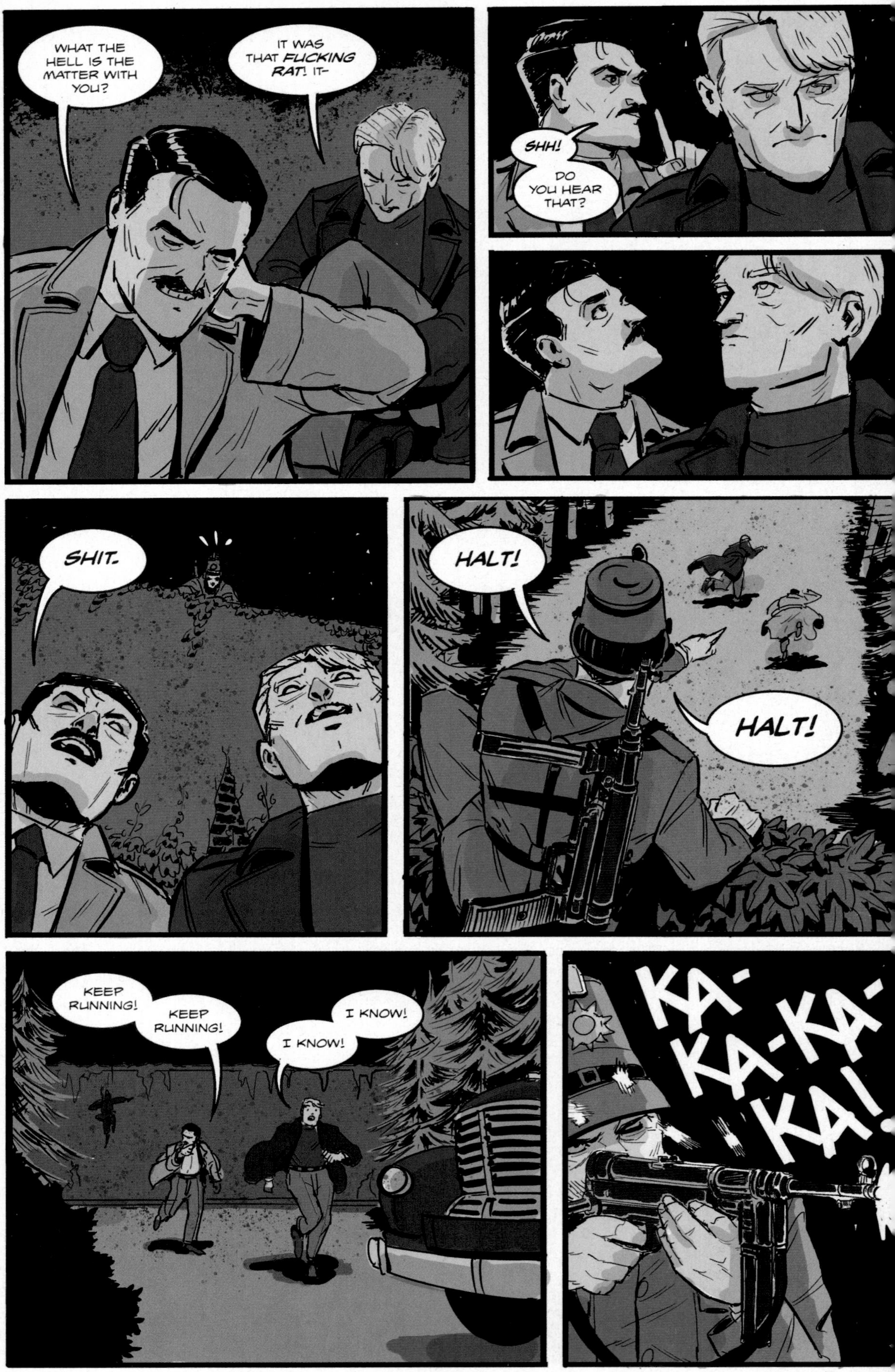
WHAT THE HELL IS THE MATTER WITH YOU?
IT WAS THAT *FUCKING RAT*! IT-
SHH!
DO YOU HEAR THAT?
SHIT.
HALT!
HALT!
KEEP RUNNING!
KEEP RUNNING!
I KNOW!
I KNOW!
KA-KA-KA-KA-KA!

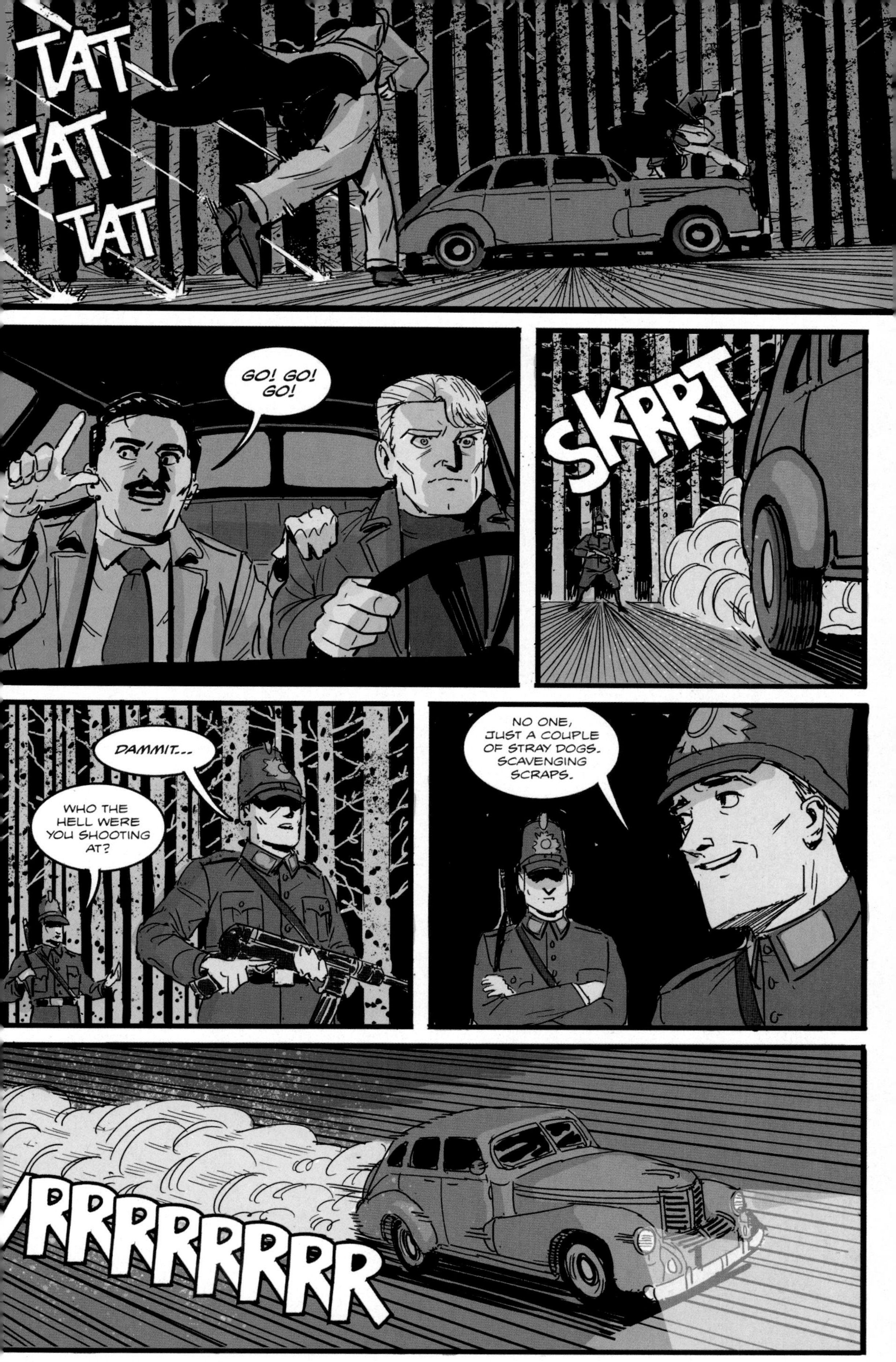
TAT
TAT
TAT
GO! GO! GO!
SKRRT
DAMMIT...
WHO THE HELL WERE YOU SHOOTING AT?
NO ONE, JUST A COUPLE OF STRAY DOGS. SCAVENGING SCRAPS.
RRRRRRRR

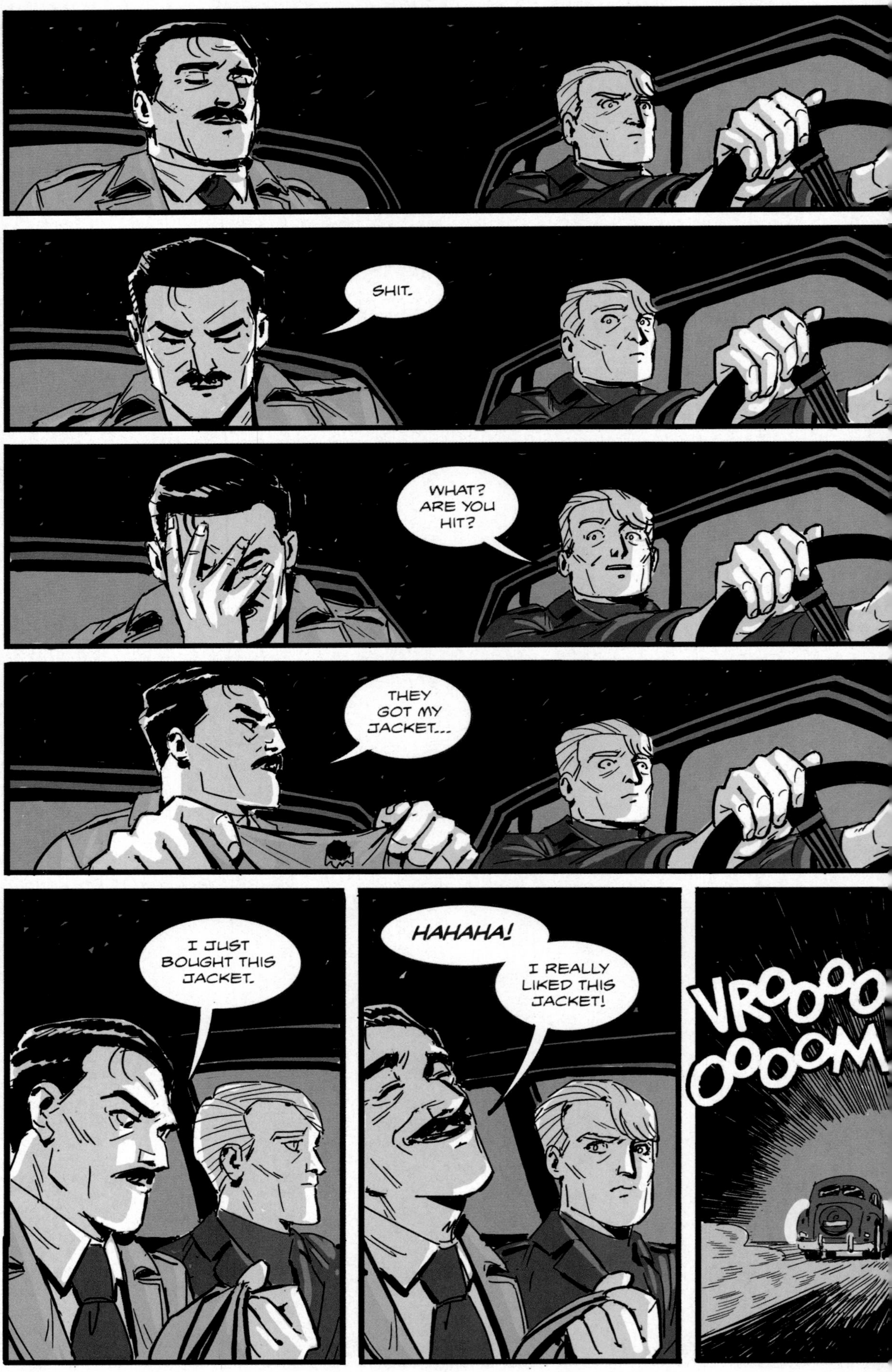
SHIT.
WHAT? ARE YOU HIT?
THEY GOT MY JACKET...
I JUST BOUGHT THIS JACKET.
HAHAHA!
I REALLY LIKED THIS JACKET!
VROOOOOOOOOM

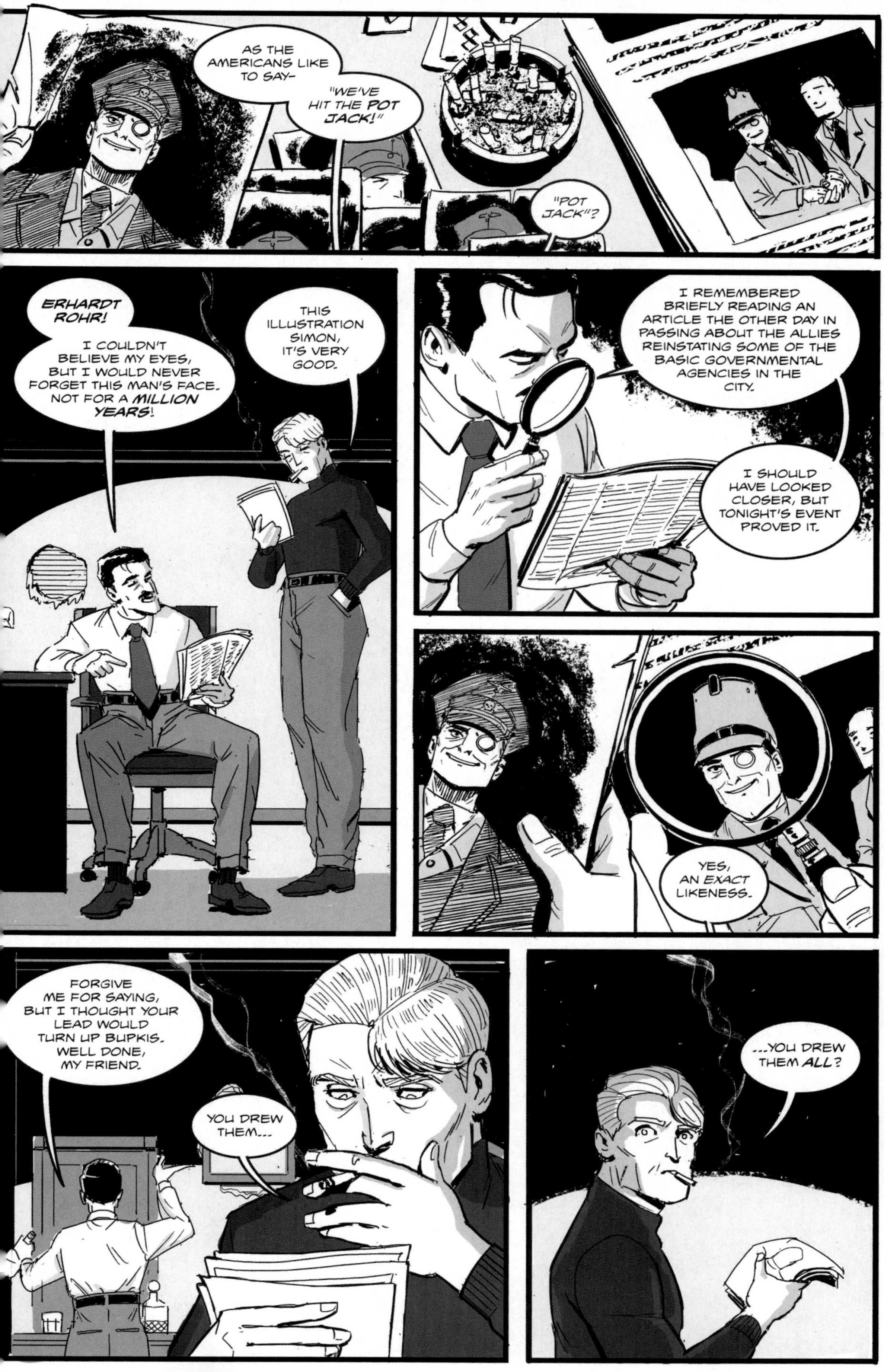
AS THE AMERICANS LIKE TO SAY-
"WE'VE HIT THE POT JACK!"
"POT JACK"?
ERHARDT ROHR!
I COULDN'T BELIEVE MY EYES, BUT I WOULD NEVER FORGET THIS MAN'S FACE. NOT FOR A MILLION YEARS!
THIS ILLUSTRATION SIMON, IT'S VERY GOOD.
I REMEMBERED BRIEFLY READING AN ARTICLE THE OTHER DAY IN PASSING ABOUT THE ALLIES REINSTATING SOME OF THE BASIC GOVERNMENTAL AGENCIES IN THE CITY.
I SHOULD HAVE LOOKED CLOSER, BUT TONIGHT'S EVENT PROVED IT.
YES, AN EXACT LIKENESS.
FORGIVE ME FOR SAYING, BUT I THOUGHT YOUR LEAD WOULD TURN UP BUPKIS. WELL DONE, MY FRIEND.
YOU DREW THEM...
...YOU DREW THEM ALL?

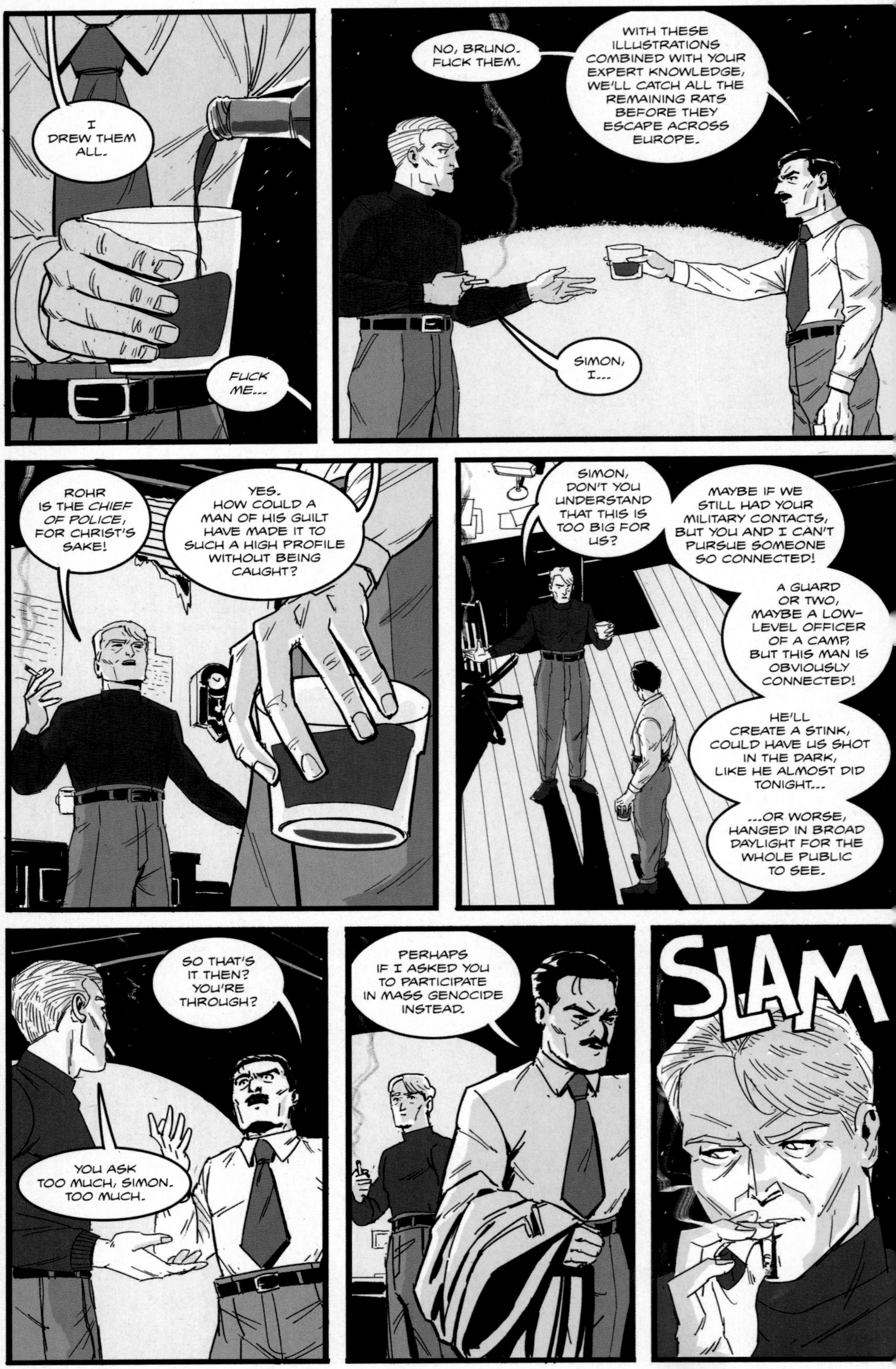
I DREW THEM ALL.
FUCK ME...
NO, BRUNO. FUCK THEM.
WITH THESE ILLUSTRATIONS COMBINED WITH YOUR EXPERT KNOWLEDGE, WE'LL CATCH ALL THE REMAINING RATS BEFORE THEY ESCAPE ACROSS EUROPE.
SIMON, I...
ROHR IS THE *CHIEF OF POLICE*, FOR CHRIST'S SAKE!
YES. HOW COULD A MAN OF HIS GUILT HAVE MADE IT TO SUCH A HIGH PROFILE WITHOUT BEING CAUGHT?
SIMON, DON'T YOU UNDERSTAND THAT THIS IS TOO BIG FOR US?
MAYBE IF WE STILL HAD YOUR MILITARY CONTACTS, BUT YOU AND I CAN'T PURSUE SOMEONE SO CONNECTED!
A GUARD OR TWO, MAYBE A LOW-LEVEL OFFICER OF A CAMP, BUT THIS MAN IS OBVIOUSLY CONNECTED!
HE'LL CREATE A STINK, COULD HAVE US SHOT IN THE DARK, LIKE HE ALMOST DID TONIGHT...
...OR WORSE, HANGED IN BROAD DAYLIGHT FOR THE WHOLE PUBLIC TO SEE.
SO THAT'S IT THEN? YOU'RE THROUGH?
YOU ASK TOO MUCH, SIMON. TOO MUCH.
PERHAPS IF I ASKED YOU TO PARTICIPATE IN MASS GENOCIDE INSTEAD.
SLAM

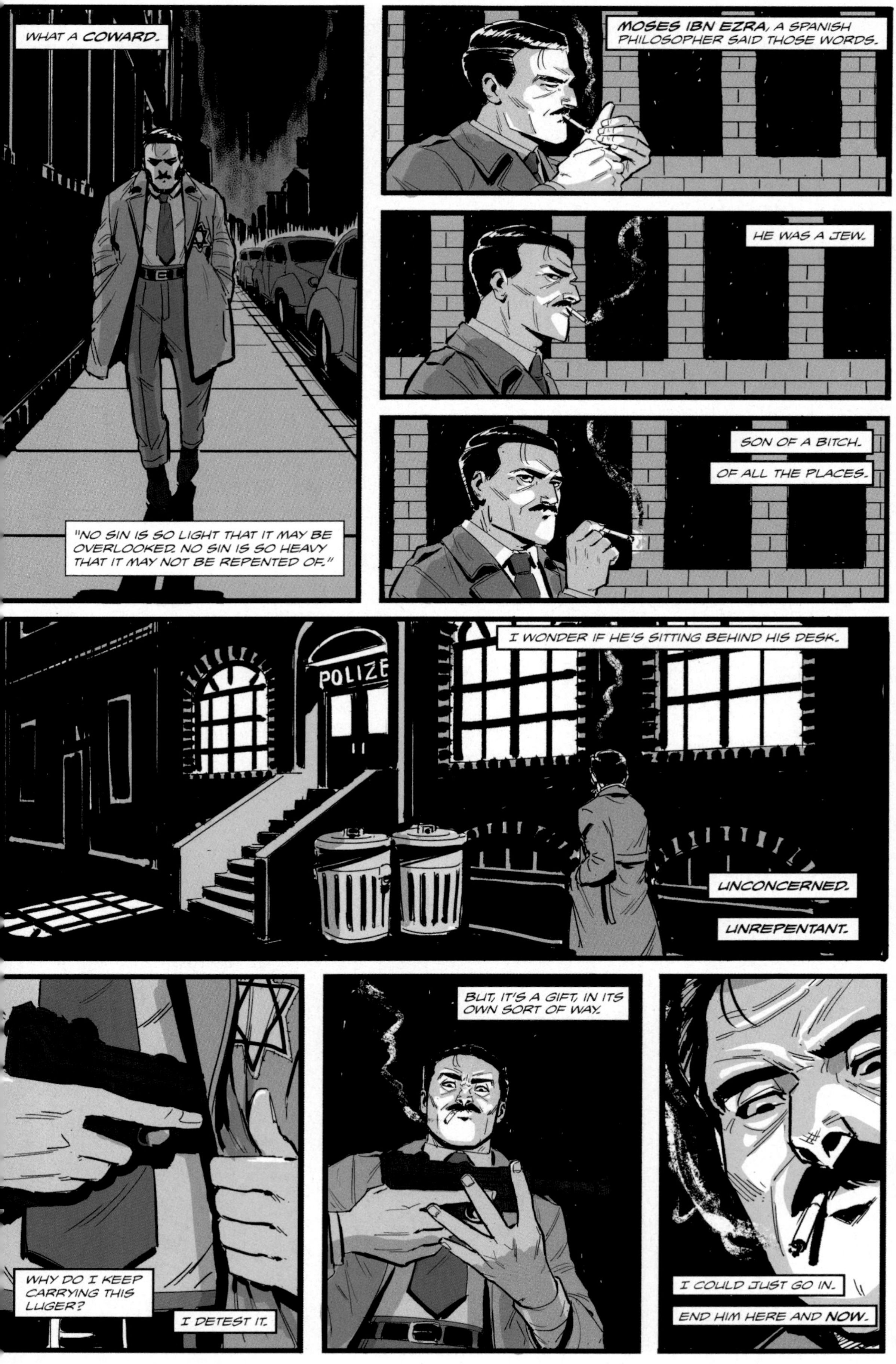

WHAT A COWARD.
"NO SIN IS SO LIGHT THAT IT MAY BE OVERLOOKED. NO SIN IS SO HEAVY THAT IT MAY NOT BE REPENTED OF."
MOSES IBN EZRA, A SPANISH PHILOSOPHER SAID THOSE WORDS.
HE WAS A JEW.
SON OF A BITCH.
OF ALL THE PLACES.
POLIZE
I WONDER IF HE'S SITTING BEHIND HIS DESK.
UNCONCERNED.
UNREPENTANT.
WHY DO I KEEP CARRYING THIS LUGER?
I DETEST IT.
BUT, IT'S A GIFT, IN ITS OWN SORT OF WAY.
I COULD JUST GO IN.
END HIM HERE AND NOW.

BUT, OF COURSE, I CANNOT.

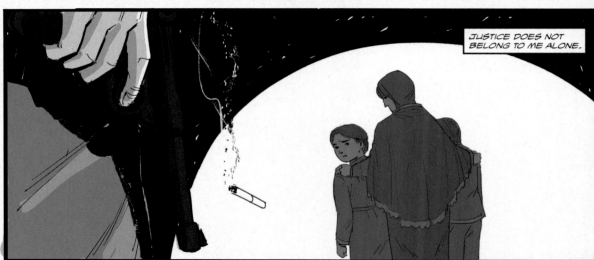

JUSTICE DOES NOT BELONG TO ME ALONE.

THE EYES OF THOSE WHO CAN NO LONGER SEEK JUSTICE ARE FULL OF EXPECTATION.

I MUST SPEAK FOR THOSE THAT HAVE BEEN SILENCED.

IN TIME, MY OWN JUSTICE WILL COME.

BUT NOT YET.

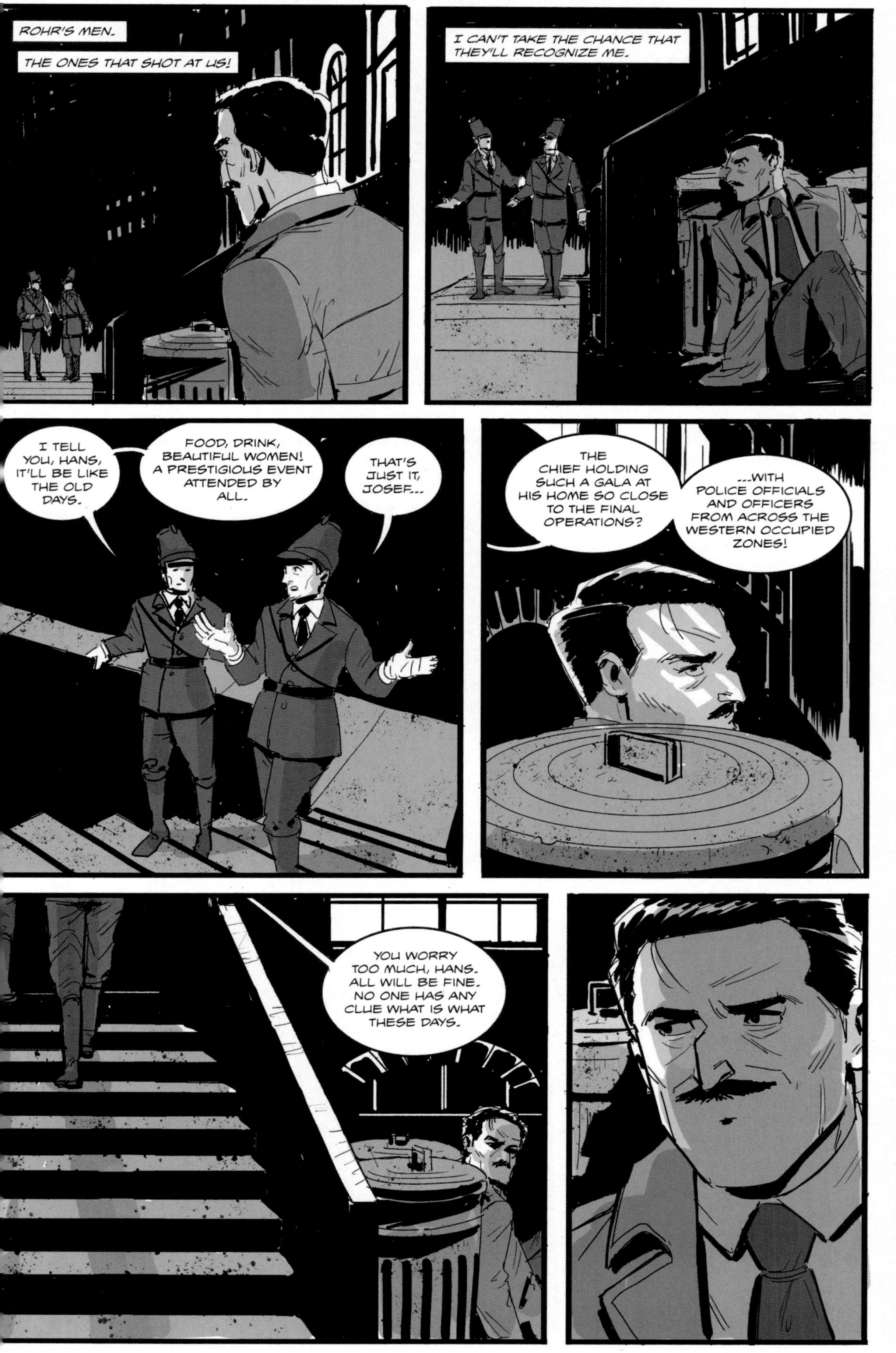
ROHR'S MEN.
THE ONES THAT SHOT AT US!
I CAN'T TAKE THE CHANCE THAT THEY'LL RECOGNIZE ME.
I TELL YOU, HANS, IT'LL BE LIKE THE OLD DAYS.
FOOD, DRINK, BEAUTIFUL WOMEN! A PRESTIGIOUS EVENT ATTENDED BY ALL.
THAT'S JUST IT, JOSEF...
THE CHIEF HOLDING SUCH A GALA AT HIS HOME SO CLOSE TO THE FINAL OPERATIONS?
...WITH POLICE OFFICIALS AND OFFICERS FROM ACROSS THE WESTERN OCCUPIED ZONES!
YOU WORRY TOO MUCH, HANS. ALL WILL BE FINE. NO ONE HAS ANY CLUE WHAT IS WHAT THESE DAYS.

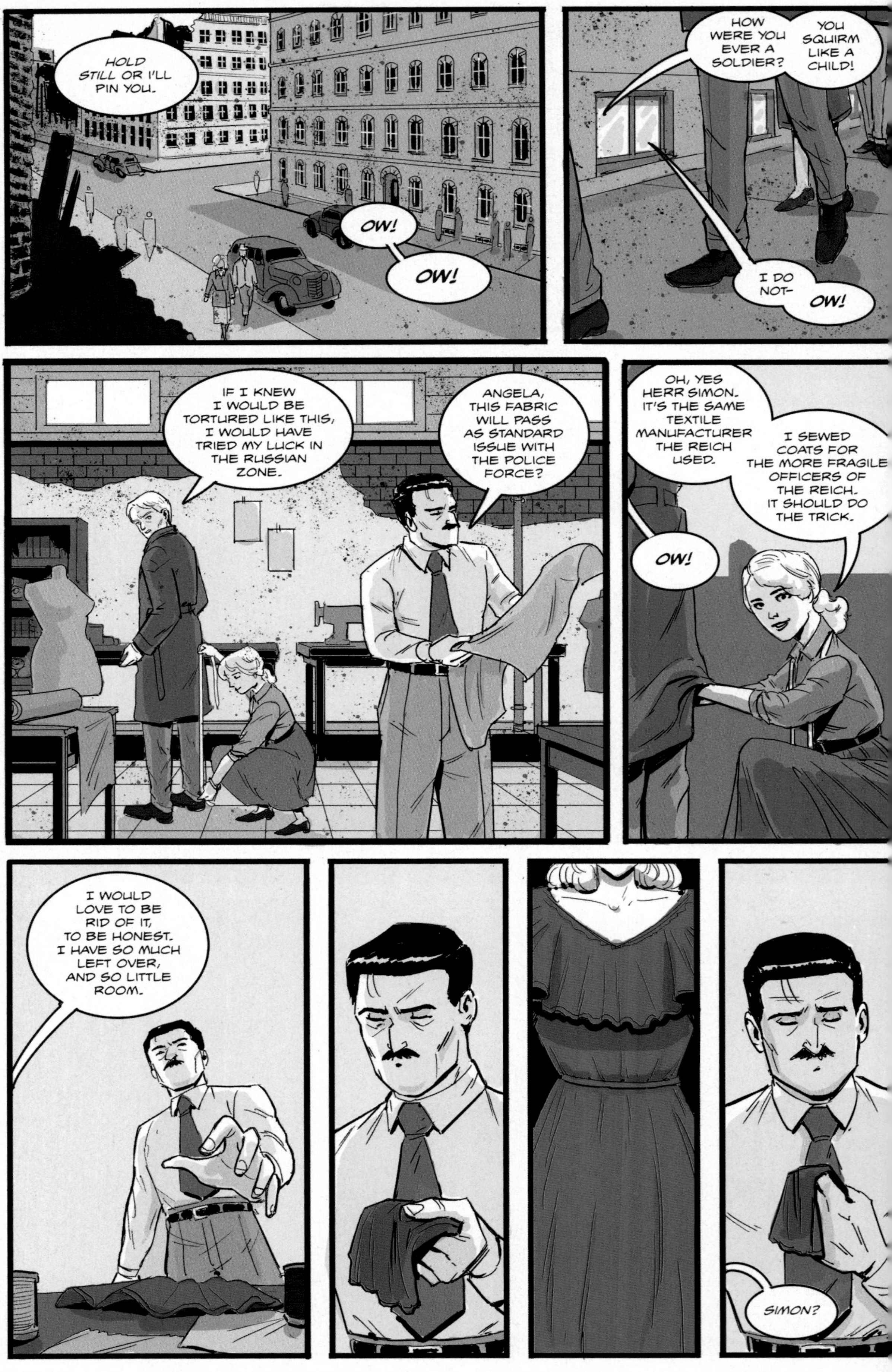

HOLD STILL OR I'LL PIN YOU.
OW!
OW!
HOW WERE YOU EVER A SOLDIER?
YOU SQUIRM LIKE A CHILD!
I DO NOT-
OW!
IF I KNEW I WOULD BE TORTURED LIKE THIS, I WOULD HAVE TRIED MY LUCK IN THE RUSSIAN ZONE.
ANGELA, THIS FABRIC WILL PASS AS STANDARD ISSUE WITH THE POLICE FORCE?
OH, YES HERR SIMON. IT'S THE SAME TEXTILE MANUFACTURER THE REICH USED.
I SEWED COATS FOR THE MORE FRAGILE OFFICERS OF THE REICH. IT SHOULD DO THE TRICK.
OW!
I WOULD LOVE TO BE RID OF IT, TO BE HONEST. I HAVE SO MUCH LEFT OVER, AND SO LITTLE ROOM.
SIMON?

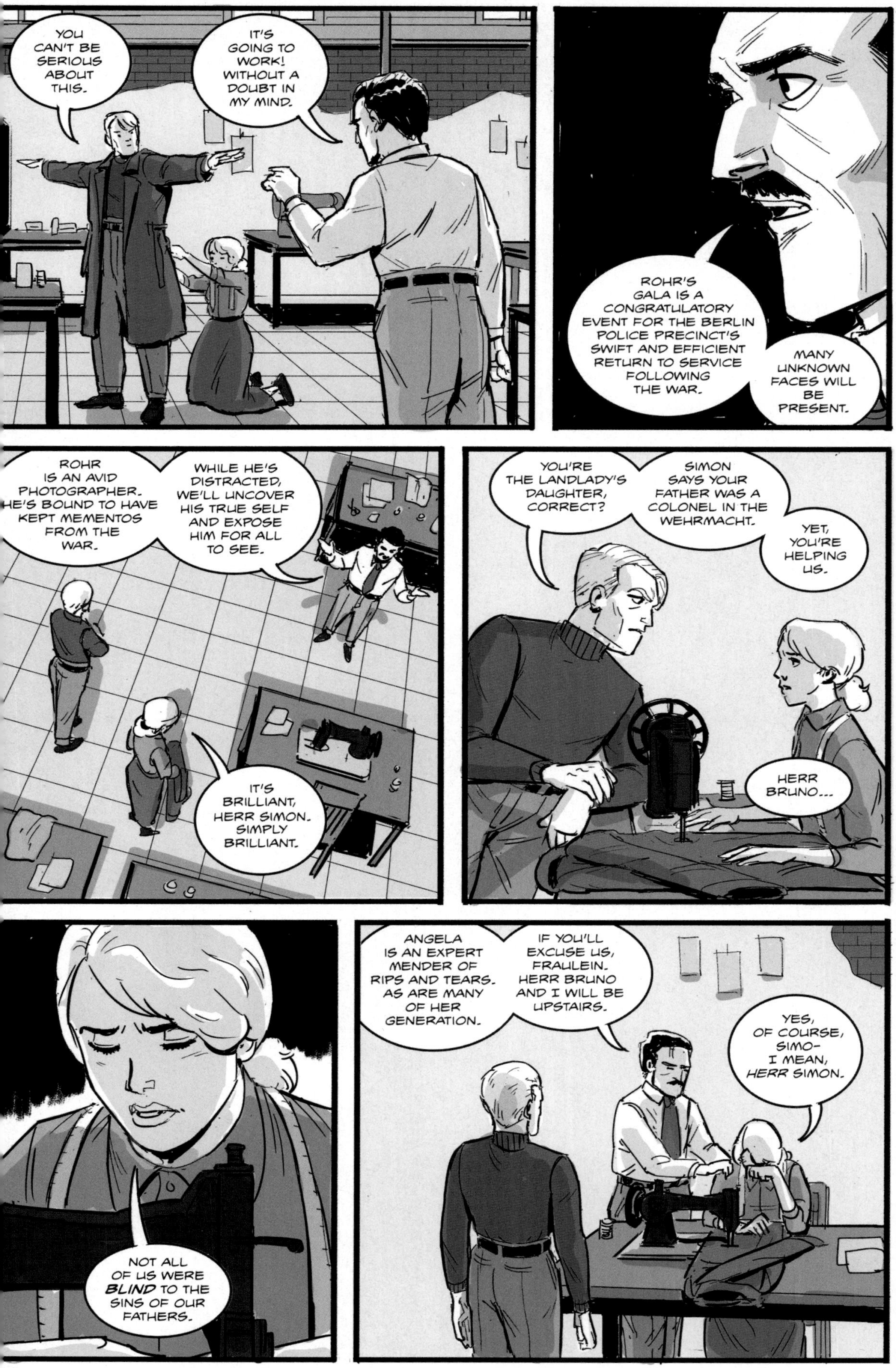
YOU CAN'T BE SERIOUS ABOUT THIS.
IT'S GOING TO WORK! WITHOUT A DOUBT IN MY MIND.
ROHR'S GALA IS A CONGRATULATORY EVENT FOR THE BERLIN POLICE PRECINCT'S SWIFT AND EFFICIENT RETURN TO SERVICE FOLLOWING THE WAR.
MANY UNKNOWN FACES WILL BE PRESENT.
ROHR IS AN AVID PHOTOGRAPHER. HE'S BOUND TO HAVE KEPT MEMENTOS FROM THE WAR.
WHILE HE'S DISTRACTED, WE'LL UNCOVER HIS TRUE SELF AND EXPOSE HIM FOR ALL TO SEE.
IT'S BRILLIANT, HERR SIMON. SIMPLY BRILLIANT.
YOU'RE THE LANDLADY'S DAUGHTER, CORRECT?
SIMON SAYS YOUR FATHER WAS A COLONEL IN THE WEHRMACHT.
YET, YOU'RE HELPING US.
HERR BRUNO...
NOT ALL OF US WERE *BLIND* TO THE SINS OF OUR FATHERS.
ANGELA IS AN EXPERT MENDER OF RIPS AND TEARS. AS ARE MANY OF HER GENERATION.
IF YOU'LL EXCUSE US, FRAULEIN. HERR BRUNO AND I WILL BE UPSTAIRS.
YES, OF COURSE, SIMO— I MEAN, *HERR SIMON.*

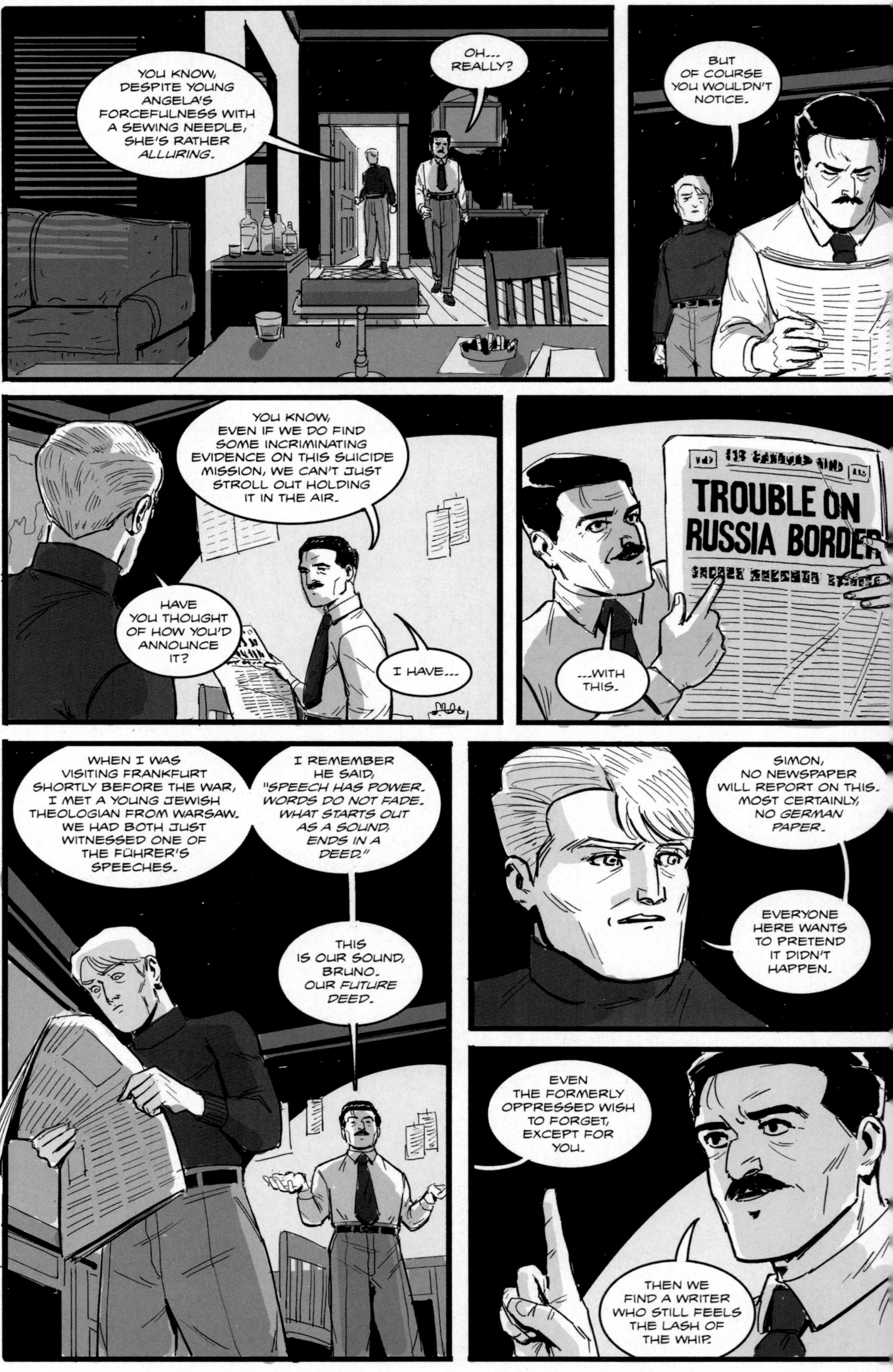
YOU KNOW, DESPITE YOUNG ANGELA'S FORCEFULNESS WITH A SEWING NEEDLE, SHE'S RATHER *ALLURING*.
OH... REALLY?
BUT OF COURSE YOU WOULDN'T NOTICE.
YOU KNOW, EVEN IF WE DO FIND SOME INCRIMINATING EVIDENCE ON THIS SUICIDE MISSION, WE CAN'T JUST STROLL OUT HOLDING IT IN THE AIR.
HAVE YOU THOUGHT OF HOW YOU'D ANNOUNCE IT?
I HAVE...
TROUBLE ON RUSSIA BORDER
...WITH THIS.
WHEN I WAS VISITING FRANKFURT SHORTLY BEFORE THE WAR, I MET A YOUNG JEWISH THEOLOGIAN FROM WARSAW. WE HAD BOTH JUST WITNESSED ONE OF THE FÜHRER'S SPEECHES.
I REMEMBER HE SAID, *"SPEECH HAS POWER. WORDS DO NOT FADE. WHAT STARTS OUT AS A SOUND, ENDS IN A DEED."*
THIS IS OUR SOUND, BRUNO. OUR FUTURE DEED.
SIMON, NO NEWSPAPER WILL REPORT ON THIS. MOST CERTAINLY, NO *GERMAN* PAPER.
EVERYONE HERE WANTS TO PRETEND IT DIDN'T HAPPEN.
EVEN THE FORMERLY OPPRESSED WISH TO FORGET, EXCEPT FOR YOU.
THEN WE FIND A WRITER WHO STILL FEELS THE LASH OF THE WHIP.

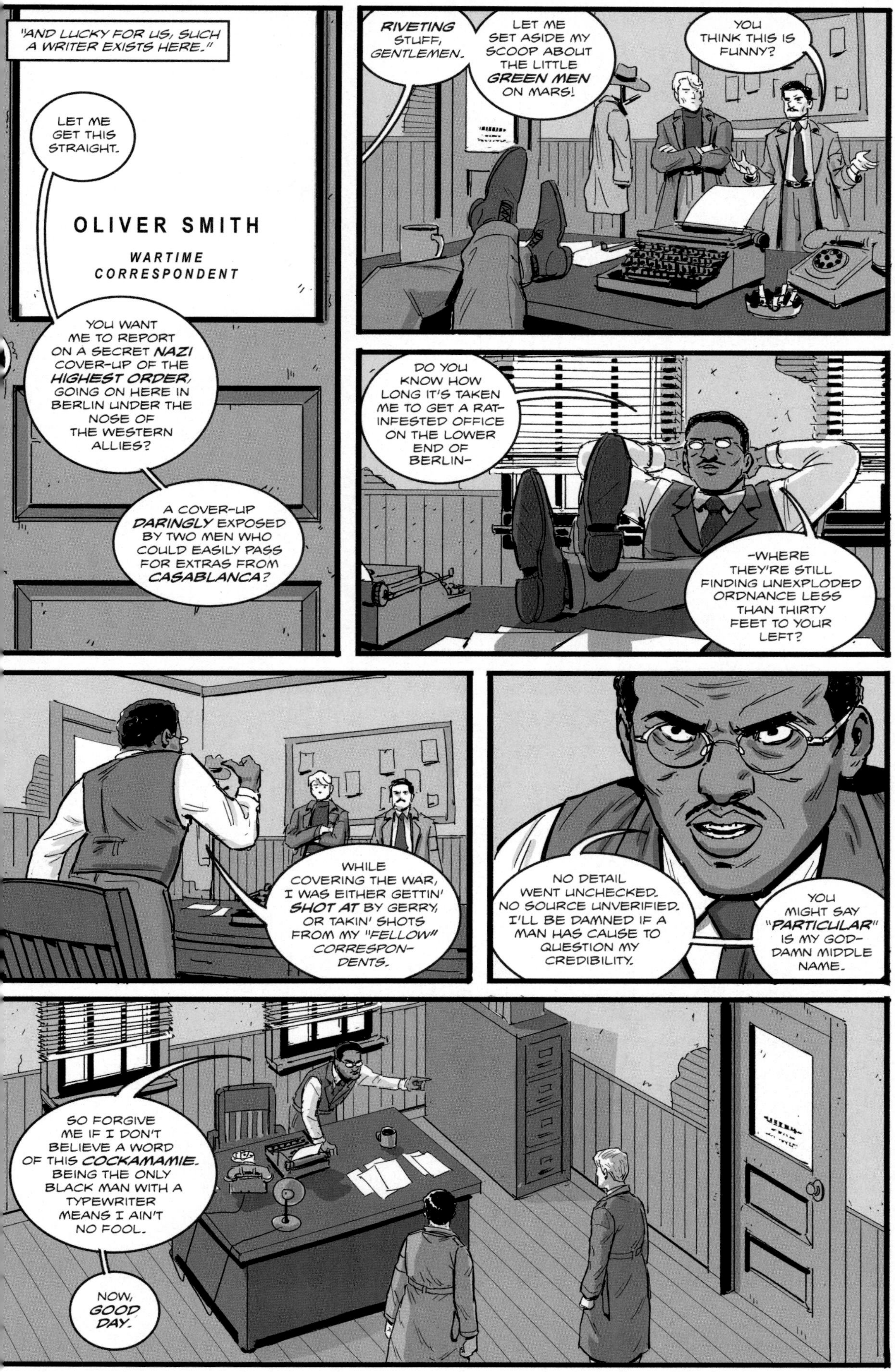
"AND LUCKY FOR US, SUCH A WRITER EXISTS HERE."
LET ME GET THIS STRAIGHT.
OLIVER SMITH
WARTIME CORRESPONDENT
YOU WANT ME TO REPORT ON A SECRET NAZI COVER-UP OF THE HIGHEST ORDER, GOING ON HERE IN BERLIN UNDER THE NOSE OF THE WESTERN ALLIES?
A COVER-UP DARINGLY EXPOSED BY TWO MEN WHO COULD EASILY PASS FOR EXTRAS FROM CASABLANCA?
RIVETING STUFF, GENTLEMEN.
LET ME SET ASIDE MY SCOOP ABOUT THE LITTLE GREEN MEN ON MARS!
YOU THINK THIS IS FUNNY?
DO YOU KNOW HOW LONG IT'S TAKEN ME TO GET A RAT-INFESTED OFFICE ON THE LOWER END OF BERLIN-
-WHERE THEY'RE STILL FINDING UNEXPLODED ORDNANCE LESS THAN THIRTY FEET TO YOUR LEFT?
WHILE COVERING THE WAR, I WAS EITHER GETTIN' SHOT AT BY GERRY, OR TAKIN' SHOTS FROM MY "FELLOW" CORRESPON-DENTS.
NO DETAIL WENT UNCHECKED. NO SOURCE UNVERIFIED. I'LL BE DAMNED IF A MAN HAS CAUSE TO QUESTION MY CREDIBILITY.
YOU MIGHT SAY "PARTICULAR" IS MY GOD-DAMN MIDDLE NAME.
SO FORGIVE ME IF I DON'T BELIEVE A WORD OF THIS COCKAMAMIE. BEING THE ONLY BLACK MAN WITH A TYPEWRITER MEANS I AIN'T NO FOOL.
NOW, GOOD DAY.

LET ME JUST—

ALLOW ME.

MR. SMITH, I, TOO, BELIEVED MY COLLEAGUE'S ACCUSATIONS TO BE *UNFOUNDED.*

HIS ACTIONS, AT TIMES, SEEM SUICIDAL. BUT HE ONLY SOUNDS CRAZY.

LOOK CLOSER. WHAT YOU SEE IS A MAN WHO *SURVIVED* MAUTHAUSEN.

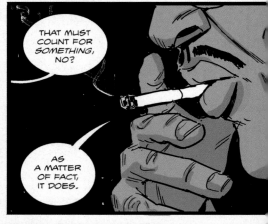

THAT MUST COUNT FOR SOMETHING, NO?

AS A MATTER OF FACT, IT DOES.

YOU WERE AT *MAUTHAUSEN?*

OH YEAH.

I KNOW THAT *DEAD* STARE.

I WAS EMBEDDED WITH THE U.S. 11TH ARMORED DIVISON WHEN WE CRACKED OPEN THAT ROTTEN EGG.

THEY ALL HAD THAT SAME LOOK.

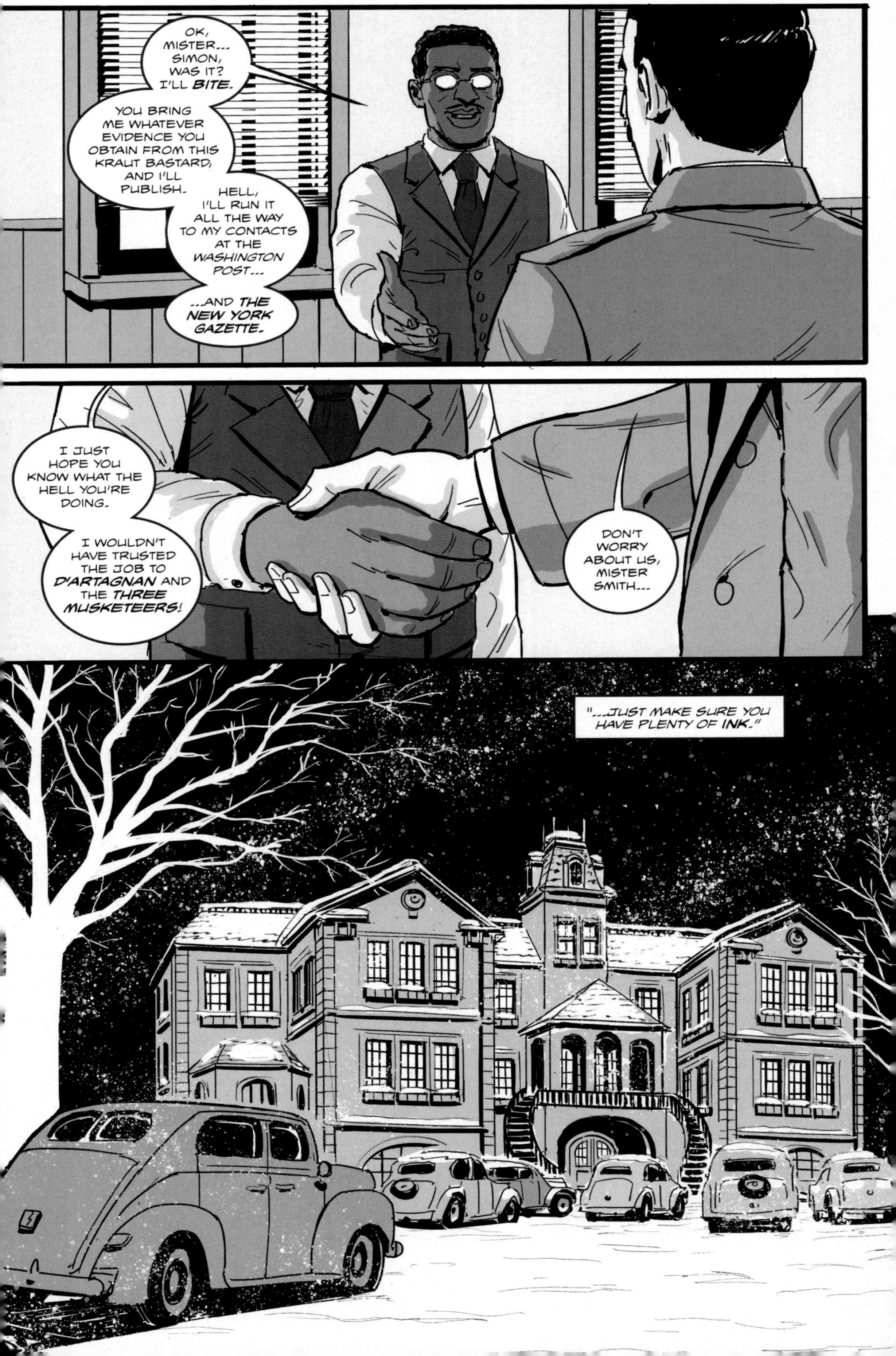

OK, MISTER... SIMON, WAS IT? I'LL *BITE*.
YOU BRING ME WHATEVER EVIDENCE YOU OBTAIN FROM THIS KRAUT BASTARD, AND I'LL PUBLISH.
HELL, I'LL RUN IT ALL THE WAY TO MY CONTACTS AT THE *WASHINGTON POST*...
...AND *THE NEW YORK GAZETTE*.
I JUST HOPE YOU KNOW WHAT THE HELL YOU'RE DOING.
I WOULDN'T HAVE TRUSTED THE JOB TO *D'ARTAGNAN* AND THE *THREE MUSKETEERS*!
DON'T WORRY ABOUT US, MISTER SMITH...
"...JUST MAKE SURE YOU HAVE PLENTY OF **INK**."

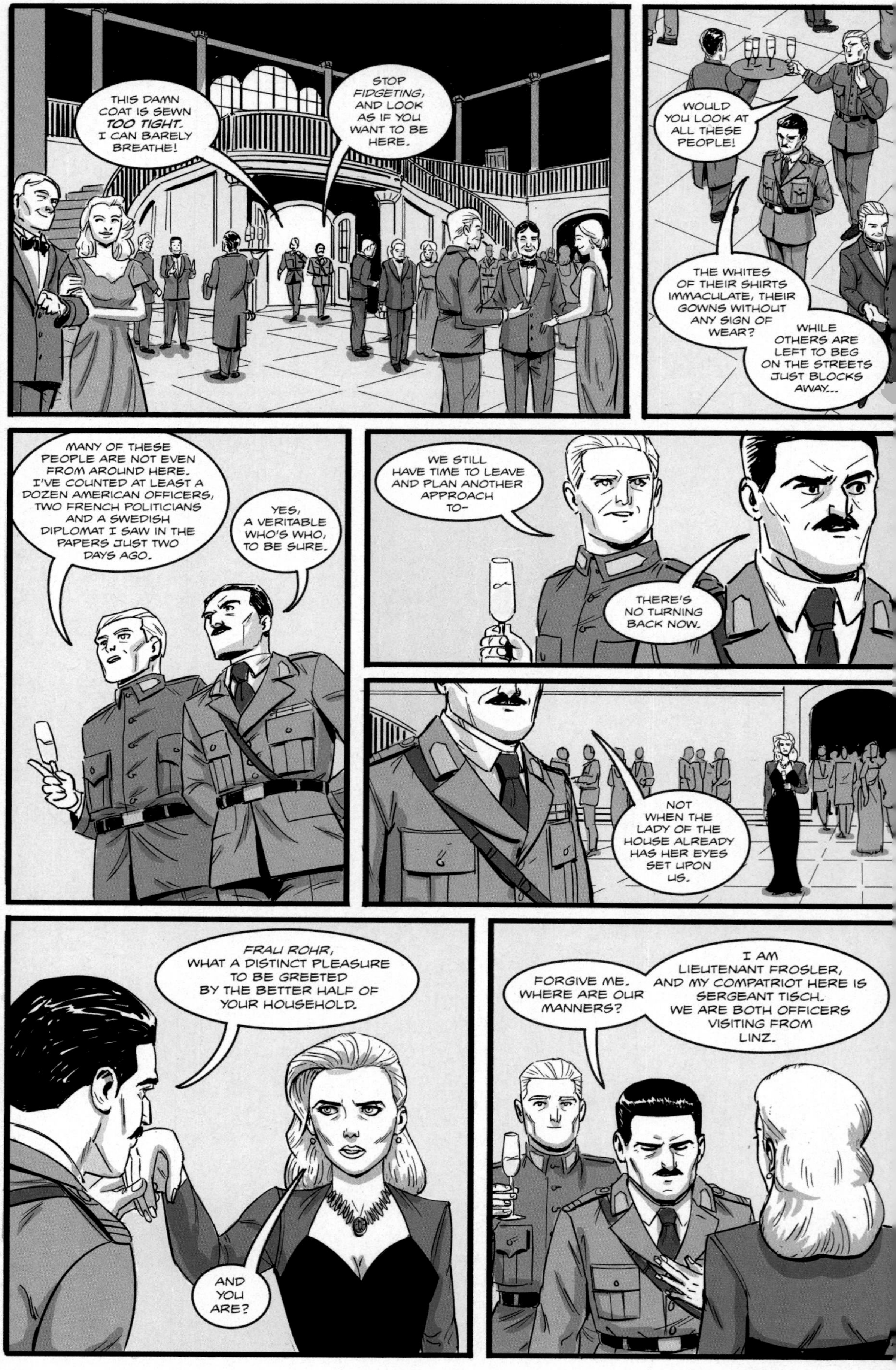
THIS DAMN COAT IS SEWN TOO TIGHT. I CAN BARELY BREATHE!
STOP FIDGETING, AND LOOK AS IF YOU WANT TO BE HERE.
WOULD YOU LOOK AT ALL THESE PEOPLE!
THE WHITES OF THEIR SHIRTS IMMACULATE, THEIR GOWNS WITHOUT ANY SIGN OF WEAR?
WHILE OTHERS ARE LEFT TO BEG ON THE STREETS JUST BLOCKS AWAY...
MANY OF THESE PEOPLE ARE NOT EVEN FROM AROUND HERE. I'VE COUNTED AT LEAST A DOZEN AMERICAN OFFICERS, TWO FRENCH POLITICIANS AND A SWEDISH DIPLOMAT I SAW IN THE PAPERS JUST TWO DAYS AGO.
YES, A VERITABLE WHO'S WHO, TO BE SURE.
WE STILL HAVE TIME TO LEAVE AND PLAN ANOTHER APPROACH TO-
THERE'S NO TURNING BACK NOW.
NOT WHEN THE LADY OF THE HOUSE ALREADY HAS HER EYES SET UPON US.
FRAU ROHR, WHAT A DISTINCT PLEASURE TO BE GREETED BY THE BETTER HALF OF YOUR HOUSEHOLD.
AND YOU ARE?
FORGIVE ME. WHERE ARE OUR MANNERS?
I AM LIEUTENANT FROSLER, AND MY COMPATRIOT HERE IS SERGEANT TISCH. WE ARE BOTH OFFICERS VISITING FROM LINZ.

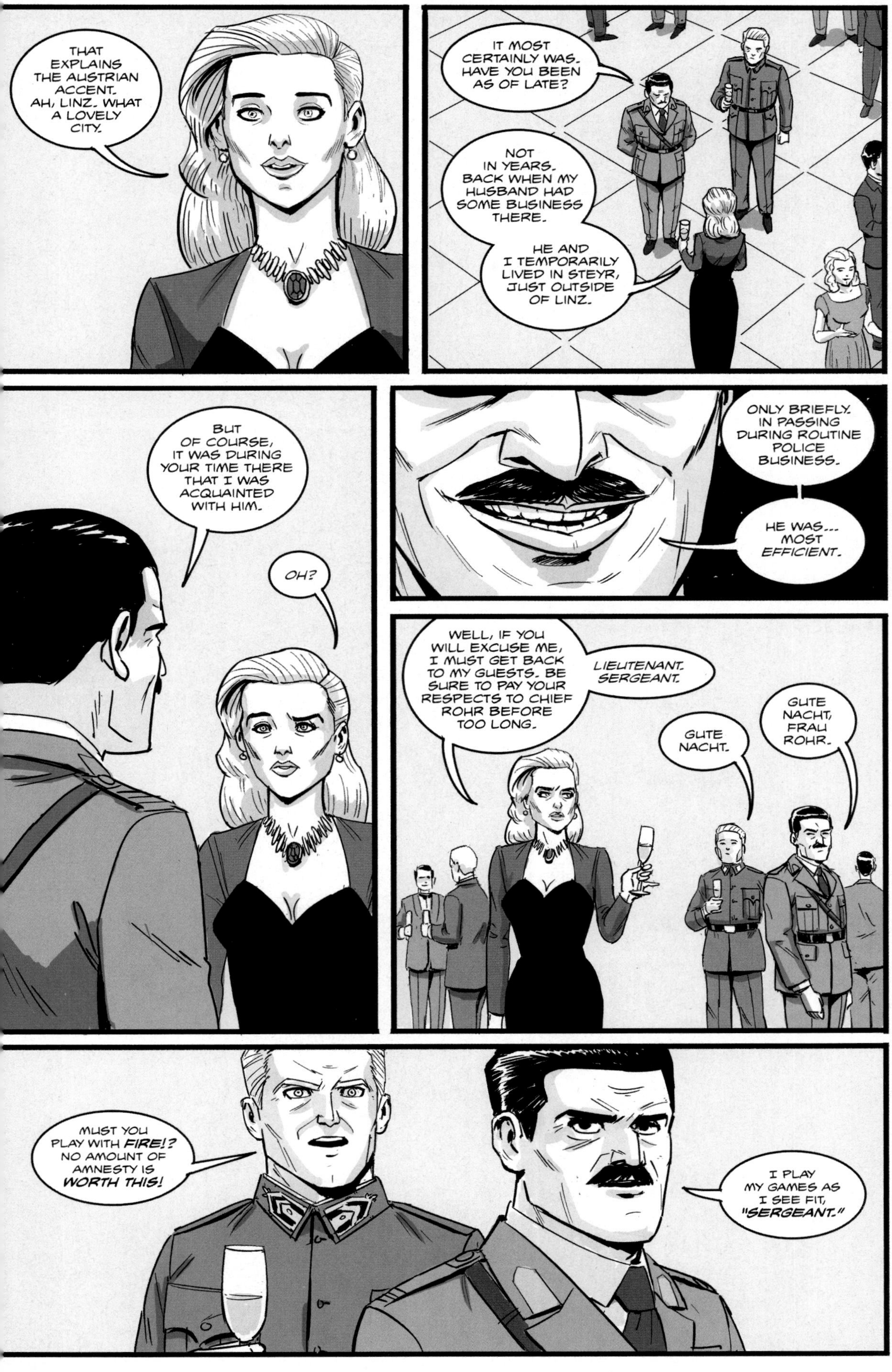
THAT EXPLAINS THE AUSTRIAN ACCENT. AH, LINZ. WHAT A LOVELY CITY.
IT MOST CERTAINLY WAS. HAVE YOU BEEN AS OF LATE?
NOT IN YEARS. BACK WHEN MY HUSBAND HAD SOME BUSINESS THERE.
HE AND I TEMPORARILY LIVED IN STEYR, JUST OUTSIDE OF LINZ.
BUT OF COURSE, IT WAS DURING YOUR TIME THERE THAT I WAS ACQUAINTED WITH HIM.
OH?
ONLY BRIEFLY. IN PASSING DURING ROUTINE POLICE BUSINESS.
HE WAS... MOST EFFICIENT.
WELL, IF YOU WILL EXCUSE ME, I MUST GET BACK TO MY GUESTS. BE SURE TO PAY YOUR RESPECTS TO CHIEF ROHR BEFORE TOO LONG.
LIEUTENANT. SERGEANT.
GUTE NACHT.
GUTE NACHT, FRAU ROHR.
MUST YOU PLAY WITH FIRE!? NO AMOUNT OF AMNESTY IS WORTH THIS!
I PLAY MY GAMES AS I SEE FIT, "SERGEANT."

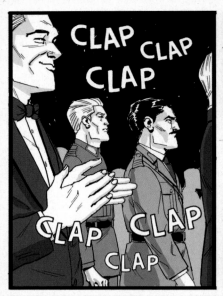

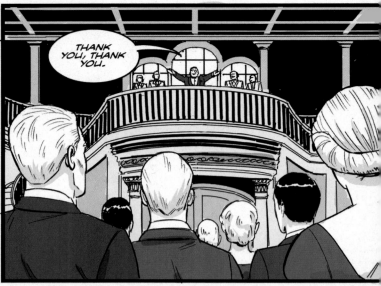

CLAP CLAP
CLAP
CLAP CLAP
CLAP
THANK YOU, THANK YOU.
THANK YOU ALL FOR COMING TONIGHT TO CELEBRATE A NEW ERA OF JUSTICE IN BERLIN.
THANKS TO THE ALLIED FORCES, WE HAVE SAVED OUR COUNTRY FROM THE BRINK OF DARKNESS...
...AND HAVE SHOWN THAT THE TRUE EFFICIENCY OF GERMANY IS BEST ACHIEVED IN THE LIGHT OF DAY, FOR THE PURPOSES OF GOOD.
A GERMANY FOR ALL, NOT A SELECT FEW.
ROHR, IT IS MY DISTINCT PRIVILEGE, ALONGSIDE THE MAYOR OF BERLIN, TO BESTOW UPON YOU THE SYMBOLIC KEY TO THE CITY...
...IN HONOR OF THE SUCCESSFUL TASK OF REAFFIRMING ORDER AND BRINGING ABOUT A NEW ERA OF PEACE AND PROSPERITY.
MAY IT LAST.
THANK YOU, GENERAL. I CHERISH THIS GREATLY.
WHERE ARE YOU GOING?
REMAIN HERE, AND KEEP YOUR EYES ON OUR RECENTLY LAVISHED FRIEND.

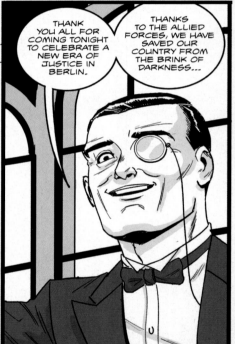

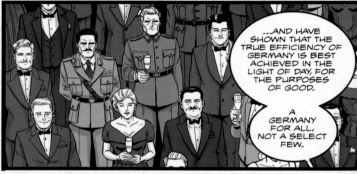

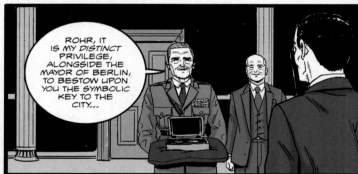

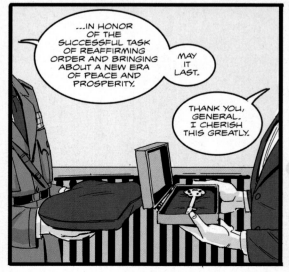

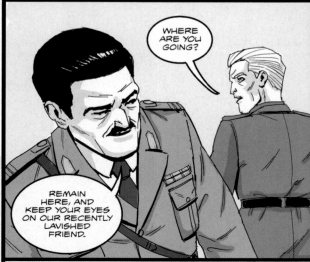

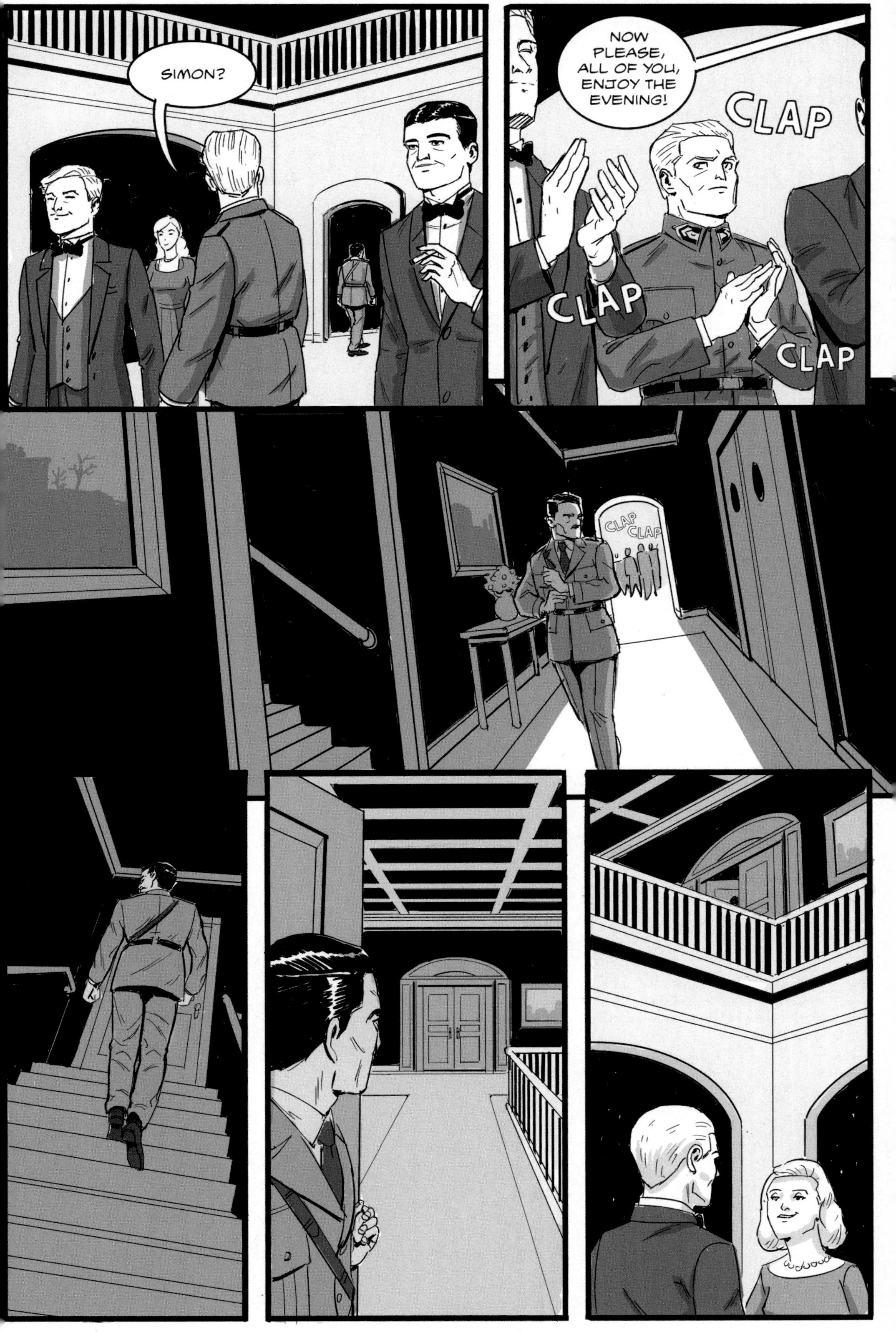
SIMON?
NOW PLEASE, ALL OF YOU, ENJOY THE EVENING!
CLAP
CLAP
CLAP
CLAP CLAP

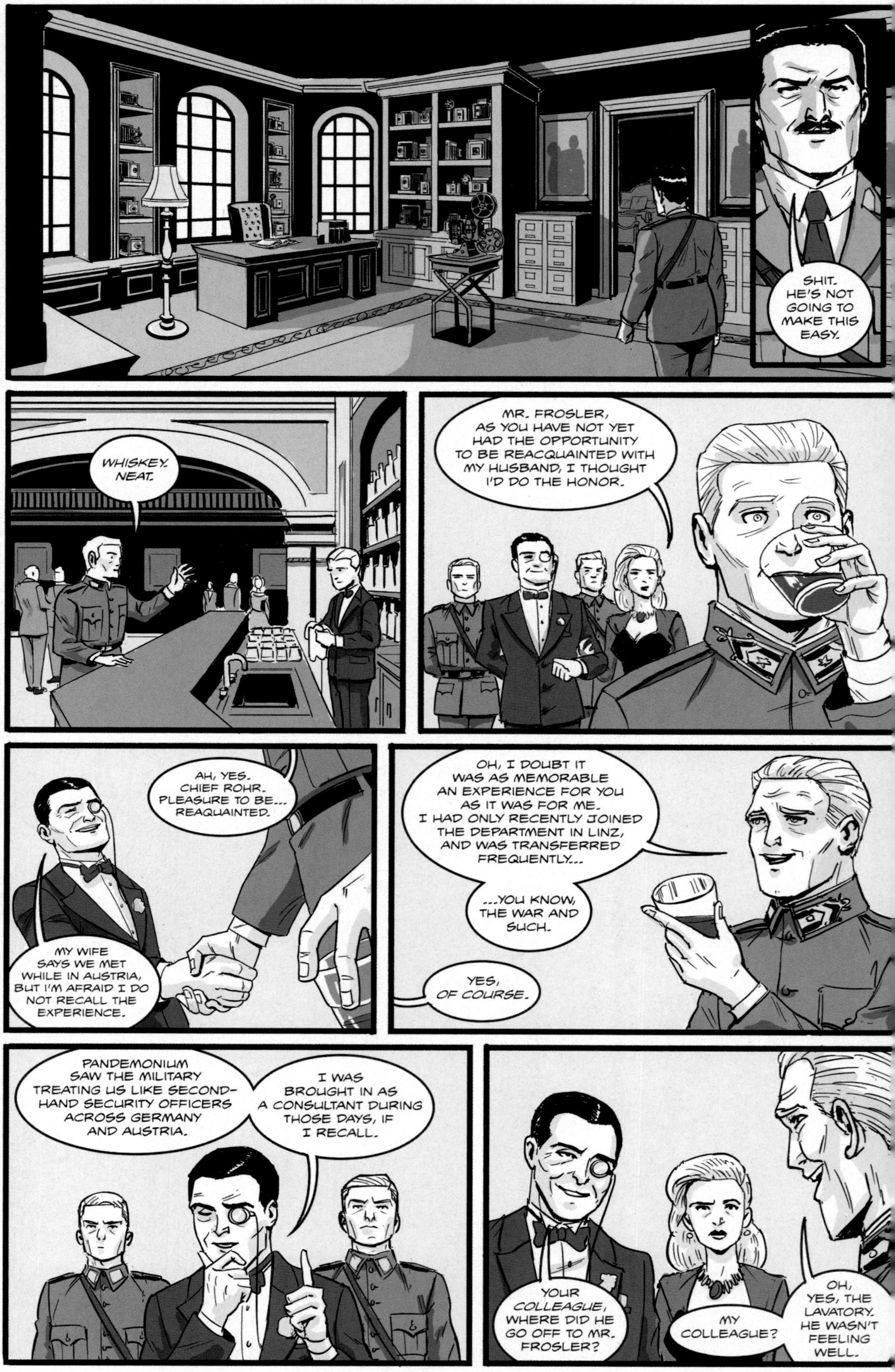
SHIT. HE'S NOT GOING TO MAKE THIS EASY.
WHISKEY. NEAT.
MR. FROSLER, AS YOU HAVE NOT YET HAD THE OPPORTUNITY TO BE REACQUAINTED WITH MY HUSBAND, I THOUGHT I'D DO THE HONOR.
AH, YES. CHIEF ROHR. PLEASURE TO BE... REAQUAINTED.
MY WIFE SAYS WE MET WHILE IN AUSTRIA, BUT I'M AFRAID I DO NOT RECALL THE EXPERIENCE.
OH, I DOUBT IT WAS AS MEMORABLE AN EXPERIENCE FOR YOU AS IT WAS FOR ME. I HAD ONLY RECENTLY JOINED THE DEPARTMENT IN LINZ, AND WAS TRANSFERRED FREQUENTLY...
...YOU KNOW, THE WAR AND SUCH.
YES, OF COURSE.
PANDEMONIUM SAW THE MILITARY TREATING US LIKE SECOND-HAND SECURITY OFFICERS ACROSS GERMANY AND AUSTRIA.
I WAS BROUGHT IN AS A CONSULTANT DURING THOSE DAYS, IF I RECALL.
YOUR COLLEAGUE, WHERE DID HE GO OFF TO MR. FROSLER?
MY COLLEAGUE?
OH, YES, THE LAVATORY. HE WASN'T FEELING WELL.

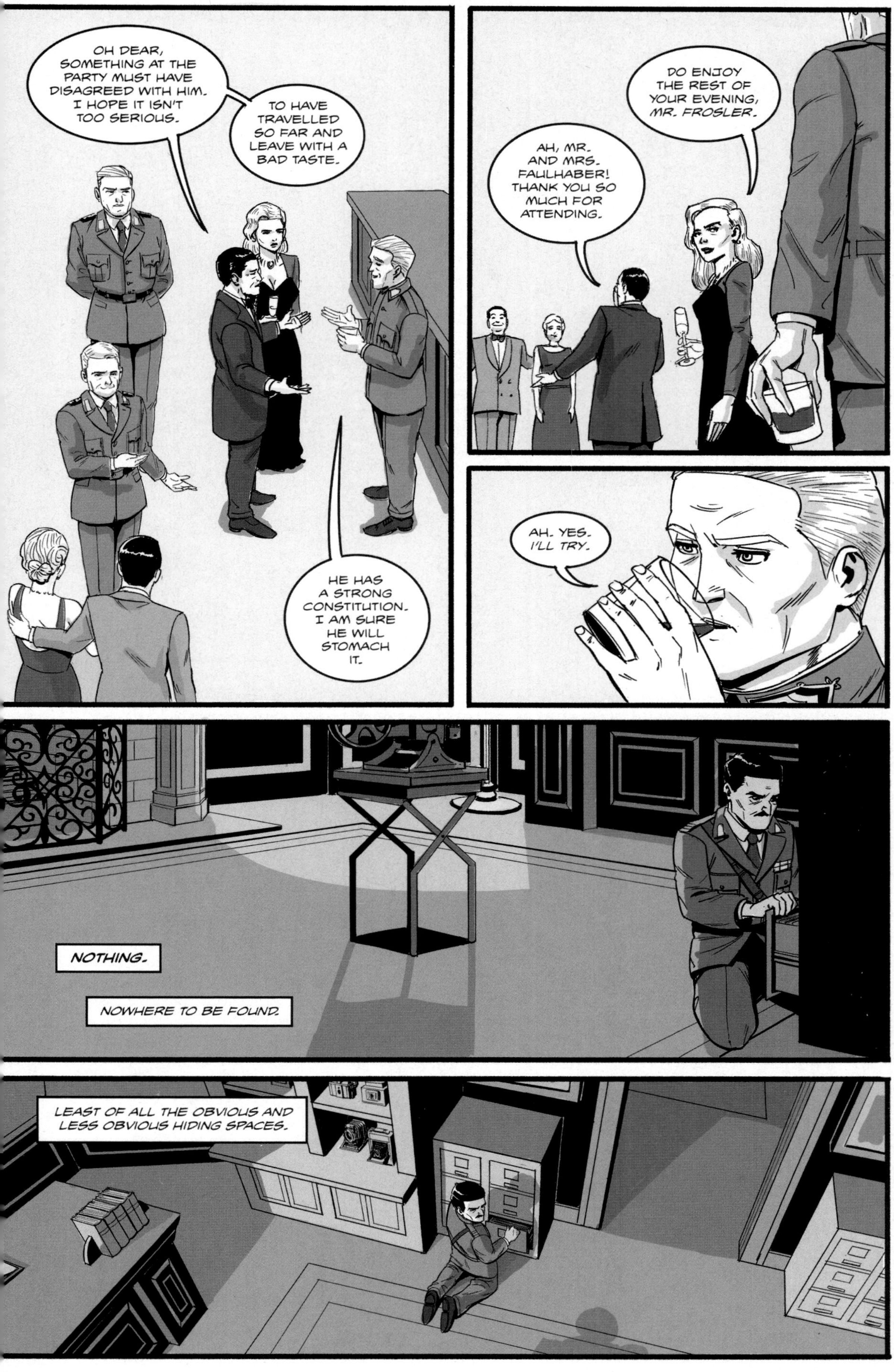

OH DEAR, SOMETHING AT THE PARTY MUST HAVE DISAGREED WITH HIM. I HOPE IT ISN'T TOO SERIOUS.
TO HAVE TRAVELLED SO FAR AND LEAVE WITH A BAD TASTE.
HE HAS A STRONG CONSTITUTION. I AM SURE HE WILL STOMACH IT.
DO ENJOY THE REST OF YOUR EVENING, MR. FROSLER.
AH, MR. AND MRS. FAULHABER! THANK YOU SO MUCH FOR ATTENDING.
AH. YES. I'LL TRY.
NOTHING.
NOWHERE TO BE FOUND.
LEAST OF ALL THE OBVIOUS AND LESS OBVIOUS HIDING SPACES.

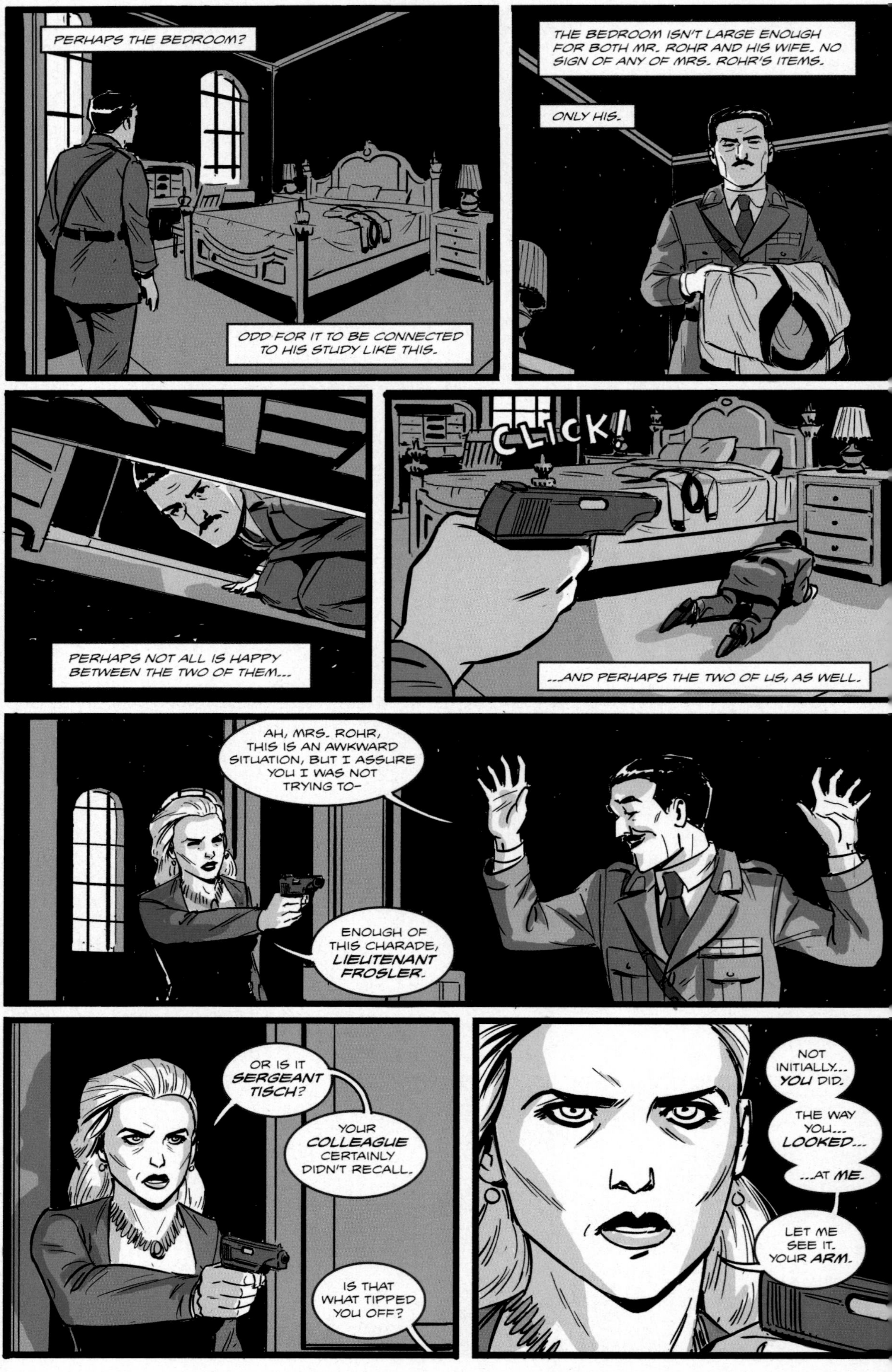
PERHAPS THE BEDROOM?
ODD FOR IT TO BE CONNECTED TO HIS STUDY LIKE THIS.
THE BEDROOM ISN'T LARGE ENOUGH FOR BOTH MR. ROHR AND HIS WIFE. NO SIGN OF ANY OF MRS. ROHR'S ITEMS.
ONLY HIS.
PERHAPS NOT ALL IS HAPPY BETWEEN THE TWO OF THEM...
CLICK!
...AND PERHAPS THE TWO OF US, AS WELL.
AH, MRS. ROHR, THIS IS AN AWKWARD SITUATION, BUT I ASSURE YOU I WAS NOT TRYING TO–
ENOUGH OF THIS CHARADE, LIEUTENANT FROSLER.
OR IS IT SERGEANT TISCH?
YOUR COLLEAGUE CERTAINLY DIDN'T RECALL.
IS THAT WHAT TIPPED YOU OFF?
NOT INITIALLY... YOU DID.
THE WAY YOU... LOOKED...
...AT ME.
LET ME SEE IT. YOUR ARM.

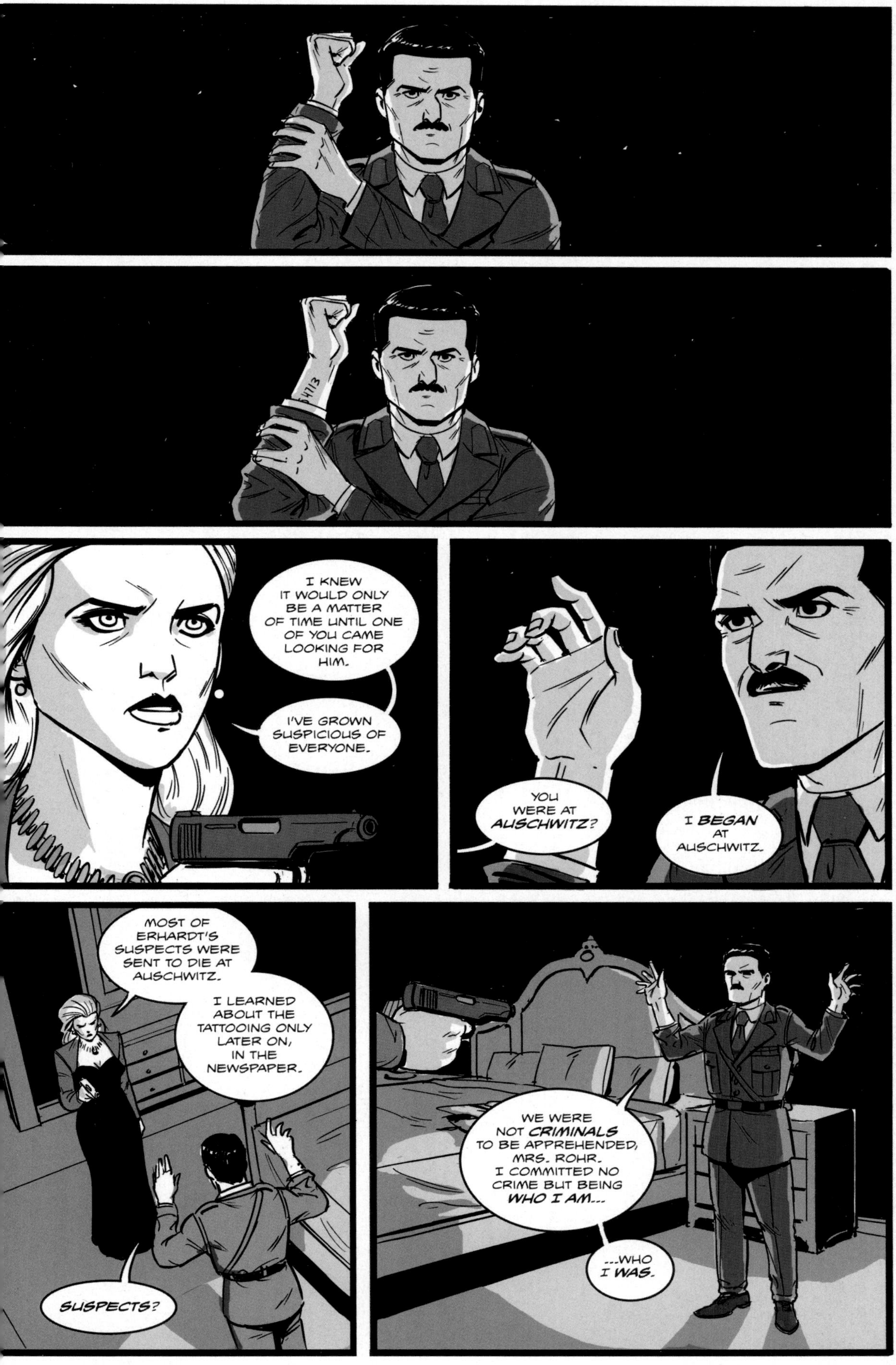

I KNEW IT WOULD ONLY BE A MATTER OF TIME UNTIL ONE OF YOU CAME LOOKING FOR HIM.
I'VE GROWN SUSPICIOUS OF EVERYONE.
YOU WERE AT AUSCHWITZ?
I BEGAN AT AUSCHWITZ.
MOST OF ERHARDT'S SUSPECTS WERE SENT TO DIE AT AUSCHWITZ.
I LEARNED ABOUT THE TATTOOING ONLY LATER ON, IN THE NEWSPAPER.
SUSPECTS?
WE WERE NOT CRIMINALS TO BE APPREHENDED, MRS. ROHR. I COMMITTED NO CRIME BUT BEING WHO I AM...
...WHO I WAS.

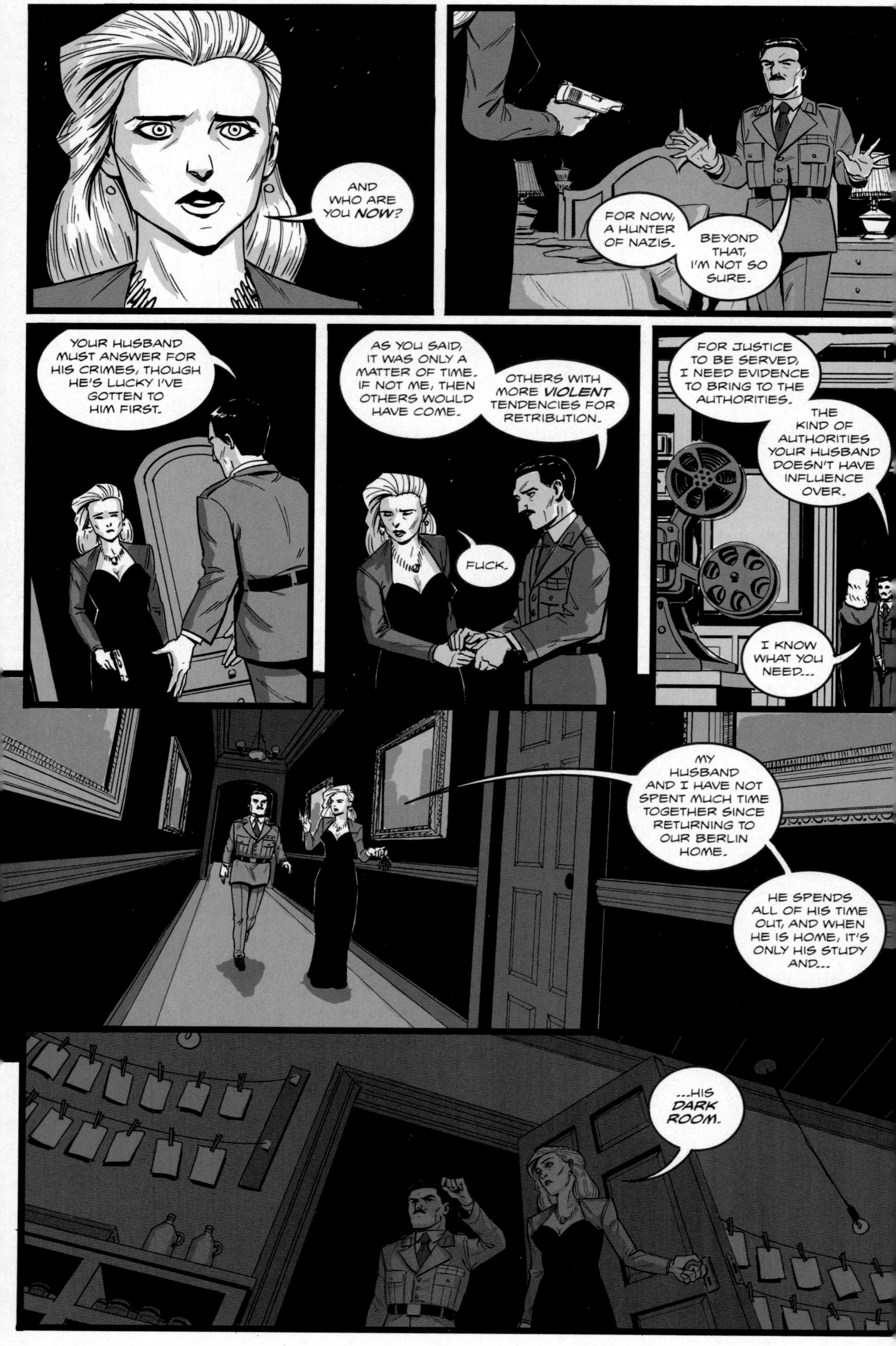
AND WHO ARE YOU *NOW*?
FOR NOW, A HUNTER OF NAZIS.
BEYOND THAT, I'M NOT SO SURE.
YOUR HUSBAND MUST ANSWER FOR HIS CRIMES, THOUGH HE'S LUCKY I'VE GOTTEN TO HIM FIRST.
AS YOU SAID, IT WAS ONLY A MATTER OF TIME. IF NOT ME, THEN OTHERS WOULD HAVE COME.
OTHERS WITH MORE *VIOLENT* TENDENCIES FOR RETRIBUTION.
FUCK.
FOR JUSTICE TO BE SERVED, I NEED EVIDENCE TO BRING TO THE AUTHORITIES.
THE KIND OF AUTHORITIES YOUR HUSBAND DOESN'T HAVE INFLUENCE OVER.
I KNOW WHAT YOU NEED...
MY HUSBAND AND I HAVE NOT SPENT MUCH TIME TOGETHER SINCE RETURNING TO OUR BERLIN HOME.
HE SPENDS ALL OF HIS TIME OUT, AND WHEN HE IS HOME, IT'S ONLY HIS STUDY AND...
...HIS *DARK ROOM*.

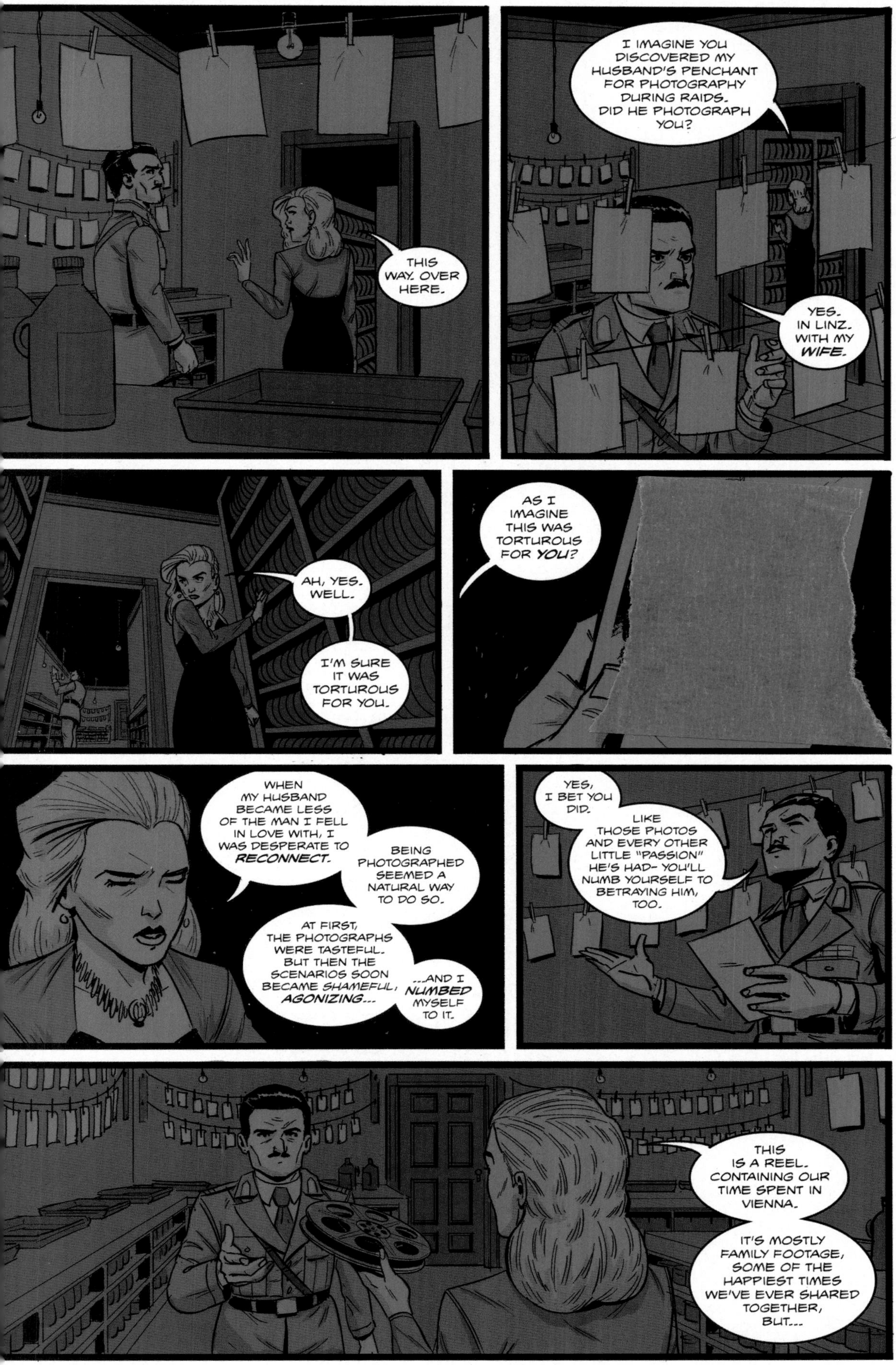
THIS WAY. OVER HERE.
I IMAGINE YOU DISCOVERED MY HUSBAND'S PENCHANT FOR PHOTOGRAPHY DURING RAIDS. DID HE PHOTOGRAPH YOU?
YES. IN LINZ. WITH MY *WIFE.*
AH, YES. WELL.
I'M SURE IT WAS TORTUROUS FOR YOU.
AS I IMAGINE THIS WAS TORTUROUS FOR *YOU?*
WHEN MY HUSBAND BECAME LESS OF THE MAN I FELL IN LOVE WITH, I WAS DESPERATE TO ***RECONNECT.***
BEING PHOTOGRAPHED SEEMED A NATURAL WAY TO DO SO.
AT FIRST, THE PHOTOGRAPHS WERE TASTEFUL. BUT THEN THE SCENARIOS SOON BECAME *SHAMEFUL,* ***AGONIZING...***
...AND I ***NUMBED*** MYSELF TO IT.
YES, I BET YOU DID.
LIKE THOSE PHOTOS AND EVERY OTHER LITTLE "PASSION" HE'S HAD- YOU'LL NUMB YOURSELF TO BETRAYING HIM, TOO.
THIS IS A REEL. CONTAINING OUR TIME SPENT IN VIENNA.
IT'S MOSTLY FAMILY FOOTAGE, SOME OF THE HAPPIEST TIMES WE'VE EVER SHARED TOGETHER, BUT...

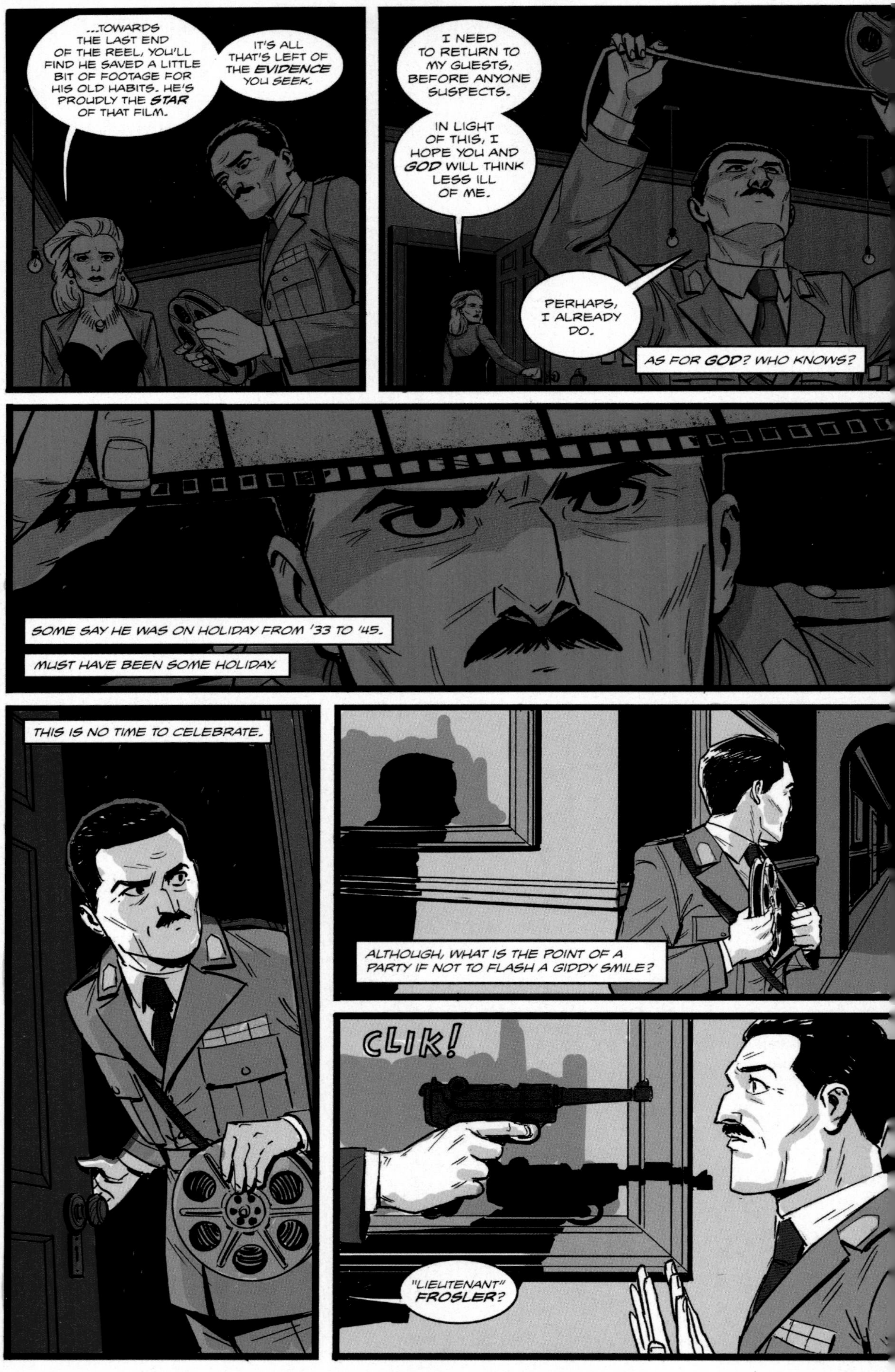
...TOWARDS THE LAST END OF THE REEL, YOU'LL FIND HE SAVED A LITTLE BIT OF FOOTAGE FOR HIS OLD HABITS. HE'S PROUDLY THE STAR OF THAT FILM.
IT'S ALL THAT'S LEFT OF THE EVIDENCE YOU SEEK.
I NEED TO RETURN TO MY GUESTS, BEFORE ANYONE SUSPECTS.
IN LIGHT OF THIS, I HOPE YOU AND GOD WILL THINK LESS ILL OF ME.
PERHAPS, I ALREADY DO.
AS FOR GOD? WHO KNOWS?
SOME SAY HE WAS ON HOLIDAY FROM '33 TO '45.
MUST HAVE BEEN SOME HOLIDAY.
THIS IS NO TIME TO CELEBRATE.
ALTHOUGH, WHAT IS THE POINT OF A PARTY IF NOT TO FLASH A GIDDY SMILE?
CLIK!
"LIEUTENANT" FROSLER?

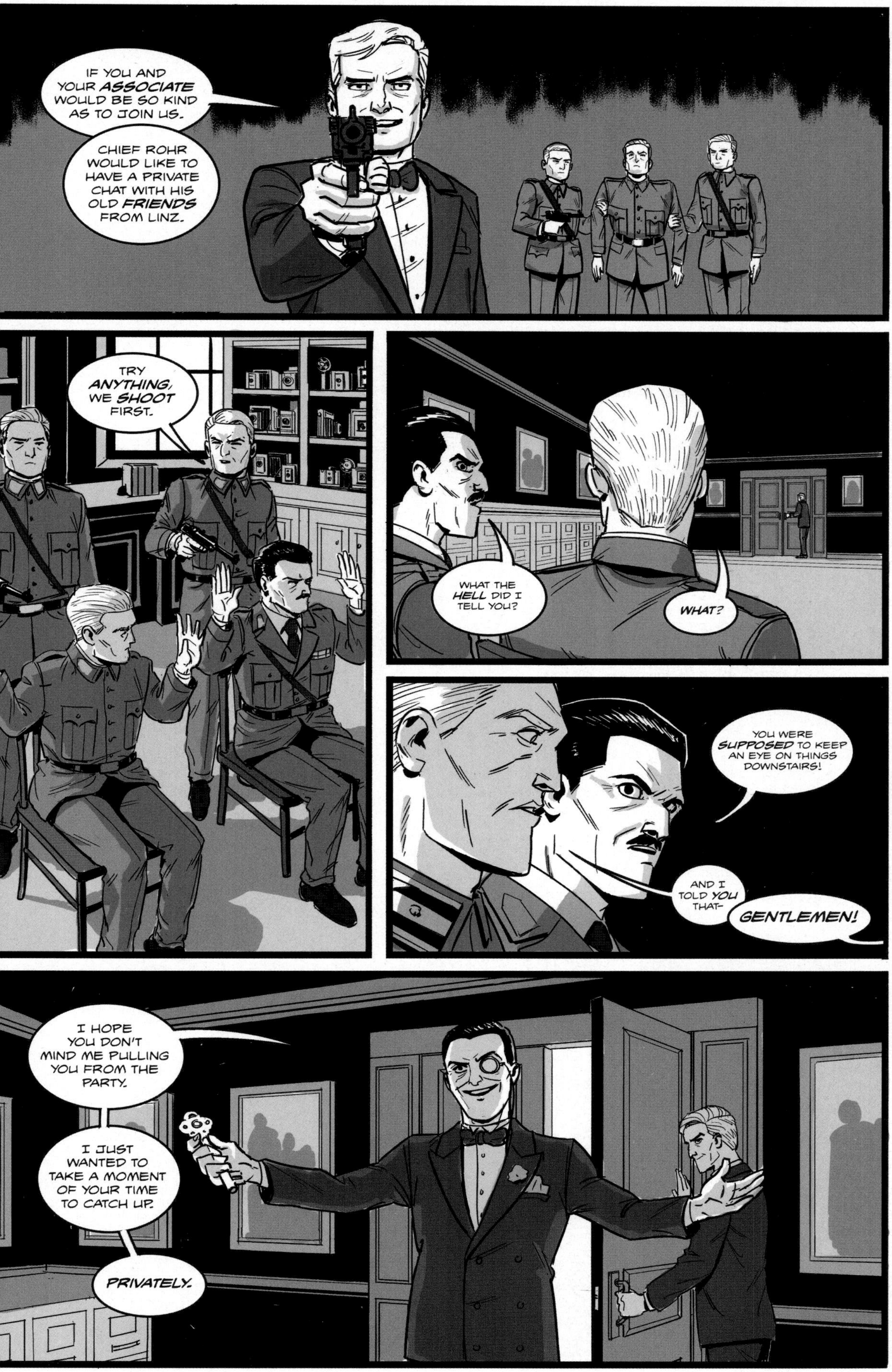
IF YOU AND YOUR ASSOCIATE WOULD BE SO KIND AS TO JOIN US.
CHIEF ROHR WOULD LIKE TO HAVE A PRIVATE CHAT WITH HIS OLD FRIENDS FROM LINZ.
TRY ANYTHING, WE SHOOT FIRST.
WHAT THE HELL DID I TELL YOU?
WHAT?
YOU WERE SUPPOSED TO KEEP AN EYE ON THINGS DOWNSTAIRS!
AND I TOLD YOU THAT-
GENTLEMEN!
I HOPE YOU DON'T MIND ME PULLING YOU FROM THE PARTY.
I JUST WANTED TO TAKE A MOMENT OF YOUR TIME TO CATCH UP.
PRIVATELY.

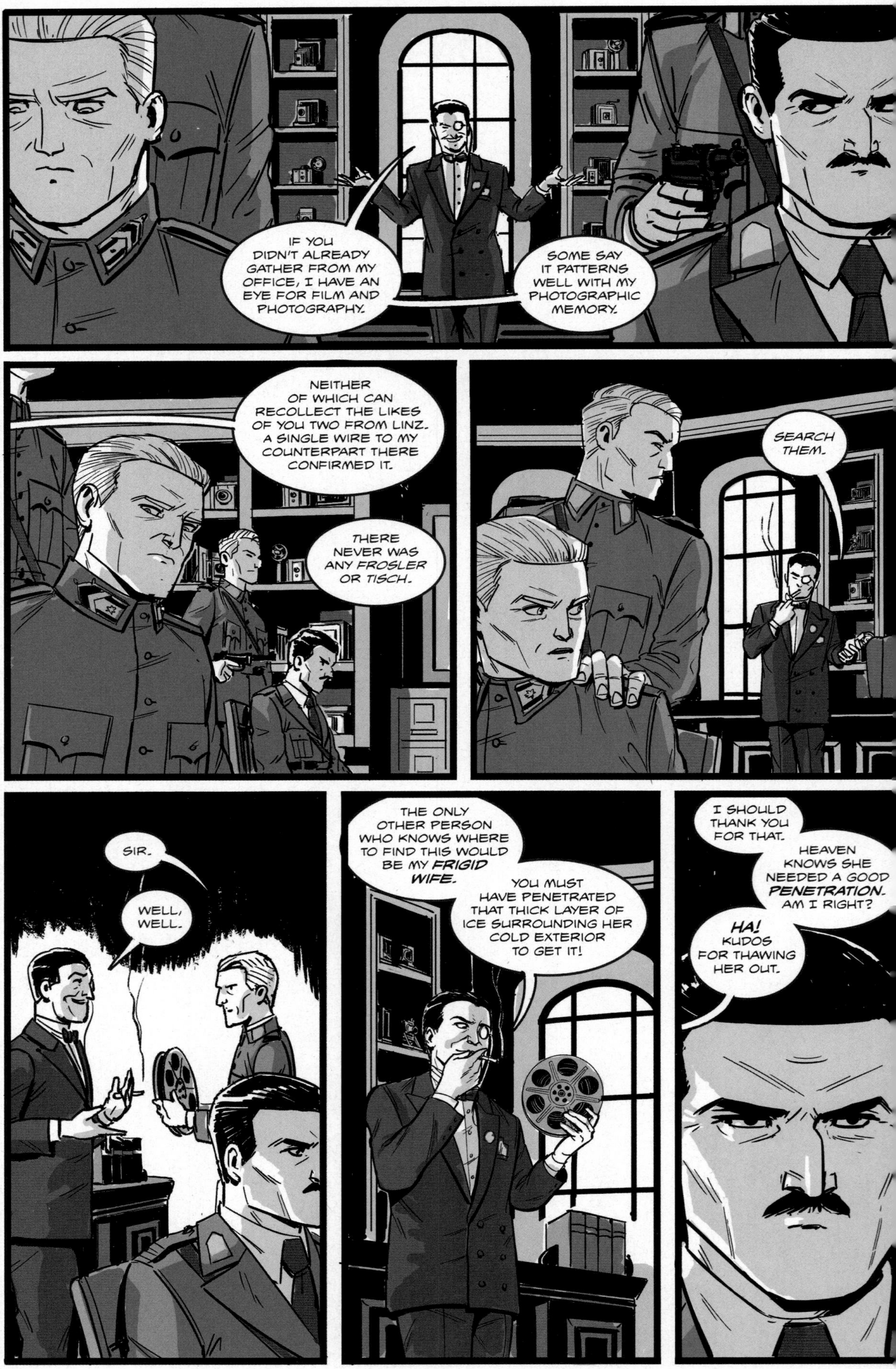
IF YOU DIDN'T ALREADY GATHER FROM MY OFFICE, I HAVE AN EYE FOR FILM AND PHOTOGRAPHY.
SOME SAY IT PATTERNS WELL WITH MY PHOTOGRAPHIC MEMORY.
NEITHER OF WHICH CAN RECOLLECT THE LIKES OF YOU TWO FROM LINZ. A SINGLE WIRE TO MY COUNTERPART THERE CONFIRMED IT.
THERE NEVER WAS ANY FROSLER OR TISCH.
SEARCH THEM.
SIR.
WELL, WELL.
THE ONLY OTHER PERSON WHO KNOWS WHERE TO FIND THIS WOULD BE MY FRIGID WIFE.
YOU MUST HAVE PENETRATED THAT THICK LAYER OF ICE SURROUNDING HER COLD EXTERIOR TO GET IT!
I SHOULD THANK YOU FOR THAT.
HEAVEN KNOWS SHE NEEDED A GOOD PENETRATION. AM I RIGHT?
HA! KUDOS FOR THAWING HER OUT.

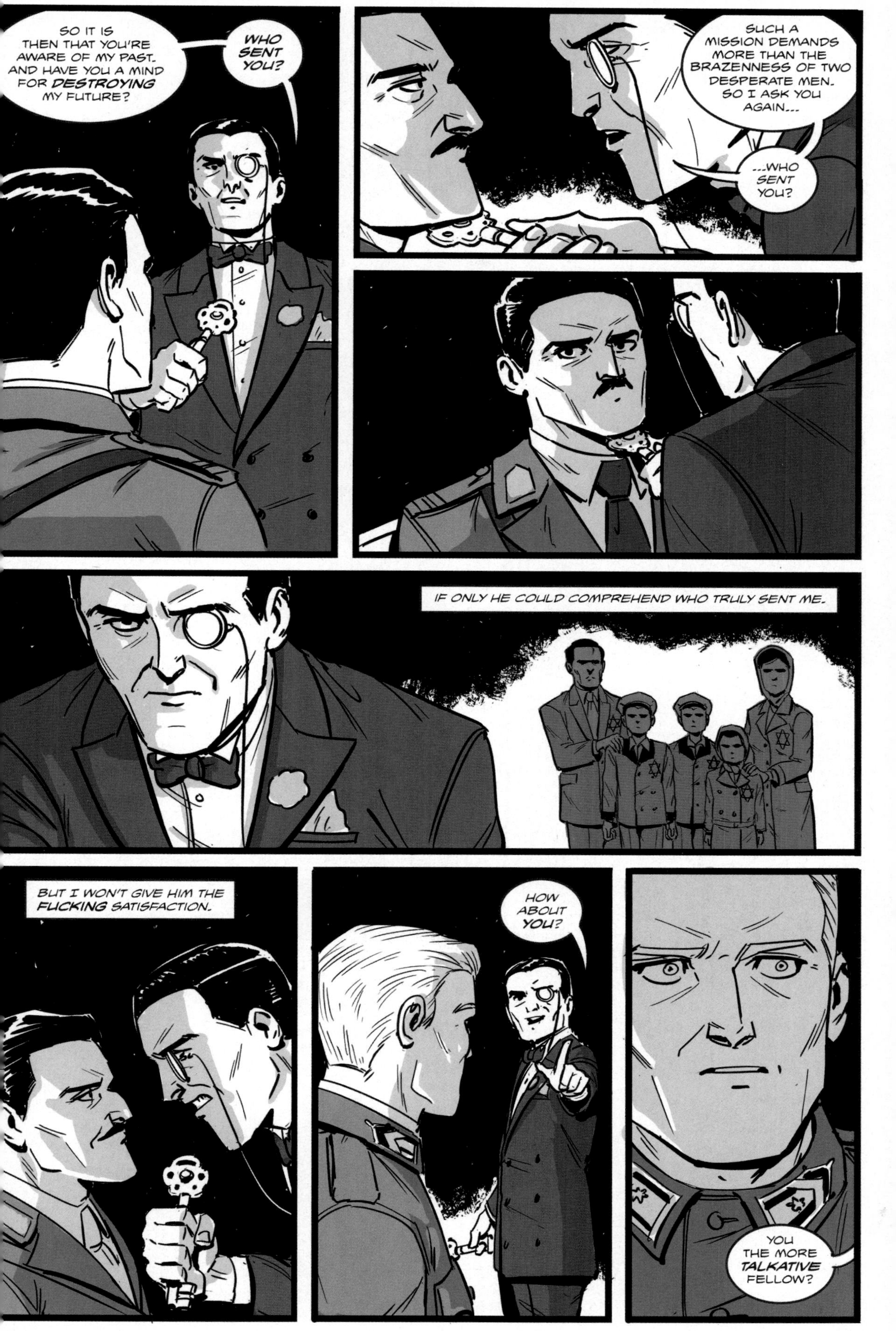
SO IT IS THEN THAT YOU'RE AWARE OF MY PAST. AND HAVE YOU A MIND FOR DESTROYING MY FUTURE?
WHO SENT YOU?
SUCH A MISSION DEMANDS MORE THAN THE BRAZENNESS OF TWO DESPERATE MEN. SO I ASK YOU AGAIN...
...WHO SENT YOU?
IF ONLY HE COULD COMPREHEND WHO TRULY SENT ME.
BUT I WON'T GIVE HIM THE FUCKING SATISFACTION.
HOW ABOUT YOU?
YOU THE MORE TALKATIVE FELLOW?

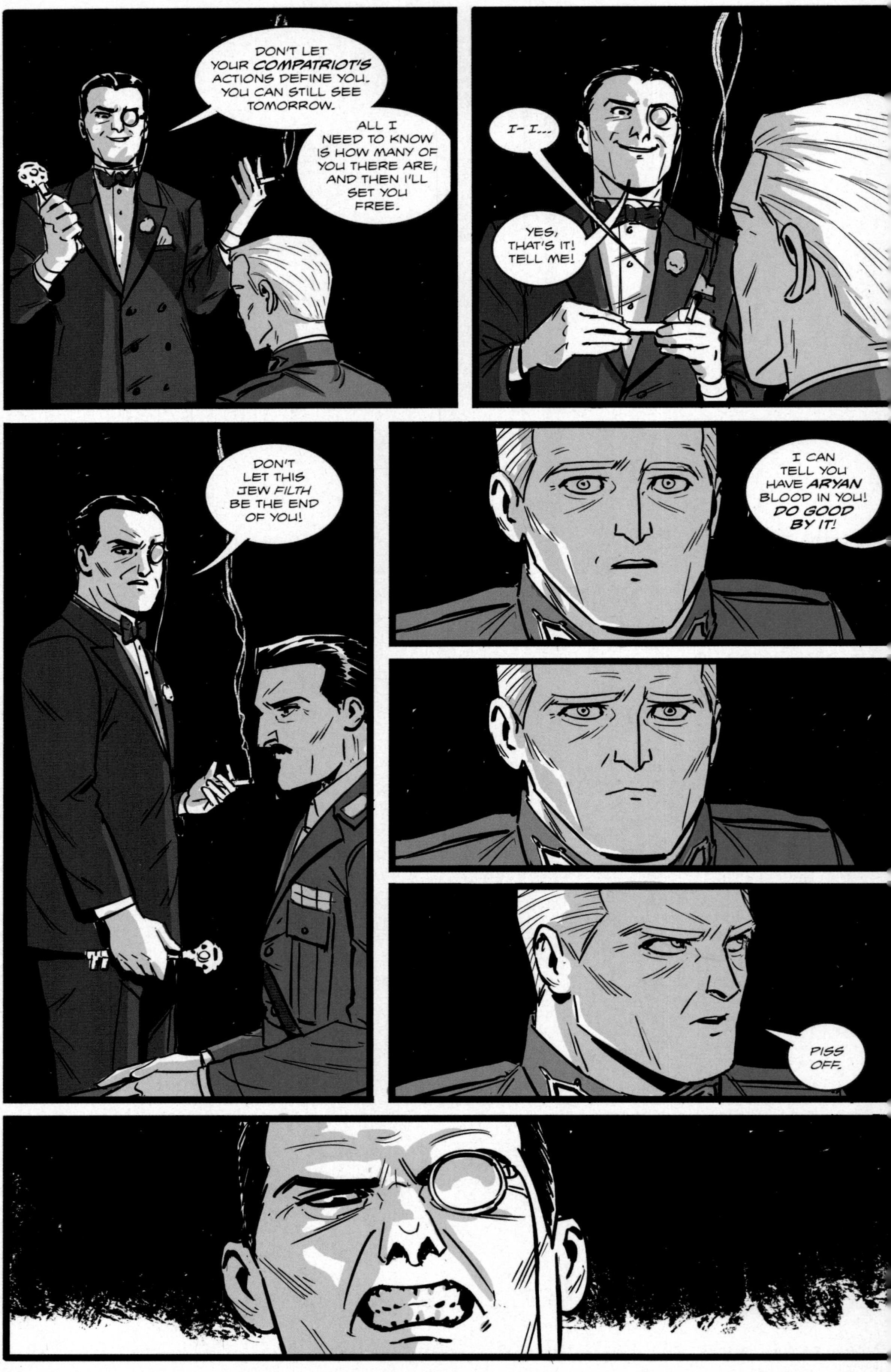
DON'T LET YOUR COMPATRIOT'S ACTIONS DEFINE YOU. YOU CAN STILL SEE TOMORROW.
ALL I NEED TO KNOW IS HOW MANY OF YOU THERE ARE, AND THEN I'LL SET YOU FREE.
I- I...
YES, THAT'S IT! TELL ME!
DON'T LET THIS JEW FILTH BE THE END OF YOU!
I CAN TELL YOU HAVE ARYAN BLOOD IN YOU! DO GOOD BY IT!
PISS OFF.

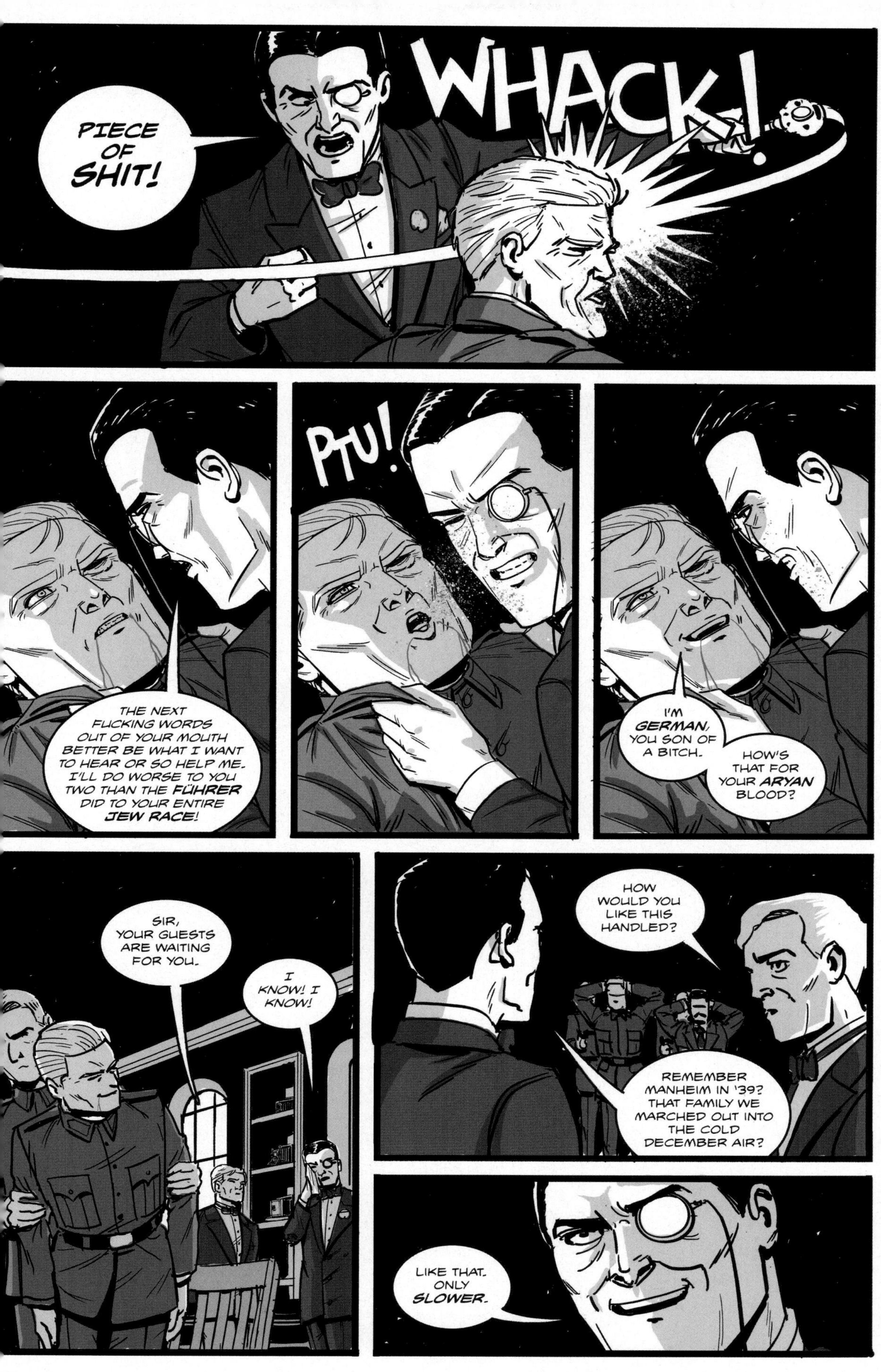
PIECE OF SHIT!
WHACK!
THE NEXT FUCKING WORDS OUT OF YOUR MOUTH BETTER BE WHAT I WANT TO HEAR OR SO HELP ME. I'LL DO WORSE TO YOU TWO THAN THE FÜHRER DID TO YOUR ENTIRE JEW RACE!
PTU!
I'M GERMAN, YOU SON OF A BITCH.
HOW'S THAT FOR YOUR ARYAN BLOOD?
SIR, YOUR GUESTS ARE WAITING FOR YOU.
I KNOW! I KNOW!
HOW WOULD YOU LIKE THIS HANDLED?
REMEMBER MANHEIM IN '39? THAT FAMILY WE MARCHED OUT INTO THE COLD DECEMBER AIR?
LIKE THAT. ONLY SLOWER.

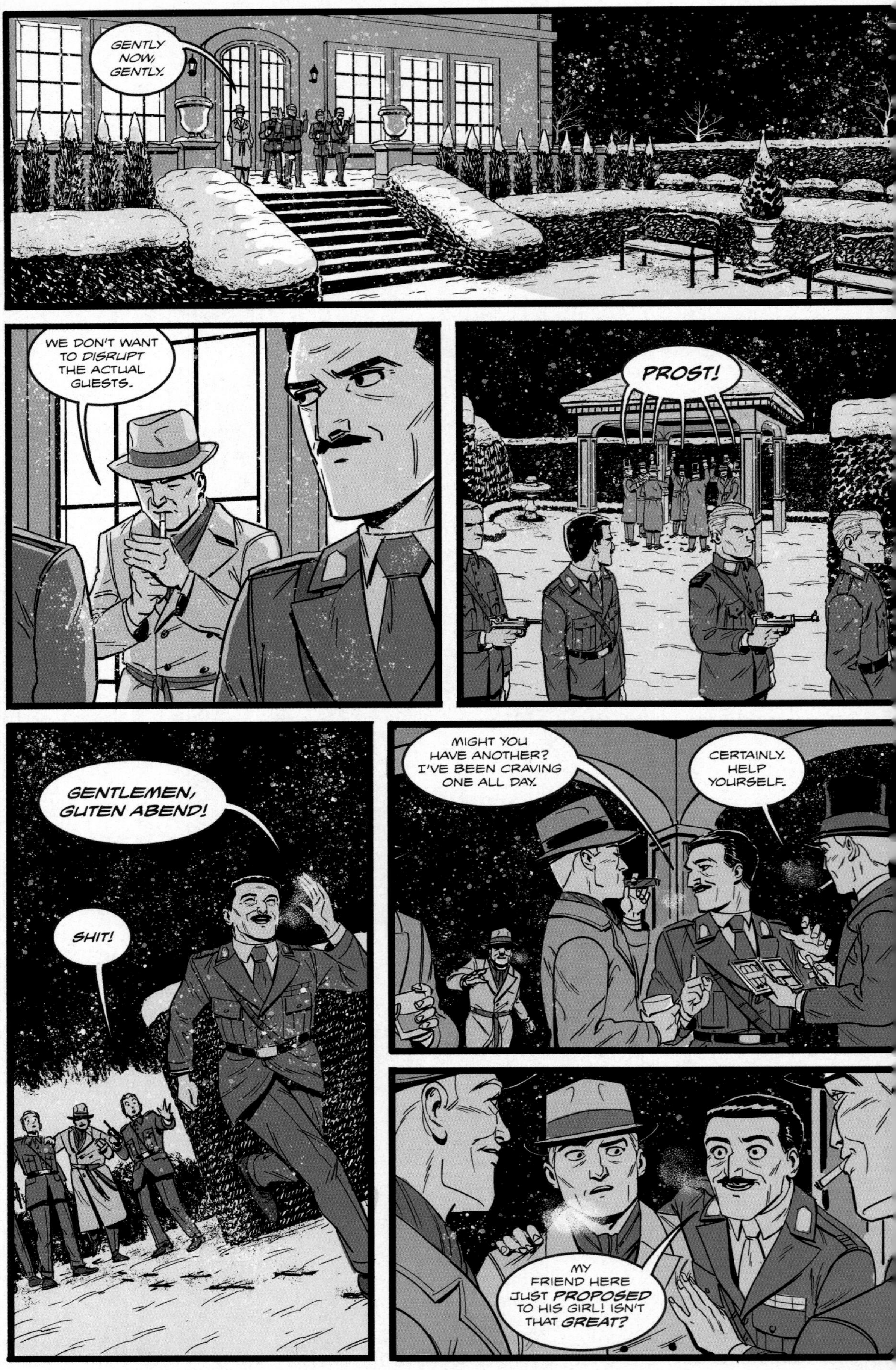
GENTLY NOW, GENTLY.
WE DON'T WANT TO DISRUPT THE ACTUAL GUESTS.
PROST!
GENTLEMEN, GUTEN ABEND!
SHIT!
MIGHT YOU HAVE ANOTHER? I'VE BEEN CRAVING ONE ALL DAY.
CERTAINLY. HELP YOURSELF.
MY FRIEND HERE JUST PROPOSED TO HIS GIRL! ISN'T THAT GREAT?

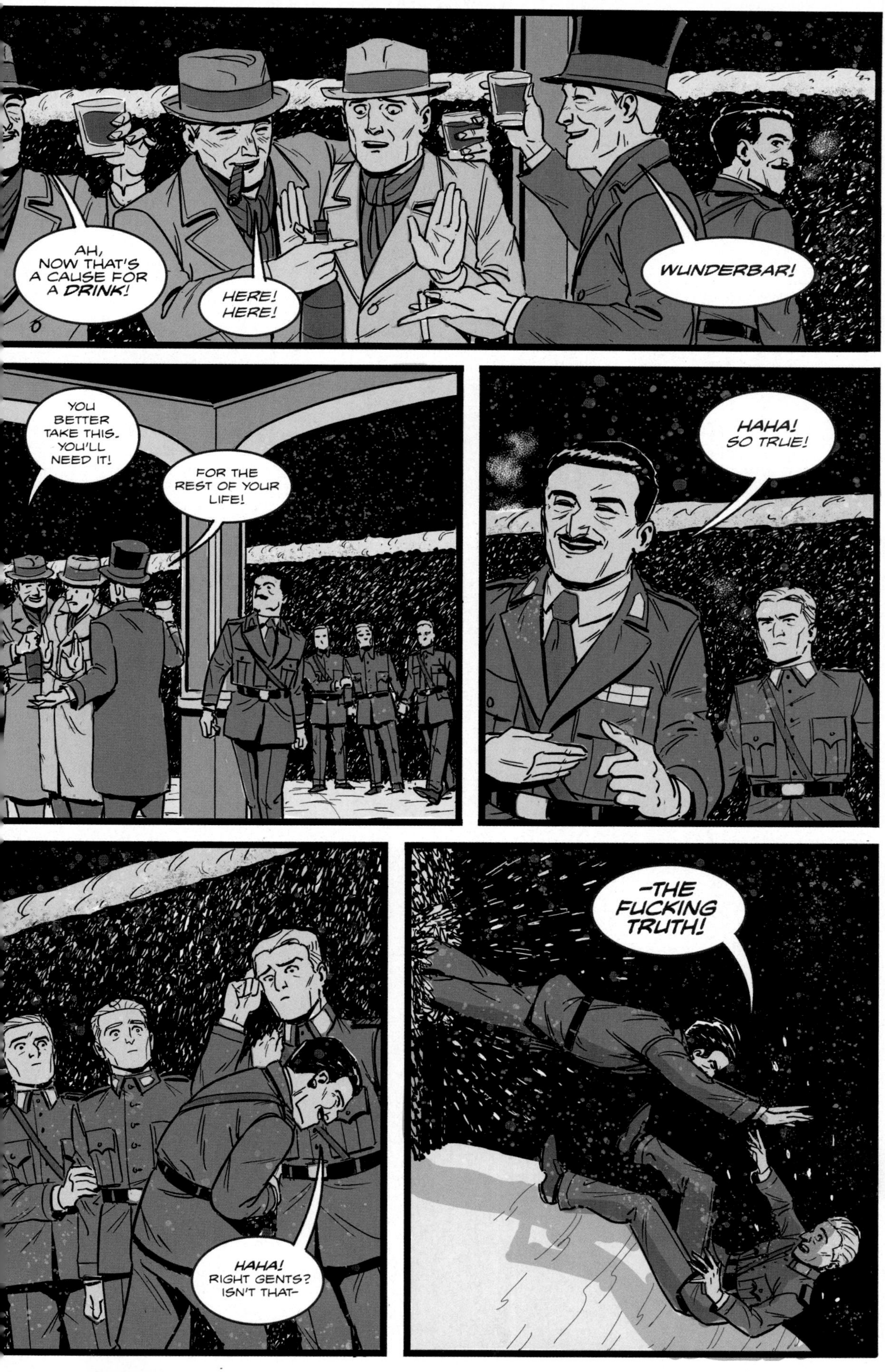
AH, NOW THAT'S A CAUSE FOR A DRINK!
HERE! HERE!
WUNDERBAR!
YOU BETTER TAKE THIS. YOU'LL NEED IT!
FOR THE REST OF YOUR LIFE!
HAHA! SO TRUE!
HAHA! RIGHT GENTS? ISN'T THAT-
-THE FUCKING TRUTH!

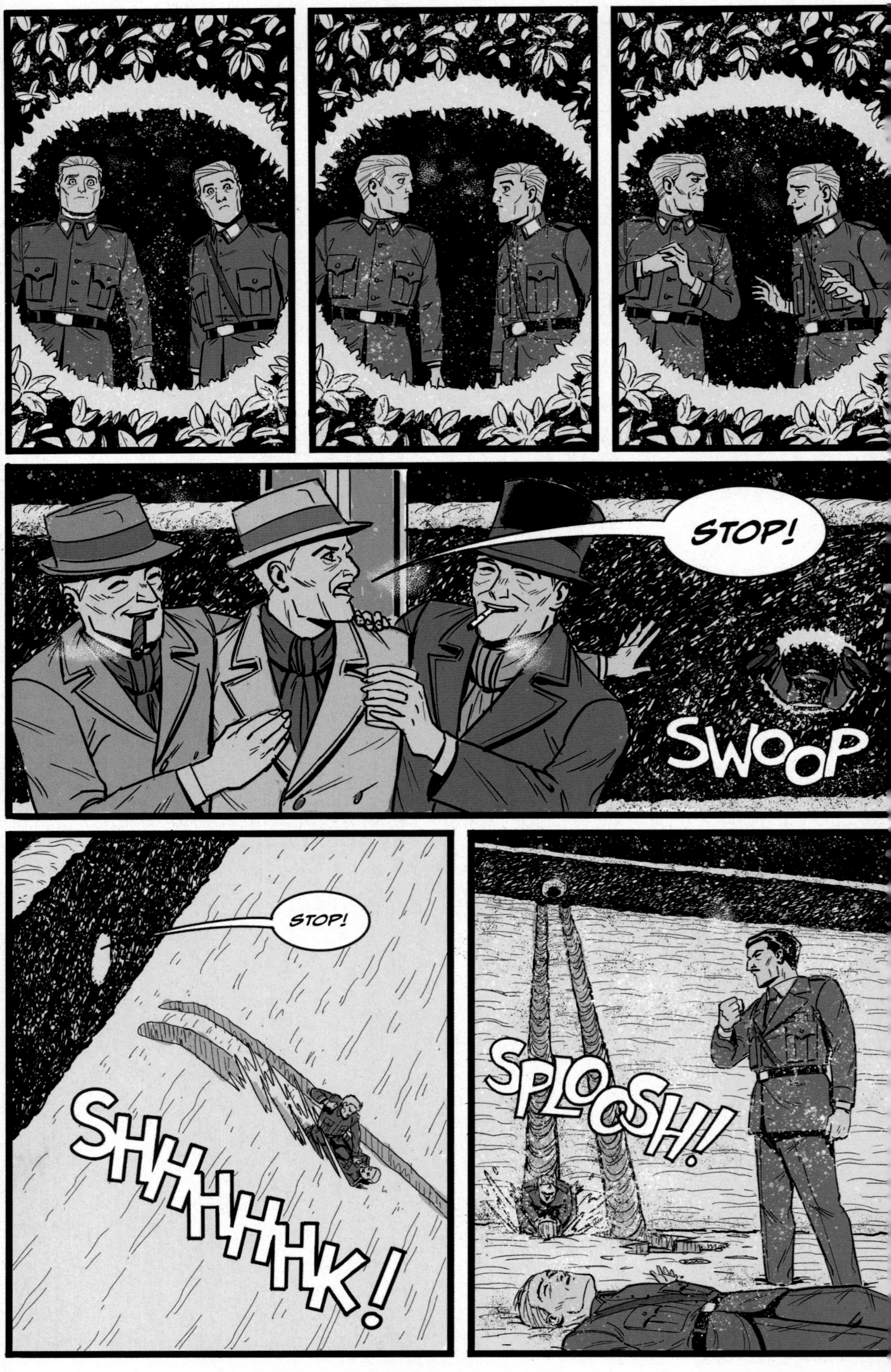
STOP!
SWOOP
STOP!
SHHHHHHK!
SPLOOSH!!

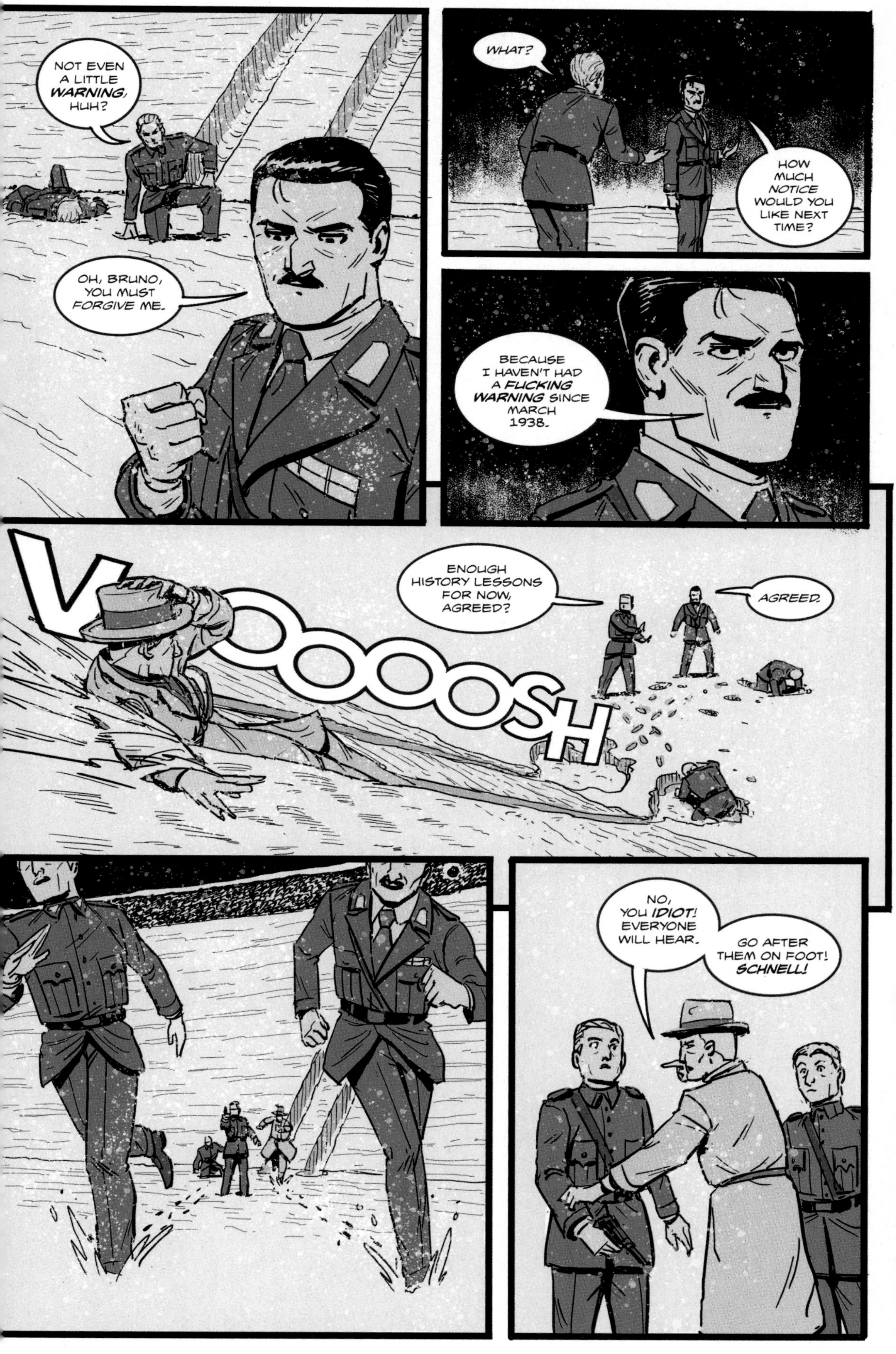
NOT EVEN A LITTLE *WARNING*, HUH?
OH, BRUNO, YOU MUST FORGIVE ME.
WHAT?
HOW MUCH *NOTICE* WOULD YOU LIKE NEXT TIME?
BECAUSE I HAVEN'T HAD A *FUCKING WARNING* SINCE MARCH 1938.
VOOOOOSH
ENOUGH HISTORY LESSONS FOR NOW, AGREED?
AGREED.
NO, YOU *IDIOT*! EVERYONE WILL HEAR.
GO AFTER THEM ON FOOT! *SCHNELL!*

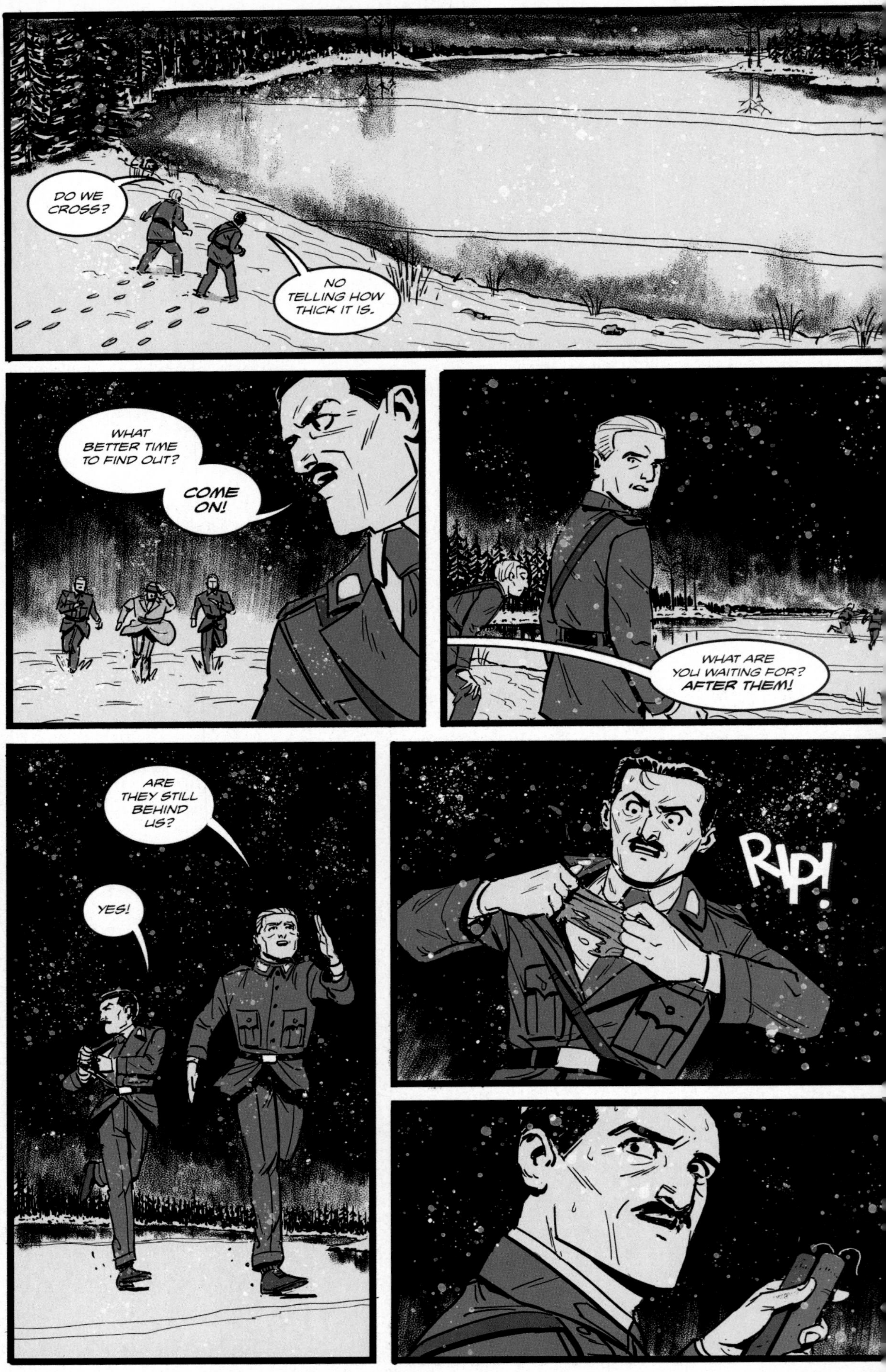
DO WE CROSS?
NO TELLING HOW THICK IT IS.
WHAT BETTER TIME TO FIND OUT?
COME ON!
WHAT ARE YOU WAITING FOR? AFTER THEM!
ARE THEY STILL BEHIND US?
YES!
RIP!

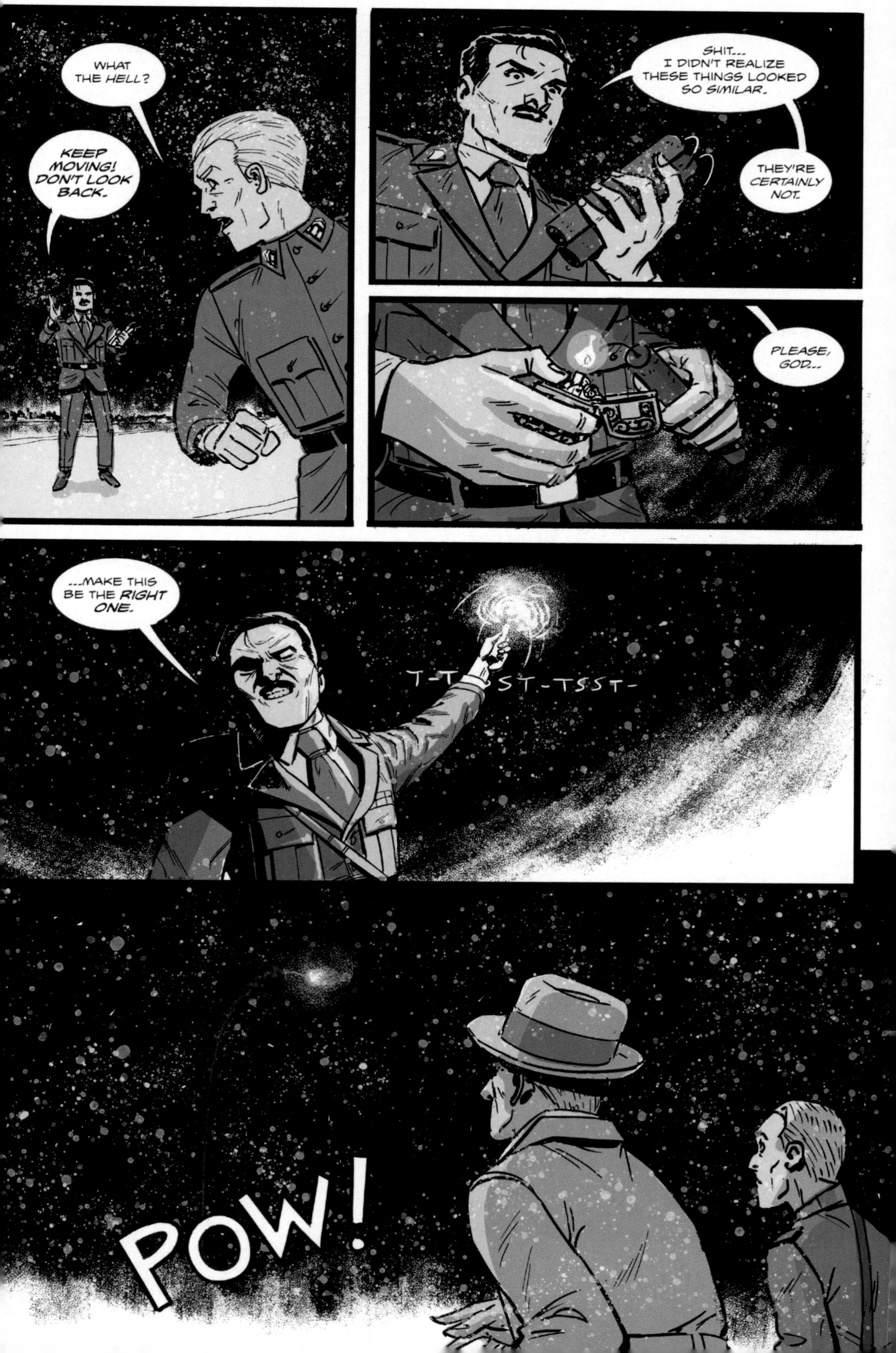
WHAT THE *HELL*?
KEEP MOVING! DON'T LOOK BACK.
SHIT... I DIDN'T REALIZE THESE THINGS LOOKED SO *SIMILAR*.
THEY'RE *CERTAINLY NOT*.
PLEASE, GOD...
...MAKE THIS BE THE *RIGHT ONE*.
T-T SST-TSST-
POW!

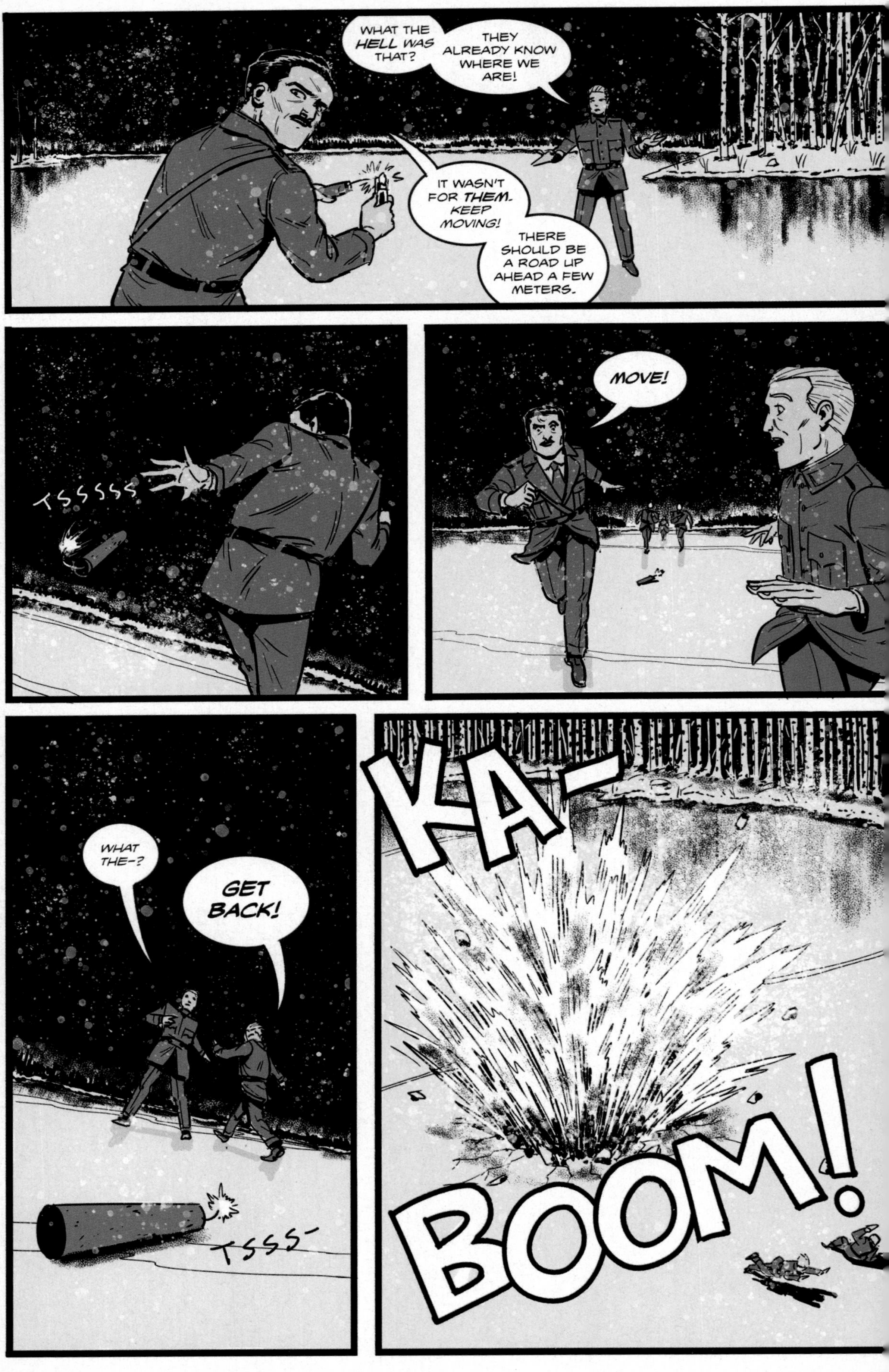
WHAT THE HELL WAS THAT?
THEY ALREADY KNOW WHERE WE ARE!
IT WASN'T FOR THEM. KEEP MOVING!
THERE SHOULD BE A ROAD UP AHEAD A FEW METERS.
TSSSSS
MOVE!
WHAT THE-?
GET BACK!
TSSS-
KA-BOOM!

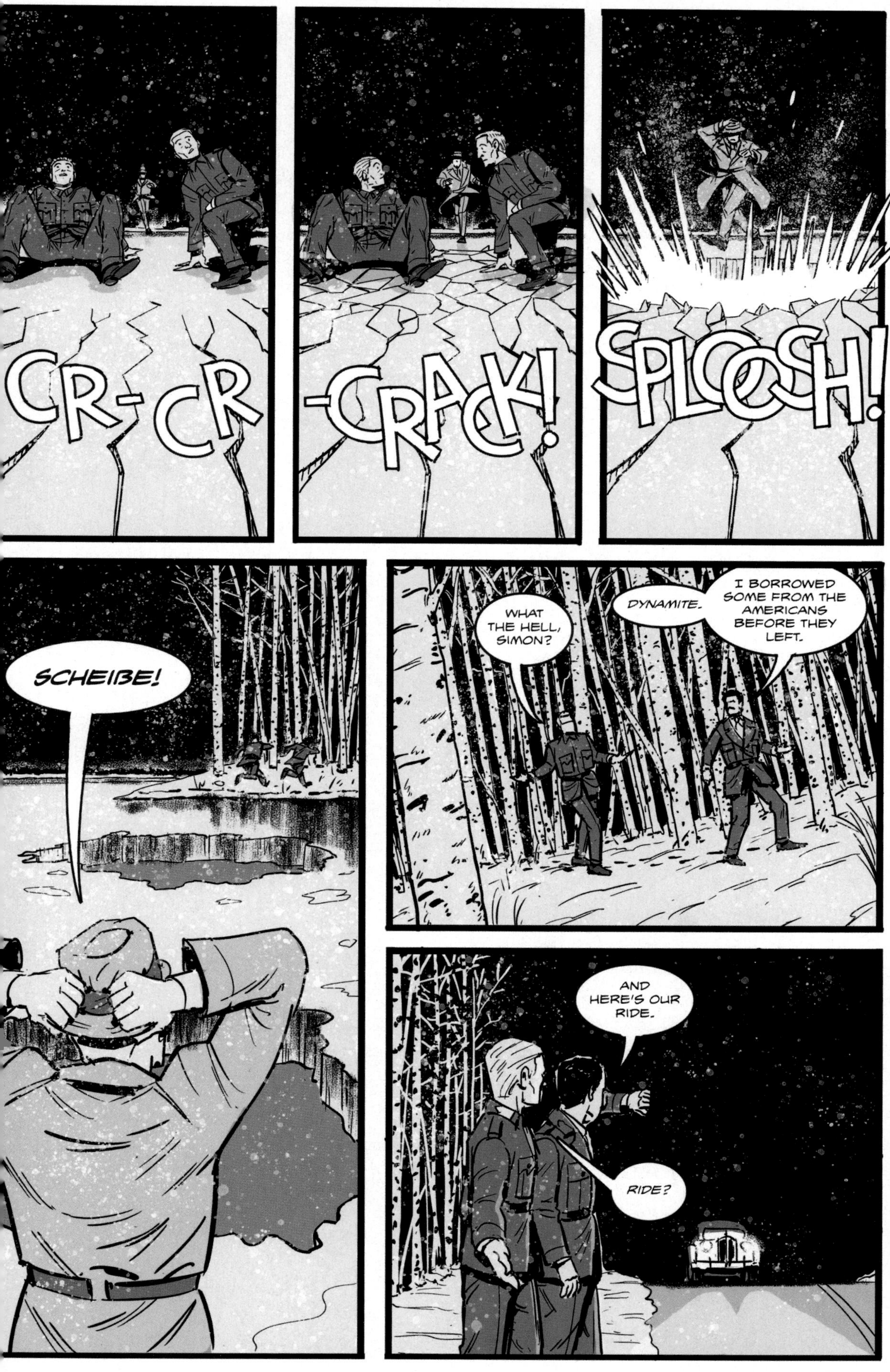
CR-CR
-CRACK!
SPLOOSH!
SCHEIBE!
WHAT THE HELL, SIMON?
DYNAMITE.
I BORROWED SOME FROM THE AMERICANS BEFORE THEY LEFT.
AND HERE'S OUR RIDE.
RIDE?

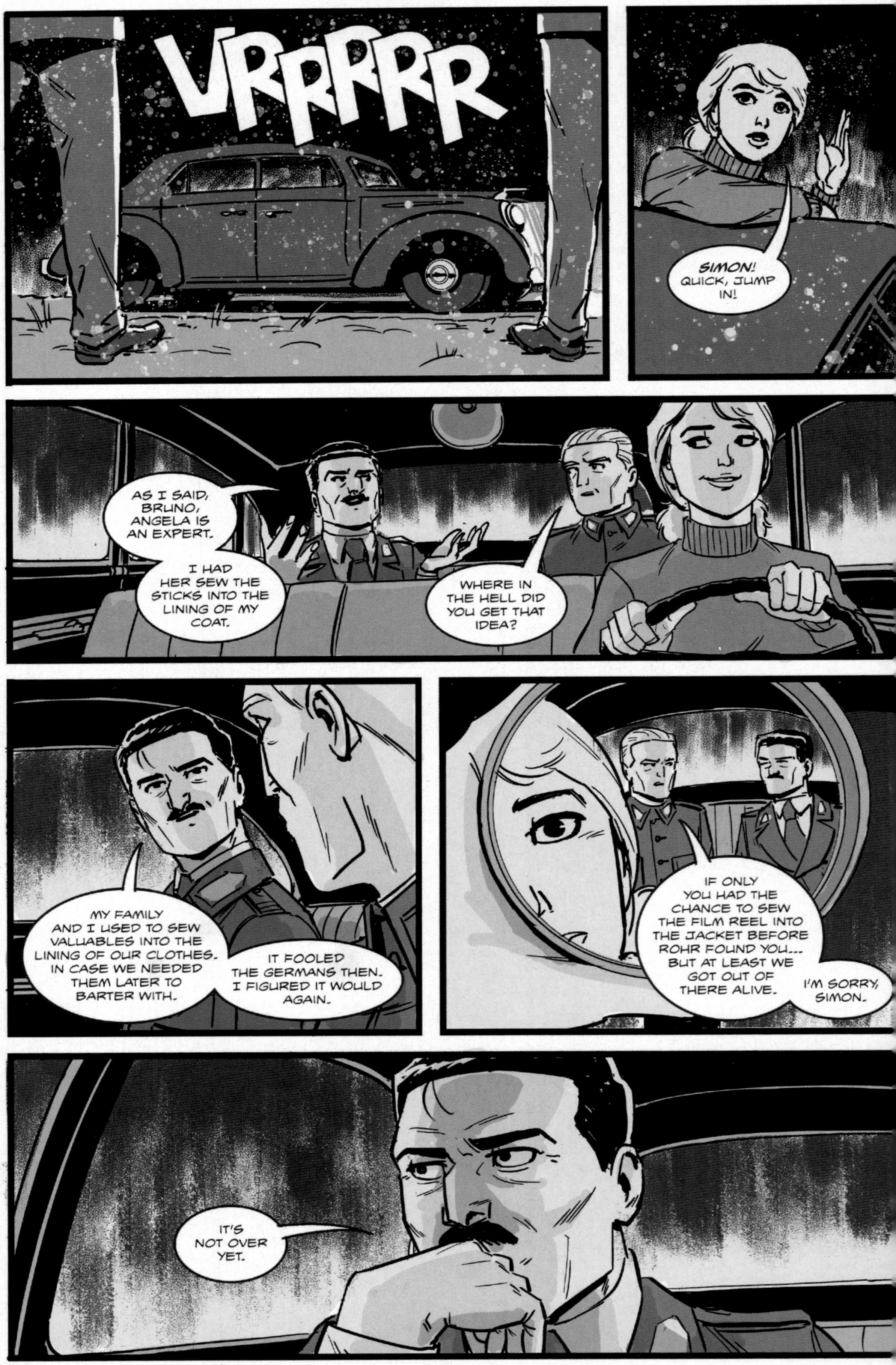
VRRRRR
SIMON! QUICK, JUMP IN!
AS I SAID, BRUNO, ANGELA IS AN EXPERT.
I HAD HER SEW THE STICKS INTO THE LINING OF MY COAT.
WHERE IN THE HELL DID YOU GET THAT IDEA?
MY FAMILY AND I USED TO SEW VALUABLES INTO THE LINING OF OUR CLOTHES. IN CASE WE NEEDED THEM LATER TO BARTER WITH.
IT FOOLED THE GERMANS THEN. I FIGURED IT WOULD AGAIN.
IF ONLY YOU HAD THE CHANCE TO SEW THE FILM REEL INTO THE JACKET BEFORE ROHR FOUND YOU... BUT AT LEAST WE GOT OUT OF THERE ALIVE.
I'M SORRY, SIMON.
IT'S NOT OVER YET.

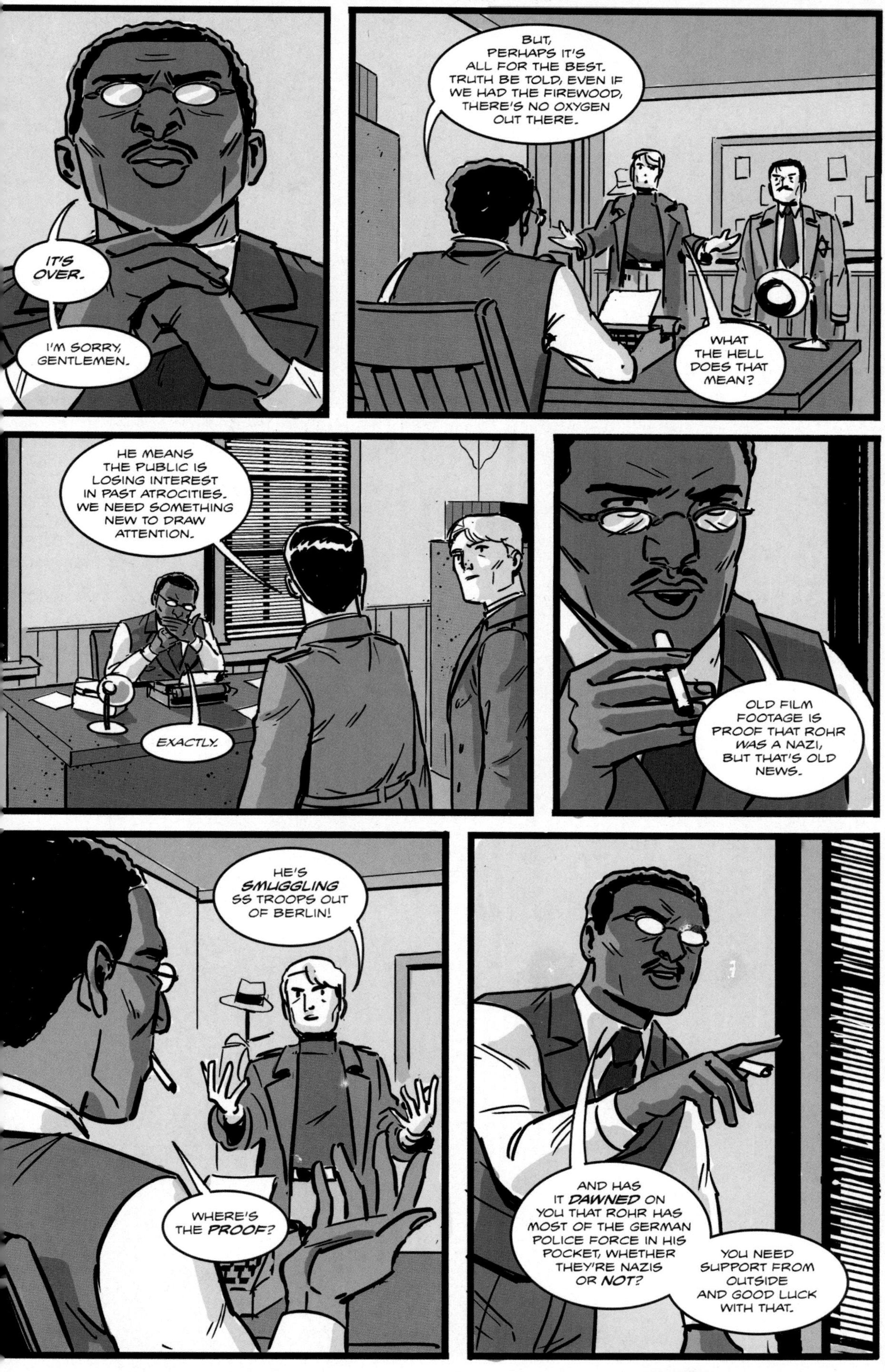
IT'S OVER.
I'M SORRY, GENTLEMEN.
BUT, PERHAPS IT'S ALL FOR THE BEST. TRUTH BE TOLD, EVEN IF WE HAD THE FIREWOOD, THERE'S NO OXYGEN OUT THERE.
WHAT THE HELL DOES THAT MEAN?
HE MEANS THE PUBLIC IS LOSING INTEREST IN PAST ATROCITIES. WE NEED SOMETHING NEW TO DRAW ATTENTION.
EXACTLY.
OLD FILM FOOTAGE IS PROOF THAT ROHR WAS A NAZI, BUT THAT'S OLD NEWS.
HE'S SMUGGLING SS TROOPS OUT OF BERLIN!
WHERE'S THE PROOF?
AND HAS IT DAWNED ON YOU THAT ROHR HAS MOST OF THE GERMAN POLICE FORCE IN HIS POCKET, WHETHER THEY'RE NAZIS OR NOT?
YOU NEED SUPPORT FROM OUTSIDE AND GOOD LUCK WITH THAT.

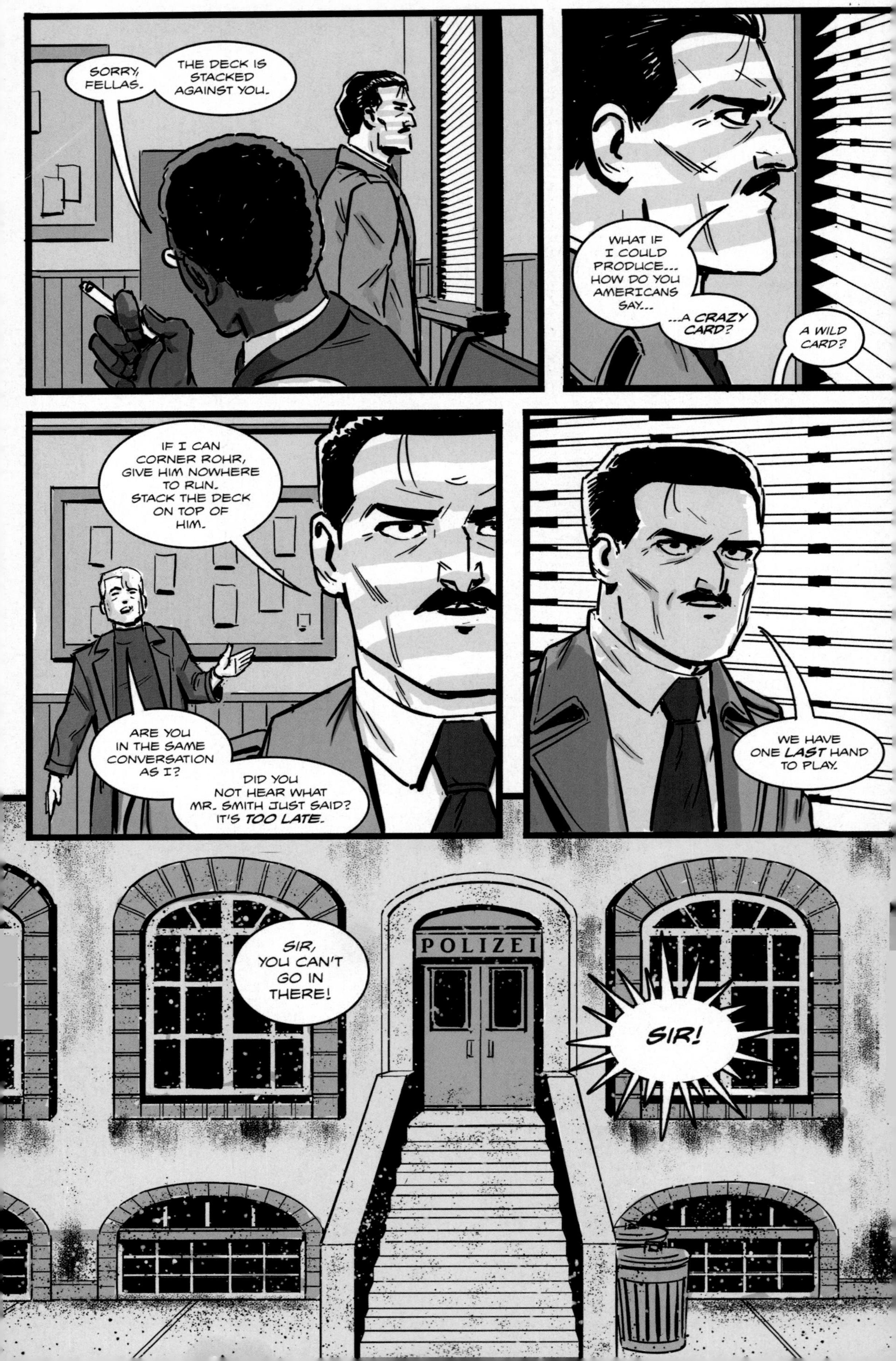
SORRY, FELLAS.
THE DECK IS STACKED AGAINST YOU.
WHAT IF I COULD PRODUCE... HOW DO YOU AMERICANS SAY...
...A CRAZY CARD?
A WILD CARD?
IF I CAN CORNER ROHR, GIVE HIM NOWHERE TO RUN. STACK THE DECK ON TOP OF HIM.
ARE YOU IN THE SAME CONVERSATION AS I?
DID YOU NOT HEAR WHAT MR. SMITH JUST SAID? IT'S TOO LATE.
WE HAVE ONE LAST HAND TO PLAY.
POLIZEI
SIR, YOU CAN'T GO IN THERE!
SIR!

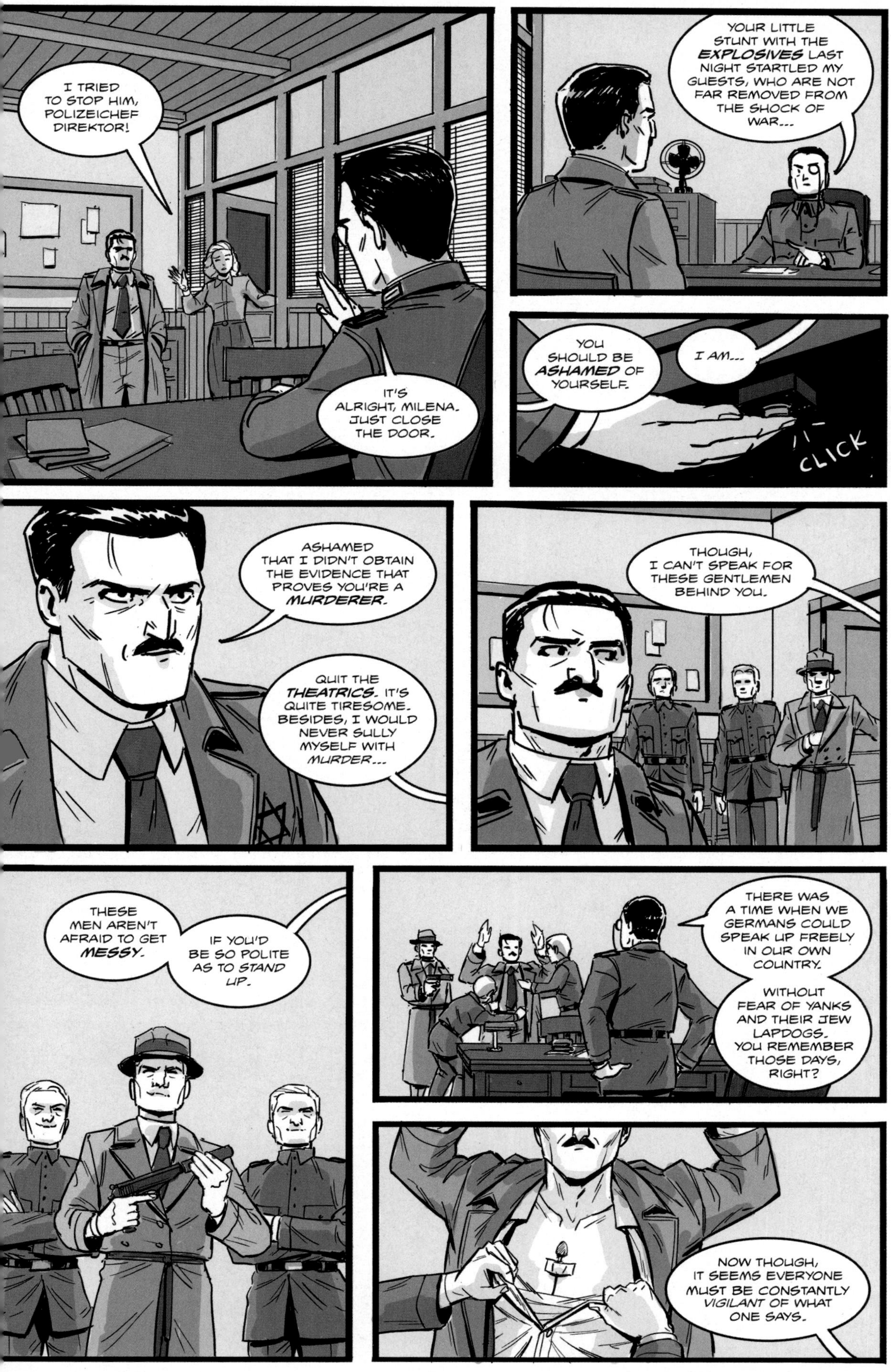
I TRIED TO STOP HIM, POLIZEICHEF DIREKTOR!
IT'S ALRIGHT, MILENA. JUST CLOSE THE DOOR.
YOUR LITTLE STUNT WITH THE EXPLOSIVES LAST NIGHT STARTLED MY GUESTS, WHO ARE NOT FAR REMOVED FROM THE SHOCK OF WAR...
YOU SHOULD BE ASHAMED OF YOURSELF.
I AM...
CLICK
ASHAMED THAT I DIDN'T OBTAIN THE EVIDENCE THAT PROVES YOU'RE A MURDERER.
QUIT THE THEATRICS. IT'S QUITE TIRESOME. BESIDES, I WOULD NEVER SULLY MYSELF WITH MURDER...
THOUGH, I CAN'T SPEAK FOR THESE GENTLEMEN BEHIND YOU.
THESE MEN AREN'T AFRAID TO GET MESSY.
IF YOU'D BE SO POLITE AS TO STAND UP.
THERE WAS A TIME WHEN WE GERMANS COULD SPEAK UP FREELY IN OUR OWN COUNTRY.
WITHOUT FEAR OF YANKS AND THEIR JEW LAPDOGS. YOU REMEMBER THOSE DAYS, RIGHT?
NOW THOUGH, IT SEEMS EVERYONE MUST BE CONSTANTLY VIGILANT OF WHAT ONE SAYS.

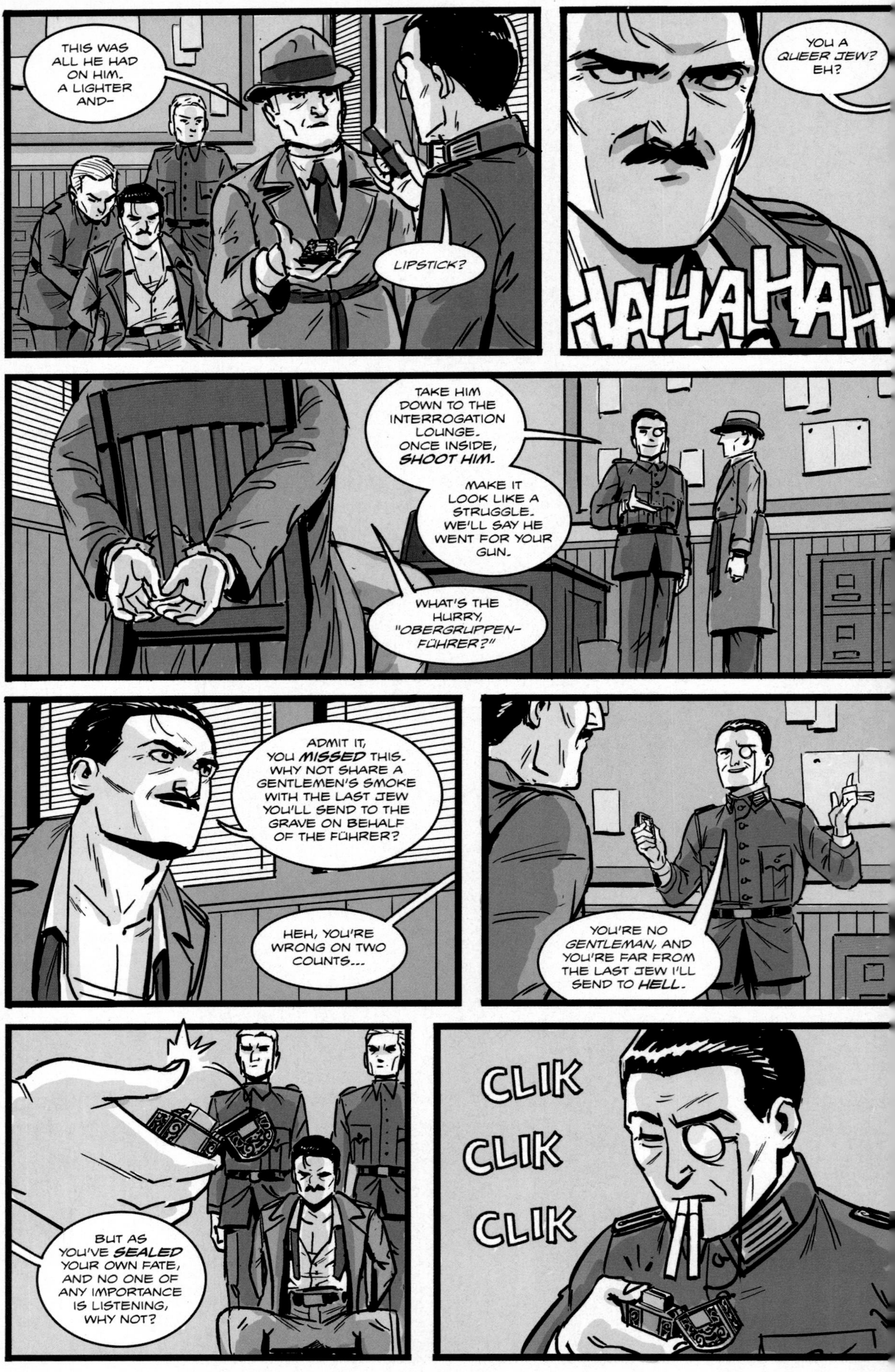
THIS WAS ALL HE HAD ON HIM. A LIGHTER AND-
LIPSTICK?
YOU A QUEER JEW? EH?
HAHAHAH
TAKE HIM DOWN TO THE INTERROGATION LOUNGE. ONCE INSIDE, SHOOT HIM.
MAKE IT LOOK LIKE A STRUGGLE. WE'LL SAY HE WENT FOR YOUR GUN.
WHAT'S THE HURRY, "OBERGRUPPEN-FÜHRER?"
ADMIT IT, YOU MISSED THIS. WHY NOT SHARE A GENTLEMEN'S SMOKE WITH THE LAST JEW YOU'LL SEND TO THE GRAVE ON BEHALF OF THE FÜHRER?
HEH, YOU'RE WRONG ON TWO COUNTS...
YOU'RE NO GENTLEMAN, AND YOU'RE FAR FROM THE LAST JEW I'LL SEND TO HELL.
BUT AS YOU'VE SEALED YOUR OWN FATE, AND NO ONE OF ANY IMPORTANCE IS LISTENING, WHY NOT?
CLIK
CLIK
CLIK

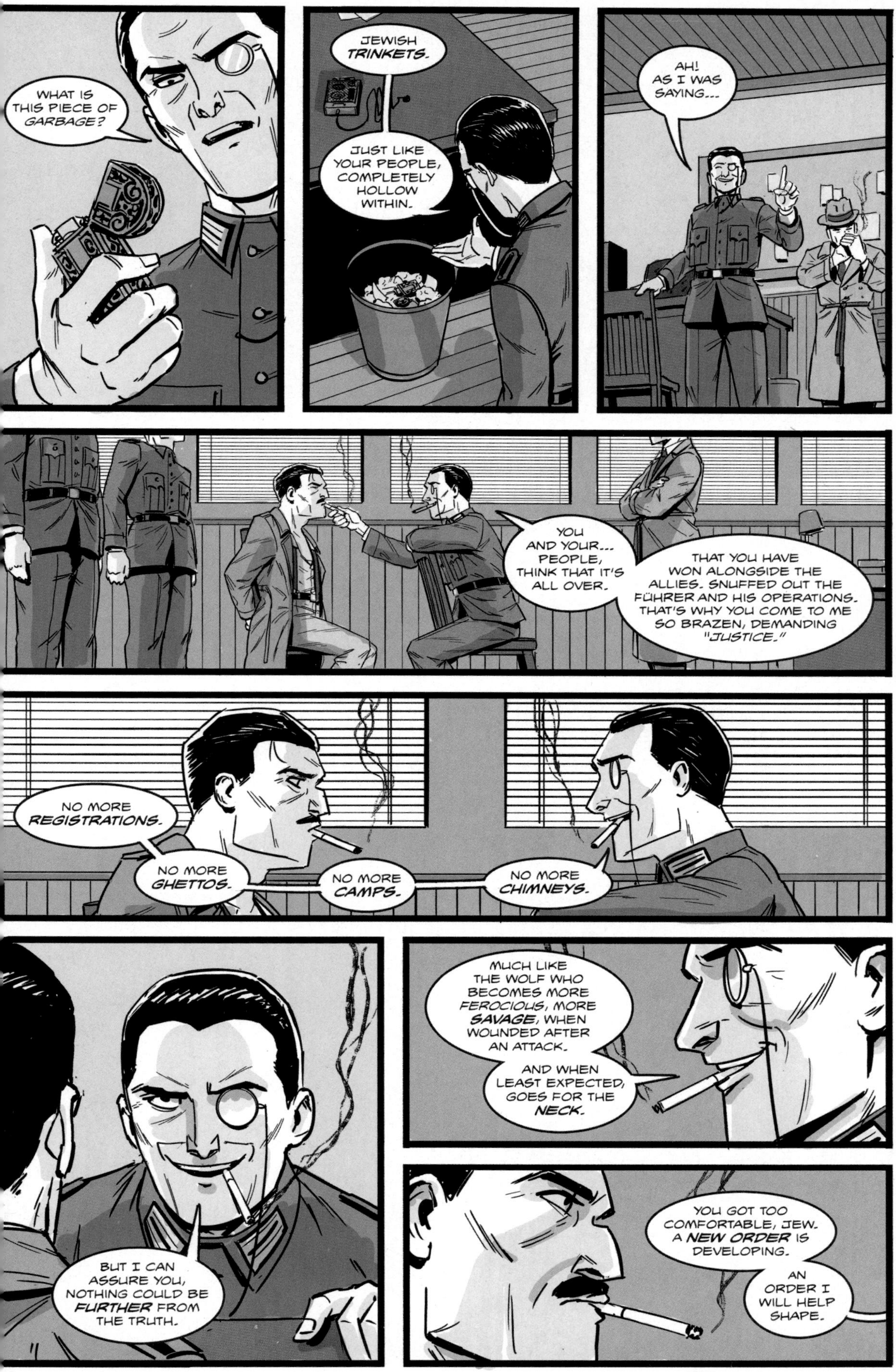
WHAT IS THIS PIECE OF GARBAGE?
JEWISH TRINKETS.
JUST LIKE YOUR PEOPLE, COMPLETELY HOLLOW WITHIN.
AH! AS I WAS SAYING...
YOU AND YOUR... PEOPLE, THINK THAT IT'S ALL OVER.
THAT YOU HAVE WON ALONGSIDE THE ALLIES. SNUFFED OUT THE FÜHRER AND HIS OPERATIONS. THAT'S WHY YOU COME TO ME SO BRAZEN, DEMANDING "JUSTICE."
NO MORE REGISTRATIONS.
NO MORE GHETTOS.
NO MORE CAMPS.
NO MORE CHIMNEYS.
BUT I CAN ASSURE YOU, NOTHING COULD BE FURTHER FROM THE TRUTH.
MUCH LIKE THE WOLF WHO BECOMES MORE FEROCIOUS, MORE SAVAGE, WHEN WOUNDED AFTER AN ATTACK.
AND WHEN LEAST EXPECTED, GOES FOR THE NECK.
YOU GOT TOO COMFORTABLE, JEW. A NEW ORDER IS DEVELOPING.
AN ORDER I WILL HELP SHAPE.

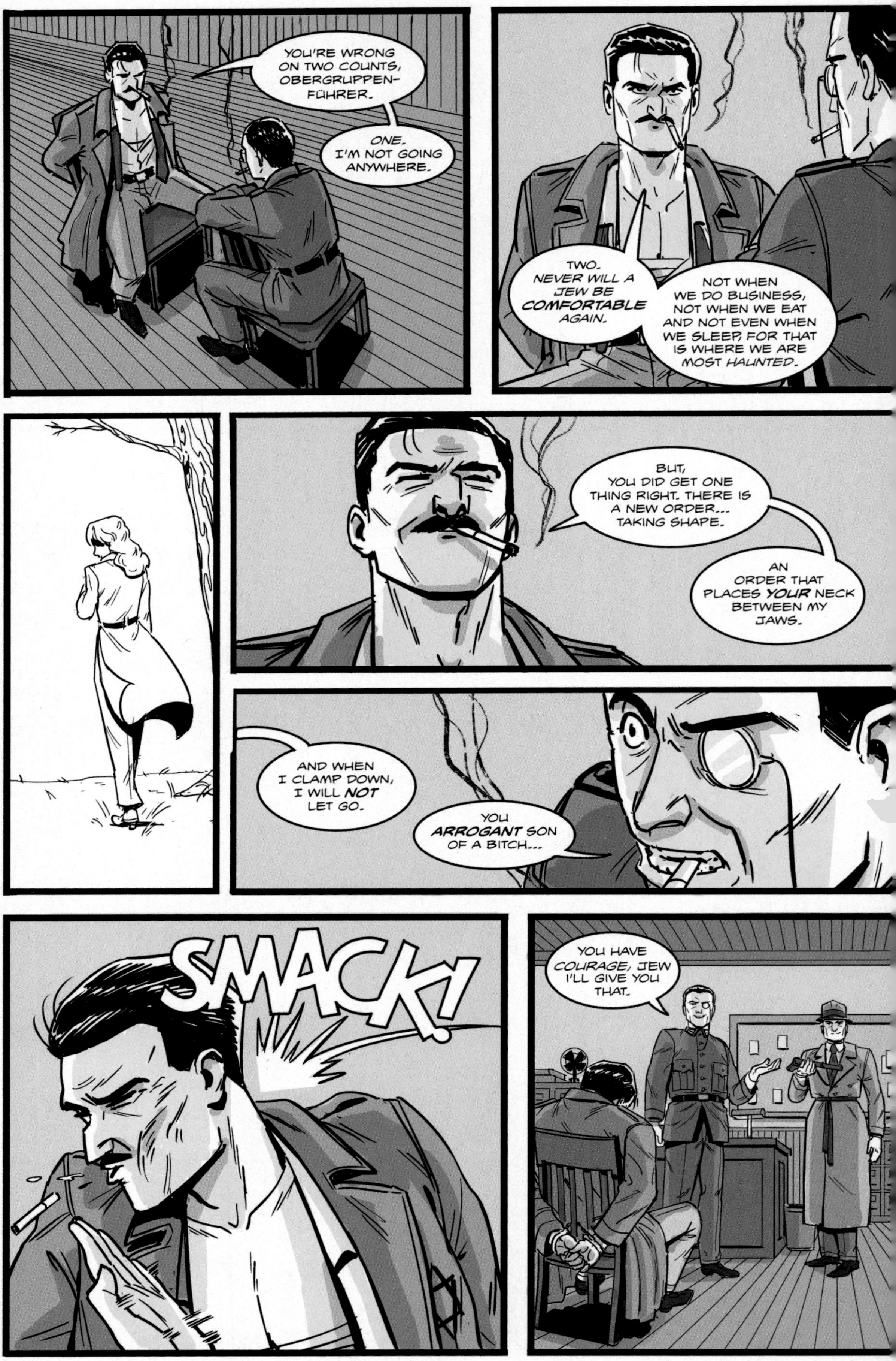
YOU'RE WRONG ON TWO COUNTS, OBERGRUPPEN-FÜHRER.
ONE. I'M NOT GOING ANYWHERE.
TWO. NEVER WILL A JEW BE COMFORTABLE AGAIN.
NOT WHEN WE DO BUSINESS, NOT WHEN WE EAT AND NOT EVEN WHEN WE SLEEP, FOR THAT IS WHERE WE ARE MOST HAUNTED.
BUT, YOU DID GET ONE THING RIGHT. THERE IS A NEW ORDER... TAKING SHAPE.
AN ORDER THAT PLACES YOUR NECK BETWEEN MY JAWS.
AND WHEN I CLAMP DOWN, I WILL NOT LET GO.
YOU ARROGANT SON OF A BITCH...
SMACK!
YOU HAVE COURAGE, JEW I'LL GIVE YOU THAT.

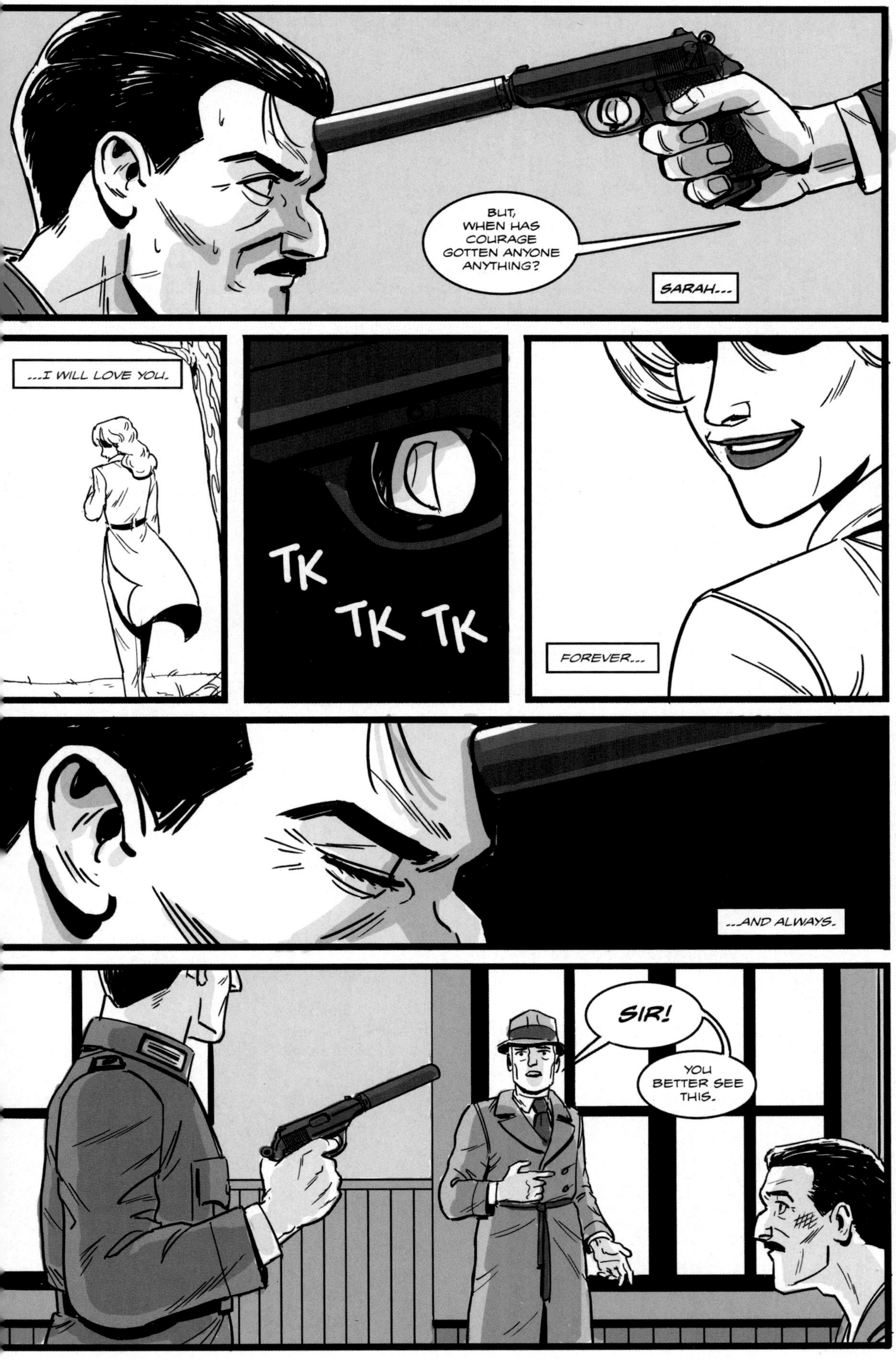
BUT, WHEN HAS COURAGE GOTTEN ANYONE ANYTHING?
SARAH...
...I WILL LOVE YOU.
TK
TK TK
FOREVER...
...AND ALWAYS.
SIR!
YOU BETTER SEE THIS.

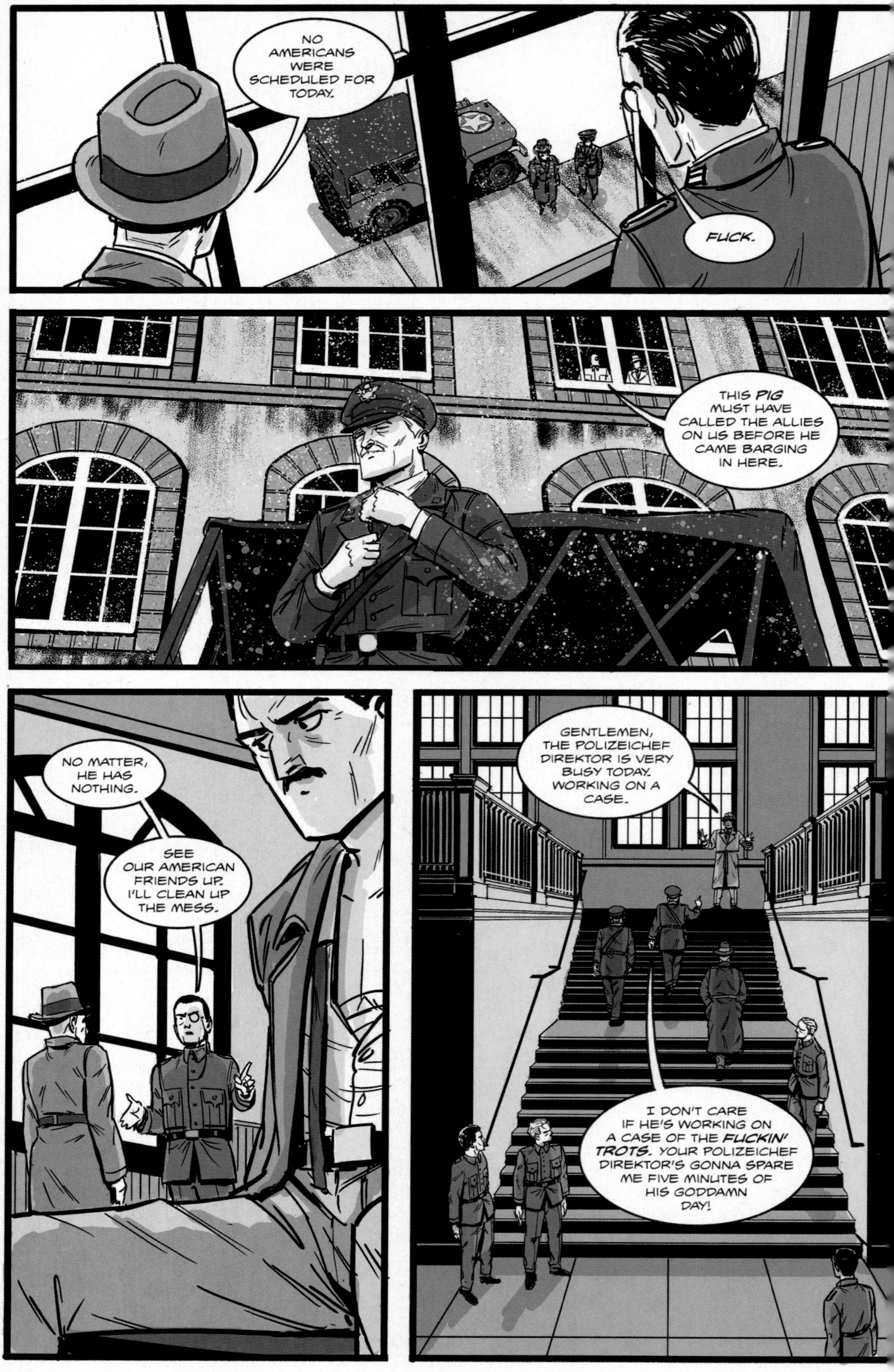
NO AMERICANS WERE SCHEDULED FOR TODAY.
FUCK.
THIS PIG MUST HAVE CALLED THE ALLIES ON US BEFORE HE CAME BARGING IN HERE.
NO MATTER, HE HAS NOTHING.
SEE OUR AMERICAN FRIENDS UP. I'LL CLEAN UP THE MESS.
GENTLEMEN, THE POLIZEICHEF DIREKTOR IS VERY BUSY TODAY. WORKING ON A CASE.
I DON'T CARE IF HE'S WORKING ON A CASE OF THE FUCKIN' TROTS. YOUR POLIZEICHEF DIREKTOR'S GONNA SPARE ME FIVE MINUTES OF HIS GODDAMN DAY!

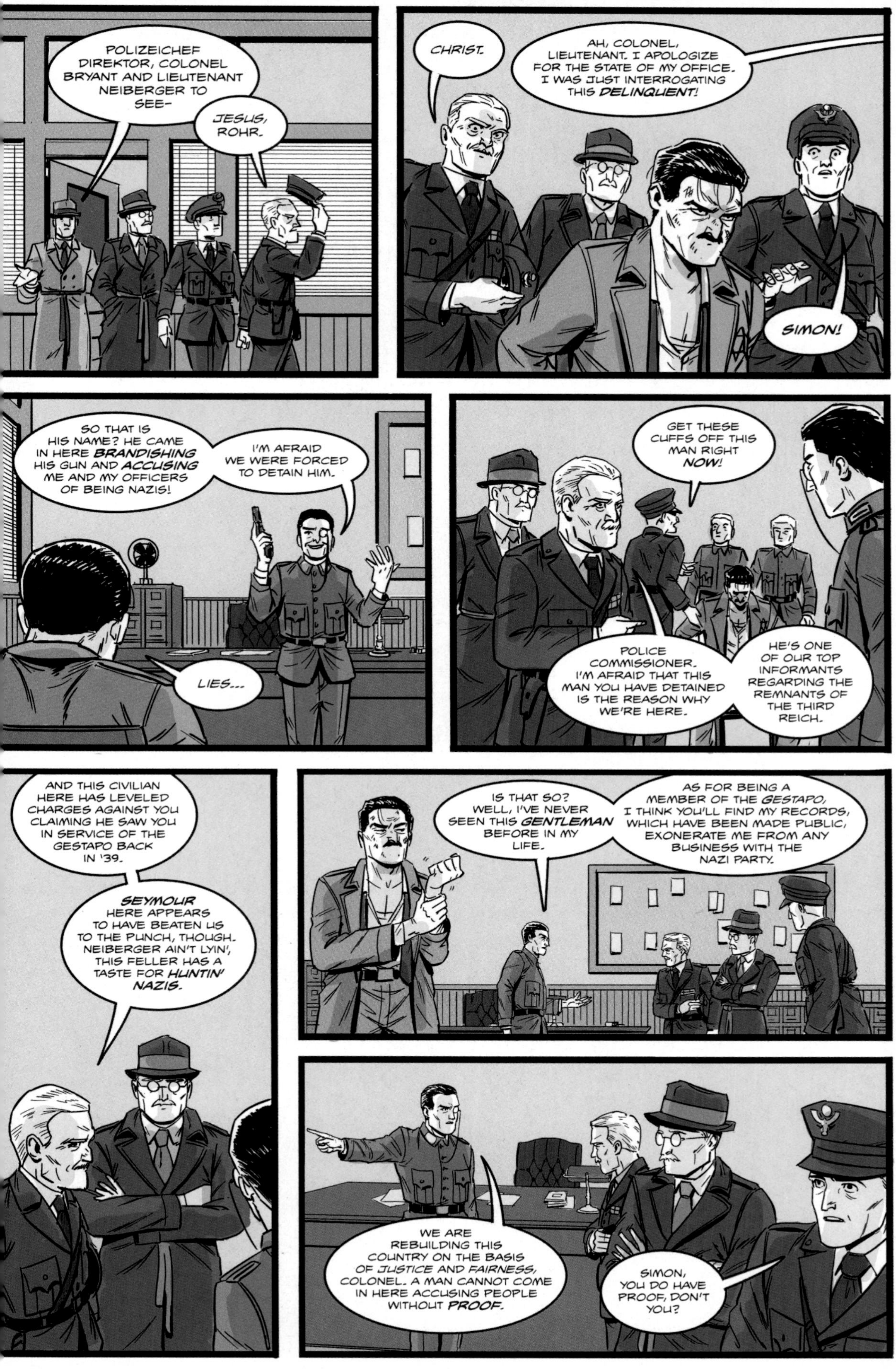
POLIZEICHEF DIREKTOR, COLONEL BRYANT AND LIEUTENANT NEIBERGER TO SEE-
JESUS, ROHR.
CHRIST.
AH, COLONEL, LIEUTENANT. I APOLOGIZE FOR THE STATE OF MY OFFICE. I WAS JUST INTERROGATING THIS DELINQUENT!
SIMON!
SO THAT IS HIS NAME? HE CAME IN HERE BRANDISHING HIS GUN AND ACCUSING ME AND MY OFFICERS OF BEING NAZIS!
I'M AFRAID WE WERE FORCED TO DETAIN HIM.
LIES...
GET THESE CUFFS OFF THIS MAN RIGHT NOW!
POLICE COMMISSIONER. I'M AFRAID THAT THIS MAN YOU HAVE DETAINED IS THE REASON WHY WE'RE HERE.
HE'S ONE OF OUR TOP INFORMANTS REGARDING THE REMNANTS OF THE THIRD REICH.
AND THIS CIVILIAN HERE HAS LEVELED CHARGES AGAINST YOU CLAIMING HE SAW YOU IN SERVICE OF THE GESTAPO BACK IN '39.
SEYMOUR HERE APPEARS TO HAVE BEATEN US TO THE PUNCH, THOUGH. NEIBERGER AIN'T LYIN', THIS FELLER HAS A TASTE FOR HUNTIN' NAZIS.
IS THAT SO? WELL, I'VE NEVER SEEN THIS GENTLEMAN BEFORE IN MY LIFE.
AS FOR BEING A MEMBER OF THE GESTAPO, I THINK YOU'LL FIND MY RECORDS, WHICH HAVE BEEN MADE PUBLIC, EXONERATE ME FROM ANY BUSINESS WITH THE NAZI PARTY.
WE ARE REBUILDING THIS COUNTRY ON THE BASIS OF JUSTICE AND FAIRNESS, COLONEL. A MAN CANNOT COME IN HERE ACCUSING PEOPLE WITHOUT PROOF.
SIMON, YOU DO HAVE PROOF, DON'T YOU?

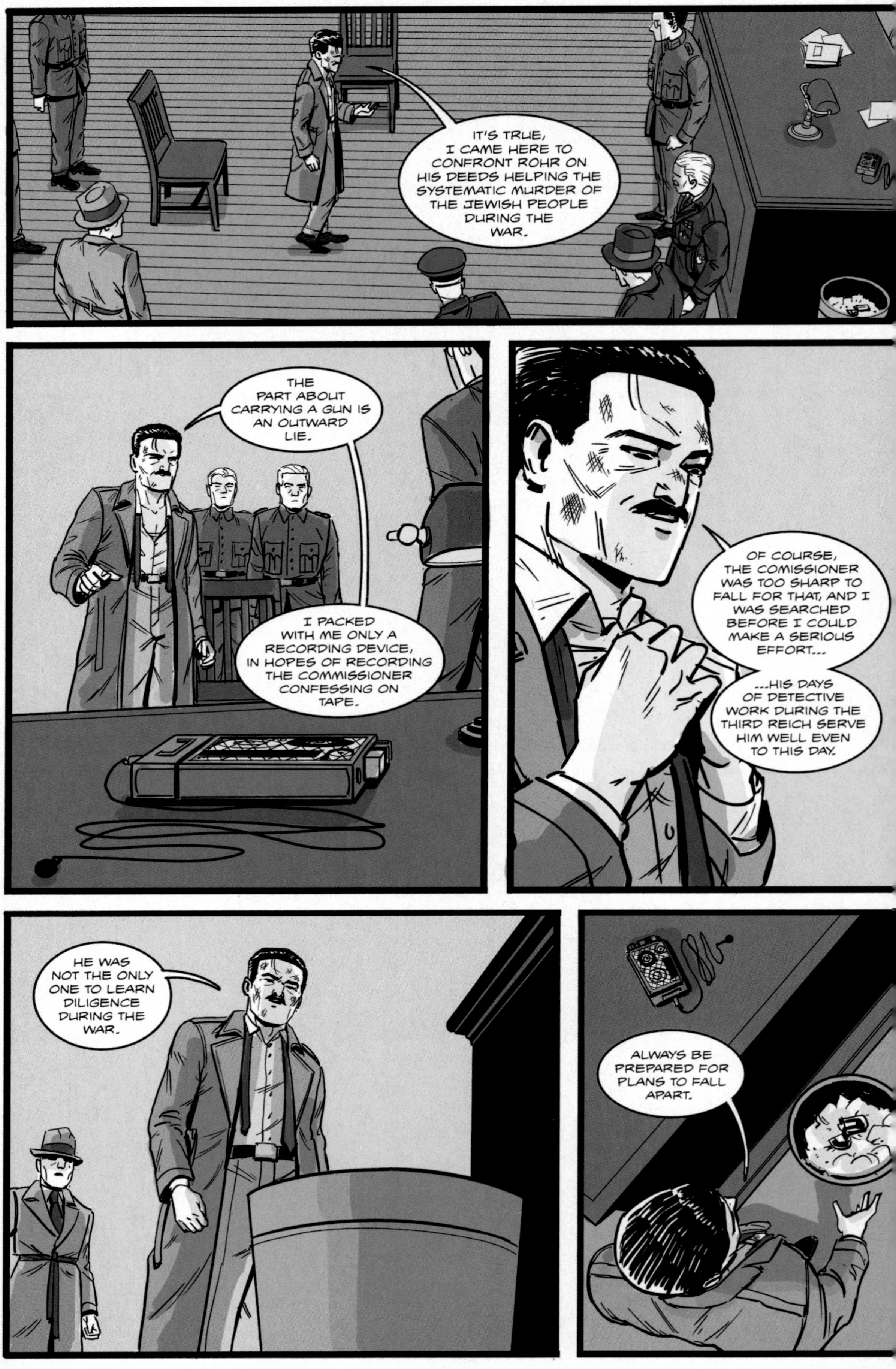
IT'S TRUE, I CAME HERE TO CONFRONT ROHR ON HIS DEEDS HELPING THE SYSTEMATIC MURDER OF THE JEWISH PEOPLE DURING THE WAR.
THE PART ABOUT CARRYING A GUN IS AN OUTWARD LIE.
I PACKED WITH ME ONLY A RECORDING DEVICE, IN HOPES OF RECORDING THE COMMISSIONER CONFESSING ON TAPE.
OF COURSE, THE COMISSIONER WAS TOO SHARP TO FALL FOR THAT, AND I WAS SEARCHED BEFORE I COULD MAKE A SERIOUS EFFORT...
...HIS DAYS OF DETECTIVE WORK DURING THE THIRD REICH SERVE HIM WELL EVEN TO THIS DAY.
HE WAS NOT THE ONLY ONE TO LEARN DILIGENCE DURING THE WAR.
ALWAYS BE PREPARED FOR PLANS TO FALL APART.

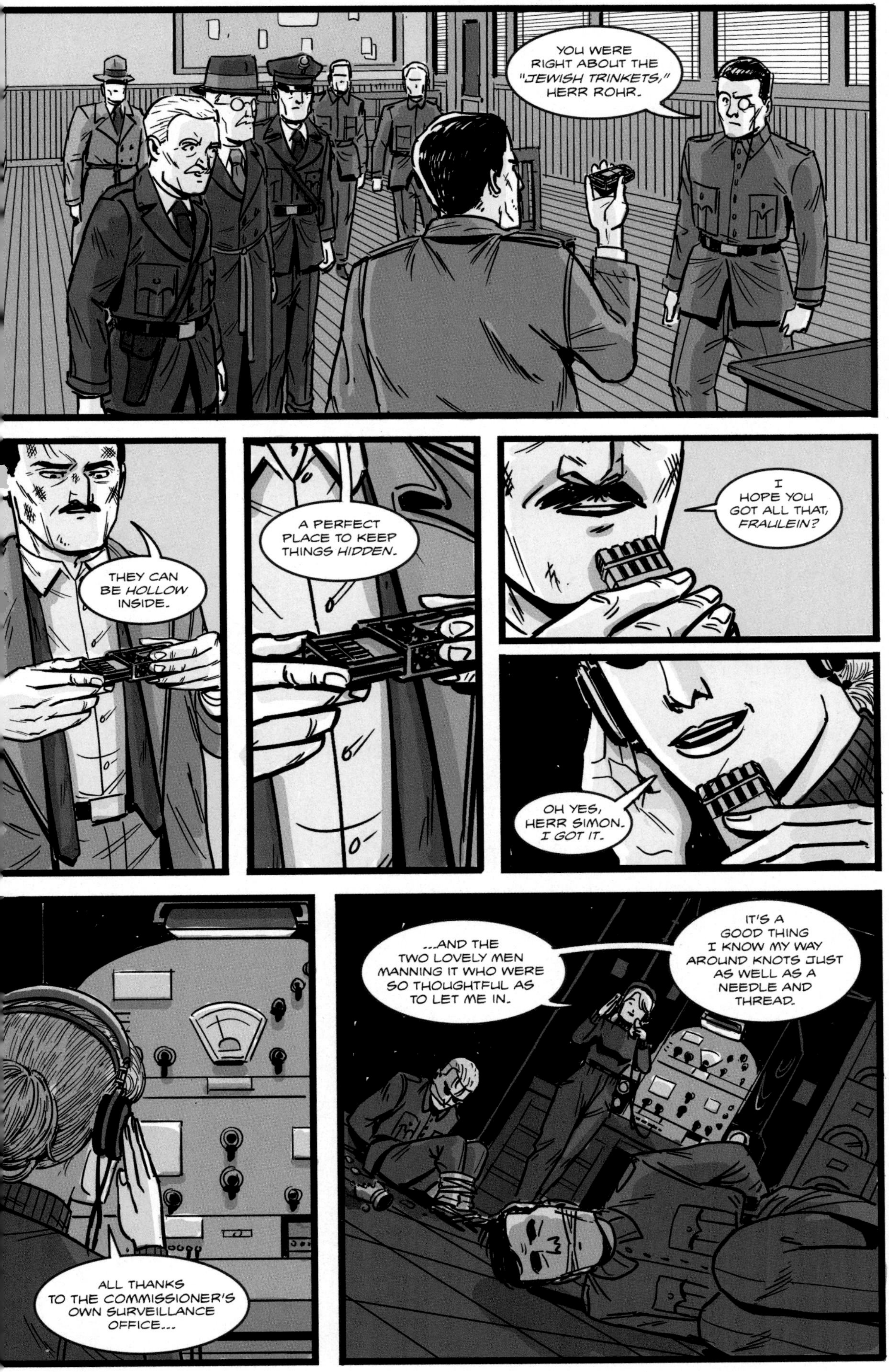
YOU WERE RIGHT ABOUT THE "JEWISH TRINKETS," HERR ROHR.
THEY CAN BE HOLLOW INSIDE.
A PERFECT PLACE TO KEEP THINGS HIDDEN.
I HOPE YOU GOT ALL THAT, FRAULEIN?
OH YES, HERR SIMON. I GOT IT.
ALL THANKS TO THE COMMISSIONER'S OWN SURVEILLANCE OFFICE...
...AND THE TWO LOVELY MEN MANNING IT WHO WERE SO THOUGHTFUL AS TO LET ME IN.
IT'S A GOOD THING I KNOW MY WAY AROUND KNOTS JUST AS WELL AS A NEEDLE AND THREAD.

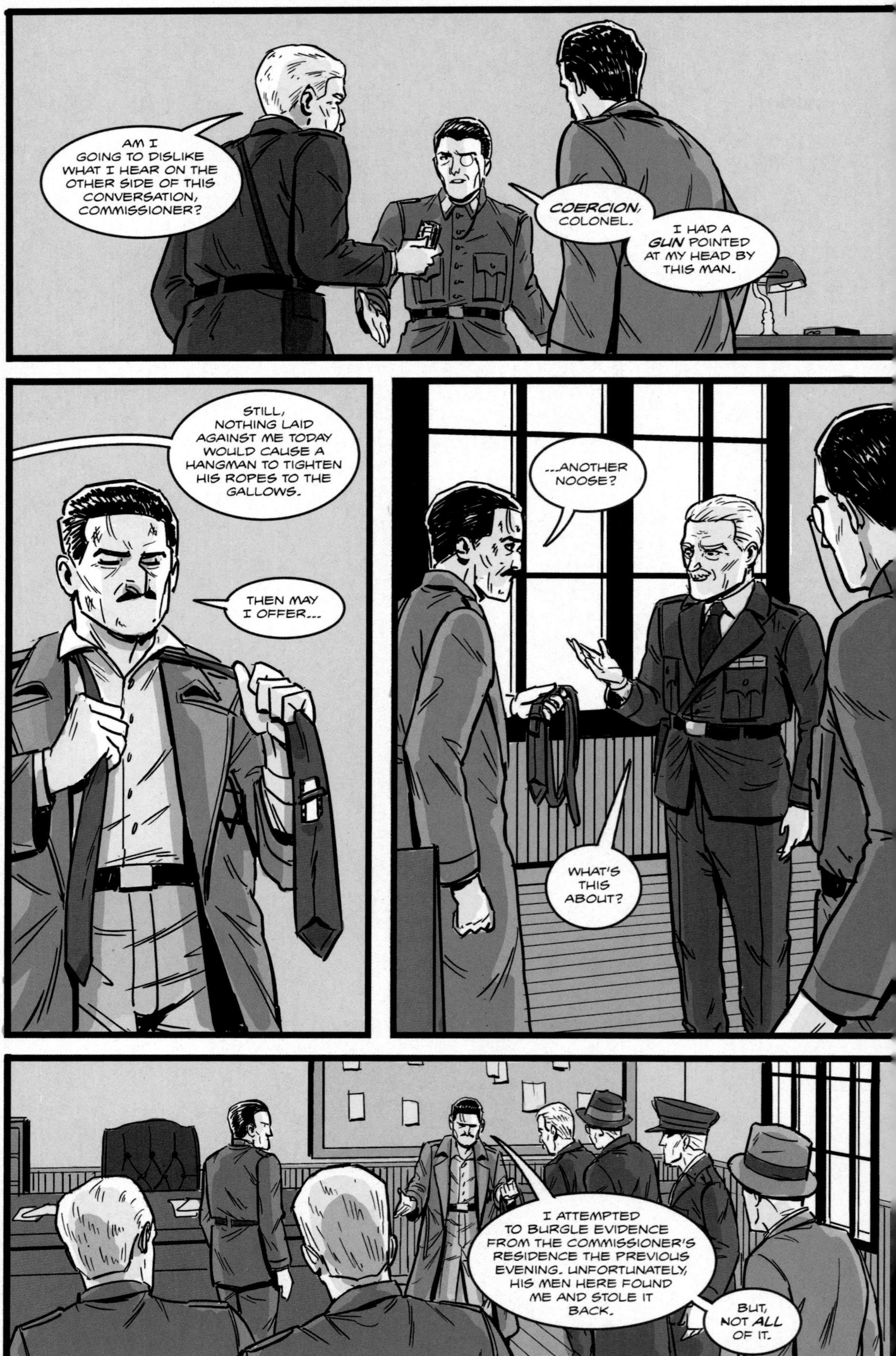
AM I GOING TO DISLIKE WHAT I HEAR ON THE OTHER SIDE OF THIS CONVERSATION, COMMISSIONER?
COERCION, COLONEL.
I HAD A GUN POINTED AT MY HEAD BY THIS MAN.
STILL, NOTHING LAID AGAINST ME TODAY WOULD CAUSE A HANGMAN TO TIGHTEN HIS ROPES TO THE GALLOWS.
THEN MAY I OFFER...
...ANOTHER NOOSE?
WHAT'S THIS ABOUT?
I ATTEMPTED TO BURGLE EVIDENCE FROM THE COMMISSIONER'S RESIDENCE THE PREVIOUS EVENING. UNFORTUNATELY, HIS MEN HERE FOUND ME AND STOLE IT BACK.
BUT, NOT ALL OF IT.

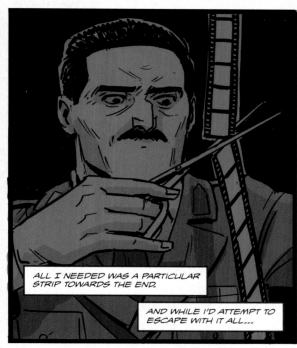

I KNEW IF I WAS CAUGHT I'D LOSE **EVERYTHING**. THERE WAS NO REASON TO LEAVE EVERYTHING TO CHANCE.

ALL I NEEDED WAS A PARTICULAR STRIP TOWARDS THE END.

AND WHILE I'D ATTEMPT TO ESCAPE WITH IT ALL...

I'D SUCCEED IN ESCAPING WITH SOME, WHICH I HID HERE.

I BELIEVE NOW, YOU HAVE ENOUGH.

HOLY SHIT. WELL, IF SIMON SAYS...

ROHR, I'M PLACING YOU AND YOUR MEN UNDER ARREST.

COLONEL, I THINK YOU WILL FIND THAT WHILE YOU OUTRANK ME...

...WE OUTGUN YOU.

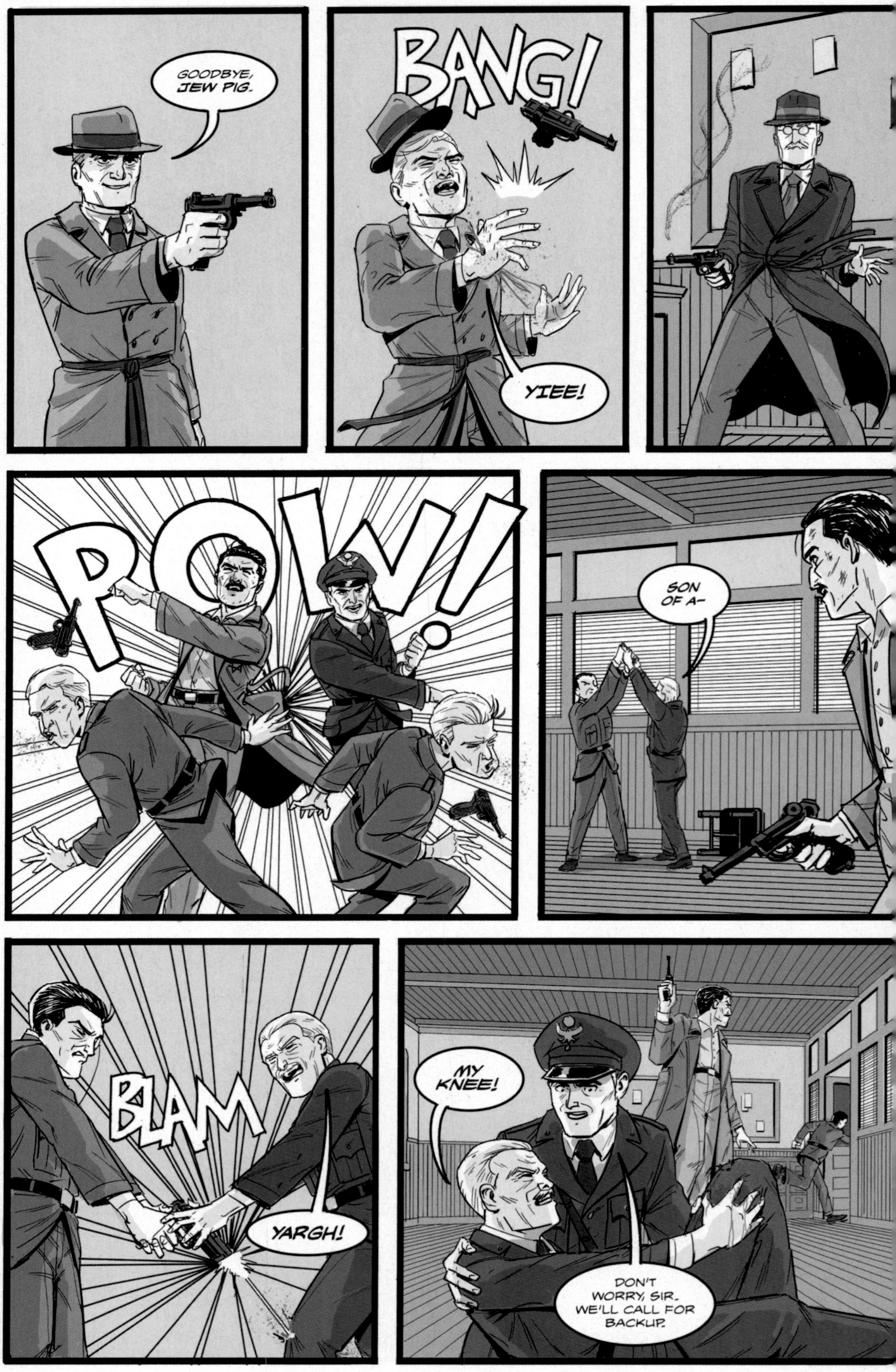
GOODBYE, JEW PIG.
BANG!
YIEE!
POW!
SON OF A—
BLAM
YARGH!
MY KNEE!
DON'T WORRY, SIR. WE'LL CALL FOR BACKUP.

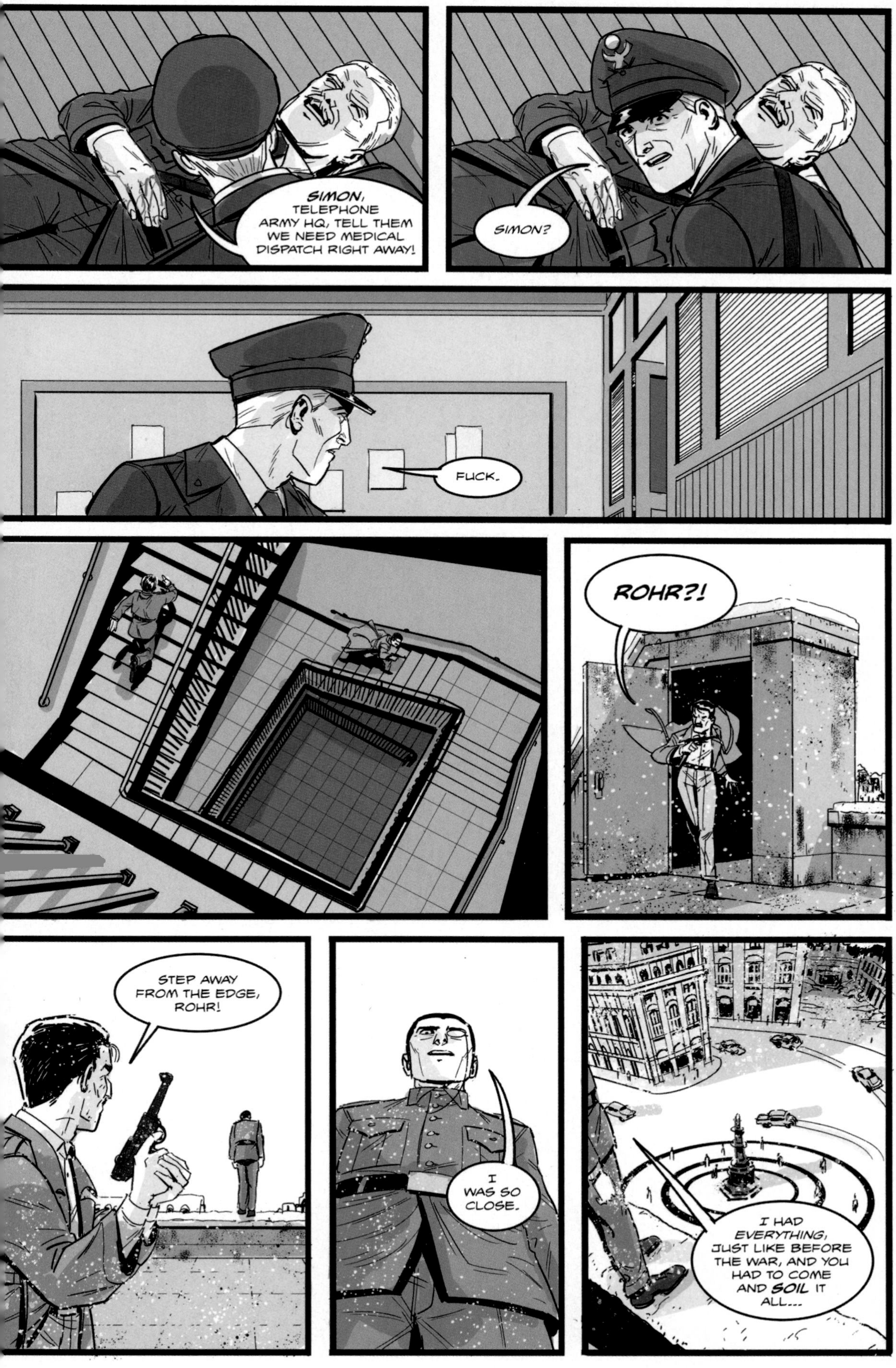
SIMON, TELEPHONE ARMY HQ, TELL THEM WE NEED MEDICAL DISPATCH RIGHT AWAY!
SIMON?
FUCK.
ROHR?!
STEP AWAY FROM THE EDGE, ROHR!
I WAS SO CLOSE.
I HAD EVERYTHING, JUST LIKE BEFORE THE WAR, AND YOU HAD TO COME AND SOIL IT ALL...

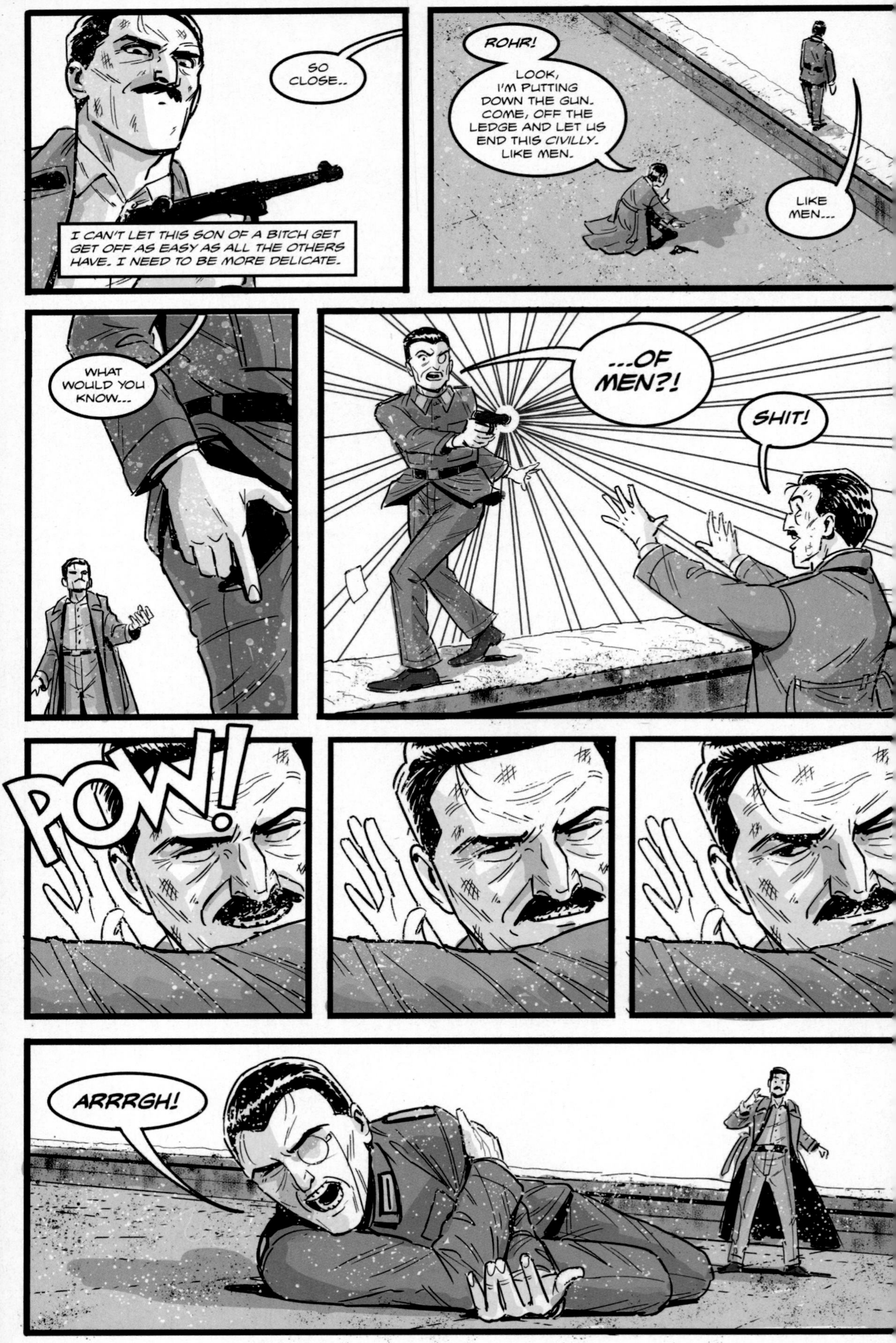
SO CLOSE..
I CAN'T LET THIS SON OF A BITCH GET GET OFF AS EASY AS ALL THE OTHERS HAVE. I NEED TO BE MORE DELICATE.
ROHR!
LOOK, I'M PUTTING DOWN THE GUN. COME, OFF THE LEDGE AND LET US END THIS CIVILLY. LIKE MEN.
LIKE MEN...
WHAT WOULD YOU KNOW...
...OF MEN?!
SHIT!
POW!!
ARRRGH!

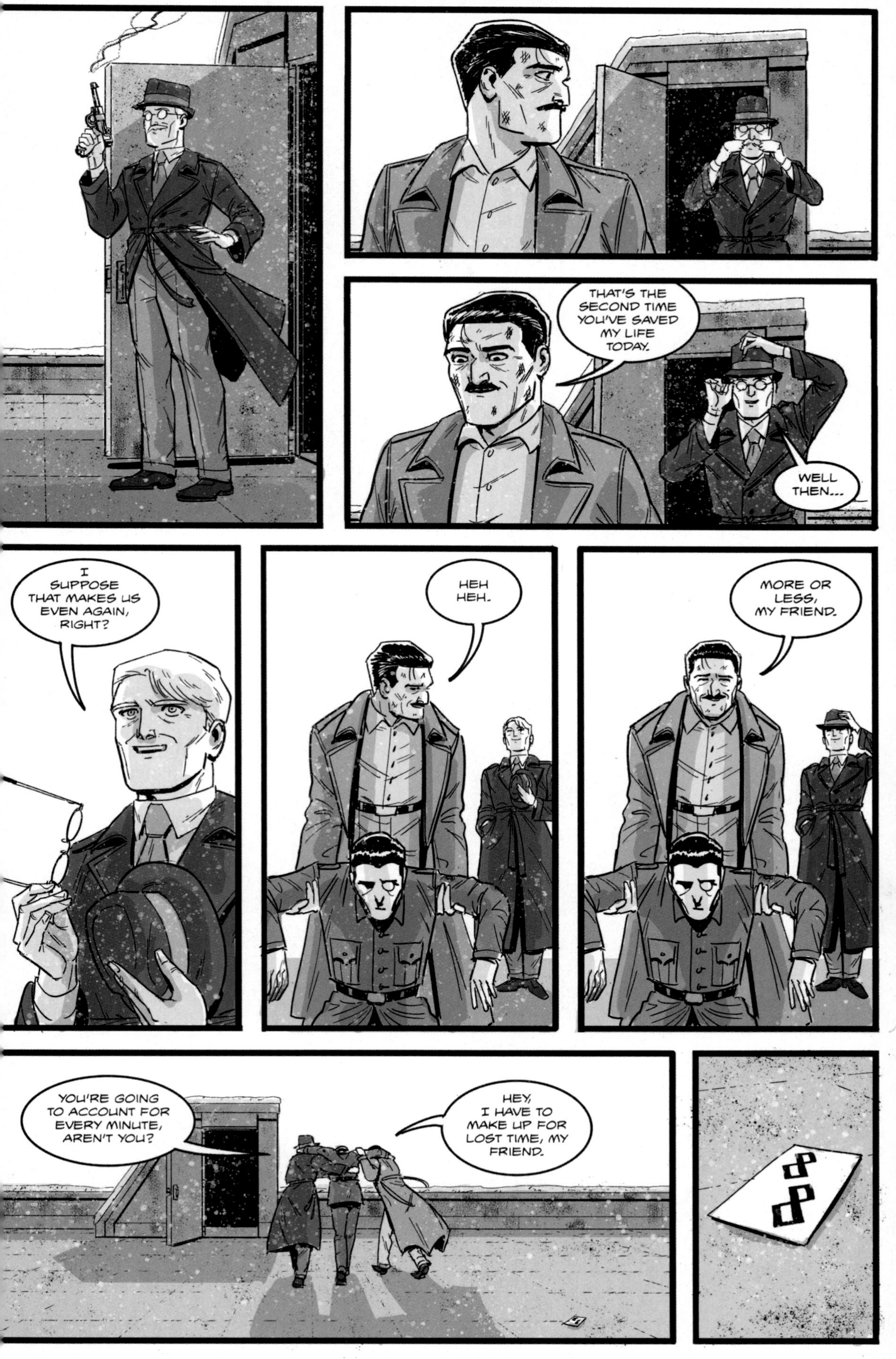
THAT'S THE SECOND TIME YOU'VE SAVED MY LIFE TODAY.
WELL THEN...
I SUPPOSE THAT MAKES US EVEN AGAIN, RIGHT?
HEH HEH.
MORE OR LESS, MY FRIEND.
YOU'RE GOING TO ACCOUNT FOR EVERY MINUTE, AREN'T YOU?
HEY, I HAVE TO MAKE UP FOR LOST TIME, MY FRIEND.

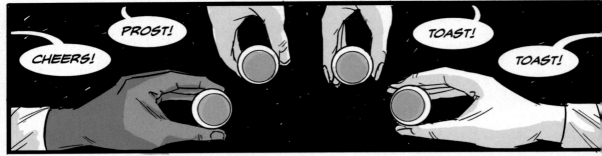

CHEERS!

PROST!

TOAST!

TOAST!

NOT HALF FUCKING BAD!

HACK *HACK*

EEHK!

The New York Gazette

NAZI HUNTER'S BRANDED JUSTICE
SURVIVOR TAKES DOWN CORRUPT POLICE COMMISSIONER

THE DRINK IS GOOD, TOO.

ANOTHER! ANOTHER!

YES, AND THIS TIME, TO YOU ALL.

WITHOUT EACH OF YOUR INDIVIDUAL CONTRIBUTIONS, WE COULD NOT HAVE SEEN THIS MISSION THROUGH. I CAN'T THANK YOU ALL ENOUGH.

IT IS ONLY A BEGINNING, THOUGH.

PROOF THAT WE CAN TAKE UP THE TASK THAT OTHERS HAVE RELINQUISHED.

LET US NEVER FORGET.

CLINK!

CLINK!

CLINK!

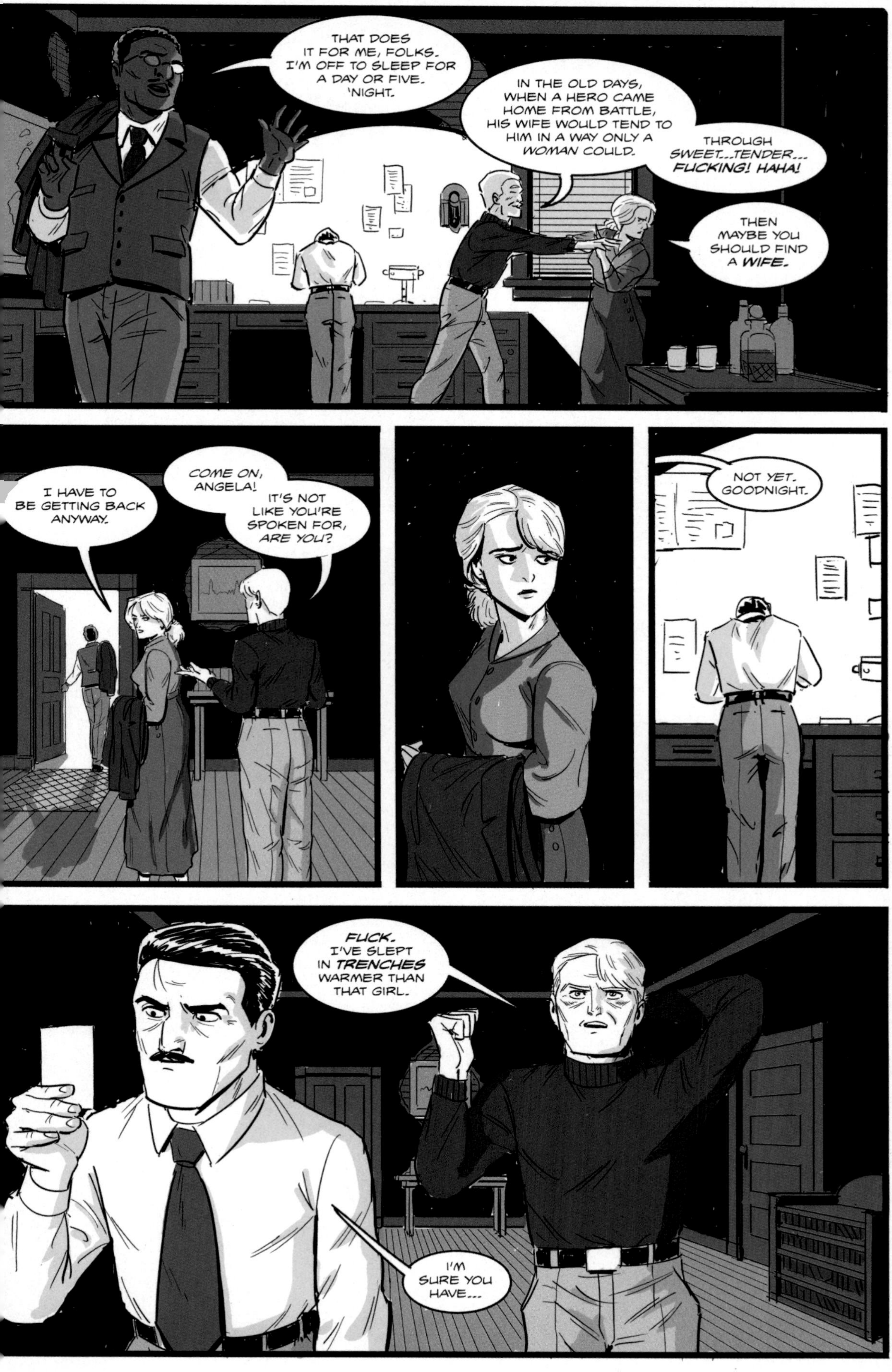
THAT DOES IT FOR ME, FOLKS. I'M OFF TO SLEEP FOR A DAY OR FIVE. 'NIGHT.
IN THE OLD DAYS, WHEN A HERO CAME HOME FROM BATTLE, HIS WIFE WOULD TEND TO HIM IN A WAY ONLY A WOMAN COULD.
THROUGH SWEET...TENDER... FUCKING! HAHA!
THEN MAYBE YOU SHOULD FIND A WIFE.
I HAVE TO BE GETTING BACK ANYWAY.
COME ON, ANGELA!
IT'S NOT LIKE YOU'RE SPOKEN FOR, ARE YOU?
NOT YET. GOODNIGHT.
FUCK. I'VE SLEPT IN TRENCHES WARMER THAN THAT GIRL.
I'M SURE YOU HAVE...

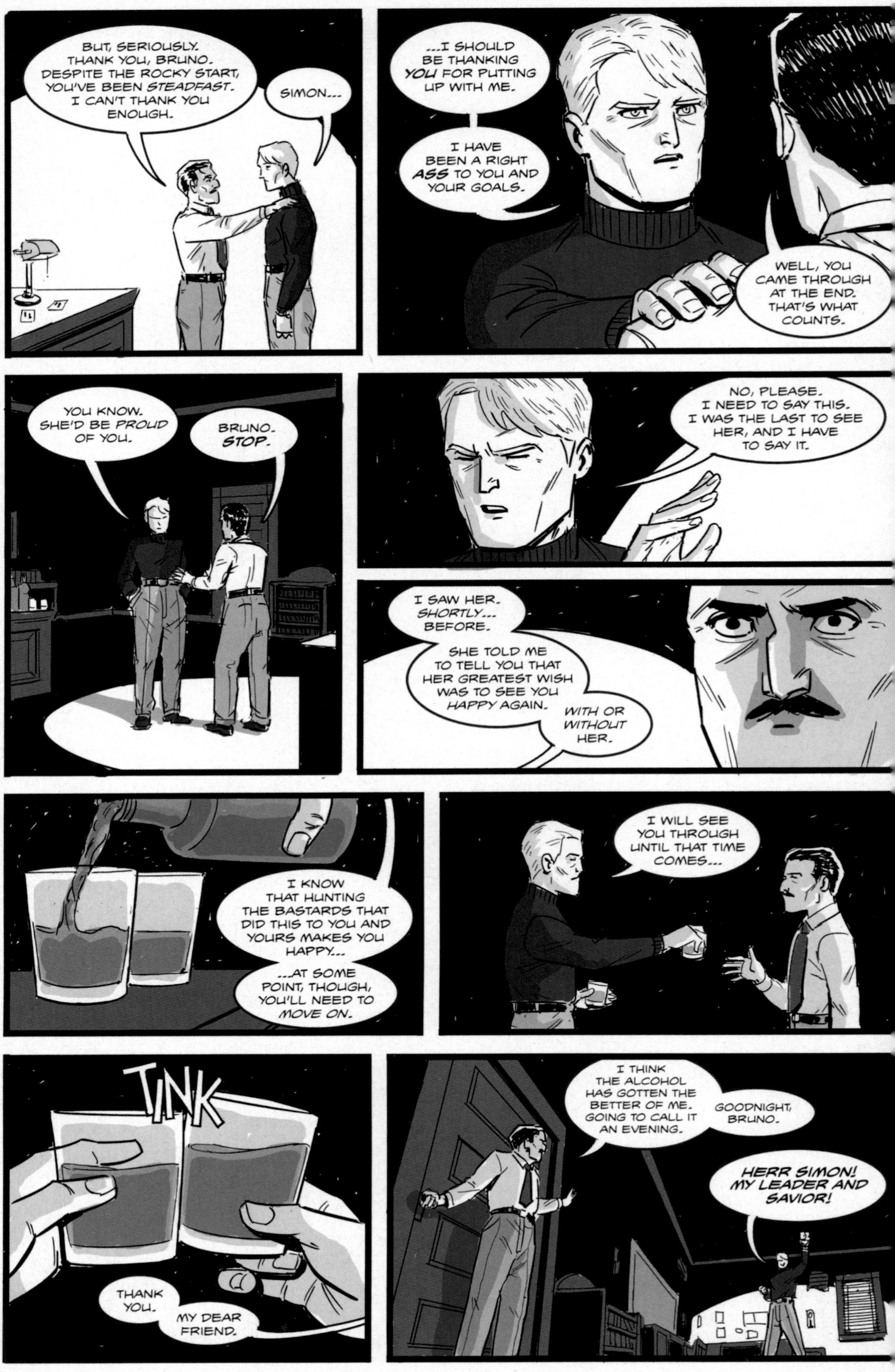
BUT, SERIOUSLY. THANK YOU, BRUNO. DESPITE THE ROCKY START, YOU'VE BEEN STEADFAST. I CAN'T THANK YOU ENOUGH.
SIMON...
...I SHOULD BE THANKING YOU FOR PUTTING UP WITH ME.
I HAVE BEEN A RIGHT ASS TO YOU AND YOUR GOALS.
WELL, YOU CAME THROUGH AT THE END. THAT'S WHAT COUNTS.
YOU KNOW. SHE'D BE PROUD OF YOU.
BRUNO. STOP.
NO, PLEASE. I NEED TO SAY THIS. I WAS THE LAST TO SEE HER, AND I HAVE TO SAY IT.
I SAW HER. SHORTLY... BEFORE.
SHE TOLD ME TO TELL YOU THAT HER GREATEST WISH WAS TO SEE YOU HAPPY AGAIN.
WITH OR WITHOUT HER.
I KNOW THAT HUNTING THE BASTARDS THAT DID THIS TO YOU AND YOURS MAKES YOU HAPPY...
...AT SOME POINT, THOUGH, YOU'LL NEED TO MOVE ON.
I WILL SEE YOU THROUGH UNTIL THAT TIME COMES...
TINK
THANK YOU.
MY DEAR FRIEND.
I THINK THE ALCOHOL HAS GOTTEN THE BETTER OF ME. GOING TO CALL IT AN EVENING.
GOODNIGHT, BRUNO.
HERR SIMON! MY LEADER AND SAVIOR!

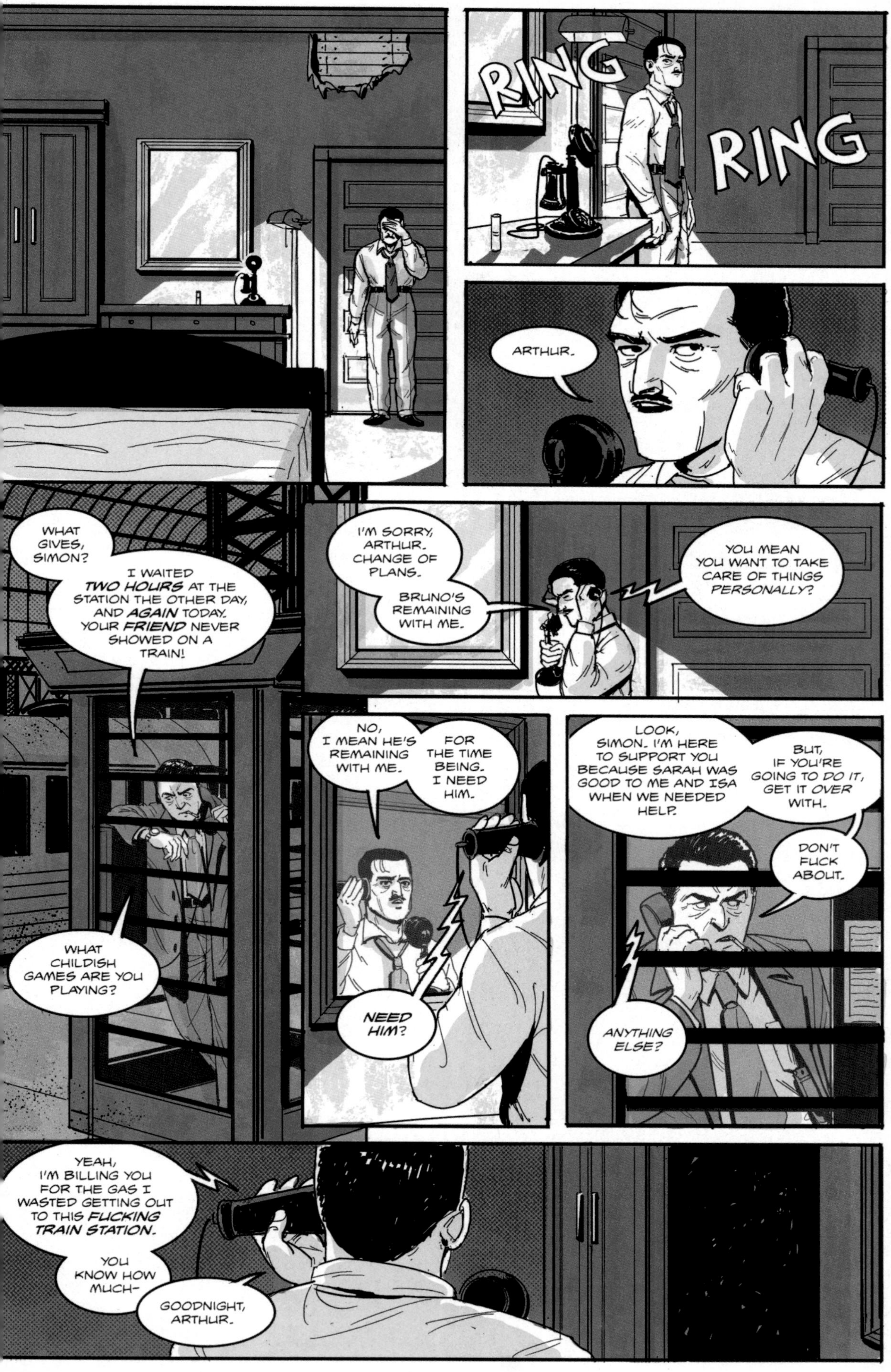
RING
RING
ARTHUR.
WHAT GIVES, SIMON?
I WAITED **TWO HOURS** AT THE STATION THE OTHER DAY, AND **AGAIN** TODAY. YOUR **FRIEND** NEVER SHOWED ON A TRAIN!
WHAT CHILDISH GAMES ARE YOU PLAYING?
I'M SORRY, ARTHUR. CHANGE OF PLANS.
BRUNO'S REMAINING WITH ME.
YOU MEAN YOU WANT TO TAKE CARE OF THINGS *PERSONALLY*?
NO, I MEAN HE'S REMAINING WITH ME.
FOR THE TIME BEING. I NEED HIM.
NEED HIM?
LOOK, SIMON. I'M HERE TO SUPPORT YOU BECAUSE SARAH WAS GOOD TO ME AND ISA WHEN WE NEEDED HELP.
BUT, IF YOU'RE GOING TO *DO IT*, GET IT *OVER* WITH.
DON'T FUCK ABOUT.
ANYTHING ELSE?
YEAH, I'M BILLING YOU FOR THE GAS I WASTED GETTING OUT TO THIS ***FUCKING TRAIN STATION.***
YOU KNOW HOW MUCH-
GOODNIGHT, ARTHUR.

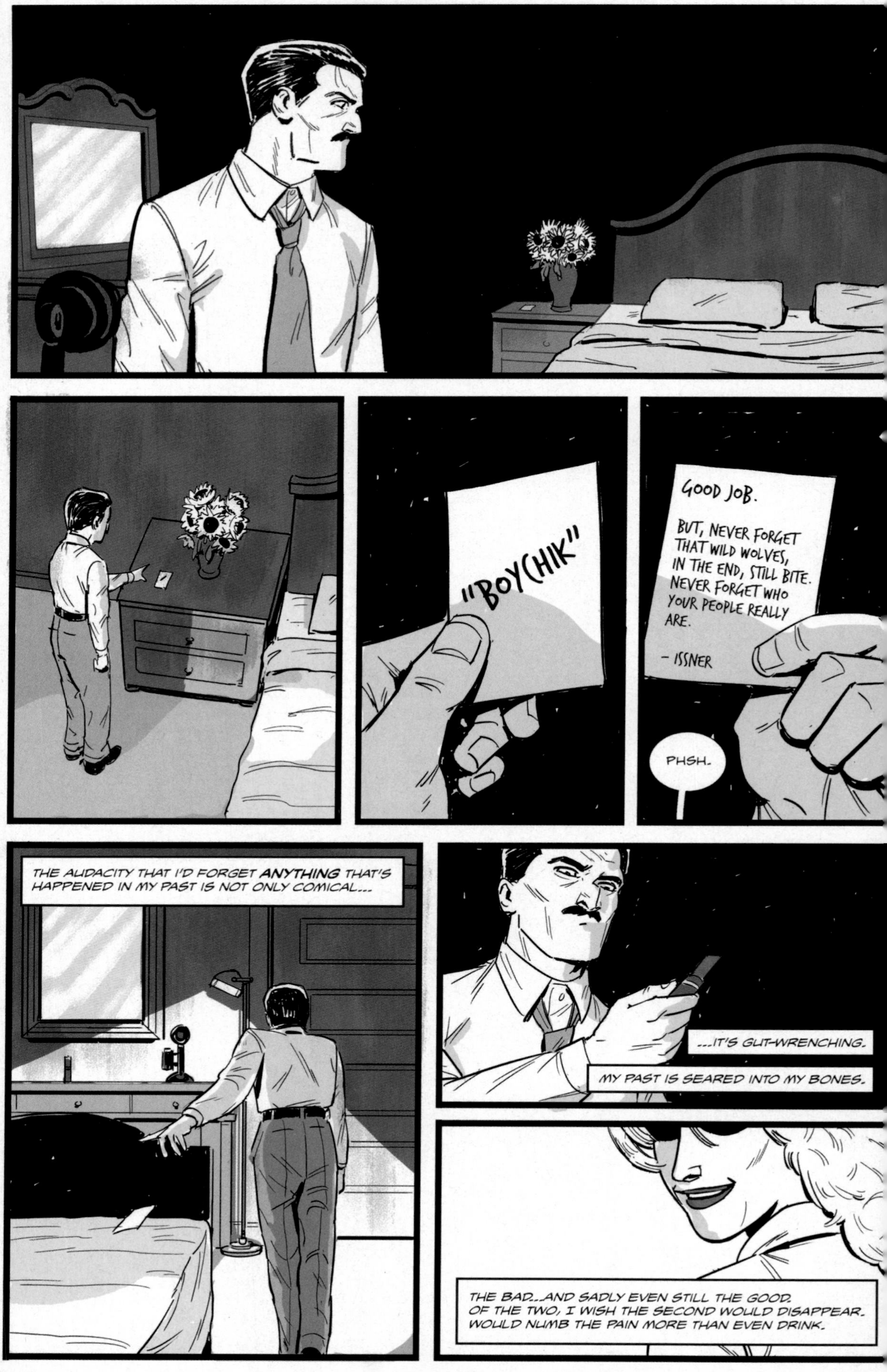
"BOYCHIK"
GOOD JOB.
BUT, NEVER FORGET THAT WILD WOLVES, IN THE END, STILL BITE. NEVER FORGET WHO YOUR PEOPLE REALLY ARE.
- ISSNER
PHSH.
THE AUDACITY THAT I'D FORGET ANYTHING THAT'S HAPPENED IN MY PAST IS NOT ONLY COMICAL...
...IT'S GUT-WRENCHING.
MY PAST IS SEARED INTO MY BONES.
THE BAD...AND SADLY EVEN STILL THE GOOD. OF THE TWO, I WISH THE SECOND WOULD DISAPPEAR. WOULD NUMB THE PAIN MORE THAN EVEN DRINK.

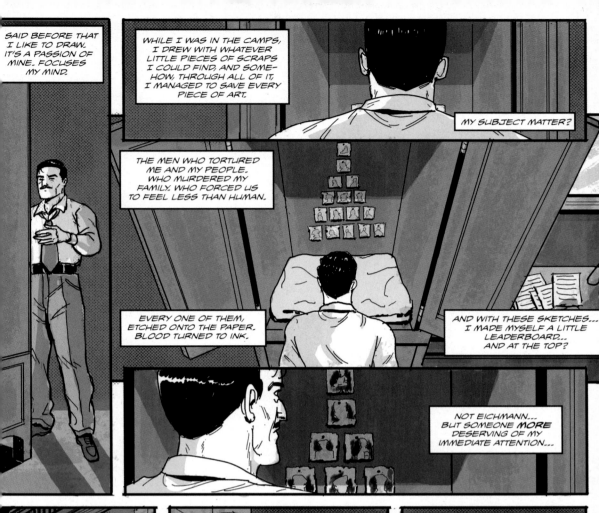

SAID BEFORE THAT I LIKE TO DRAW. IT'S A PASSION OF MINE. FOCUSES MY MIND.

WHILE I WAS IN THE CAMPS, I DREW WITH WHATEVER LITTLE PIECES OF SCRAPS I COULD FIND, AND SOME-HOW, THROUGH ALL OF IT, I MANAGED TO SAVE EVERY PIECE OF ART.

MY SUBJECT MATTER?

THE MEN WHO TORTURED ME AND MY PEOPLE. WHO MURDERED MY FAMILY. WHO FORCED US TO FEEL LESS THAN HUMAN.

EVERY ONE OF THEM, ETCHED ONTO THE PAPER. BLOOD TURNED TO INK.

AND WITH THESE SKETCHES... I MADE MYSELF A LITTLE LEADERBOARD... AND AT THE TOP?

NOT EICHMANN... BUT SOMEONE *MORE* DESERVING OF MY IMMEDIATE ATTENTION....

THIS IS CRAZY, COOPER.

AIN'T NEVER GONNA FIND THIS GUY.

PROBABLY HALFWAY TO *TIMBUKTU.*

YEAH. PROBABLY RIGHT.

TELL YA WHAT, LET'S HIT THAT LITTLE KRAUT BAR DOWN A WAYS.

HEARD THEY GOT SOME OF THAT VAT 69 THE CAPTAIN'S ALWAYS TRYIN' TO GET HIS HANDS ON.

HAH!

IF THEY DO, WE BETTER SMUGGLE A COUPLE BACK TO THE BARRACKS TO KEEP FROM GETTING SLAPPED FOR BOOZIN' AFTER HOURS.

I WON'T ARGUE WITH THAT IDEA!

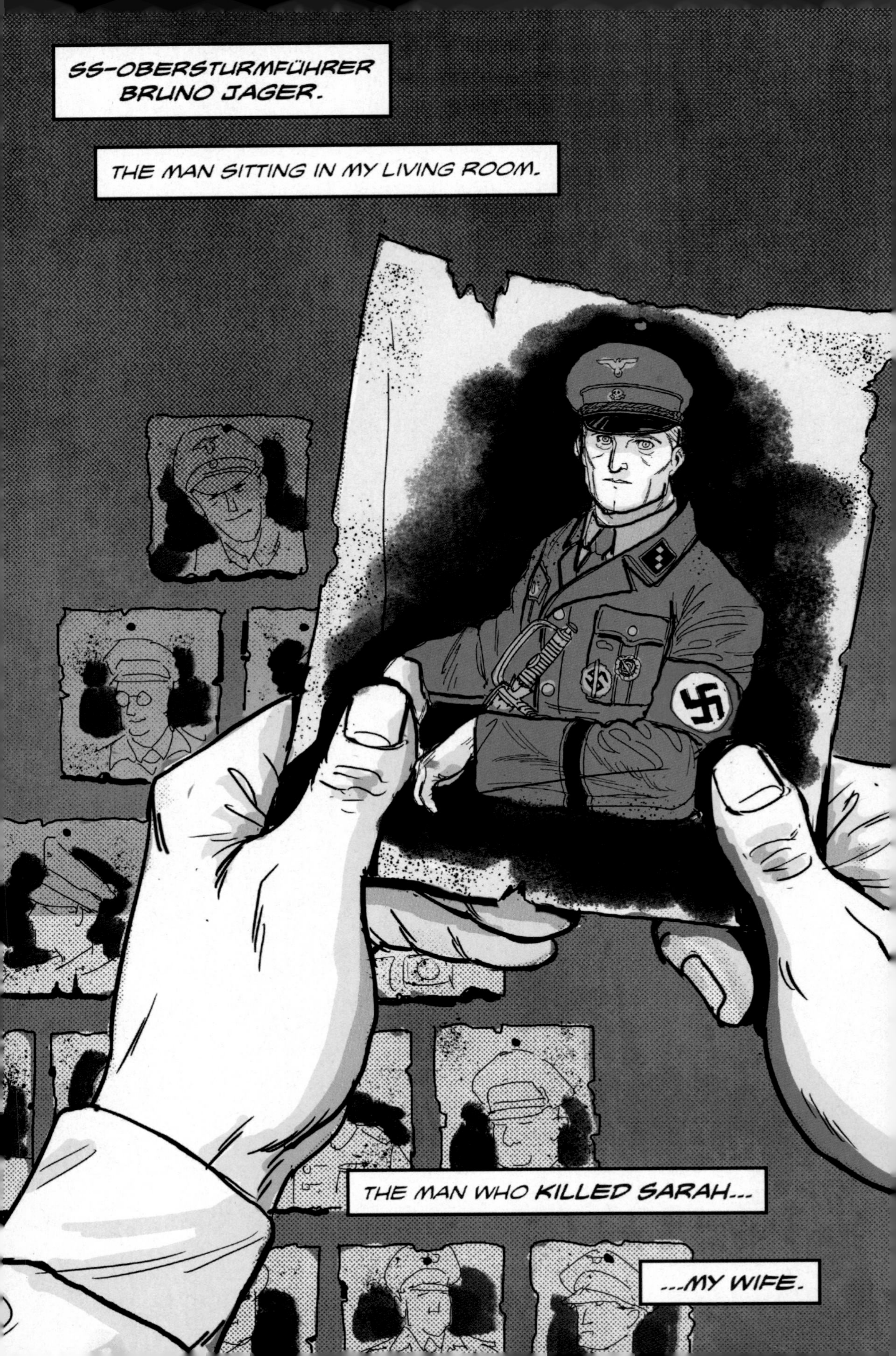
SS-OBERSTURMFÜHRER BRUNO JAGER.
THE MAN SITTING IN MY LIVING ROOM.
THE MAN WHO **KILLED SARAH**...
...MY WIFE.

"FOR EVIL TO FLOURISH, IT ONLY REQUIRES GOOD MEN TO DO NOTHING..."

– SIMON WIESENTHAL

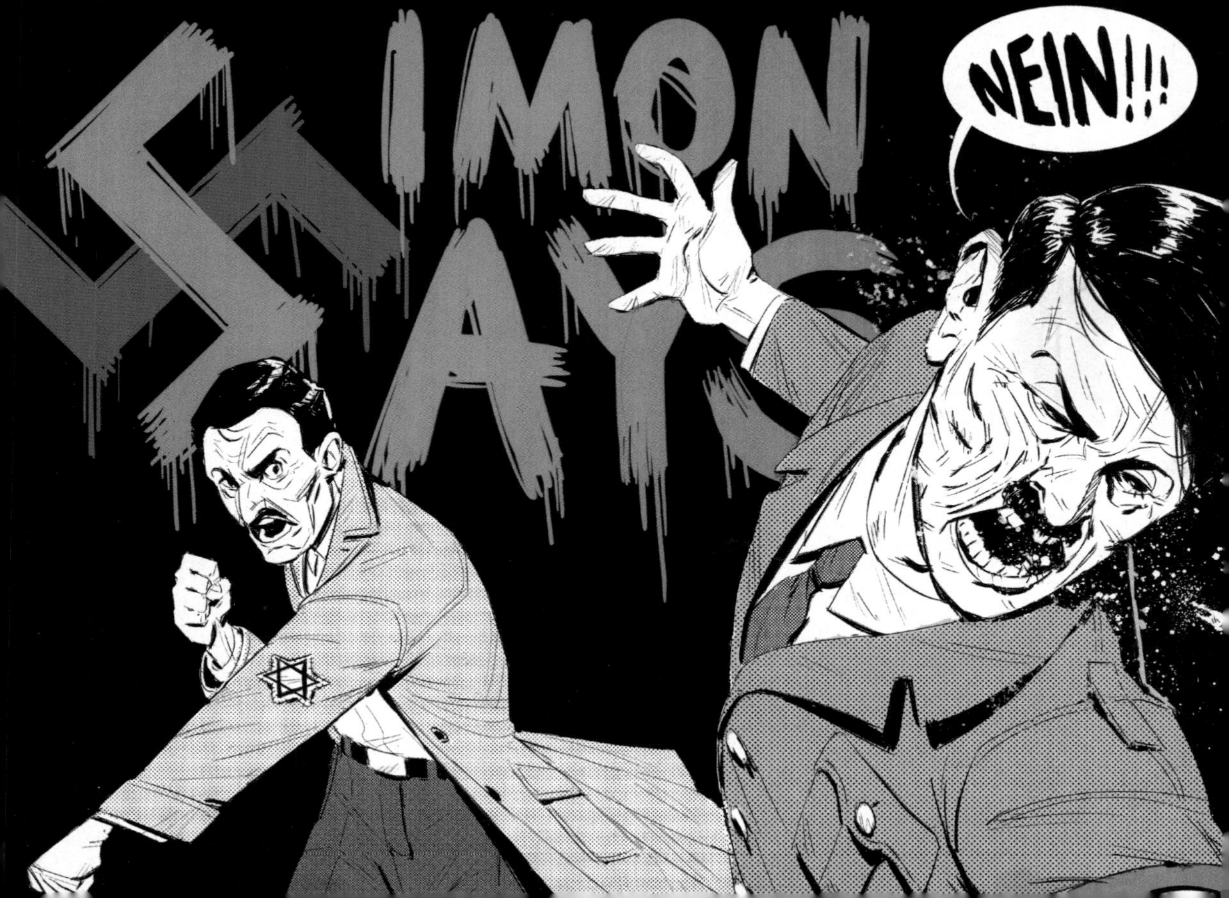
IMON
AYS
NEIN!!!

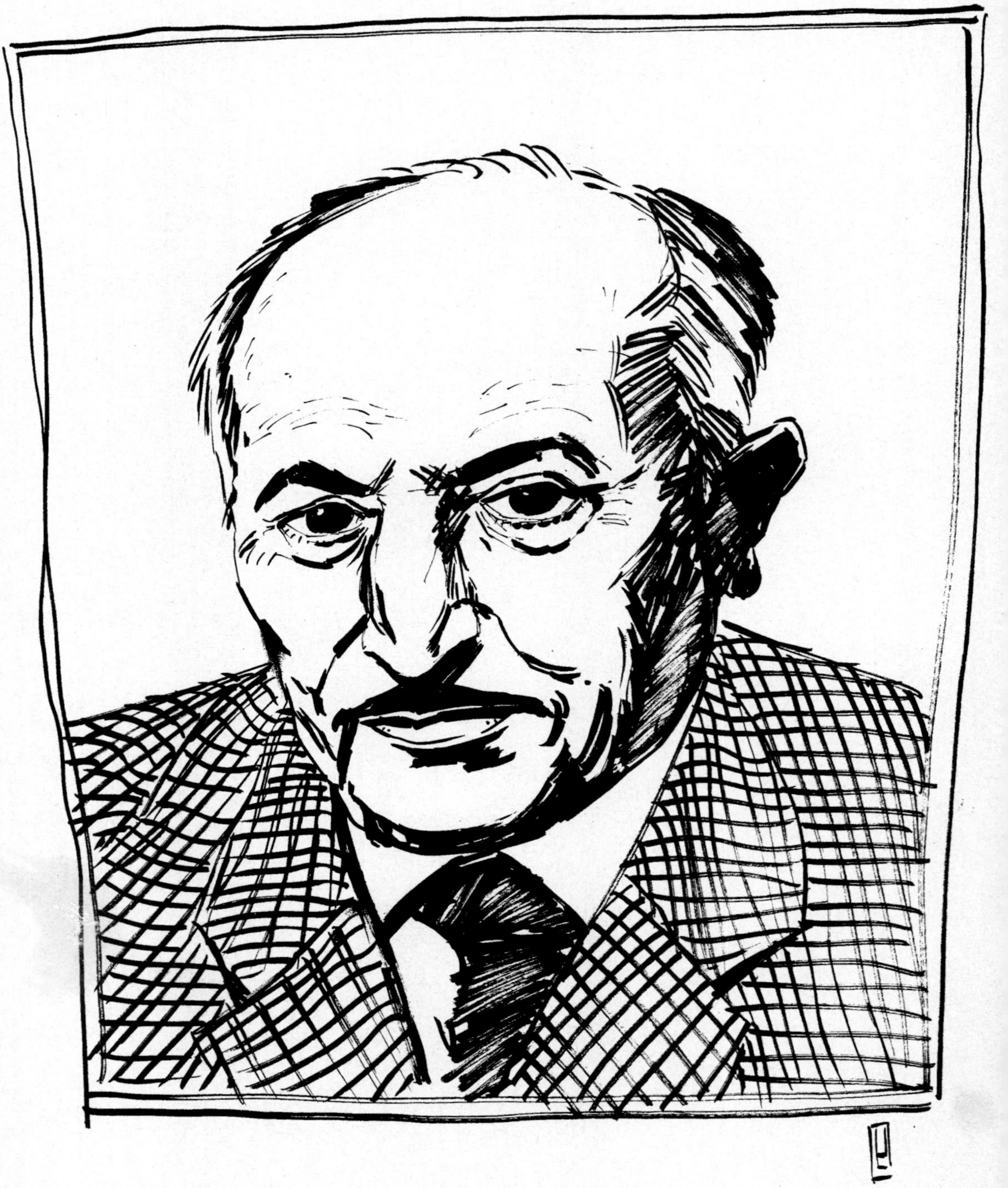

ORIGINAL PITCH PAGES 2015

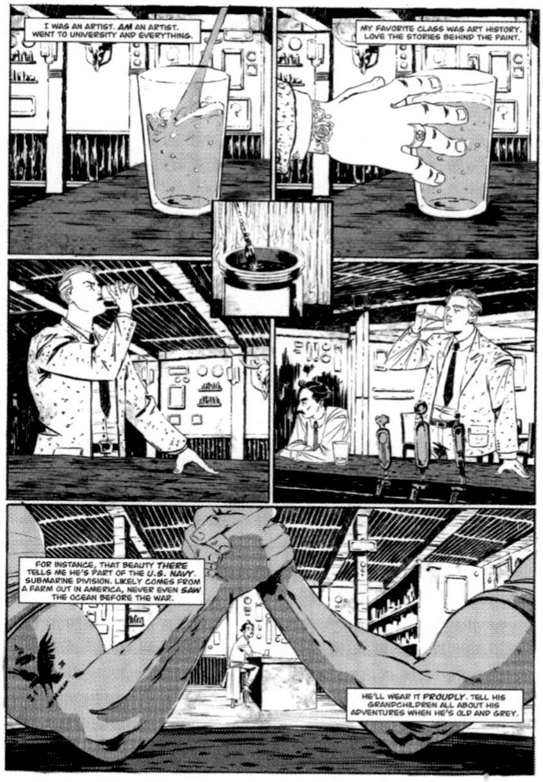
I WAS AN ARTIST. AM AN ARTIST. WENT TO UNIVERSITY AND EVERYTHING.
MY FAVORITE CLASS WAS ART HISTORY. LOVE THE STORIES BEHIND THE PAINT.
FOR INSTANCE, THAT BEAUTY THERE TELLS ME HE'S PART OF THE U.S. NAVY. SUBMARINE DIVISION. LIKELY COMES FROM A FARM OUT IN AMERICA, NEVER EVEN SAW THE OCEAN BEFORE THE WAR.
HE'LL WEAR IT PROUDLY. TELL HIS GRANDCHILDREN ALL ABOUT HIS ADVENTURES WHEN HE'S OLD AND GREY.

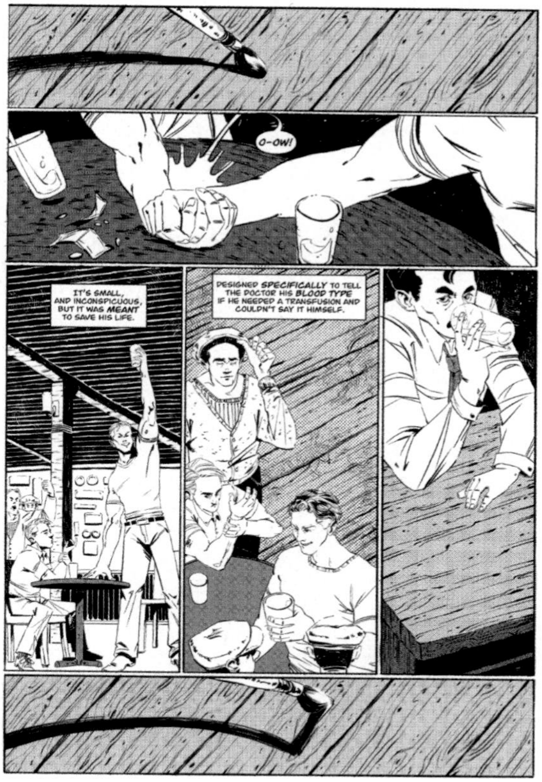
O-OW!
IT'S SMALL, AND INCONSPICUOUS, BUT IT WAS MEANT TO SAVE HIS LIFE.
DESIGNED SPECIFICALLY TO TELL THE DOCTOR HIS BLOOD TYPE IF HE NEEDED A TRANSFUSION AND COULDN'T SAY IT HIMSELF.

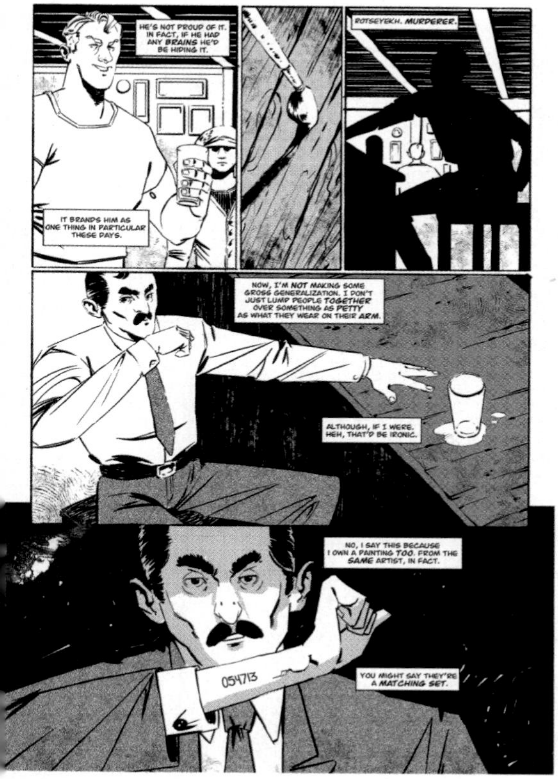
HE'S NOT PROUD OF IT. IN FACT, IF HE HAD ANY BRAINS HE'D BE HIDING IT.
IT BRANDS HIM AS ONE THING IN PARTICULAR THESE DAYS.
ROTSEYECH. MURDERER.
NOW, I'M NOT MAKING SOME GROSS GENERALIZATION. I DON'T JUST LUMP PEOPLE TOGETHER OVER SOMETHING AS PETTY AS WHAT THEY WEAR ON THEIR ARM.
ALTHOUGH, IF I WERE. HEH, THAT'D BE IRONIC.
NO, I SAY THIS BECAUSE I OWN A PAINTING TOO. FROM THE SAME ARTIST, IN FACT.
054713
YOU MIGHT SAY THEY'RE A MATCHING SET.

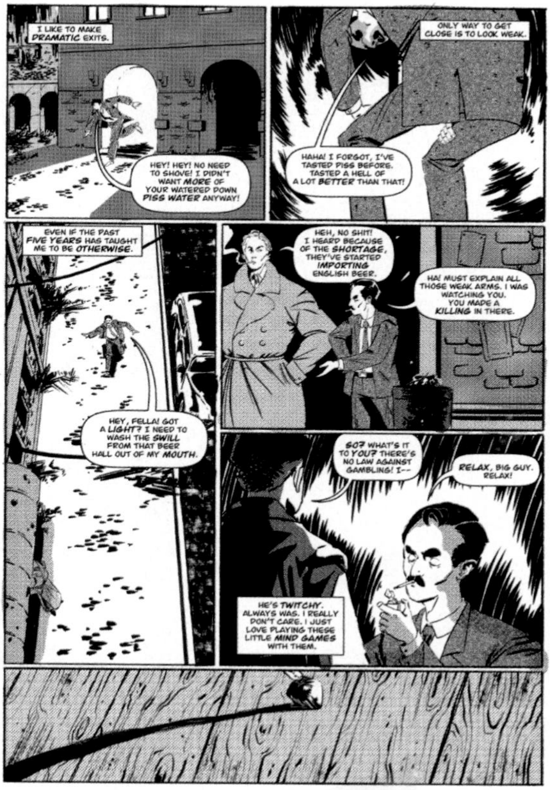
I LIKE TO MAKE DRAMATIC EXITS.
HEY! HEY! NO NEED TO SHOVE! I DIDN'T WANT MORE OF YOUR WATERED DOWN PISS WATER ANYWAY!
ONLY WAY TO GET CLOSE IS TO LOOK WEAK.
HAHA! I FORGOT, I'VE TASTED PISS BEFORE. TASTED A HELL OF A LOT BETTER THAN THAT!
EVEN IF THE PAST FIVE YEARS HAS TAUGHT ME TO BE OTHERWISE.
HEY, FELLA! GOT A LIGHT? I NEED TO WASH THE SWILL FROM THAT BEER HALL OUT OF MY MOUTH.
HEH, NO SHIT! I HEARD BECAUSE OF THE SHORTAGE, THEY'VE STARTED IMPORTING ENGLISH BEER.
HA! MUST EXPLAIN ALL THOSE WEAK ARMS. I WAS WATCHING YOU. YOU MADE A KILLING IN THERE.
SO? WHAT'S IT TO YOU? THERE'S NO LAW AGAINST GAMBLING! I--
RELAX, BIG GUY. RELAX!
HE'S TWITCHY. ALWAYS WAS. I REALLY DON'T CARE. I JUST LOVE PLAYING THESE LITTLE MIND GAMES WITH THEM.

ART BY ANDREW SIDES

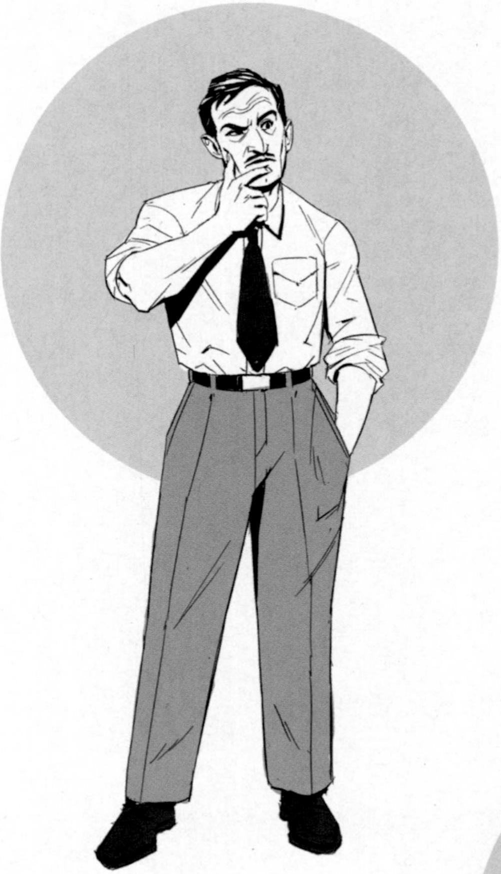

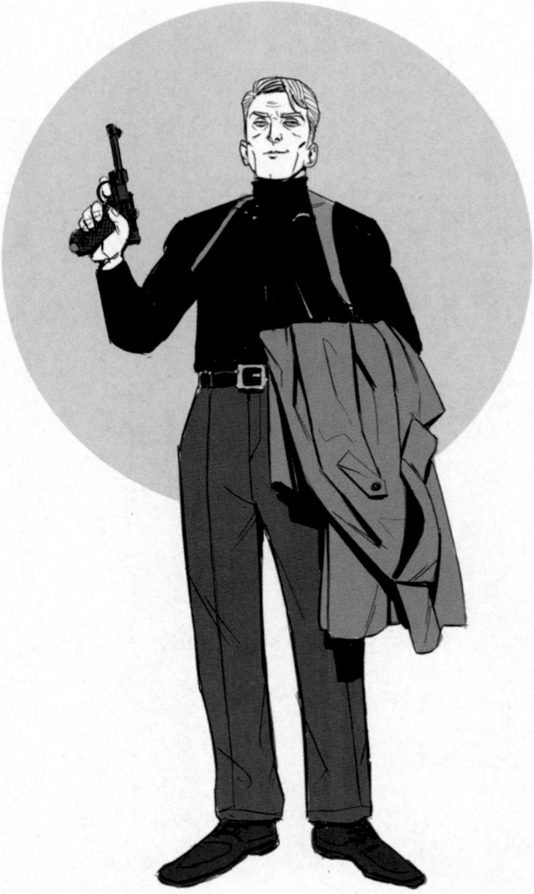

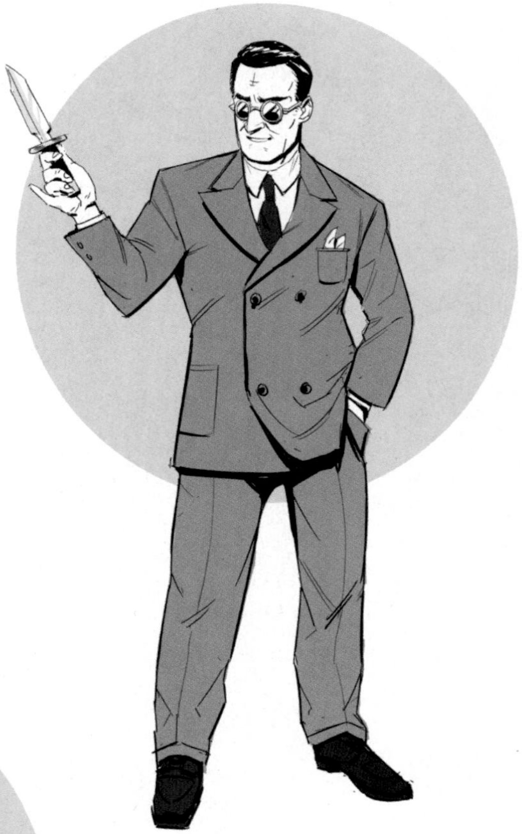

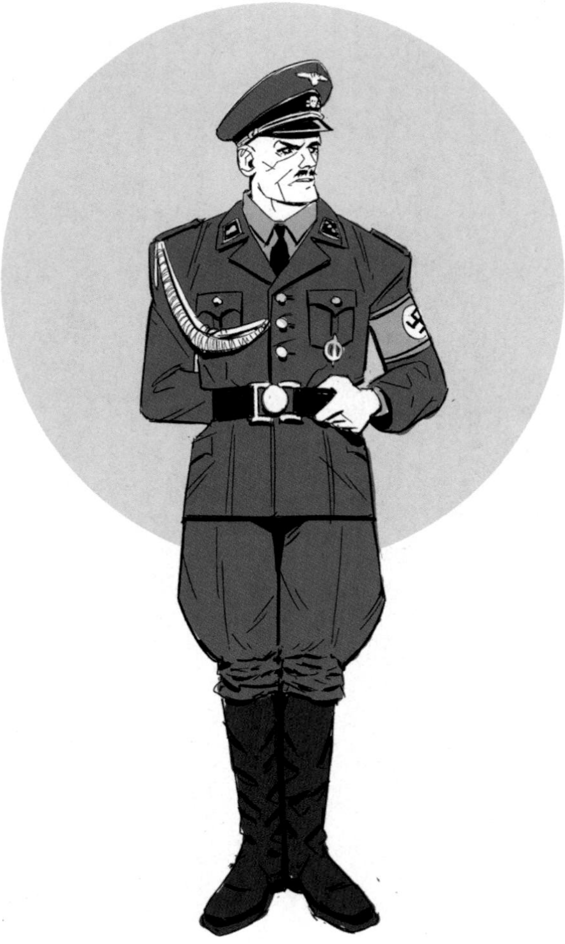

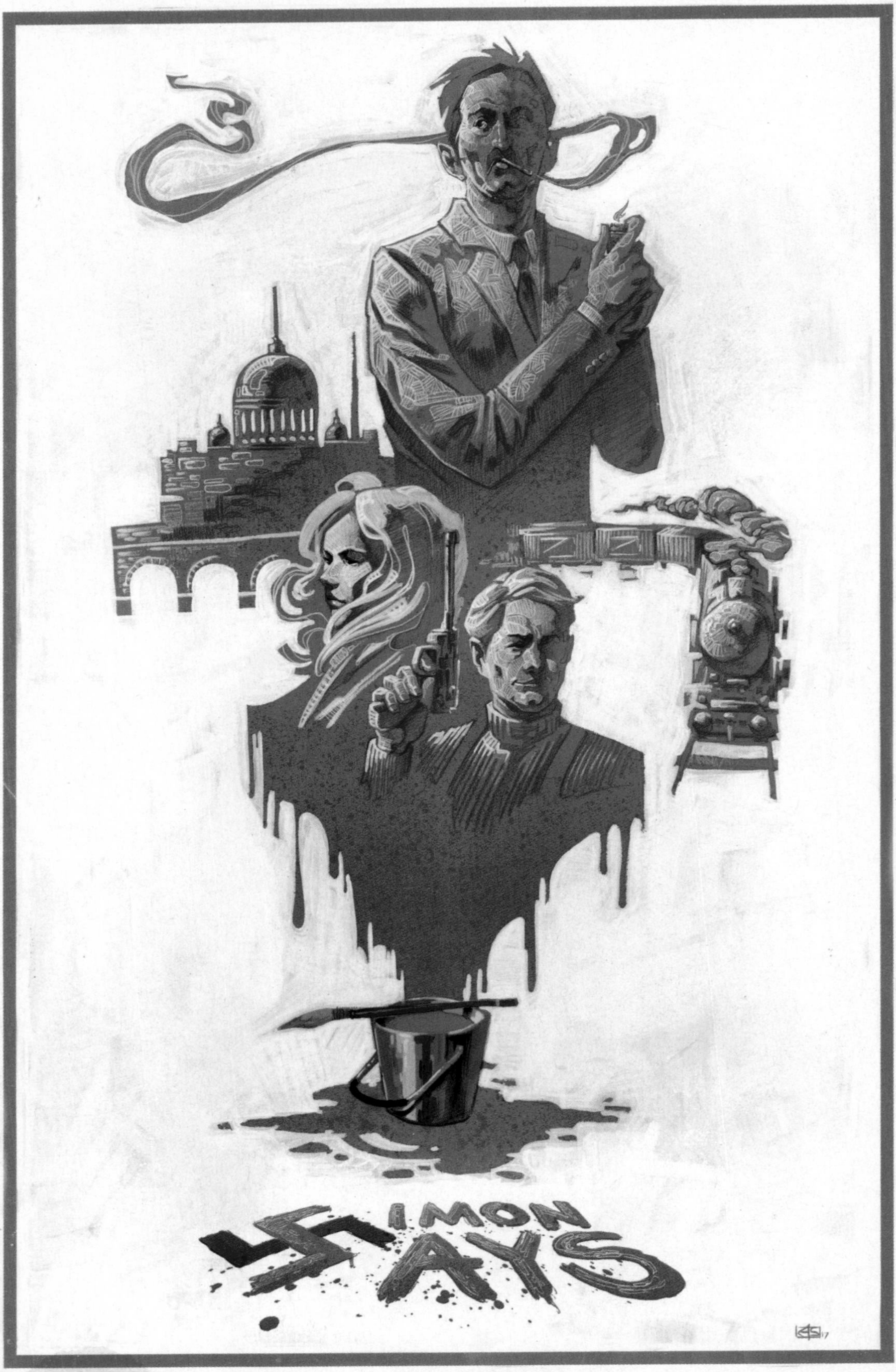
IMON
AYS